THE SECRET RETIREE:

DRUGS AND DEATH

THE SECRET RETIREE:

DRUGS AND DEATH

By Rupert Nelson

iUniverse, Inc.
New York Bloomington

THE SECRET RETIREE: DRUGS AND DEATH

This is a work of fiction. All of the characters, names, incidents, organizations, and dialogue in this novel are either the products of the author's imagination or are used fictitiously.

iUniverse books may be ordered through booksellers or by contacting:

iUniverse
1663 Liberty Drive
Bloomington, IN 47403
www.iuniverse.com
1-800-Authors (1-800-288-4677)

Because of the dynamic nature of the Internet, any Web addresses or links contained in this book may have changed since publication and may no longer be valid. The views expressed in this work are solely those of the author and do not necessarily reflect the views of the publisher, and the publisher hereby disclaims any responsibility for them.

ISBN: 978-1-4401-4517-9 (pbk)
ISBN: 978-1-4401-4518-6 (ebk)

Printed in the United States of America

iUniverse rev. date: 6/3/2009

THIS BOOK IS DEDICATED TO THE ETHNIC MINORITIES,
KNOWN AS THE MOUNTAIN TRIBES, WHO LIVE IN THE
UPLANDS OF NORTHERN THAILAND.

Cover photo is a Hmong Tribeswoman in her opium field, circa 1970.

This book is a work of fiction. Some locations in Thailand and the United States are real. Some events that occurred in Thailand are real. The characters that we meet in the book are fictitious.

GLOSSARY OF FOREIGN WORDS

Note: No particular system of transliterating words has been used in this book. The author has simply spelled foreign words in a manner that approximates their sound. For the convenience of the reader, the English meaning of the foreign word is given each time a foreign word is used. The Asian languages used in this book are all tonal; no attempt was made to show the tone.

Farang (Thai): A foreigner, Caucasian

Hakka (Chinese): One of the Chinese language groups

Khaow tom (Thai): Watery rice gruel

Pak pung fai daeng (Thai): A green vegetable, related to morning glory, fried in oil over a hot fire

Kapi (Thai): A fish based salty paste used as a condiment

Chow Khaow (Thai): People of the mountains, mountain tribes

Mia noi (Thai): minor wife

Tsiah bwe (Swatow dialect Chinese): A greeting, literally have you eaten

Lop Cheung (Cantonese Chinese): A red Chinese sausage

Ang mo (Swatow dialect Chinese): Caucasian, literally red head

Jin Haw (Thai): Chinese from Yunnan Province

Bok Kwei (Cantonese Chinese): White Devil

Rote (Thai): motor vehicle

Mow rote (Thai): car sick

Keh baan (Northern Thai): village headman

Pu yai baan (Thai): village headman

Fawn (Northern Thai): barking deer

Per (Karen)" grandfather

Pi (Karen): grandmother

Aw mae (Karen): eat, literally eat rice

Kin khaow (Thai): eat, eat rice

Kalawa (Karen): white person

Y'wa (Karen): Creator God

Kam Muang (Northern Thai): Northern Thai dialect

Ow anyang (Northern Thai): what do you want

Wai (Thai): A Thai curtsy with folded hands lifted to one's face

Khaow nung (Northern Thai): steamed glutinous rice

Pak pung (Thai): A common green vegetable related to morning glory

Rong kha sot (Thai): abattoir

Wan pra (Thai): Buddhist holy days on the four quarters of the moon

Pinto (Thai): stacked food container

Nalika (Thai): watch/clock

Cha cha (Thai): slowly

Nam pla (Thai): fish sauce

Pla kheng (Thai): salted fish sold in small baskets

Kuomintang (Chinese): abbr. KMT, the Chinese Nationalist Party

Krengjai (Thai): to be careful of others feelings

Haw dza-aw (Akha): eat, literally eat rice

Fin (Thai): opium

Joi (Chinese): a measure of weight, 1.6 kilograms

Hui (Thai): small stream, gully

Sawng (Thai): brothel

Khai tua (Thai): sell one's body for prostitution

Tio sawng (Thai): visit a brothel

Chow khaow sokaprok (Thai): dirty hill tribe person

Khun pa (Thai): aunt

Ai (northern Thai): elder brother

Sao borisut (Thai): virgin

Dip (Thai): green/ raw (not the color green)

Tu kopkhaw (Thai): food cupboard

Dio dio (Thai): wait a minute

Kai yang (Thai): barbequed chicken

Som tam (Thai): spicy Thai salad

Nong (Thai): younger sibling, younger sister, often used to address young girls

Mu sam chan (Thai): three layered pork, belly meat

Jek (Thai): pejorative for a Chinese person

Aw taw nya (Karen): eat pork

Thra (Karen): teacher, minister

Nai amphur (Thai): district officer

Ok rong (Thai): a mango variety

Songkran (Thai): traditional Thai New Year

Sanuk (Thai): fun

Khaow mun kai (Thai): chicken with rice cooked with chicken fat

Pern chow (Thai): hired gun

Kop khaow (Thai): food eaten with rice

Khaow daeng (Thai): rice with much of the bran still on the grains, literally red rice

Toklong (Thai): agree

Ngo kwai (Thai): stupid like a buffalo

Glua pi (Thai): afraid of spirits

Khun paw (Thai): father

Dawk pumalai (Thai): flower garland

Soi (Thai): side street

Ngaw (Thai): rambutan fruit

Nua sawan (Thai): dried beef, literally heavenly meat

Mun wai (Thai): engagement (to be married)

Kanom pang ping sawng chin (Thai): two pieces of toast

Klong Toey (Thai): Bangkok Port area

Pasin (Thai): sarong

Ti rak (Thai): my love

TABLE OF CONTENTS

BURMA

MAESALONG

MAECHAN

LAOS

CHIANG MAI

CHIANG MAI

LAMPOON

MAESARIANG

BANGKOK

MAHACHAI

THAILAND

CHAPTER ONE

A BODY IN THE GARDEN

Most residents of the Palm Gardens Retirement Community were still in bed that early Sunday morning when the usual quietness was broken by the intrusive sirens of emergency vehicles. The sound of sirens was not all that unusual; after all, it was a retirement community and emergencies caused by strokes, heart attacks and other illnesses common to elderly people, occurred all too often. What was unusual, however, was the ever increasing number of police vehicles parked around Pratt Garden, a tree shaded retreat within the confines of the Community. "What do you suppose is going on over there?" was a question asked in many nearby homes that morning. "Maybe I'll go take a look." Entry to the garden, however, was already forbidden by uniformed police, who had put up yellow tape around the perimeter of the garden.

The Palm Garden Retirement Community was located in the Southern California college town of Ashmore. Most such communities in California were rather new; rarely more that 50 years old. Palm Gardens, however, was soon to celebrate its 100th anniversary. It had been built like an old European village, with winding streets and a variety of house styles constructed over the years. Many trees and shrubs had been planted around the houses in a somewhat haphazard fashion. Gardens, shaded by ancient live oak trees, provided quiet retreats. The place was owned by a church denomination and the residents, from a variety of church groups, were all former clerics, seminary professors, or missionaries to foreign lands. They had come to Palm Gardens to live out the remainder of their lives in a safe and caring environment. They were people who had been community leaders, academics and world travelers. Many had been social activists, and continued to find ways to further their causes. They took an active part in the administration of their community. They were not a regimented or docile group of people.

It was not surprising, therefore, that a growing number of people gathered around, what appeared to be, a crime perimeter within the shaded garden. "What's going on here?" several people demanded. A police captain explained very little. "It appears a crime has been committed here. We are conducting an investigation and an announcement will be made at a later time. Has anyone here seen anything unusual?" A resident, Marvin Schuster, cleared his throat, "I'm the one who called the police this morning." "Oh yes," replied the captain. "Please come with me to my car, I want to talk to you." Marvin told his story, leaving out no details, especially about his dog.

Marvin was good to his dog, a cocker spaniel mix of indeterminate age, adopted from the local shelter. He was not a beautiful dog, and Marvin had named him Caliban, after a character in Shakespeare's play, "The Tempest", who was described as being "neither fish nor fowl." Caliban's mixed ancestry had not blended well, but the dog didn't seem to care. As long as Marvin fed and walked him he was happy. He was a curious dog and demanded at least three walks a day, so he could check out the doggy news on trees, bushes and fire hydrants. He never failed to leave his own message.

Caliban's first walk of the day was early, just as it was getting light. That was his favorite time of day. Many things, besides other dogs, excited his curiosity. The musky odor of raccoons and opossums and the wild scent of visiting coyotes brought out the canine instincts deep in his DNA, imbedded there since the time his ancestors joined the migratory humans around their fires many thousands of years ago.

Early that frightful Sunday morning in January Caliban had roused the blanket covered Marvin from the depths of his bed. "It's too cold Caliban," moaned Marvin. "Go lay on your rug." Caliban would not wait. He began to bark, which soon brought a reaction from the other covered body in that bed. Marvin's wife, Emily, tolerated the dog, but made it known it was her husband's responsibility. Emily was not a morning person. "For God's sake Marvin walk your dog." Inwardly complaining, of both spouse and dog, Marvin got up, turned on the bathroom lights, and, like a well trained husband, lifted up the toilet seat before using it, and put it down again after use. He washed his face, got dressed and put on a heavy jacket. Although he lived in Southern California the morning air was cold, with an occasional frost in January. "Hold your horses Caliban, we're going, we're going. Where's your leash?" Finally, jacketed and gloved Marvin was pulled out the door by the ever eager Caliban.

It was really Marvin who was taken for a walk. He had recovered from a stroke the previous year, which left him with diminished strength. He allowed his dog to go where it wanted and he followed, leash in hand. Palm Gardens, with tree lined streets and flower gardens, was a good place for walks. As usual, Caliban found many intriguing scents that morning, and left his own. He chased an early rising squirrel up a tree, nearly yanking Marvin off his feet. "Slow down you dumb dog," complained Marvin. "You'll never catch those squirrels." Not the least bit subdued, Caliban forged ahead into a shaded retreat, known as Pratt Garden, where he stopped abruptly. The early morning light barely penetrated under the canopy of live oak and ash trees. "Let's go," mumbled Marvin with a tug on the leash. "I don't like it in here." Caliban wouldn't go. He was sniffing at something on the ground. Marvin could see there was something there, old clothes perhaps. Caliban barked, something he rarely did. "What have you got there boy? Leave it alone." Caliban wouldn't leave. Marvin used his cane to poke at the form on the ground. It wasn't just old rags. There was something there. He leaned over for a close look and saw what it really was. "My God," he breathed. "It's Clifford, and he's dead."

Marvin rushed home after his gruesome discovery, called the

police, and hurried to the toilet. The sounds of Marvin being sick woke up Emily. "What are you doing in there?" she demanded. No reply. Irritated, she got up and opened the unlocked bathroom door. "Marvin, are you sick?"

"Oh my God, Emily, Caliban found something this morning."

"So, what was it this time, another dead rat?"

"No, Emily, it was Clifford Johnson. I found him dead."

"You found Clifford dead?"

"Well, it was really Caliban who found him in that shaded garden near the dining hall."

"What are you talking about? How do you know he was dead?"

"Oh, he was dead alright. Must have been hit on the head hard; his brains were oozing out, and one eye had popped out of its socket. Made me sick."

"Well don't just stand there. Call the police."

"I did. They're coming."

That's what had happened, and Marvin told it as best he could. Captain Gallager listened patiently. "Thank you Mr. Schuster. You may go now, but don't leave town. You'll be asked to come down to the station to make an official report."

CHAPTER TWO

CLIFFORD

Clifford Johnson was a new arrival at Palm Gardens. He soon found that the friendly long-time residents were interested in learning who he was. However, he remained rather noncommittal when asked the usual questions, such as "Where do you come from? What universities and theological seminaries did you attend? Where did you work?" Clifford frequently encountered those questions, especially when seated around a table in the dining hall during dinner. The residents all ate together for their noon meal. It was required. Well, not really required, but it was required to pay for it, so, of course, the residents did all come together and sat at tables of six or eight. Dinner was the primary social occasion at Palm Gardens. Information was shared, announcements made, and there were lively conversations at each table.

It was quite normal to share personal information during those conversations around the tables. After all, the residents were well acquainted with each other, and newcomers were soon drawn into the prevailing culture at Palm Gardens. Many residents had attended well known universities and theological seminaries. Indeed, several were former professors at those institutions. They were not reticent about speaking of former glories, and had a natural curiosity about other residents. Frequently, it was discovered that some residents had crossed paths in former times. These conversations helped to meld the residents together into a social group that really did care for one another.

Clifford usually answered such questions by replying that he had attended a small mid-western college, that no one had ever heard of, and that he had spent his career abroad. That really was not enough to satisfy the more persistent questioners, but it was all the information they could obtain. They were too polite to pry further. Clifford did not tell lies. He was a graduate of Sioux Rapids College in South Dakota. He was right; no one had ever heard of that place. It was also true that he had spent his career abroad. Indeed, he had lived in northern Thailand for 30 years as a missionary with the Asian Inland Mission, known by its acronym, AIM. He never supplied that information to anyone at Palm Gardens, assuming that such a small mission organization would only bestow negative prestige to anyone associated with it.

He was right. Not only would it be unknown at Palm Gardens, but members of so-called Faith Missions, such as AIM, had to raise their own support. AIM did not pay any of their missionaries a salary; they simply forwarded funds raised by their missionaries. A missionary with a dynamic message and a charismatic presence could raise adequate support from a number of churches. Alas, Clifford was neither dynamic nor charismatic. He had barely raised enough funds to maintain himself in Thailand, and had never married, not wanting to inflict such penury on a wife and children.

Back home in South Dakota, where he had been born, he had been a loner. He was an only child in a family that did not socialize much with their neighbors. His parents were often ill and died a few months apart when he was a senior in high school. He inherited the family home and lived there alone. A local church hired him as a janitor, and although he had no close friends he was drawn into the life of the church and attended regularly. After his graduation from high school he attended the nearby Sioux Rapids College, where, for four years he managed to pay his school expenses by being the assistant janitor. During his senior year, at the age of 21, he felt the call of God to be a missionary, attended an unaccredited Bible School for three years, managed to raise some funds from sympathetic people in his home church, and in 1959 flew off to Thailand, a land he knew nothing about, except that it had few followers of the Christian faith.

Clifford discovered he had a flair for languages and learned them easily. He lived in the capitol city of Bangkok for one year, attending a Thai language school, and during that time mastered the Thai language. His teachers were amazed. They had never encountered a *Farang* (foreigner) who had learned their tonal language so well in such a short time. The Thai language has five tones, and each syllable must be spoken with the right pitch. No problem for Clifford. It helped, of course, that he had no social life and spent his time either studying or walking through the markets listening to people speak. Many of the market people were immigrants from China and he even began to pick up words from five Chinese dialects. For the first time in his life, he fit in. He felt at home in his adopted country, and when he heard about the minority groups living in the northern uplands, known as the Mountain Tribes, he knew that's where he wanted to spend the rest of his life.

He purchased an ancient Land Rover from a Chinese man he met in one of the markets. It was a good deal. The vehicle was old, but the engine had been overhauled and was good for many more miles. The shop owner wanted to buy a new van, and, besides, he felt sorry for the *Farang* who had no family and always wore old clothes and rubber sandals. He was also impressed that Clifford could speak a few words of Hakka, his native dialect from his old home in China. Anyone who could speak Hakka deserved a good deal!

One hot, humid day in July of 1960, the day after his last day of Thai language school, Clifford loaded his few belongings in his Land Rover and headed north, past Don Muang Airport and into the heart of Thailand, or Siam, as the country used to be called. He had no definite destination. His future was uncertain, but he had a feeling of exhilaration. He knew he had acquired two valuable things: a new language and a reliable vehicle. Two things he had never owned before. He wasn't ready to acknowledge it yet, but he was also free of well meaning neighbors and church members back home who had felt sorry for the "poor orphan boy" and kept a close watch over him. Now he was free to explore new worlds, and eager to do so.

Neither his vehicle or the road condition allowed for a speedy trip.

He cruised along at about 50 mph on the good stretches where there was a macadam surface, but much slower where the road was broken up and saturated by recent rains. It was the beginning of the monsoon season and rice planting time. All along the way that day family groups were standing in the flooded rice paddies transplanting rice shoots. It was tiresome stoop labor, but they often stopped to give a cheery wave as he drove by. Clifford was driving through the rice basket of Thailand; a great alluvial bowl 300 miles long that surely had been created for rice. The clay soil held the water that farmers released from canals onto their fields. The water itself, diverted from rivers and streams, carried nutrients to the rice roots, and the hot sun provided the energy to convert those raw materials into a food grain that sustained all the people of Southeast Asia and beyond.

Fish came into the paddies from the water released from the canals and fattened in the shallow water during the growing season. Later, when the water was drained to permit harvest, the fish were collected and dried to provide protein throughout the year. The first two lines of an ancient song were often on the farmer's lips:

> *"Nai na me khaow,*
> *Nai nam me pla."*
> "In the fields are rice,
> In the water are fish."

Clifford knew that somewhere ahead was the provincial town of Chiang Mai, sometimes called the gateway to the northern mountains. In Bangkok he had seen photographs of Hill Tribe people on the streets of that town. They dressed differently from the lowland Thai and spoke different languages. He decided to stop for the night there and explore the town. Maybe he would stay. Maybe he wouldn't. He knew he needed time to learn how to approach the Tribal people in the uplands.

It was just getting dark when Clifford arrived at the outskirts of Chiang Mai. He was greatly relieved to see the lights, as he feared to continue on the unfamiliar road. He was beginning to worry he had missed the town completely. He drove on in to the market area in the center of the town, where he found an inexpensive hotel called the *Suk Niran*. He knew that name meant Eternal Happiness, but what he didn't know was that the hotel was a favorite of traveling salesmen, because it also served as a brothel. The clerk at the front desk assigned Clifford a room on the third floor and a bus boy carried his suitcase up the stairs to his room. Clifford was rather embarrassed when the bus boy suggested he could arrange for a young lady to come to his room. "I have no interest in such things," he asserted, as he showed the bus boy out, and quickly double locked his door. He ignored the raps on his door that came with some regularity for the next few hours.

Other than the unwanted solicitations, Clifford was satisfied with his accommodations. It was a three storey concrete building without a lift. The entire center of the building was open from the ground floor up to a ceiling of translucent roofing that let in light. Each floor had an interior balcony from which entry was made to the small rooms. It reminded Clifford of a prison cell block he once visited with his church group back in South Dakota, but here there were no bars. In the open area on the ground floor was a restaurant and small shops selling knick knacks. There was a hood and vent over the restaurant stove, but still, delicious odors wafted upward to Clifford's third floor room, reminding him that he was hungry. The midday bowl of noodles he had eaten at a roadside food shop was not going to sustain him through the night.

It was about 10 P.M. when, between taps on his door, he ventured out of his room and descended to the restaurant. The food was to Clifford's liking: plain, delicious and cheap. It was basically a Chinese restaurant, but with some adjustments for Thai tastes. The place was full, in spite of the late hour, and many of the patrons were ordering *khao tom,* as did Clifford. *Khao tom* is a watery rice gruel commonly eaten for breakfast or late at night. It is quite tasteless by itself, but is usually eaten together with side dishes of salty, sour or peppery hot foods that add flavor. Clifford ordered small pork ribs with garlic that were fried crispy, a salted duck egg and tiny dried fish fried to a crisp and eaten whole, head and all. He also ordered *pak pung fai daeng,* a local vegetable related to morning glory that is rapidly fried in a very hot wok with oil, chilies and garlic. The oil catches fire, but just when it seems all is lost the cook empties the wok contents onto a plate. Within five minutes every dish, piping hot, was in front of Clifford, who bowed his head and gave thanks to God for a safe journey and for a blessing on the food.

CHAPTER THREE

CHIANG MAI

Clifford was an early riser. Early enough to see young ladies emerging from some of the rooms as he descended the stairs to the street below, where he discovered many other people were early risers. Buddhist monks in their saffron robes had already emerged from their temples and were walking through market and residential areas with large black bowls held in both hands. Some people, mostly women, had prepared food to place in the monk's bowls, which they did after lowering their head and raising their arms in a prayerful position. The monks took the food back to their various temples and shared it among themselves. Breakfast was their main meal of the day. They might eat again before the noon hour, but after that they were prohibited from eating until the following morning.

A market near the hotel was already a buzz of activity. A large wooden building, built by the city, was divided into stalls and rented to shopkeepers and those selling fresh produce. Clifford was always interested in markets and walked all around this one. Enclosed shops along the outside perimeter of the building were tended mostly by Chinese entrepreneurs selling farm and household necessities. Some Indian cloth sellers were arranging bolts of brightly colored cloth to attract the eyes of women shoppers. Most of the building, however, consisted of tables displayed with a great variety of vegetables and fruit. A seller, usually a local woman, stood behind each table and sold her wares. One end of the market was reserved for meat and fish. Here there were both men and women sellers. Hogs, cattle, chickens and ducks had been killed and eviscerated at a slaughterhouse and brought to the market before light. The sellers were busy cutting up the meat with sharp butcher knives and selling to customers. Some of the beef was actually water buffalo, identifiable by its darker color and courser texture.

Clifford was amused to see one male customer get a good scolding. He had purchased a piece of pork which the seller wrapped up in a section of banana leaf, a common wrapping material, and proceeded to another table where a Muslim lady was selling beef. Her table was identified with the half moon and star emblem of Islam, which meant that other Muslims could purchase meat from her and be assured it was halal (kosher). The man absentmindedly placed his bundle of pork on her table while he reached in his pocket for money. "Get that bundle of shit off my table," yelled the lady. She added a few more expletives that increased Clifford's meager vocabulary of such words.

Salt water fish, crabs, shrimp and shellfish were piled in large boxes mixed with crushed ice to keep them fresh. Local fresh water fish were splashing around in buckets of water. Salted and dried fish were hanging on lines for customers to inspect. On the edges of the fish section Clifford was distracted by the odor of *kapi*, a salty brownish- purple paste made from crabs or shrimp. The women sellers had mounded the paste up in large white enamel dishpans and sold it in small amounts. As Clifford well knew, a little goes a long way It was smelly, but fried with vegetables it adds flavor and salt.

Returning to the main part of the market Clifford walked past the people, mostly Chinese, selling rice. Many grades of rice was offered to customers. First, there were two major types. The Northern Thai people prefer glutinous rice, which is steamed, not boiled. It is very sticky, so must be eaten with one's fingers. The other major type of rice is the kind most familiar to Westerners. Both kinds of rice were further subdivided by variety, and by the percentage of broken kernels. The cheapest rice, separated out at the rice mills, contained many broken kernels. New rice of the non-glutinous type was also cheaper than the previous year's rice. The reason being that rice in storage for a year shrinks slightly, so a liter of old rice actually contains more rice than a liter of new rice. Clifford had already learned many of these things by hanging out in the markets of Bangkok, but there were differences here in the north. Some of the fruits and vegetables were different, there were more women sellers, dress was different, and there was the language. Clifford, ever mindful of languages, immediately noticed that Northern Thai was quite different from Bangkok Thai. There was some different vocabulary and familiar words were pronounced with a different tone.

The sidewalks outside the market were also full of women selling their produce. These were people who could not afford to rent a stall, but simply brought their goods in baskets and arrayed them on a piece of plastic on the sidewalk. Clifford stopped to buy a hand of bananas from one such vendor. That was his breakfast. The lady had no trouble understanding Clifford's Bangkok Thai and even congratulated him for speaking so correctly.

"I've just arrived from the South, but hope to learn your Northern way of speaking," replied Clifford.

"Oh, we'll understand you alright. All schools teach in the official language like you speak."

"Did you go to school?"

"Yes, but my village school only went to the fourth grade and that was long ago. I'm an old lady now."

Clifford guessed she was about 50. His parents had been that age when they died, but had looked much younger than this white haired lady. It was also obvious she was a betal nut chewer, and had a cud in her mouth. Her lips were stained red, and her teeth were nearly black from chewing on the nut of the areca palm. Clifford had tried it once when offered a chew in a Bangkok market. He had placed the piece of nut, wrapped in a betal leaf smeared with a lime paste, in his mouth and chewed on it, much to the amusement of the people in the market. It was supposed to be a mild stimulant, but Clifford didn't like the taste and soon spit it out.

"Do any of the Mountain Tribal people come to this market?" enquired Clifford.

"Oh yes, I see some most every day. Do you want to take a photograph of them?"

"No, I just want to meet them."

"You might not be able to talk to them, mostly they just speak their own language."

"Where is a good place to find them," enquired Clifford.

"Try that shop owned by the old Chinese man." She pointed down the street. "He buys things from the *Chow khao* (mountain people)."

"What kind of things?" Clifford was interested.

"Things they grow in their hill fields, like chili peppers and sesame."

"Is that all?"

"No, they bring in things from the forest, like animal hides and medicinal herbs. That old Chinese man is clever. He sells those things for a lot of money, a lot more than he pays for them."

Clifford thanked the market lady and walked on down the street, pausing to look into each shop. Most of them had a shelf on a rear wall with an ancestral tablet, a food offering and joss sticks, so he knew the owners were Chinese. Many had been born in Thailand, but kept their own traditions. Finally, he came to the shop that he was sure was the one he was looking for. It was a messy place; herbs were spread out to dry on a mat placed on the sidewalk in front of the shop, causing pedestrians to detour onto the street to avoid stepping on the mat. Animal hides were stacked in one corner of the shop, and large baskets of chili peppers were stacked up and ready to be sent to Bangkok, according to an address label on them. As Clifford stood watching, two Tribal men came walking into the shop, each with a huge basket of dried peppers on their backs. Even in the morning coolness they were perspiring, and slipped out of their baskets with a sigh of relief. Clifford knew they were Tribal by their clothing. He had seen pictures of such people. They were dressed in black homespun cloth with red and yellow embroidery on their tunics. They spoke to one another in a language Clifford had never heard before.

Without a word the Chinese shopkeeper folded up one of the herb drying mats on the sidewalk and wheeled out a large scale, on which he placed one of his empty baskets. He motioned to the two men to empty their baskets into it. As they did so, the shop owner inspected the chilies, feeling them with his fingers. When both of the men's baskets were emptied, he weighed them and wrote down a figure on a note pad. Next, he picked up an abacus from a cluttered desk and deftly moved the beads around making a calculation. The "clack, clack, clack" of the abacus was the only sound to be heard.

"I will pay you four hundred and fifty Baht," said the merchant, speaking in the Northern Thai dialect to the two Tribal men. When they didn't seem to comprehend he wrote down that figure on his note pad and showed it to them. The men assented and the transaction was completed. Clifford was standing close by watching the procedure and noticed the smoky smell of the peppers. Evidently, they had been dried over a wood fire. Even the clothing of the men had that same smoky smell. Not a bad smell, but intriguing. It was not an urban odor, but took Clifford back to a day in his childhood when he had helped his father burn some tree branches around their house. Wood smoke.

The men divided their money, wrapped it in plastic bags, and placed it in their shoulder bags. They shouldered their empty baskets and continued on to the market. The shop owner's wife came out from the rear of the shop and helped her husband prepare another basket of chilies to send to Bangkok. Clifford heard them speak to one another, and although he could not understand their conversation, he knew they were speaking *Teochiu*, a Chinese dialect he had often heard spoken in Bangkok. Most of the Chinese in Thailand were *Teochiu*, who had immigrated from southern China. "*Tsiah bwe*," ventured Clifford, which he knew was a *Teochiu* word meaning "have you eaten," but commonly used as a greeting. The couple stared at him in surprise. "*Tsiah bwe*," repeated Clifford. Finding their tongues the shopkeepers replied, "*Tsiah bwe*," and continued speaking in Chinese. Clifford switched to Thai and explained that he really didn't know *Teochiu*, only a word or two.

"Where did you learn even a few words of our language?" the man asked. "I have never heard a *Farang* speak even a word."

"I lived in Bangkok a year and liked to visit the markets, so I heard *Teochiu* spoken a good bit. Sounds like a hard language to learn."

"No, very easy," the merchant smiled. "I have spoken it since I was a child. Sit down here and have a cup of tea." The woman went back to the rear of the shop.

He cleared off a place on his old desk and set the tea service between them. It was the traditional Chinese method of serving tea, very different from how it is done in the West. Several very tiny cups without handles were placed on a round metal tray. The tray had two levels; cups on top and space underneath to hold spilled tea or water. The merchant stuffed a small teapot full of tea leaves, placed it on the tray, and opened a thermos of very hot water brought in by his wife. He poured hot water into two cups to warm them up and filled the teapot. Next, he dumped the water out of the cups into the tray and refilled them with tea. He picked up one cup, signaling Clifford to do the same, and they both sipped their tea. It was strong, aromatic and refreshing. Once again the merchant filled the pot with water and poured them each a cup.

"So, what are you doing up here in the North?" he wanted to know. "You must be either a teacher or a missionary."

"I am a missionary," replied Clifford, "and maybe you can help me."

"No, your foreign religion is not for me."

"That's not what I meant. I would like to work among the Tribal people, and I see they come to your store. Can you help me meet them?"

The merchant saw an opportunity. "Yes, I can help you. We make a deal, o.k.?"

"That depends on the deal. What do you have in mind?"

"I help you meet the *Chow Khow* (Mountain People), and you send them to my shop. Good deal, eh? I make money and you make converts."

Clifford was beginning to like this guy. He spoke the Thai language brokenly, but he was straightforward and obviously had a sense of humor. He decided to join the game.

"Not a good deal. If you pay too low a price I lose my reputation with the Mountain People and you make too much money."

"No no, never happen. I'm a poor man. Look at this shop, it's falling apart. I can't even afford a *mia noi* (minor wife).

"If you tried that I'd chop off your *lop cheung* (Chinese sausage)," came a voice from the rear of the shop.

"Ai ya, that woman gives me no freedom. What's a man to do?"

"Maybe you could build your wife a nice new house."

"If I did that the government revenue people would think I was making money and increase my tax."

"These chilies sell for a good price in Bangkok," Clifford waved his arm to a stack of baskets. "What do you do will all your money?"

"My children have cost me a lot of money. Look at all seven of them hanging on the wall."

Clifford looked at the seven pictures hanging above the desk and realized they were the seven children of this couple, each receiving their university diploma from the hand of His Majesty the King. Clifford had heard that His Majesty personally gave the diploma to each person graduating from the two Thai universities in Bangkok, but had never seen evidence of it before. There they were, four sons and three daughters, children of a Chinese immigrant couple who bought chilies and forest products and sacrificed to send their children to the best universities in Thailand.

With obvious pride the man pointed to each of his children, and giving their Thai names, told what they were doing. Two were medical doctors, one of whom was doing advanced study in the United States. The others were all in good professions.

"In Thailand I am nothing," continued the merchant. "I can't even speak good Thai like you. I never had the opportunity to receive an education, but that old woman back there and I, we sent all our children to school. Now we don't have to work so hard, they will help us in our old age. That's the Chinese way."

Clifford realized the merchant really did appreciate his wife, they just liked to banter with one another.

"I'll tell you what I can do," continued the merchant, "One of those men who were just here told me they saw some men from a different tribe that were coming here to sell their dried peppers. Just wait here and you can meet them."

"I didn't think they spoke Thai."

"They don't, but one of those men speaks a little *Jin Haw* (Yunnanese), so I understood what he meant."

"What kind of language is that?"

"Oh, it's what they speak in Yunnan Province, China and is similar to the central Chinese language of Mandarin; not very proper Chinese.

That province is a long way from Beijing, and really not so far from us. Many Tribal people live there too."

Clifford was learning a lot from this merchant and decided to wait. He had discovered his name was Nai Lee, and had just completed his fifth 12 year cycle, which made him 60 years old. In both Thailand and China years are grouped in 12 year cycles. Clifford watched Nai Lee's wife light joss sticks on the ancestral alter and place a small cup of tea on it. With the ancestors taken care of, she joined her husband in cleaning debris out of a basket of dried leaves dumped on a mat.

"What are those leaves for?"

"This is an herbal medicine we will send to a Chinese medicine store in Bangkok. Very good for people with diabetes."

"Where do you get it?"

"I ask the Hill Tribe people to collect it. These leaves come from a plant that grows in the mountains. I use it myself."

"Do you have diabetes?"

"Yes."

"How do you know? Have you seen a doctor?"

"No need, I can find out myself."

"How do you do that?"

"I piss on the ground. If ants are attracted to my urine I know there is sugar in it."

"Does that really work?"

"Works for me. We Chinese were using this medicine when you *Ang Mo* (redheads) were still living in the forest and wearing animal skins," he said with a sly grin.

His wife murmured something to him in Chinese causing him to laugh. "My old lady just told me not to speak to you like that. I was just joking. You know that don't you?"

Clifford was still thinking up a good reply when two Tribal men walked up in front of the store with two huge baskets of dried chillies on their backs. They eased the baskets off their backs and the merchant went out to talk to them. Their dress was different from the two who had come earlier to sell chilies. Those men wore darker clothes, almost black, but these two wore red pullover homespun tunics with some yellow and black mixed in. Nai Lee spoke to the younger man in the local Northern Thai dialect. After some bargaining, they agreed on a price, the chilies were weighed and the men received their money. They were about to leave, when Nai Lee spoke to the young man at some length. The Northern dialect is similar enough to Central Thai, so Clifford could understand most of the conversation.

"You see this Foreigner here," Nai Lee lifted his chin toward Clifford, "He would like to get to know you mountain people. Why don't you let him go home with you?"

"I don't think a foreigner could live with us," replied the younger man. "I have heard they are rich people. How could they eat our food and sleep on the floor of our bamboo houses. No, it wouldn't work. We couldn't even talk to him."

"Now wait a minute. I don't think this man is rich and he does speak good Thai like they speak in Bangkok. You'd get along o.k."

The older person nudged the younger and spoke in their language. Clifford assumed he wanted to know what was being said. Finally, the young man spoke to Nai Lee. "I don't know why, but my wife's father seems to be interested. He said something about an old tradition concerning the White People. He can come with us, but I don't think he'll stay long."

"Did you understand what was said?" Nai Lee spoke to Clifford in Central Thai.

"Yes, I think so. I can go with them to their village, right?"

"Yes, that's right. Do you know what tribe they belong to?"

"No."

"In Northern Thai we call them Yang, but in Central Thai they are known as Kariang."

Clifford had read about these people, who also lived in Burma. The English word for them was, Karen. He turned his attention to the younger man, "Thank you for allowing me to come to your village. Are you ready to go now?"

"My father-in-law and I have some things to buy in the market, let's meet here at this Chinese shop when the sun is right above us."

"Sounds good, and by the way I have a Landrover parked at the hotel. Can I take you back to your village?"

"What's that?"

"Oh, its like a small truck."

Once again the two men conferred, and the younger replied, "There is no road to our village, but we can drive part way and leave your *rot* (motor vehicle) at a Thai village where the trail to our village begins.

"So, you have a truck. That's good, maybe you can transport more chilies and things to my store," smiled Nai Lee.

"We'll see about that. But what do I need to take with me to the village?"

"Not much, maybe a blanket and flashlight. They'll feed you, but I'd take some food to share with them."

"Nai Lee, thank you very much. You have been a big help." Clifford returned to the market and purchased a blanket, a kilo of dried fish, oranges and a backpack. On the way back to the hotel he stopped at a food stall and ate a plate of rice and chicken curry. At the hotel he checked out, reclaimed his Landrover and drove back to the store. The men were waiting. Without a word they placed their purchases in the truck and started to crawl in.

"No, no, sit up front with me in the cab," said Clifford. They didn't seem to know how to open the door, so Clifford opened it for them. The young man crawled in first, straddling the gear shift lever. The older man followed, and Clifford reached across to open his window. They were ready to go.

CHAPTER FOUR

ASCENT TO THE HILLS

Neither man said much; the young man directed Clifford by pointing out the streets leading to a higbway heading west out of town. After driving for about an hour he again pointed to a side road, and Clifford entered a very different kind of road. It was a dirt track that appeared to have been used only by ox carts. It was a winding road with many hairpin curves. Suddenly, the older man stuck his head out the window and threw up. His son-in-law looked like he would soon do the same, so Clifford stopped while they all got out. "*Mow rot,*" (car sick) murmured the young man. They rested a while in the shade of teak trees, but soon crawled back in the vehicle and Clifford proceeded at a slower pace.

They soon came to a small Thai village and Clifford was directed to a house a bit larger than most. "House of *Gae Ban,* you can leave your truck here." Clifford parked near the house, but had no idea what those words meant. Seeing his confusion, the young man explained, "I think in Bangkok Thai you would say *Pu Yai Ban,*" which Clifford recognized as meaning the village headman.

The village headman's house, like all the other houses, was constructed of the local teakwood and elevated about six feet off the ground. The headman himself appeared on a veranda and the young

Karen man suggested to Clifford that he ask permission to leave his truck. Clifford did so, and the headman gave permisssion.

"Are you going with these men to their village?" he asked.

"Yes, I am," replyed Clifford, not really knowing what his role was in this negotiation.

"How long will you be there?"

"I don't know, maybe a few days."

"Well, good luck. Your truck will be safe here while you're in Huey Fawn Village."

"Huey Fawn; what does that mean?"

"That's the Thai name for the Karen village."

Later, Clifford was to learn that *fawn* is the Northern Thai word for the small deer known in English as barking deer, so the name meant Barking Deer Creek.

The two Karen men were already retriving their belongings from the truck, so Clifford shrugged on his backpack, picked up a water canteen he kept in the truck and followed the men, who were already leaving. The young man explained, "It's a long walk to our village so we want to get there before dark."

The trail straggled out of one end of the village and immediately went through the flooded rice paddies of the Thai villagers, following the bunds, or dikes, separating the paddy fields. Beyond the fields the trail went uphill through scattered hardwood trees and low underbrush. At first, Clifford was exhilarated by the thought he had made contact with these people and was actually on his way to a mountain village. Soon, however, following two men with seemingly iron legs brought him back to reality. Their pace was not rapid, but it was relentless. Uphill, downhill, across log bridges over streams, they never slowed. A year of no physical exertion during language study in Bangkok had not prepared Clifford for this day. His legs ached, he was breathing hard, and perspiration soaked his clothe. Only the thought of being left behind on the trail kept him going.

Coming to a small stream, the men stopped for a drink, cupping the water in both hands and bringing it to their mouths. Clifford flopped to the ground, breathing hard. The two men looked at him and spoke among themselves in low voices. He assumed they were talking about him, and resolved to keep going, no matter how difficult it became. After washing his face in the stream and drinking from his canteen he stood up on shakey legs. The men resumed their pace and Clifford followed. The trail was not so steep at that point and was shaded by giant bamboo. Clifford had never seen such bamboo. Some were at least 12 inches in diameter at the base and nearly 100 feet tall. Occasionally, the men stopped to dig up young bamboo shoots just emerging from the ground. Clifford welcomed the rest breaks and felt his strength returning.

The afternoon sun was getting low, but the day was far from over. The trail once again became steep and Clifford struggled to keep up. In spite of his aching legs, however, he noticed a great difference in the vegetation around them. The leafy trees of the lower elevations were replaced by pine trees, and the fallen needles on the trail made a welcome cushion to walk on.

It was nearly evening when they emerged from the pine trees and Clifford was amazed to see bare hillsides on which young rice seedlings were emerging. "Our fields," explained the young man. The trail went straight through one of the fields, and Clifford could see the trees had been cut and burned. Some stumps and partially burned logs remained, with the rice coming up around them. He realized these were not the flooded rice paddies of the lowlanders, but the upland fields of the hill people. The rice had been planted into the ashes of the burned trees, and Clifford could see there were also a few plants of corn, cucumbers and Chinese cabbage interplanted with the rice.

In the gathering darkness, Clifford could smell the village before he saw it. It was a good smell of burning firewood as the evening meal was being cooked in the grass thatched houses clustered together just below a ridgeline. Glimpses of the cooking fires could be seen through the split bamboo walls of the houses, which were elevated off the ground like the Thai houses in the valley, but these were smaller and of a simpler construction.

Clifford followed the two men to a house in the middle of the village. They kicked off their rubber slippers and and climbed the stairs, more like a ladder, up to a kind of veranda or porch. Clifford had to sit on the lower step to remove his shoes before ascending to the porch. Two women and three young children came out of an inner room to stare at Clifford. One of the women lit a kerosene lamp and set it on the floor. The older of the two men now spoke at some length to the women, with an occasional gesture toward Clifford who assumed they were talking about him. Finally, the older of the two women picked up a mat and unrolled it on the floor next to a wall, motioning for Clifford to rest on it.

Clifford lay down on the mat with his head on a hard pillow that had been provided for him. It felt wonderful. He gave a sigh of relief as his tired legs ceased to tremble and he took stock of his situation. The seven occupants of the house sat on the floor and continued their conversation. The children never took their eyes off the prostrate foreigner. Clifford's eyes moved around the room, noting the large bamboo that had been split and spread open to make the floor and walls. There was a fire burning on an earth filled box in a smaller room at one end of the porch near the stairs. He assumed that was the kitchen. A pot, supported on an iron tripod, was boiling with the flames licking around it. Smoke from the fire went up and passed through the grass thatch roof. Behind Clifford was another room, which he could not see into.

Clifford sat up with his back against the bamboo partition when the younger man began talking to him in the Northern Thai dialect. "None of the women and children in this village have ever seen a white foreigner. The children are even a little afraid of you," he said with a smile. "They think you are a giant."

"I'm not that big," replied Clifford in astonishment.

"No, but there are some old Karen stories about 'giants' who are very fearful creatures. Sometimes we tell our children to be good or the 'giants' will get them."

"Oh yes, my mother used to threaten me in the same way with the 'boogyman'."

"Boogyman?"

"Yeah, something like your 'giants'. Tell your children I'm just an ordinary human being who came from a distant land."

The young man spoke to the children, who seemed to relax somewhat, but still kept wary eyes on Clifford.

"My name if Clifford," ventured the owner of that name. "What's yours?"

"I was named Pa Heh, but now people call me Wa Paw Pa."

"Why the change?"

23

"Our people, the Karen people, like to call each other by the name of our first child. That girl," he pointed to the oldest child, "is named Wa Paw, so I am now known as Wa Paw Pa, which means father of Wa Paw."

"That's nice," exclaimed Clifford. "I like that."

"You don't think it's funny?"

"No, not at all. Is this your wife?" Clifford asked, indicating the younger woman.

"Yes, her name is Naw Baw, but now she is known as Wa Paw Mo, mother of Wa Paw."

"Oh yes, now I'm beginning to understand. What about the older couple?"

"They are my wife's parents," replied Pa Heh, who was pleased that Clifford was interested in his family. "You can call her father *Per*, which means grandfather, and call her mother, *Pi*, which means grandmother.

"Do they live with you?"

"Yes," but he added, "Actually, this is their house. We live with them."

"Is that the custom?"

"Yes, all Karen men join their wive's family when they marry. Now we have three children, so we need to build a house for ourselves, but we will always stay in this village."

"Couldn't you live in your home village?"

"No, that is not the Karen way. Anyway, our fields are here."

"Didn't you have fields in your home village?"

"No, my mother did, but they went to my sisters."

"Oh, you mean the land is passed on from mother to daughter."

"That's right. That's the Karen way. Is it like that among your people?"

"Well, sometimes." Clifford thought about it. "We really don't have a system like that. Property can go to all the children in a family, but farmland more commonly to a son."

Pa Heh thought such an indefinite system could make for problems in a family, but kept his thoughts to himself. He looked at the two younger children. "I have two more children, both sons. The middle one is Ti Heh, and the youngest one is…" ,he paused with an embarrassed look. "Well, when he is little we call him *Taw Ae.*"

"Does that have any meaning?"

"Yes, it means pig turds."

Clifford was shocked. That did not sound like a term of endearment that any parent would give to a child.

With a glance at his mother-in-law, Pa Heh continued, "We know there are many evil spirits around us. They make life difficult and take things from us. Many of our children die when they are small. An evil spirit gets in them, so they sicken and die. Maybe those spirits will not want to take a child called Pig Turd. When he gets older we'll give him another name."

Pa Heh stood up, ending the conversation, and moved a low table into the center of the room. The women had gone into the room with the fire and came out carrying bowls of rice and vegetables, which they placed on the table. "*Aw mae, aw mae,*" Pa Heh said, as he urged Clifford to his feet and motioned for him to sit at the table. The table was only about 10 inches high, and Clifford found it awkward to sit on the floor with his legs folded up. The family members did it easily, and Pa Heh placed a heaping plate of rice in front of him. "*Aw mae,*" he repeated, and added the Thai translation "*kin khaow,* which Clifford knew meant to eat. The words literally mean to eat rice, but since rice is eaten at every meal, they simply mean to eat. He had learned his first Karen words.

Soup spoons were provided, and everyone started to eat. Clifford was hungry, and joined in. The rice was somewhat red in color because the bran layer had not been entirely milled off. It had a nutty flavor and was delicious. Clifford commented on how good the rice tasted, and Pa Heh replied, "It's our own rice from the hill fields. Hill rice always tastes better than the lowland padi rice grown in water."

There were two other large bowls on the table; one containing soup and the other boiled vegetables with bits of fish in it. Clifford did not recognize the vegetable; it was somewhat bitter but went well with the rice. The soup turned out to be a communal bowl. From time to time the family members would dip out a spoonful and transfer it directly to their mouths. It was a clear soup with some of the vegetable leaves floating in it, and some unrecognizable bones in the bottom of the bowl. It was salty, and also went well with the rice. Clifford knew that some of his American acquaintances might have trouble eating such a meal, especially the communal soup, but Clifford was a flexible fellow, and really did want to get to know these people of the hills.

There was also a small bowl on the table of something green and mashed up into a kind of paste. Clifford had no idea what it was, but took a spoonful and spread it on his rice as he had seen the others doing. He soon learned what it was; a chili pepper sauce that made him feel like the top of his head was coming off, and made tears come to his eyes. "That stuff is hot," he gasped, to the great amusement of the two older children, who covered their giggles with their hands. Even Naw Baw suppressed a smile.

"You may not be able to eat our food," commented Pa Heh. "We only eat what we grow in our fields, or find in the forest."

"No, I like it. I really do. That's the best rice I've ever eaten, and I have learned to be careful with the chilies."

The leftover rice was collected and returned to the kitchen. Clifford remembered the oranges and dried fish he had brought with him, so he dug them out of his back pack, placing the oranges on the table and handing the fish to Naw Baw, who took them to the kitchen. The children were very pleased with the oranges, and everyone sat down again to peel and eat them.

CHAPTER FIVE

KAREN TRADITIONS

Per, the grandfather, spoke to his son-in-law at some length, and when he had finished Saw Pa Heh turned to Clifford, "*Per* wants to ask you some questions. He is very interested in the *Galawa* people."

"*Galawa?*" enquired Clifford.

"Yes, that means a white foreigner like you."

"What does he want to know?"

"He has been telling me some of the ancient stories of our people. I must tell you that we respect our old people, and from them we learn the sayings of our elders that had descended to them from former generations. *Per* said he heard them from his grandfather when he was a boy and still living across the border in Burma where there are many Karen people, and that some of these old stories are about you, the White People, whom we consider to be our younger brothers."

The old man spoke late into the night, and Clifford was fascinated by what he heard. *Per* told of their fears. They are afraid of the spirits, who, although unseen, can enter a village or a house causing sickness and death. He told of the coming of an evil spirit to this village many years before. First, the spirit entered into a chicken. That chicken made odd sounds, unlike the normal sounds of chickens. They knew the spirit came in that chicken, because soon people started to get sick with high fevers. Many died. It was a time of great sadness. The villagers came together and sacrificed other chickens to the spirit, but the illness persisted. Finally, they sacrificed several pigs. After the flesh and blood of the pigs were offered to the spirits, the meat was cooked and everyone came together to eat. They "ate to the spirits" and the elders called upon the spirits to accept their offering and depart. They did so, and the illness went away.

The villagers wanted to know what they had done wrong that caused the punishment from the spirits. One man confessed. He was a married man, but had slept with another woman one night in a field house. *Per* explained that the Karens do not sanction such misbehavior. Since that time they have strictly adhered to their beliefs: one man one wife, no sex before marriage, and no sex outside of marriage. Also, he explained that some of the old women had grown lax in tending to the household spirits. It is the duty of the oldest woman in each house to make small offerings to the spirit of that house. "Once a year," he explained, "we have a big spirit ceremony in which pigs are sacrificed. Everyone must participate, and the village is closed to outsiders on those days. Before planting rice in our hill fields the male head of each family sacrifices a chicken and sprinkles its blood on the ground. Together with a glass of rice whiskey, that is an offering to the spirits of the land so they will be content and grant us a good crop."

Per also explained their fear of outsiders. "Back in Burma we Karens feared the Burmese who were often cruel to us. The Thai people are kinder, but still we know they look down on us and think we are dirty and backward. Now they want to build a school in our village and send schoolteachers. We would prefer they not come here. We can teach our children the Karen way. That's better than having outsiders live here." Saw Pa Heh, speaking to Clifford in Thai, did not agree. "I think it would be good to have a school her." he asserted. "We live in Thailand and Thai ways are going to affect us whether we like it or not. My wife's father is of the old generation. We need to look to the future."

Per started to relate a legend he had heard from his grandfather, but first Naw Baw brought out a tray and set it on the table. Some small containers and a kind of cutting instrument, like a scissors, were on the tray. Naw Baw offered the tray to Clifford. He knew it was the ingredients for a betal nut chew and declined. He had seen some of the older market women in Bangkok chewing on it with red stained lips, frequently spitting red saliva into a spittoon, but didn't know the procedure. Naw Baw demonstrated by opening one of the containers and taking out some dried seeds, about the size of large grapes. With some difficulty, she cut some in smaller pieces with the scissors. They were evidently hard and tough. Next, she opened a small wide topped bottle containing lime paste, dug some out with her finger, and smeared it over one of several leaves on the tray, placed some of the nut pieces on the leaf, rolled it into a ball and popped it into her mouth. After chewing for a few minutes she moved the cud into her cheek and gave Clifford a big red stained smile. He had learned in the Bangkok markets that the nut was the the dried seed of the areca nut palm, and the leaf was from the betal vine. The lime seemed to stimulate the flow of saliva. He had tried it once in a Bangkok market and thought it tasted terrible. He vowed never to use it again. Naw Baw's father and husband each prepared a chew, and when it was tucked into their cheeks Per proceeded with the legend.

"When Y'wa (God) created the world he took three handfuls of earth and threw them around him. From one sprang the Burmese, from another the Karens, and from the third the *Kalas*, the White People. The Karens were talkative and made more noise than all the others, so the Creator believed there were too many of them, so he threw another handful of earth to the Burmans, who thus gained such supremecy that they were able to overcome the Karens and have oppressed them ever since," (Marshall, Rev. Harry, The Karen People of Burma: A Study in Anthropology and Ethnology, University of Ohio Bulletin, vol. 26, No. 13, 1922.)

Per continued, "I have also heard from the old ones a story that is a little different. In the beginning *Y'wa* created three races of people; the Karens, the dark skinned people like the Indians, and the White People. Thus, the Karens are the elder brother, and the White People are the younger brother. At that time the Karens had the 'Golden Book', sometimes called the 'Book of Life'. However, the Karens did not realize the value of that book and carelessly left it laying around. The younger brother picked up the book and took it away with him to the land of the White People. To this day our younger brother has not returned with the Book, but we believe that he will come with it someday and return it to us." (Cross, Rev. E.B., "The Karens", <u>Journal of the American Oriental Society</u>, Vol. V. 1854.)

The hour was late. The children had fallen asleep on the floor of the house, so Naw Baw scoopped them up and retired to the inner sleeping room. Per had one more tale to tell. He told about a time long ago when Karens lived in a nice place and were happy. The soil was good, many kinds of fruits grew in the forest and food was easy to obtain. No one went hungry. However a large serpent also lived in the forest. He was tricky and sometimes did cruel things. He had noticed a newly married couple living in a house at the edge of their village near the forest. Those two loved one another very much. One day, when the man was working in their fields, the serpent came to the house and carried the woman off to his den. When the husband returned home he discovered his wife was gone, and a fearful neighbor related he had seen the serpent take her away. The villagers believed the serpent had a den in a mountainside deep in the forest, so the man armed himself with a large knife and went in search of the den. He found it in a dark and gloomy canyon shaded by large trees. "Serpent, do you have my wife," he shouted into the den. A rustling noise was heard from within the den, and the serpent spoke. "What if I do, what can you do about it?"

"I will come down after you and cut you to pieces."

"Ho, ho, ho," laughed the serpent. "If you enter my den you will never see your wife again, and I will squeeze the life out of you in my coils."

"Serpent, have pity on me. Return my wife to me and I will never bother you again."

"There is only one thing you can do that will make me release your wife."

"Tell me, and I will do it."

"I'll tell you, but I don't think you love your wife enough to do it."

"Tell me," demanded the man. "I will do anything."

With a great roar the serpent replied, "When your blood flows down into my den I will let your wife go."

"I'll do it," replied the husband, "but first I must return home."

"I don't think I'll see you again," mocked the serpent.

The man had a plan. He returned home, took one of his best chickens and hurried back to the serpent's den.

"Serpent, I'm back, and here is my blood about to run down into your den. When you see the blood release my wife as you have promised."

The man quickly cut the chicken's neck, and let the blood flow into the den.

A great roar echoed from the depths, "You cannot fool me with chicken blood you stupid man. I only want your blood. Now you will never see your wife again."

"Wait," cried the man. "You shall have my blood, but first I must return home."

Once again the man ran home, caught their only pig, and led it back to the den. "Serpent, I am ready. Now release my wife." He cut the throat of the pig, and blood gurgled down into the den.

Now the serpent was really angry. "You foolish man, do you think you can fool me with the blood of a pig. I see you love yourself more than your wife. You have failed to do what I demanded. Your wife will be mine forever."

"Serpent, I truly love my wife." With those words, the man cut his own throat and his blood went down into the den.

"I see you really do," murmered the serpent, and he released the woman. (dramatized by a Pwo Karen dance troupe from Burma)

"Now you see," said Per, as if talking to himself. "We can only use the blood of chickens or pigs to appease the spirits, "Who is there, who would shed his blood for us?"

Clifford was amazed by those stories, and unprepared for the old man's question directed at him, "Younger Brother, have you heard of these things?"

Clifford was tired, but that night he could not sleep. The question, "Have you heard of these things?" spun around and around in his brain. Of course he had heard of those things. He knew the Hebrew word for God was *Yaweh*, so similar sounding to the Karen word for their Creator God. Also, there were the creation stories he had just heard where *Y'wa* had created humankind from earth, the ancient story of the Golden Book, and the good land that sounded like a virtual

Eden. Finally, there was the Serpent, the bad guy. He remembered Per murmering about sacrificing the blood of pigs and chickens, all they could do to propitiate the spirits who held them in a bondage of fear, and wondering if there was another way. Clifford was confused. He had never dreamed that these people living in such an isolated place would have such concepts and traditions. He thought he was here to teach them, but they already knew so very much.

Clifford knew he had been naïve about their culture, and that the tribal traditions he had just heard gave him an opportunity to be manipulative. He reasoned it might be easy for him to graft into these ancient beliefs his version of the Holy One. He knew the Asian Inland Mission would applaud him for doing so. He could even become famous! Clifford, howver, was basically an honest man. The very thought of manipulating a belief system was repugnant to him. He vowed to get to know these people better, learn their language, and, finally, share with them his own concept of God. He would tell the stories he knew from the "Golden Book", his Bible, but he would not force his beliefs on anyone. These people would come to their own conclusions. He heard a rooster's first announcement of the coming dawn before he slept.

It was already light when Clifford was awakened by a loud noise. "Kerplunk", a brief pause, and "kerplunk" again. The noise continued, even shaking the house with each "kerplunk". Clifford quickly pulled on his pants and went down the stairs to see what was making that noise. He found Naw Baw using a heavy wooden contraption that reminded him of a see-saw. Naw Baw stepped on one end of a wooden beam, which lifted up the other end. Attached to that end was a verticle piece of rounded wood. When she stepped off her end of the beam, the other end fell with the loud "kerplunk" sound. The rounded piece of wood dropped into a hollowed out piece of wood partially dug into the ground under the house. Rice was in that hollow, and each time the rounded piece of wood dropped into it the rice was hulled. It was really a very large foot operated mortar and pestle. Wa Paw was helping her mother by pushing the rice around in the hollow so it all got hulled, and, when finished, she scooped out the rice and loose hulls and placed them on a round winnowing tray. By flipping the tray up and down she was able to separate the contents into three piles. The outer rice hulls were discarded, the bran layer was saved to feed their pigs, and the white rice grains were immediately put in a pot over the open fire in the kitchen.

Saw Pa Heh appeared and Clifford asked, "Does your wife do this every morning?"

"Yes, she pounds the rice most mornings."

"Why not do a lot one day and keep it to use for several days?"

"We think freshly hulled rice tastes better, also when the hull is removed weevils can easily infest the hulled rice."

Clifford was learning about village life. Next, Pi, the old grandmother, came down to feed the two pigs in a covered pen behind the house. Clifford had noticed the 20 liter can propped up on rocks with a fire beneath it when he had arrive the day before, but gave it no attention. Now, he could seer it contained some cooked weeds, old cabbage leaves and some of the rice bran. Pi poured the contents of the can into a wooden trough in the pig pen, where it was noisily slurped up by the pigs, acting like pigs.

"*Aw meh, aw meh,*" called Naw Baw from up in the house. Clifford remembered his two words of the Karen language, "eat rice, eat rice." Once again they squatted around the low table, and there it was, rice, the staple of life in Thailand. To go with the rice was a bowel of bamboo shoots boiled with some of the dried fish Clifford had brought. He remembered that Saw Pa Heh and Per had stopped along the trail the day before and dug up the bamboo shoots. Here they were, bambook shoots and the salty dried fish. Delicious, with just a tiny bit of the hot chili sauce.

Clifford was just finishing his breakfast when a little boy appeared at the foot of the stairs. He spoke to Clifford in Karen, and, of course, Clifford understood nothing, although, he thought he did rercognize the words *aw meh*. He looked at Saw Pa Heh, who, in turn, addressed Clifford. "The boy says to go to his house to eat."

"But I just finished eating."

"Never mind, just follow the boy."

Clifford followed the boy to a nearby house that was smaller than the one he had slept in the previous night. There was no table, but bowls of rice, soup, chili sauce, and something different; a bowl of boiled black snails, were set on a woven reed mat. A man stood up to greet him, and once again Clifford heard those words, "*aw meh, aw meh.*" The two of them ate together in silence, and although Clifford was already full, he forced himself to eat another bowel of rice, into which he had spooned some of the soup to make it go down easier. He had no idea how to eat the snails, so followed the example of his host, who sucked out the snail from its shell. It was not easy, and required a strong suck. He had just finished, when a little girl came to that house and spoke to him. Clifford looked at his host, who smiled, and with a wave of his hand, indicated that Clifford should go with the girl. Clifford feared it would be another breakfast. It was. He was not surprised when he saw more bowls of rice, and what appeared to be a bowl of rice gruel mixed with bits of meat. "Oh no, rice with rice," he groaned to himself.

Clifford ate breakfast six times in six different houses. In the last three houses he was able, with great effort, to eat only one or two spoonfuls. After the sixth house he beat a hasty retreat back to where he had slept, hoping to avoid more children with invitations. "How come I was asked to so many houses?" he asked Saw Pa Heh.

"People are just being hospitable."

"In my country," Clifford replied, "someone may invite you to their place to eat, but no one else will invite you for the same meal."

"If people knew you were staying for a long time they might do it like that too, but they think you may be leaving soon and want to invite you to eat in their homes before you leave."

"That's nice, but my stomach may burst."

"We have a saying, " grinned Saw Pa Heh, "better a broken stomach than left over food."

"When I came into this village yesterday," ventured Clifford, "the people did not seem friendly. No one spoke to me."

"They have been watching you, and you seem harmless. Remember, I told you last night that the Karen people are a bit suspicious of outsiders."

"What about you?"

"I get out more often. I go to the city to sell things and visit the Thai people at the village where you parked your car. That's how I learned to speak *kam muang*, the northern Thai dialect."

Naw Baw came out of the kitchen and unfolded some threads

attached to a contraption next to an outer wall. Only when she sat down, unfolded the thing and started to weave did Clifford realize it was a loom. He had seen frame looms before, but never a body loom. It was attached to wall posts, but could be folded up and laid aside when not in use. Naw Baw had unrolled the loom, which was attached to a deer skin belt. She fastened the belt around her and leaned back when she started to weave, which applied tension to the threads. Each time she pulled a bobbin through the work in progress she pounded it in tightly with a sword shaped piece of hardwood, which gave the fabric a tight weave. She was weaving a white piece of material with an occasional red thread added. "What is she making," Clifford wanted to know.

"She's making a dress for Wa Paw, our daughter."

"Wouldn't she like a little more color?"

"No, no, all girls and unmarried women wear white. That's our custom."

Clifford realized he had seen only two kinds of women's clothing in the village, but had assumed it was just a lack of choice. For the first time he really looked at the clothing worn by Naw Baw. It consisted of two pieces; a pull-over blouse and a wrap-round skirt, both of a rusty red color with threads of blue and yellow in geometric designs, much more intricate and colorful than the white one-piece shifts worn by the girls.

"Does it ever happen that a woman never marries?" asked Clifford.

"Seldom."

"If it does happen, does she wear white all her life?"

"Yes, of course. She could never wear the clothing of a married woman. It couldn't be done. Not our custom."

"What about men? Can boys and married men wear the same kind of clothes?"

Saw Pa Heh thought the question was funny, "Yes, no difference for men." Clifford had already admired the red pull-over shirts worn by the men with vertical threads of white, yellow or blue.

"So," noted Clifford, "a Karen man can always tell which women are married and who is single."

"For sure. How can you know in your country?"

"Well," Clifford was taken aback, "if we don't know I guess we have to ask, not the woman but someone who knows her." Saw Pa Heh didn't think much of that way of doing things, but continued.

"My wife makes all our clothes; for herself, for me and for our children."

"What about your pants," asked Clifford. "They don't appear to be made at home."

"No, they're not. Most men buy pants because its easier. Years ago men wore long shirts to their knees, but now we just buy these dark blue pants in the market."

Clifford was learning a lot from these people who had so graciously taken him in, and he hated to leave, but he had seen other villagers heading for their fields with hoes on their shoulders. Surely, Saw Pa Heh had more to do than talk to him.

"Saw Pa Heh, the time has come for me to return to town."

"No need to be in a rush. You are welcome to stay with us."

"Thank you. This has been a great experience for me. I have really enjoyed getting to know you and the people in this village. May I come again sometime?"

"Of course, anytime you want."

"Anyway," continued Clifford, "I had better get my Landrover at the Thai village, before the Headman thinks I left it for him."

"Oh, your truck will be all right, but I'll go with you."

"No need to do that. I can find my way. I just follow the trail don't I?"

"Yes, just follow the trail. You'll be all right."

Clifford went back up to the house to collect his backpack. Naw Baw and her oldest daughter, Wa Paw, were ready to go work in their fields. They were wearing large straw hats and carrying hoes and machetes. Naw Baw reached in her shoulder bag and took out a package wrapped in a banana leaf which she gave to Clifford. "*Bo meh*," she said. Clifford turned to Saw Pa Heh, who had returned to the house. "That means a bundle of rice," he explained, "something for you to eat at midday."

Clifford marched out of the village with a sense of exhilaration. He had accomplished something all by himself in finding his way to this village and making friends with Saw Pa Heh and his family. Now he had a sense of purpose. He knew he had to find a house to rent in

Chiang Mai and establish himself in this Northern Region of Thailand. He wanted to visit the other Mountain Tribes and learn their languages. He set difficult goals, but on that sunny morning he knew he could do it. Nothing seemed impossible, even finding his way back to the Thai village. He went through the hill fields, through the pine trees, and into the bamboo forest. The trail was familiar and he was confident he could take care of himself.

That was before he came to a fork in the trail. He stopped and looked down both branches of the trail. Nothing seemed familiar. He realized that following someone who knew the way was not the same as walking alone. There was a crude bench made of bamboo right where the trail forked. It was about noon, so Clifford decided to sit and eat the bundle of rice while he thought about which fork to take. He untied the strips of bamboo used to tie up the banana leaf and opened the package. There was about a double handful of rice, with most of the red bran layer still attached to the kernels. A piece of the salted fish he had brought with him to the village was placed on top of the rice. A small leaf packet revealed a dab of chili sauce. It was a great midday repast. As he sat on the bench the sounds of the forest, quieted by his arrival, started up again. Birds sang from the tree tops and insects buzzed all around him. A flock of small parrot-like birds, a bit larger than parakeets, flew into a tree and noisily ate the fruit hanging from it. Clifford was startled when something with fur on it swooped down just above him and landed on the trunk of a nearby tree. It was a flying squirrel. Clifford had heard of such creatures, but had never seen one. He knew they didn't really fly, but when they jumped off a tree branch they spread out their legs, which opened skin between their legs enabling them to glide from tree to tree.

It was nice to sit in the quietness of the forest, but he still had a long walk ahead of him, and he knew he had a problem. He really didn't know which fork to take. Shouldering his pack he took the one to his left, which soon descended to a small creek, which he easily stepped over. From there the trail ascended to a grassy area with a thin stand of trees, and Clifford surprised a band of gibbons. They fled from him, partly on the ground and partly swinging from tree to tree. Later, from the forest higher up the mountain he heard them calling, "hooooo, hooooo, hooooo." It was a very wild, eerie sound, which did not help

Clifford's state of mind. He thought he might be going in the wrong direction. He had a queasy feeling in his stomach that people get when they began to realize they may be lost. Still, he kept going, thinking that he had to explore this trail for a ways before giving up on it and retracing his steps back to the fork.

He soon came to some old hill fields that had been abandoned, and that made him feel better. Perhaps there is a nearby village, he thought, so he kept going. Sure enough, coming out of some trees he spotted a village on a ridge top about a mile away. He hurried on, and as he entered the village he could see the people were not Karen. The houses were not elevated, but built of rough wood planks right on the ground. Through open doors he could see the floors were of hard packed earth. The men were wearing wide, baggy pants drawn up at the waist with a belt, and shirts made of a black shiny cloth material. They wore embroidered skull caps and heavy silver necklaces. The women wore embroidered blouses and pleated skirts that had batik designs on them. Clifford stopped in the center of the village hoping someone would greet him, but no one did. The villagers were busy with various tasks, but at the same time were watching Clifford with wary eyes.

Clifford spoke in Thai to one man who was sharpening his machete with a whetstone. "I seem to be lost," Clifford said, "can you direct me to the Thai village?" The man did not reply, but yelled something toward one of the houses. After a short wait, a man strolled out of that house and approached Clifford. He was wearing clothes similar to the other men, but his clothe were new and instead of rubber sandals or bare feet, he was wearing polished dress shoes "*Ow anyang?*" (what do you want) he asked in a rather discourteous manner in the Northern Thai dialect. "I seem to have taken the wrong trail," replied Clifford. "I was coming down from a Karen village and came to a fork in the trail. I took the left fork which led me here. Can you tell me how to get to the Thai village?" The man eyed Clifford suspiciously, but replied, "Take this trail you came on back to that fork and take the right fork. That will take you to the Thai village."

"Yes, I'm sure that's true, but isn't there a shortcut I can take?"

"No, stay on the trail you came on."

Clifford thanked him and turned to leave, but the man asked, "How come you, a *farang*, are up here in these mountains alone? Do you have business here?" "No," replied Clifford, "just visiting my friend in the Karen village. Sorry to bother you."

It was late afternoon when Clifford hurried back down the trail to the fork. He took the right fork, which proceeded downhill, and immediately he began to recognize things he had seen two days before on his way to the Karen village. He was relieved to be on the correct trail, but worried about the coming darkness. He thought about the man who had given him directions, and how unfriendly he seemed. That was unusual; most people he met in Thailand were friendly. He also recalled that he had said he was visiting a friend in the Karen village. "That's true," Clifford spoke to himself, "I do consider Saw Pa Heh my friend. I will come back to visit him soon."

CHAPTER SIX

THE THAI VILLAGE

It was just getting dark, when much to Clifford's relief, he arrived at the Thai village. He went to the Headman's house, followed by barking dogs, and saw his Landrover was still parked where he had left it. The Headman came out to see who was coming and saw Clifford.

"So, you are back. I wondered who the dogs were barking at."

"Yes, I made it back o.k., now I had better drive back to Chiang Mai."

"Too late for that. The road up here is not very safe at night. There have been robberies. Better if you stay in my house tonight."

"I don't want to bother you."

"No bother, my family and I were just going to eat. Come join us."

Clifford followed the Headman up the stairs into the house. It was built of teakwood, including the polished floor. He introduced Clifford to an attractive woman who appeared to be about 40 years old. "My wife," said the Headman. The woman gave Clifford a graceful *wai*, a Thai greeting, which Clifford returned. "Sit, here at the table," commanded the Headman, who was both friendly and brusk. Clifford was reluctant to join the family. They had certainly not been expecting him, but they insisted, so he sat. It was a low round table like in the Karen village homes, but larger and also made of teak. Two children, a boy and a girl, dressed in school uniforms were also sitting at the table. "My children," explained the Headman, with his usual brevity. They also greeted Clifford in the Thai manner. The girl, who was the oldest of the children, went back to the kitchen and brought back a basket made with split bamboo, which she placed close to Clifford. It contained glutinous steamed rice, which the Northern Thai call *khaow nung*. Clifford knew it by its Central Thai name, *khaow niow*. Clifford had already learned in the Chiang Mai market that Northern Thai people mostly ate this type of rice. It is sticky, and must be eaten with one's fingers. Clifford observed the family members reaching into other baskets, taking out some rice and rolling it into a ball, which they used to pick up food from dishes in white enamel bowls. Clifford did likewise.

The food was centered around rice, of course, but there were several side dishes in the bowls. There was a common vegetable, *pak bung*, stir fried with garlic, a chicken curry, and a fried fish. A bottle of fish sauce and a small bowl of chili sauce was also on the table. The children did not stare at Clifford, obviously they had seen foreigners before. "I see your children are both in school," remarked Clifford.

"Yes," replied the headman, "they're going to our village school, but next year my daughter will go to high school at the district town down on the main road. Either her mother or I will have to take her everyday on my motorcycle." That was a rather long speech for the Headman. The girl gave her father an impish grin. "You don't have to take me. I can drive myself." The Headman rolled his eyes. He had heard that request before!

After eating, the girl and her mother cleared the table. The Headman got up and brought back a bottle of whiskey and two glasses, which he proceeded to fill. "Have a drink," invited the Headman.

"No thanks," replied Clifford, "I don't use alcohol."

"I thought you Foreigners all drank a lot of whiskey."

"Well, some do, but not me."

Not wanting to seem unappreciative of the man's hospitality, Clifford added, "It makes me dizzy."

"Makes me feel good," replied the Headman, and added, "Where's your Hill Tribe friends? Did you come back alone?"

"Yes," replied Clifford, "I didn't think I would have any trouble, but I was kind of lost for a while."

Clifford went on to describe how he took the wrong fork in the trail, and finally came to another village, which was neither Karen or Thai.

"Must have been that Meo village," said the Headman, as he looked at Clifford carefully. "Anything going on there?"

"No, not much, but the people didn't help much. Only one man seemed to speak Thai and he was not very friendly."

"What did he look like?"

Clifford described the man, mentioning that he did wear Tribal clothe, which was new and elegant, and also that he was the only villager he saw wearing nice leather dress shoes.

"That sounds like Sae Yang," murmured the Head Man with a worried look. "He must be out of jail."

"Jail?"

"Yes, he's a drug dealer. You had better stay away from that village. They plant opium and the man you met has gotten rich selling heroin."

"Where does the heroin come from?"

"Heroin is refined from opium. Takes 10 kilograms of opium to make one kilogram of heroin. Pure poison that stuff is. I've never known anyone addicted to heroin to break the habit."

"Is it easy to make?"

"No, not so easy. They must have a little factory hid away somewhere. They need some special chemicals and someone who knows how to do it. Sometimes those people bring in a Hong Kong Chinese chemist.

"Don't the police do anything?"

"The police must have their suspicions, they've asked me about that village, but I don't want to get involved. Too dangerous. People like that," he lowered his voice, "will take revenge on your family if you inform on them. They have no heart. Stay away from them."

Clifford was thinking about that village. The Headman had called them Meo, but he remembered seeing pictures of a tribe called Hmong that looked like them.

"Are those people sometime called Hmong?" he asked.

"Yes, I think so," replied the Headman draining his glass, "don't go near them. You might come across their factory by mistake."

While they were talking the Headman's wife had prepared a sleeping place for Clifford in one end of the room. She opened a thin mattress on the floor and covered it with a blanket. Clifford got up, opened his back pack and took out his own blanket, which he placed on the mattress. Clifford was impressed, he knew the mattress would be more comfortable than the thin mat he had slept on in the Karen village. His sleeping place was in a part of the room elevated about a foot from the rest of the floor. On the wall was a shelf with a Buddha image and some smoldering joss sticks. While still in Bangkok, Clifford had learned something about etiquette in a Thai Buddhist house, so he went to bed with his head to the image, not his feet. That night Clifford slept well under the impassive gaze of the Buddha.

The following morning, Clifford was served a breakfast of *khao tom* (watery boiled rice) enlivened with pickled vegetables, salted duck egg, and some dried fish. Clifford was grateful for the hospitality he had received at the Headman's house. Before leaving he thanked both the Headman and his wife.

CHAPTER SEVEN

GETTING SETTLED IN CHIANG MAI

Clifford drove back to Chiang Mai with no further adventures and returned to the Suk Niran Hotel where he had stayed before. He was now convinced that he should stay in Chiang Mai and needed to rent a house. Late in the afternoon he went to visit Nai Lee at his little shop.

Nai Lee was glad to see him, "Well, you made it back, I see neither the tigers or the bedbugs ate you."

"No, I had a good time. No tigers, no bedbugs and I even learned two Karen words."

"What did you learn?"

"I learned to say *aw meh*, which means to eat rice."

"That's a very necessary word. From there you can learn other important words, like 'where's the toilet', and 'I love you', which you can say to a pretty girl."

Clifford blushed, and Nai Lee laughed at him. Mrs. Lee, however, had some kind words for him. "That's all right," she asserted, "only men with good hearts blush. Women have to watch out for men who don't blush."

Clifford, eager to change the subject, said, "I've decided to stay in

Chiang Mai, so I need to find an inexpensive house to rent. Do you know of any?"

The Lees conversed together in Chinese, and finally spoke to Clifford. "We know a lady who may have a house to rent behind her own house. Most *Farangs* would want a nicer house, but this one may be suitable for you. We can talk to her tonight and let you know what we find out. We'll tell her you're a shy *Farang* who has no wife."

Clifford grinned and said he would come back tomorrow.

After another night, at what Clifford hoped was his last night at the Suk Niran Hotel, he returned to the Lees shop at mid-morning in his Land Rover. "Ah, here you are," greeted Nai Lee, Let's go look at the house." Clifford was directed down some narrow roads away from the shopping area and into the front yard of a medium sized wooden house. "Keep driving," instructed Nai Lee, and there, in the back yard, was a smaller wooden house. "Park here," added Nai Lee, "I'll get the owner."

Clifford looked over the exterior of the house while he was waiting. It was elevated off the ground on concrete posts. The remains of an old ox cart was under the house, but Clifford thought it could be removed so he could park his Land Rover there. The house had been painted brown with a wood stain that resists termites. He noted, with approval, that the roof was made of cement shingles, not the more common corrugated metal used on many such houses. Clifford had learned that metal roofs were hotter and also very noisy during a rain storm.

Nai Lee came back with the house owner, a middle-aged Thai woman, and introduced her to Clifford. "This is Khun Pa Chintana (Aunt Chintana) .She will show you the house." The woman had a set of keys in her hand, but made no move toward the house. Clifford acknowledged her presence with the traditional Thai curtsy of folded hands lifted to his chin and she returned the curtsy. "Before we look at the house I have some questions," she said to Clifford. "Will you be staying for some time? I don't want to bother with someone who rents the house one month and leaves the next month."

"Yes," replied Clifford, "I will be staying for several years I think."

"Oh, that's good. Nai Lee has told me you are single, but do you have a wife who will be coming later?

"No, I have no wife."

"You must understand that you must not bring in any woman of bad reputation. Do you agree to that?"

"Yes, I certainly agree with that."

Clifford blushed again when Nai Lee said with a broad grin, "He's bashful."

Chintana ignored the shop keeper and walked up the steps to the locked door, which she opened and beckoned Clifford to follow.

After Chintana unbolted and opened some of the window shutters he could see the house was clean. There were metal bars on the windows to keep out robbers, but no screens. There was a kitchen protruding out from the side of the house and somewhat separated from the main structure. Clifford knew that Thais like their kitchens to be separated from the rest of the house, perhaps to keep out the odor of frying garlic and chilies, which are used with most meals. The kitchen contained a sink with a water faucet over it, and a charcoal stove. Chintana explained, "if it's more convenient for you to use gas I will take out this charcoal stove and you can buy your own gas stove."

There were three other rooms and Chintana showed them to Clifford without comment. One was a small room near the kitchen, where Clifford thought he would likely eat his meals. It contained a small table. The other two rooms had no furniture. A door from one of those empty rooms led to a Thai style bathroom, which had a cement floor, a sink, a squat toilet and a large crock filled with water to dip from when bathing. A light bulb hung from the ceiling of each room.

"I have no furniture," commented Clifford.

"I have a single bed I can lend you, but you will have to get your own mattress."

"How much is the rent?"

"It will be 1,000 Baht a month."

Clifford mentally calculated that would be $50 in American money. He looked at Nai Lee who said, "I think that is a good deal."

Clifford enquired of Chintana, "What about the cost of water and electricity?"

"I will pay for the water. The meter for both houses is near my house, but you will have to pay your own electric bill."

"Sounds all right to me. I'll take it. When can I move in?"

"Anytime you want, but I would like a down payment of the first month's rent please."

"I can do that as soon as I open up a bank account."

"Where are your possessions?"

"Don't have much but a couple of suitcases. I'll have to do some shopping."

"I know a good place to get furniture," spoke up Nai Lee, "you can buy what you need at the Provincial Prison."

Chintana gave Clifford a key for the padlock on the door, and reminded him that the first month's rent was due. Clifford took Nai Lee back to his shop and received directions to both a bank and the prison. Clifford knew he had to start with the bank, so following Nai Lee's advice, he went directly to the *Tanakan Thai Panich*, known in English as the Siam Commercial Bank, where he hoped to open a checking account. He first spoke to a bank employee at one of the windows, who directed him to the bank manager in his office. The bank manager was a cheerful man who stood up to shake Clifford's hand and spoke to him in English. "Welcome to this bank. My name is Khru Praphan, what can I do for you?"

Clifford replied, "I would like to deposit some money and open a checking account. Can a Foreigner do that?"

"Of course, of course you can," he replied as he pulled out some forms from his desk. "How much are you going to deposit?"

"I have these checks from America, can I deposit U.S. dollar checks into a Thai account?"

"Yes, no problem. Let's see what you have."

Clifford handed the bank manager six checks of various amounts that had been forwarded to him by the Asian Inland Mission before he left Bangkok. The manager called one of the bank employees and instructed him to calculate their worth in Thai Baht. "Now," the manager continued, "I will need a photo copy of your passport and the address of your residence."

Clifford pulled out his passport from his pocket and slid it across the desk. "I don't have a photo copy."

"Never mind, we can make a copy here," as he called another employee and instructed him to do so.

"I have just rented a house this morning and don't know the address."

"I will need that to complete these forms. What is your occupation?"

"I am a missionary."

"Is that so, I am a Christian myself. What mission group are you with?"

"The Asian Inland Mission."

"I never heard of it. Are there others from that mission in Thailand?"

"No, I think I'm the only one."

"Where do you intend to work?"

"I want to work among the Mountain Tribes People. I just came back from visiting a Karen village in the mountains."

"That's amazing. I'm a Karen myself."

Now it was Cliffords turn to be amazed. "Can that be? I thought all Karens lived in the mountains and were not…." He was about to say, "not educated," but realized that would not sound good.

The bank manager laughed, "Many people think that, but some Karens live in lowland areas and do attend school. I was fortunate to be able to attend a Christian school here in Chiang Mai. I became a teacher in a village school and people still call me *Khru*, which means teacher, but I later started working as a clerk in this bank and am now the manager."

Clifford was further amazed when the Manager broke into song and sang all verses of the Christian hymn, Amazing Grace. "Where did you learn that hymn?" asked Clifford. He was not expecting such hospitality in a Thai bank. "I learned it in the Christian school I attended. Did you know there is also a Thai version?" To prove that fact, he sang it through again in Thai. About that time, one of the bank clerks entered the office and gave the manager some forms and Clifford's passport.

"Well, now we must get down to business. Today the exchange rate is Baht 20.31 for one U.S. Dollar, so we have credited your new account with 11,376 Baht," declared the manager. "Usually a foreign check is not credited to your account until it is cleared, which may take two or three weeks. I think I can trust you, so I had the amount credited to your account today. Would you like some of that in cash?"

"Yes, I would. How about 3,000 Baht, so I can pay my rent and buy some furniture."

Again, the manager called in a clerk, who was hovering just outside the office, and in a few minutes Clifford was walking out of the bank with a new checkbook and 3,000 Baht in his pocket. "God works in mysterious ways," he murmered. He was also grateful to Nai Lee, who had directed him to just the right bank.

The Prison Store was located just outside the grey walls of the Provincial Prison, and Clifford made several purchases. He liked the items made from rattan, which one of the prisoners working there showed him, so he bought a couch with two matching chairs. Cushions, stuffed with kapok, came with them. Clifford thought he was done, but the storekeeper was a natural salesman.

"How about a bed?" he asked.

"Don't need one. The house owner is lending me one."

"Does it have a mattress?"

"No, thanks for reminding me. Do you sell mattresses too?"

"Sure, right over here."

Clifford was shown to a stack of mattresses. They were the kind commonly used in Thailand that can be folded up when not in use. They were also stuffed with kapok and were rather hard. Clifford selected a mattress for a single bed.

"Do you sleep alone?" asked the curious shopkeeper, who had never had a foreign customer before. Clifford thought that was a rather personal question.

"Yes, I'm not married. Anything wrong with that?"

"No, no, sorry I asked. It does get rather lonely in here."

"Are you really a prisoner here?"

"Yes, I've been in here five years already."

"They trust you to work here in the store?"

"They kind of trust me. There's still a guard outside the door, and if I attempted to escape I'd get five years added to my term."

"How much longer you got?"

"Two years, but I'm hoping for a pardon on his Majesty the King's birthday."

"What are you in for?" Clifford thought he could ask personal questions too.

"Drugs. I should have known better, but I got involved with a guy who said he could make me rich. Now he's rich and I'm in jail."

"Did you sell the stuff?"

"No, I just transported it. Took it all over the country. Mostly heroin, that was made in the mountains around here. The Hill Tribe guy that hired me was jailed too. Somebody snitched on us."

Clifford had another question, "What about the man who hired you, is he still in jail?"

"No, he had a lot of money, a lot of contacts in high places. He's out."

Clifford thought it was not possible, but he asked anyway, "Is his name Sae Yang?"

The prisoner reacted with a sharp look at Clifford. "Who are you anyway? Get out of here, I don't want to talk to you."

Clifford was surprised by the man's reaction, but realized that the prisoner had formerly had an association with Sae Yang; an association that had obviously soured, and now he was suspicious of Clifford. "Wait," Clifford urged, "I'm sorry, but I think I accidentally met this man who you worked with." Clifford had a soft spot for lonely people. He had known loneliness himself and was beginning to like this talkative prisoner, who was confined to a cell when not working in the store. Clifford described his visit to the Karen village, how he got lost on the way back and ended up in the Hmong village. He described the man he had met there, and that he had learned his name from the Thai Headman. The prisoner listened, and seemed to accept Clifford's explanation. "O.k., but my advice is to stay away from that guy. He's dangerous."

That was the second warning Clifford had received about the man he had met in the Hmong village. "Thank you," Clifford replied, "I will surely never go to that village again. By the way, what is your name? I may come back for more furniture."

"My name is Prasong, and by the way, how are you going to get your furniture to your house?"

"I don't know. I hadn't thought about that."

"I'll get you a truck."

"How can you do that?"

"Watch me!"

Prasong went to the door and yelled at someone sleeping under a mango tree. "Hey *Ai Tia*, this *Farang* needs to have his furniture delivered." To Clifford's amazement, the man walked to a nearby pickup truck and drove up to the shop, even if Clifford thought his nickname was a bit demeaning. It meant "Shorty" He was short and stocky, so the name fit.

Clifford paid 900 Baht for the furniture, which amounted to about $45.00. The truck driver looked at Clifford's purchases and said he would deliver for 100 Baht. Clifford was about to agree when he noticed Prasong, who was standing behind the driver, shake his head negatively. Clifford caught on and bargained, "Too much, I'll give you 60 Baht." The driver readily agreed, so Clifford realized he had still overpaid. Still, both the furniture and delivery charge seemed very low. He was also glad to see that Prasong was seemingly not suspicious of him anymore and willing to be a friend. Prasong could see the foreigner was harmless, but still planned to ask *Ai Tia* for a 5 Baht "finders fee" when he returned.

Clifford, followed by the truck, returned to his rented dwelling where the two of them carried the furniture up into the house. After paying the driver, Clifford sat on one of the chairs with a sense of satisfaction. He had a bank account, he had a home, and he had made some friends, He was ready for the next step, whatever that was.

After one sleepless night in his house, swatting mosquitos, he realized that next step needed to be a practical one. He returned to the market, where he purchased a mosquito net, a small refrigerator, some pots and pans, food, a gas burner and a tank of bottled gas. Clifford really didn't want to deal with the old charcoal stove in his house, which required some expertise to start and keep burning at the right temperature. Back at his house, he and Chintana removed the stove in the kitchen and set up the two burner gas stove. Chintana approved. "Much easier for you," she assented. She also asked him how much he had paid for each of his purchases. "Too much," she repeated time after time, but Clifford was satisfied. Chintana also agreed to have the old ox cart under the house removed, so Clifford could park his Land Rover there. Clifford was now ready to turn his efforts to learning the Karen language.

CHAPTER EIGHT

ANOTHER LANGUAGE

The Bank Manager was the only Karen, known to Clifford, who lived in Chiang Mai, so he returned to the bank to talk to him. Anyway, the bank needed his address on those forms he had not completely filled out. The bank manager saw Clifford when he entered the bank and waved him into his office. "So, have you spent all your money already?"

"No, not yet, but I do want to talk to you. Is this an inconvenient time?"

"No problem! What's on your mind?"

"Well, I told you before that I want to work among the Hill Tribes. I know there are many different tribes, and each have their own language, but since I have already visited a Karen village, I would like to learn that language. How can I do that?"

"I might be able to find someone who could help you," thoughtfully replied the Manager. "Next Sunday come to my house at 6:00 P.M. I live in the *Nong Prateep* area. A small group of Karen Christians come for a worship service; something like a house church."

The Manager drew a simple map that gave directions to his house and gave it to Clifford. "You must understand," he warned, "that none of those people are trained teachers. Some are gardeners for wealthy people. Some are laborers of various kinds, but they can speak both Thai and Karen. Maybe you can start with them, and also keep up your visits to Karen villages."

The next Sunday, Clifford was at the bank manager's house at 6:00 o'clock sharp and was introduced to the manager's wife, a Thai lady. Furniture in one room had been pushed against the walls and mats put on the floor for people to sit on. Clifford was the first one to arrive, and was thus able to observe the worshippers as they arrived. Most of the women wore Karen clothing, except girls who mostly wore Thai skirts and blouses. Most men wore Western trousers with a Karen woven pullover shirt. Some women with infants strapped to their backs carried large black umbrellas to shade their child from the sun. It was 6:30 before the informal service began. Clifford was offered a chair, but he chose to sit on the mats with the other worshippers who gave him curious looks, but who looked aside when he looked at them. The manager opened the service with a hymn. Clifford recognized the tune, but the words were in Karen. A number of people, both men and women, stood to offer prayers or request the singing of another hymn. Clifford was surprised by the quality of the singing. They sang with vigor in four part harmony Most sang from memory, but some used well worn hymnbooks.

The manager nodded to a young man, who came to the front of the room and read from what Clifford assumed was a Bible. He was a good reader and the people listened attentively, except for some small children who wandered around the room. Some babies started to cry, but their mothers nursed them and they quieted down. After reading from the Bible the young man spoke for about 15 minutes. When he sat down, the manager stood to open another hymn and everyone joined in. He finished with a prayer and the service ended.

As the people were leaving, the manager switched to the Thai language and introduced Clifford to the young man who had spoken during the service. "This is Swe Po, he may be able to help you learn the Karen language. He has newly arrived in Chiang Mai.

Clifford and Swe Po sat on a bench in the shade of a mango

tree and got acquainted. Clifford was curious about the Bible and hymnbooks that had been used in the service. "I didn't know that the Karen language had been reduced to writing," said Clifford, "was that done here in Thailand?"

"No", replied Swe Po, "It was done in Burma about a hundred years ago," as he took his Bible out of his shoulder bag and showed it to Clifford.

"Amazing," marveled Clifford, "The letters seem to be all circles."

"Those are Burmese letters; Baptist missionaries and Karens in Burma at that time used the Burmese alphabet to write the Karen language."

"How is it that you can read Karen? Did someone teach you?"

"Before I was born some Karen Christians from Burma came to our village and taught us about Jesus. Our whole village became Christian. They taught our people how to read and left some Bibles and hymnbooks with us when they left. The older generation taught us children, and someday I will teach my children."

"You speak Thai well. Can you read it?"

"Yes, there is a government school in my village. It only goes as far as *Prathom* 4 (fourth grade), but I did learn to speak and read Thai."

"Is your village in the mountains?"

"No, its in the lowlands near the town of Maesariang. Most of the Karens in Thailand live in the mountains, but there are no schools there."

"Why not?"

"I think Thai teachers do not like to live there. They get lonely."

"What kind of work do you do here in Chiang Mai?"

"I work in the *rong kha sat.*" (abattoir)

"What's that?"

"That's where the animals are killed and butchered to be sold for meat in the markets."

"Do you like to work there?"

"No, it's a terrible place; pigs squealing, cows bellowing, blood being collected in tubs; no, I really don't like it there."

"So, why do you work in such a place?"

"It was the only job I could find. No one else wants to work there, especially Buddhists, so at least I do have work and enough income to pay my share of the rent and food in the house four of us from my village live in."

"I suppose the Buddhists don't like to kill animals."

"That's right; its against their religion, but some do anyway. I don't have to kill the animals either, all I do is clean up the place."

"How long is your workday?"

"I work from 4:00 A.M. until noon."

"That means you really have to get up early."

"Sure does. They start killing the animals about midnight, so the meat can be in the market early in the morning. I come with the cleanup crew, and that's not so bad. It means I have the rest of the day off."

Clifford was glad to hear Po Swe's afternoons were free.

"Po Swe," Clifford continued, "I would like to learn the Karen language. Can you come to my house and teach me?"

Po Swe gave Clifford an incredulous look, "I'm not a teacher; how can I do that?"

"Well, you can speak and read Karen, and we can talk to one another in Thai, so it should be possible, and I'll pay you 20 Baht an hour. What do you think?"

"I suppose I could try it."

"Good, can you start tomorrow at 2:00 P.M.?"

"Where do you live?"

Cifford gave directions to his house and Po Swe agreed to be there, but Clifford wanted to know more about Po Swe's work. "Why aren't the animals killed in the day time and the carcasses kept under refrigeration?" he asked.

"There is no refrigeration," Po Swe replied, "The animals are killed and the meat is sold all in one day."

"What if the market sellers have meat left over?"

"That's up to them; some have refrigerators for their own use."

Clifford had often visited markets in Bangkok and had learned that animals are not killed on the four Buddhist holy days of each month, which correspond with the four quarters of the moon, so he asked Po Swe about this. "What happens on *Wan Pra* (the holy days), are animals killed here in Chiang Mai?"

"No, I get those days off, the slaughter house is always closed on *Wan Pra*. Even though I'm a Christian, Sunday is just another work day. At least, I am able to attend a worship service here at the Bank Manager's house in the afternoon."

Clifford settled into a routine of language study six days a week. He was a diligent student and guided his teacher into providing organized lessons, such as he was accustomed to at the Thai Language School in Bangkok. He soon learned to read, and the Karen Bible and Hymnbook became his text books. Po Swe warned him that those books had been translated in Burma, so he might find the local Karens speaking a little differently. Po Swe advised him to visit some of the Karen villages in the mountains around Chiang Mai, and gave directions to several. Clifford was glad to do that, and sometimes returned to visit his Karen friends in that first village he had visited. Saw Pa Heh, Naw Baw, and the children were always glad to see him. Sometimes they laughed at the proper Karen he was learning, and taught him how the mountain Karens in Thailand spoke. Per, the old grandfather, however, approved. "Good, you are learning our language correctly, like city Karens speak in Burma. Nobody will mistake you for an ignorant mountain Karen."

Pa Heh had heard there were books written in the Karen language, but had never seen one. "Can you teach me to read?" he asked Clifford.

"Well, I'm just learning myself, but I can teach you what I know," replied Clifford.

Clifford was a natural linguist who picked up languages fast. Living alone, he had time on his hands and soon learned the Karen alphabet. He was able to read the words in the Bible or Hymnal before he knew what the words meant. On one visit to his friends at the Karen village, he read to them the two creation stories found in the book of Genesis. They were quite impressed to learn that the Creator God in that book was named Y'wa, the same as their own word. They marveled that Clifford could read the Karen words, even though he still had to speak to Saw Pa Heh in Thai to communicate his thoughts. Still, Clifford was making good progress and with each visit to the Karen village was able to depend on their language more, and Thai less.

Though Clifford had made a few acquaintances he had a very limited social life. Po Swe came to teach him the Karen language, he attended the Karen Christian service at the Bank Manager's house, and sometimes when he was in the market area he stopped to visit with Nai Lee and his wife at their shop. He even had a waving relationship with the pick-up driver, Ai Tia, who had delivered his furniture purchased at the prison. He considered Saw Pa Heh and his family in the Karen village to be friends, but did not see them often. Aunt Chintana, from whom he rented his house, had kept a suspicious eye on him for some time waiting to see if any ladies of ill repute came to his house. When none did, she became friendlier and sometimes sent over some rice and curry in a *pinto* (stacked food container), which Clifford appreciated very much, since his own cooking was barely at survival level.

He had not met any foreigners like himself, although he often saw them on the streets. The most numerous were the young back packers who were touring the world on the cheap. Their dress and behaviour sometimes embarrassed Clifford. Unlike the foreigners, Thai women would never wear short shorts and halter tops. Many of the travelers wore blouses or shirts made from old flour sacks with the miller's logo prominently displayed. Only very destitute Thais would wear such poor clothing, and it would embarrass them to do so. One day in the market, Clifford was asked by a Thai woman selling vegetables, why the *Farangs* wore such clothing. "They can't be poor or they could not afford to travel. When a Thai goes abroad they would wear their best clothe so as to not bring shame to our country." She laughed when Clifford explained, "I think its the style for *Farang* young people these days."

The Thais are a very tolerant people, with a live and let live attitude, so they mostly ignored the bizarre ways of the foreigners. That was not always true when religious symbolism was involved. There are many old Buddhist temples in Chiang Mai that were visited by tourists. Groups with a tour guide were instructed on proper behaviour. Women should wear modest clothing and men a shirt. Always remove shoes before entering a temple. One group of clueless young Mormon missionaries got in serious trouble when they had a picnic in a forest near an ancient temple site. The temple building was long gone, but the old Buddha image stood alone. They had their picture taken while sitting on top of the image. Thais never reach over, or touch someone on the head, which is considered the holiest part of the body. Sitting on an image of the Lord Buddha was the worst thing they could have done. When the photos were developed in a photo shop the owner notified the police, and the group were all arrested. Their Mission supervisor bailed them out, and they were released, after a stern lecture from a police captain.

After a few months, Clifford was feeling at home in Chiang Mai. He had a house, knew where the cheap restaurants were, and was able to speak passable Karen. He picked up the Northern Thai dialect from hanging around in the markets, and also from his landlady. His financial situation, however, was a bit shakey. Clifford was supposed to raise his own financial support by writing to supporting churches back in the United States and providing glowing reports of his mission work. Clifford, however, was more diligent about language study than writing letters. Anyway, what could he write about? He studied, went to the markets, rented a house, furnished it, and made occasional trips to villages where he could barely communicate with the people. He didn't think those activities would impress anyone.

Clifford was forced to think about what he was doing in Thailand. He knew he wanted to share his Christian beliefs with the Hill People, but was honest enough to realize he could not do that until he understood their own spirituality, and he couldn't do that until he could really communicate with them at a deep level. He knew his language study was important and would not give that up just to report questionable conversions to his supporting churches. Clifford also loved his trips to the upland villages. He was curious about their way of life, their culture, beliefs and family life. He was really coming to love those people.

CHAPTER NINE

MEETING THE AKHA

One day Clifford stopped by Nai Lee's shop and saw some people who were certainly Tribal, but he couldn't identify them. Their group consisted of both men and women dressed in dark homespun with embroidered shirts and blouses. The women wore headdresses, covered with silver buttons and coins, and short pleated skirts. Clifford had never seen such short skirts worn by any women in Thailand. They were selling animal skins, dried chili peppers and some roots, which Clifford assumed were used for herbal medicine. Nai Lee told him they were Eekaw and had come from Chiang Rai Province to the north. That information prompted Clifford's memory. He had heard about these people, who called themselves Akha. When their business transaction was completed, and they had pocketed the money from the sale of their products, Clifford spoke to them in Northern Thai. They stared at Clifford, but gave no response. Nai Lee spoke to one of the men in a language Clifford could mostly understand. It was like Northern Thai, but a little different. "Some of these people understand Thai Yai," Nai Lee explained to Clifford. "The Thai Yai live in that part of Burma just to the north of Thailand. Clifford, always interested in languages, realized that the Thai Yai were also known as Shan. "How come you know all these languages?" asked Clifford.

"In my business it helps, anyway I used to live in Mae Sai on the Burma border and heard this language spoken a lot. It is very similar to Northern Thai."

"Then why didn't they respond to my question?"

"I don't think a *Farang* has ever spoken to them before. Anyway, I told them you were alright. Try again."

Clifford did try again, and the man Nai Lee had spoken to replied. "Yes, I understand. What do you want?"

"I would like to visit your village and perhaps stay a few days. May I do that?"

Clifford thought that was a simple request, but it brought on a flurry of discussion among the Akha that lasted for some time. Neither Clifford or Nai Lee could understand a word. Finally, the man who had spoken before turned to Nai Lee and asked, "Why does this foreigner want to come to our village?"

"You had better ask him," replied Nai Lee, and all eyes turned to Clifford. Clifford was a bit flustered, but managed to explain that he was a new resident in Thailand, expected to stay for several years, and would like to get to know the Akha people. "Nai Lee, who owns this shop, knows me," Clifford added. "He can tell you that I will cause you no trouble." All eyes turn back to Nai Lee. "That is true, this foreigner is a good man. I can vouch for him." There was another consultation among the Akha. Finally, the man who seemed to understand Northern Thai spoke to Clifford, "We don't know why a foreigner would want to stay in our village, but we have no objection, you may come if you wish."

"Thank you. I would like to come. When is a good time?"

"We are returning by bus tomorrow to Mae Chan. From there we walk. You had better come with us or you will never find our village."

"I have a truck, so you can all go with me. What time do you want to go?"

"In the morning; when the sun is up."

"What time is that by the clock?"

"*Baw mi nalika* (have no watch). Meet us here when the sun is up."

"I'll be here, and if you want to take anything back with you, there will be room in my truck." With a nod, the man turned and the Akha all left in the direction of the market.

As promised, Clifford returned early in the morning, and found the Akha waiting for him. "Where did you sleep?" he asked the man he had spoken to the day before. "Right here," he replied pointing to Nai Lee's shop. Nai Lee was opening the folding metal door of his shop and had heard Clifford's question . "Yes, that's true. I sometimes allow the Hill People to sleep on the floor of my shop if they have brought things to sell. They have no relatives here, so where would they go? Anyway, its good for business."

The Akha had taken advantage of Clifford's offer to take things back with them, and proceeded to load various items into the Land Rover, including hoes, machetes, blankets and an assortment of well wrapped packages. Clifford pointed to the only one who had spoken to him and asked him to sit in the front seat with him. The others climbed up into the back of the truck. Following the man's directions, Clifford started out of town going south, even though their ultimate direction was north, toward the town of Mae Chan. The Thai Highway Department was planning two new roads; one east to Lampang, where it would hook up with the main north-south highway, and one north, that would be a much shorter route to Chiang Rai, Mae Chan, and Mae Sai on the Burma border. Unfortunately, neither of those roads was completed, so Clifford had to drive south for 90 kilometers before hitting the major highway that would take them to Chiang Rai and Mae Chan. Clifford could have taken the bus with the Akhas, and saved gasoline expenses, but he thought he might explore the region north of Chiang Mai and his Land Rover would be useful. Also, transporting the Akhas and their purchases would be helpful to them and perhaps they would recipocrate.

It was a long drive; a total of 12 hours, including stops for gasoline and a lunch stop along the road under a giant rain tree that provided welcome shade. The Akhas ate the rice and chicken they had bought in the market wrapped in squares of banana leaves that served as plates when opened. Clifford had expected to stop at a roadside noodle stall, but the Akha shared their food with him. Some of his passengers had been car sick and did not eat much.

Much of the way was through rice paddies, now brown and sere after the harvest. Cattle had been released in many of the fields so they could graze on the stubble and spilt rice. Occasionally, the road went over a ridge forested with teak trees, before dropping into another valley. Clifford often had to slow for lumbering water buffalo on the road, that were now unoccupied after the rice growing season. Sometimes he passed long trains of ox-carts transporting harvested rice to a rice mill. He also shared the road with elephants and their mahouts. Elephants are fearful of motorized vehicles coming behind them, so their mahouts, riding on their backs, would command their elephants to turn and face the vehicle.

When they went through Chiang Rai Clifford wanted to stop, but the Akha man beside him said they wanted to go on to Mae Chan where they would spend the night. It was another 40 kilometers to Mae Chan and Clifford was exhausted. The road from Chiang Mai was supposed to be a major highway, but much of it was not in good shape, full of potholes and long stretches where the macadam was broken up.

Clifford was delighted to reach Mae Chan, but further disappointed when instructed to continue north. It was dark, he was bone weary and more than a bit irritated.

"I thought we were just going to Mae Chan today. We can't walk in the dark can we?"

"We'll stop soon," the Akha assured Clifford. "*Cha cha,*" (go slowly).

Almost immediately, Clifford was told to turn left. He found himself on a well maintained dirt road and proceeded in a westerly direction. His front seat companion was looking intently out the window, and motioned for Clifford to slow down again. "Turn in here," he instructed, pointing to an ill defined track through the trees. To Clifford's surprise they soon came to a rather large two story house built of brick and stucco. A Landrover, much newer than Clifford's, was parked in front.

"We'll sleep here tonight," said the Akha as he stepped out of the vehicle. "A man of few words," murmured Clifford to himself. "I don't even know the man's name." The people in the back of the truck also got out and one man went to the door of the house and cleared his throat loudly. A young woman opened the door, and the whole group began to converse in a language that Clifford assumed was Akha. During a pause in the conversation she opened the door wider and the group of Akha entered the house. The woman looked at Clifford doubtfully, but the man with whom he had shared the front seat waved him in.

They entered a large room with a concrete floor and stuccoed walls illuminated by a single light bulb dangling from the ceiling. Some old calendar pictures were attached to the otherwise bare walls. Some of the pictures were of scantily clad women, but there was also one of the Thai Royal Family. The woman who had opened the door busied herself unrolling grass mats and placing them on the floor at one end of the room. The Akha arranged themselves on the mats, but Clifford still stood by the door wondering what was going to happen next and what his role should be.

The mats in place, the young woman, who seemed to be Akha, but was dressed in Thai clothes, dipped several scoops of rice into cooking pot and washed it several times, using water from an open bucket. She disposed of the water by pouring it into an open drain on the floor next to a charcoal stove. When the rice was clean of floating hulls, she added some more water and placed the pot on the stove. There was no fire in the stove, but she threw in wood shavings for kindling and lit them with a match. When the flames flared up she placed charcoal pieces on the fire and fanned them with a bamboo fan. In just a few minutes the fire was burning hot and the rice pot began to boil.

Clifford thought this was a good time to find out a few things; like what he was doing here. He joined the Akha sitting on the mats and spoke to the man who had sat in the front seat with him. "What is your name?" he asked directly.

"My name is Lee Mui," he replied, "and what is your name?"

"My name is Cliff-ord." He elongated his name to hopefully make it more understandable.

"Cleefor," repeated Lee Mui"

"Yes, something like that, and who are these other people?"

"The two women are my wives, and the other two men are my relatives."

"What about the woman in this house, who is she?"

"She is my older wife's niece."

"What is she doing here?"

"She is married to the owner of this house. He is *Jin Haw*."

Clifford had already learned from Mr. Lee in Chiang Mai that the *Jin Haw* were Chinese from the Province of Yunnan.

"Is he here?"

"Yes."

"Where?"

"Upstairs."

"Will we meet him?"

"Maybe. My wife's niece says he has a guest and they are talking business."

"What is his business?"

"This and that. He buys and sells and has become quite rich."

Clifford had already learned that Lee Mui was not a great conversationalist, but also sensed a guardedness in talking about the Chinese businessman. He obviously did not want to say much about him.

Clifford noticed the young woman had finished cooking the rice and had removed the pot from the fire. Next, she placed a wok on the fire and emptied two cans of sardines in it, together with chopped up chili peppers and cilantro leaves. Working rapidly and efficiently, she set up a low table that had been leaning against a wall, set six bowls on the table, scooped rice into them, and brought out six sets of chopsticks. She poured the sardine mixture into another larger bowl with a spoon and placed it in the center of the table. She spoke in Akha to the group and they all got up and sat around the table. The men spooned some sardines over their rice first and Clifford followed suit. The two women were next and they all picked up their bowls and ate with chopsticks, Chinese style.

The young woman refilled each person's rice bowl two or three times, and there were enough sardines to add some flavor to each bowl of rice. Clifford was amazed at how two cans of sardines could be stretched so far. He realized that each person limited themselves to how much they took. Clifford thanked her in Thai, and when she smiled and nodded her head, he asked her name. "My name is Mee Bu," she replied. She was still cleaning up after the meal when a middle-aged man came down the stairs from the rooms above. The Akha all stood up and murmured some greetings. Obviously, this man commanded some deference. He gave Clifford a sharp look and spoke to Lee Mui in Thai. "Who is this *Farang*?"

"I met him in Chiang Mai at the shop where we sell things."

"Why did you bring him here?"

"He wanted to visit an Akha village."

The man, not knowing that Clifford understood Thai, turned and spoke to him in broken English. "Why you want to visit Akha village?"

"I'm just interested in learning about the Hill Tribes. I did not know we were going to stop here."

"What nationality are you?"

"I am American."

"So, you from the American Consul, is that so?"

"No, no. I am a missionary."

"A missionary!" the man snorted. "You'll have a hard time in that stupid Akha village. I hope you like dog meat."

"We ate well in your house tonight," Clifford responded "Your wife is a good cook."

"She not know much. Anyway, don't call her my wife. A man needs company when he lives alone. Know what I mean?" he asked with a leer.

Clifford changed the subject. "I think we go on to the village tomorrow morning"

"Good idea. I hope you're a good walker."

The *Jin Haw* turned to go back upstairs. "Mee Bu, come with me," he commanded.

On the way up the stairs he turned and spoke to Lee Mui again, "You know this is not a good time to bring in outsiders, especially an American. Send him home as soon as you can."

When he was gone, a silence descended on the Akha. "Not very friendly is he," ventured Clifford. "Would it be better if I went back to Chiang Mai?"

"No need to do that," Lee Mui responded with some heat. "We agreed you can come. That *Jin Haw* does not own us."

"So, why do you stay here?"

"It is convenient. He buys things from us, so he allows us to stay overnight here sometimes."

"What about Mee Bu?"

"What about her?"

"Is she happy here?"

"We cannot always be happy. She was an only child and her mother and father died. Here she has a place to stay and food to eat. Sometimes that's the best you can do."

Clifford was beginning to understand the situation, but he had one more question. "Why do you sell some things to Nai Lee in Chiang Mai and some things to this man?"

Lee Mui hesitated, "There are some things Nai Lee will not buy."

"Such as?"

Lee Mui avoided the question. "We have a long walk tomorrow, best we get some sleep."

Lee Mui handed Clifford two blankets from a pile left by Mee Bu. "Now it is the cold season. It will be cold tonight." With that said, Lee Mui stretched out on a mat and rolled up in two blankets. Clifford had brought his sleeping bag, so he put the blankets under him like a thin mattress

Clifford still had questions, but obviously, some must remain unanswered. The room temperature reminded him that it was January, and it really was getting cold. Clifford guessed it was about 40 degrees. Like everyone else, he slept in his clothe, curled up in his sleeping bag. The hard floor did not keep him awake long.

Clifford awoke to the aroma of cooking rice and the searing smell of chilies being stirred in a wok. He raised his head and saw Mee Bu at the charcoal stove. The rice had been cooked, and in a wok she was frying a mixture of chilies and garlic that brought tears to his eyes. She added some water to the wok, threw in a few handfuls of leafy vegetables, sprinkled on some *nam pla* (fish sauce) and covered the wok with a wooden cover. By the time Clifford was up, folded his blankets and made a trip to the outhouse behind the house, the cooked vegetables had been poured into a bowl and Mee Bu was heating four *pla kheng* (salted fish) in the wok.

Rice, vegetables and fish were placed in bowls on the mats where they had been sleeping, and they all, with the exception of Mee Bu, gathered to eat their breakfast. They ate in silence, savoring the aromatic rice, eaten in great quantities to counter the salty fish and spicey hot vegetables. When they had finished eating, Mee Bu placed the remainder of the food on six pieces of banana leaf, which she had briefly held over the fire to make the leaves more pliable. Each leaf was bundled up and tied with a strip of split bamboo. Clifford understood that was to be their midday meal.

When the Akha stepped outside, Clifford briefly remained inside to thank Mee Bu for the food. She nodded her head and averted her eyes. Clifford noticed tears in her eyes, and suspected they were not caused by the chilies. Outside, two small horses, with backpacks made from split bamboo, were standing.. All the items the Akha had purchased in Chiang Mai, plus the bundles of food, were placed in the back packs. "We go now," Lee Mui said to Clifford.

"Go where?" Clifford wanted to know.

"Doi Maesalong."

"Is that your village?"

"No, it's a Chinese town."

"I thought we were going to your village."

"Maesalong is on the way. Tomorrow we reach our village."

With that bit of news, one of the Akha men tugged on the front horse's halter rope and they were off.

Clifford felt frustrated that he never knew what was going to happen next. What was a Chinese town doing in Thailand? Where did these two horses come from? He shrugged his shoulders and followed the horses. Anyway, he didn't have to carry his own backpack and that helped. In the cool morning air he felt like he could walk all day without stopping.

They followed a major foot trail, and often met other people and horses. After skirting a Mien, sometimes called Yao, village the trail became steeper. It was noon when they reached an Akha village where there was a fork in the trail. They stopped in that village and Clifford was glad for a rest. This village was not their destination, but they were invited up on a porch of one of the bamboo houses and ate their noonday meal that Mee Bu had prepared for them. Clifford took the opportunity to ask Lee Mui some more questions.

"Lee Mui, where did these two horses come from?"

"They're my horses. I left them at the *Jin Haw's* house when we came down to go to Chiang Mai. Mee Bu took care of them."

"Mee Bu seems to be a big help to you."

"Yes, she is."

"I saw tears in her eyes this morning."

Lee Mui paused before answering, "She wanted to come home with us today."

"Why couldn't she?"

"That *Jin Haw* man paid my wife 40 silver rupees for Mee Bu to be a housekeeper. She must stay with him."

Clifford wanted to say she was evidently more than a housekeeper, but held his tongue.

"What is this Chinese town of Maesalong," he asked.

"It's a town in these mountains settled by Chinese *Kuomintang* (Chinese Nationalist Gov.) soldiers that fled here when they were defeated by the Communists in China. They've been here about 10 years now."

"This was all news to Clifford. What is the *Kuomintang?*"

"I don't know. That what's these people were called when they arrived."

Lee Mui didn't seem to know any more about the Chinese in this place called Maesalong, so Clifford realized he would just have to wait until they got there.

After eating their lunch they returned to their trek, ignoring the trail that branched to the right, and continuing on the main trail. It was late afternoon when they approached a town, which Clifford correctly assumed was Maesalong. It was no village, but a real town with shops and many two storey buildings. People, many with horses, were coming into the village from side trails joining them as they trudged down the dirt main street. Clifford noticed that many of the larger houses were walled in with earthen walls, and, likewise, many of the houses were constructed with earth walls that had been whitewashed. Clifford caught occasional glimpses through open gates of houses into an open courtyard of hard packed earth. It looked oddly familiar, and Clifford realized he was remembering pictures of villages in northern China that he had once seen in a National Geographic Magazine. On shop fronts, and some walls, only Chinese words were seen. I'm in Thailand, thought Clifford, but not a Thai word was to be seen. They walked past a large building that was evidently a school, but only Chinese ideographs were to be seen. The flag flying over the school was the old flag of the Chiang Kai Shek government in China. Near the end of the road the elevation rose sharply and on a hill overlooking the town was a large building of whitewashed stucco with the Muslim symbols of the quarter moon and star prominently placed on the roof. It was a mosque, which further confused Clifford. He had never associated Islam with China.

Clifford wanted to learn more about this place, but the Akha turned off on a side road. He followed the group to a simple house constructed of wood with a grass thatch roof. "Where are we," Clifford asked Lee Mui.

"In Maesalong"

"Yes, I know, but whose house is this?"

"These are Akha people who are relatives of mine. We stay here tonight."

Clifford had assumed that his visit to an Akha village would be similar to his visit to the Karen village; a drive and a walk all done in one day. This was different. He also wanted to learn more about Maesalong, and Lee Mui did not appear to be a good source of information.

Unlike the house of the night before, this house was elevated off the ground. The men who led the horses lifted the back packs off the horses and placed them on the porch. The horses were allowed to drink from a concrete tank filled with water. When they finished drinking, the men led them behind the house and turned them loose in a small corral, joining another horse already there. The horses nickered to one another in recognition, but soon gathered at a manger to eat grass and tree leaves that had been placed there.

An Akha woman with a child at her breast appeared to be the only one home. She spoke to Lee Mui at some length, with an occasional doubtful glance at Clifford. Lee Mui, ever a man of few words, spoke to her briefly and turned to Clifford. "My relative is working in the market. This woman is his wife. She will prepare food for us to eat when her husband returns." Clifford had not expected to be staying in so many different homes and felt a bit *grengjai*, as the Thai say, which means something like fearing to be a burden or a bother. He really wanted to see more of Maesalong, so he told Lee Mui he would go for a walk and eat in one of the food stalls he had seen.

Clifford returned to the main street and strolled back down the way they had come. He saw several Tribal people, mostly Akha, carrying heavy loads of garden produce or firewood on their wooden backpack frames. At an outdoor market people, both men and women, were buying vegetables, meat and bean curd before returning home with the ingredients for their evening meal. He passed by some food stalls that did not appeal to him, but stopped at one that had the kitchen in front of the shop. Behind the kitchen were a few round wooden tables with backless stools arranged around them.

Clifford knew his Thai language ability would not help him here, so watched the male cook prepare food, hoping to see some dishes that appealed to him. A stir fry looked good; the cook, who was also most likely the shop owner, threw garlic in a sizzling hot wok, added some pieces of pork, Chinese cabbage, and, finally, cubes of bean curd. He poured in something that appeared to be a thick black soy sauce, stirred it up one more time and emptied the wok contents into a bowl. Clifford entered the shop just as a young girl picked up the bowl to take it to a customer. He pointed to the bowl, and the cook nodded that he understood. The cook spoke in Chinese to Clifford, but when Clifford just shrugged his shoulders, he pointed to an empty table and indicated Clifford should sit there.

He had no sooner sat down when a young man wearing a white shirt and tie entered the shop. He gave his order to the cook and looked around for a table. Spotting Clifford, he came to his table, smiled, and asked in English, "May I sit with you?"

Clifford was surprised, but replied, "Yes, of course, please join me."

"My name is Teacher Chen," stated the young man. "Are you English?"

"No," replied Clifford, "I am American, will that do?"

"Oh yes, it will do very well," replied Chen. "I teach English at the school here and use textbooks from England, but I seldom have an English speaker to talk to." Clifford was delighted that this earnest young man, with wire frame glasses, who spoke rather formal English, had joined him. "I'm glad for the company. I never expected to find an English speaker here. I can speak Thai, but that does me no good here."

"I can understand that; I have lived here a year now and have no use for the Thai language at all. I seldom hear it spoken. How long have you lived in Thailand?

"Nearly two years, but where did you come from?"

"My home is in Taiwan. I volunteered to teach at the school here in Maesalong. I thought it would be a great adventure, but I don't care for my life here. Maesalong must be the most boring place in the world, and the girls are so old fashioned."

"I've just arrived," replied Clifford doubtfully, "and don't intend to live here, but it seems like a very interesting place."

"What brought you here."

"I'm a missionary and just came with some Tribal People to visit their village."

"Oh, so you're a priest. You're not supposed to think about women anyway."

"Oh, well," Clifford stammered, "I'm not really a priest. I'm a Protestant Christian and we can marry. Not that I will, but it's not forbidden." He ended in some confusion.

"Well, I came from the city of Taipei where we had nightclubs, movies, good restaurants and girls looking for a good time. Know what I mean?"

Now Clifford was embarrassed. "I like a quiet life." he murmured. "I've never seen a place like Maesalong. Can you tell me about it?"

"What do you want to know?"

"Everything. Why is it here? Why is it all Chinese? In Thailand all schools must teach in Thai, but here it seems like Chinese is used. Even the Chinese flag is flown. How can this be?"

Teacher Chen was lonely and glad for the opportunity to practice his English. Their food came and in between bites he proceeded to tell Clifford about Maesalong. Well, not everything he knew. He didn't want to run afoul of Republic of China Military Intelligence, so kept to basic facts that were of general knowledge to anyone who was interested. He told Clifford that in 1949 the Chinese *Kuomintang* government, headed by Chiang Kai Shek, evacuated to Taiwan, vowing to return. However, some units of the Chinese Army were in the landlocked province of Yunnan, located in southwest China bordering Burma. They evacuated into Burma and stayed for a few years. Burma really didn't want them, so many were air lifted to Taiwan.

Teacher Chen omitted to say that the United States assisted in that air lift. He also failed to mention, or maybe he did not know, that several non-Chinese suddenly found themselves in Taiwan. Some were Tribal women who had married Chinese soldiers. They probably went willingly, but there were others. Large numbers of the soldiers did not want to go to Taiwan, where they would be again subjected to military discipline. In Burma they were heavily involved in the drug trade. Some Tribal villages planted opium for their own use, and to sell as a cash crop. The *Kuomintang* soldiers saw an opportunity to make a lot of money, not only to support their army, but also for personal enrichment. They encouraged, and even forced, Tribal villagers to plant more opium poppies. The soldiers bought the raw opium from the villagers and transported it to places where international drug buyers would purchase it. Many of the Chinese soldiers involved in this lucrative business were on a quota to be sent to Taiwan, but instead they forced some of the Tribal people to go in their place. "Go, or we'll kill your family," was not an idle threat.

Still, Teacher Chen did tell most of the story, as he understood it. It was the 93rd Army of the KMT (*Kuomintang*) that were not sent to Taiwan. They moved overland into Thailand and settled in a remote area near a stream named Maesalong. "Chinese are more ambitious than these Tribal People around here." asserted the teacher. "Just a few years ago there was nothing here; now there is a big town."

"Did the Thai government allow so many to come?" asked Clifford.

"No problem! The Thai government asked us to come. They're afraid of the Communists you know, so we are supposed to keep the Communists out of Northern Thailand. Thai laws do not apply to us." Teacher Chen lowered his voice, "We even have a powerful short wave radio here. We're in daily contact with the Chinese Army in Taiwan."

"How are so many people able to make a living here?" Cliffford wanted to know.

"We're good traders. Most of the Chinese here are Yunnanese, who have been trading overland with Thailand for a long time. Not me. I'm not Yunnanese. They are really rather backward country people. My parents and relatives were well educated and came from east China. They lost a lot of property when they moved to Taiwan."

Teacher Chen was correct about the Chinese at Maesalong being good traders, but he neglected to specify the primary product that was traded. It was opium, and it was a big business. He was also correct about Thai laws. There was a law against buying and selling opium, but the Thai Military Government at that time had made a deal. The KMT could support themselves in the opium trade, and in return they were to be an anti-Communist shield in the north.

"Tell me about the school?" asked Clifford.

"Ah yes, the school; the reason I'm stuck here for another year."

Teacher Chen may have found his quiet life in Maesalong boring, but he did show some animation when talking about the school. "Would you like to see it? I can take you there."

"Yes, I would very much like to see your school," hastily replied Clifford.

It was a short walk to the school, and although it was now dark, a few street lights allowed Clifford to see it was a long one storey building located on about the only level place in town. "The Army commander here, General Tao, commanded every able body person, man or woman, to level this ground for the school. It was all done by hand labor, including the soccer field."

Clifford was impressed. He had never seen such a job of earth moving done without any machinery. "Do even the civilians here have to obey the General?" he asked.

"Oh yes", Teacher Chen was quick to reply. "His word is law."

Teacher Chen knew a lot about the school, although it was already constructed before he arrived. He informed Clifford that it was a full 12 year school, and that most of the students were local children, but they came from different home environments. The better students were from families where both parents were Chinese, and spoke that language at home. Many of the ordinary soldiers, however, were illiterate and did not bring wives with them. They had married Tribal women from the mountain villages. Children from those families did not speak Chinese well, if they spoke it at all.

"I teach Chinese language and history," added Teacher Chen, "but it's a tough job. These students don't have much Chinese cultural background. Very different from the Republic of China in Taiwan."

Teacher Chen also told about some students whose parents had brought them here from Bangkok or other Thai cities. The parents were mostly second generation Chinese immigrants who wanted their children to receive a traditional Chinese education. In years past, they would have sent them to China, but since that was not possible now, they took their children out of Thai schools and sent them to Maesalong. "Those students are my biggest problem," complained Teacher Chen. "They really don't want to be here and need a lot of discipline. Some even run away and return home."

The school was deserted, except for an adult education class in one room. Teacher Chen had a set of keys and showed Clifford several of the classrooms. Portraits of Sun Yet Sen, founder of the Chinese Republic, and Chiang Kai Shek were prominently displayed on the front wall of each room. Teacher Chen also opened the door to the school office and asked Clifford to sign the guest book. "Include your mailing address. I might write you a letter sometime."

Clifford knew he should get back to the house with the Akha, so he told Teacher Chen where he was staying and his plans to go to the Akha village in the morning.

"Well, you are a brave man. How well do you know the villagers you are traveling with?"

"I don't really know them; we met in Chiang Mai when they were selling things."

"What things?"

"Just animal skins, chilies, and some medicinal roots."

"That sounds alright, but you should keep in mind that this is the harvest time for opium. Did you know that?"

"No, I don't even know what it looks like."

"You may see some on your walk tomorrow. Look for stalks with light green leaves with a seed pod on top. This is not the best time to be wandering around where opium is grown. People may be suspicious."

"No one told me; I'll just stay close to the Akha I'm with."

"That may be like the rabbit staying close to the tiger for protection," laughed Teacher Chen

"Really!"

"I'm just kidding, but don't walk alone. I have heard there is a unit at the American Consul in Chiang Mai that reports on drug movements to the Thai police."

Clifford remembered the man at the house they had stayed in the day before who had questioned him about being from the American Consul. "No one tells me anything," said Clifford.

They shook hands, and Clifford returned to the Akha house. The woman's husband had returned and everyone was eating. "*Haw dza-aw,*" he was urged, which Lee Mui told him meant to eat with them.

"Thank you, but I ate in a restaurant. I'm full. I also met Teacher Chen who showed me the school." Lee Mui conveyed that information to the couple who lived in this house, and they seemed to have some questions.

"Did Teacher Chen wear glasses?" Lee Mui asked Clifford.

"Yes."

"My relatives here say that man spends a lot of time in the building with the radio that talks to Taiwan."

Clifford grunted a response. He was learning not to be surprised by anything anymore. He wanted to ask if they would see opium fields tomorrow, but refrained from doing so. "Whatever happens will happen," he murmered under his breath. Like the night before, they all slept on the floor.

It was still dark the following morning when Clifford awakened to the sounds of people moving around and pans rattling. The Akha were folding up their blankets, so Clifford rolled up his sleeping bag and went out behind the house to use the toilet. He washed his face and hands from water in a clay pot located on the edge of the porch. He shivered in the morning cold, but was ready to eat when a pot of newly cooked rice was brought out from the cooking room, together with some pumpkins stewed with green vegetables and bits of unidentifiable meat. A candle set on a stool offered scant illumination to the group as they ate their meal in silence. After drinking a cup of hot tea, poured from a soot encrusted teapot, two of the men went outside and brought the two pack ponies around to the front of the house. It was now beginning to get light, and the horse packs, which had never been emptied, were again placed on the pony's backs and securely tied down with ropes. Bundles of steaming rice wrapped in banana leaves were placed in the pony packs on top of the other items. After a few words of farewell to their hosts of the previous night they straggled out of Maesalong on a trail heading north.

Since arriving in Maesalong the day before Clifford had not had much opportunity to talk to Lee Mui. Now, as they walked together on the trail he had a lot of questions. His first concern was this day's walk. "Will we reach your village today?"

"Yes, easily."

"Will, it take all day?"

"No, we should get there about halfway between noon and dark."

"Will we go through other villages along the way?"

"Yes."

"What kind?"

"Two Akha villages and one Lahu."

Clifford had hoped that Lee Mui would expand on some of his brief answers, but he never did. He was a quiet man who gave correct, but brief, answers to Clifford's questions. Clifford was curious about the opium that, according to Teacher Chen, was planted in this area. He knew the Thai word for it was *fin*, but was hesitant to ask Lee Mui about it. He thought about it for some time and finally decided to bring Teacher Chen's name into the conversation.

"Teacher Chen at Maesalong says a lot of opium is grown around here. Will we see any today?"

Lee Mui did not immediately reply, and Clifford regretted his question, but Lee Mui had been thinking. That *Jin Haw* man, who had taken his wife's niece to live with him, was a buyer and seller of opium. That's how he had become rich, and he had criticized Lee Mui for taking a foreigner into places where opium was planted. Still, Lee Mui decided, this man, Cleefor, seems like an honest man who really is teaching the "Jesus Religion" he had heard about. "Yes," replied Lee Mui, "We will see many fields of *fin* today.

"Has it always been planted here?" Clifford wanted to know.

"For as long as I can remember there have been a few fields of opium, mostly grown for medicine and for some old men who were addicted to it."

"Is it a good medicine"

"Yes, very good. It stops pain."

"Is more being planted now?"

"Yes, much more."

"Why?"

"Some of the Chinese at Maesalong want us to plant it."

"Do they pay for it?"

"Yes, they pay us, but I know they make a lot more when they sell it."

Clifford learned that the harvest was not over, but that buyers were already coming through with pack horses to pick up the opium. Lee Mui pointed ahead to the side of a mountain where there was a patch of light green vegetation, lighter than the surrounding trees or grass. "There is a *rai fin*" (opium field), he said. "Our trail will go nearby." It took the group another hour to reach the field, and there they stopped to rest and eat in the shade of a cluster of bamboo. "This field belongs to Lahu Daeng," (Red Lahu) revealed Lee Mui. "Some of their women are working in the field now."

"I would like to see what they're doing," urged Clifford. "Will you come with me?" They walked into the field and Clifford saw the opium plants, which resembled the flowering poppies his mother had once planted around their house, were nearly waist high. Some were still in bloom, and the field of red, white and mauve blossoms were a beautiful sight. As Clifford and Lee Mui approached the women, two men stepped out of a nearby clump of bushes. They both had machetes, and one carried a muzzle loading gun. Lee Mui spoke to them and they replied. After a brief conversation, Lee Mui turned to Clifford and explained that he knew these men and was explaining that the foreigner wanted to see the opium poppies.

"Can you speak Lahu?" asked Clifford.

"Yes, many of us Akha can speak Lahu."

"Would they mind if I look closely at what the women are doing?"

"No, they won't mind. I asked them already."

Clifford watched the women closely. One had a three bladed knife in her hand, with which she scratched 3 cuts along one side of the circular seed pods. Some of the pods were already dry and the scratches were easily visible, but this woman was choosing only the green pods that had not yet been cut. As soon as she cut into the pod, a milky sap oozed out of the cuts. The other woman had a curved knife with a broad blade in her hand and was scraping off the brown substance that had exuded from the cuts. Lee Mui explained that the brown substance was what came out of the cuts made the day before. "The sap-like material coming out of today's cuts will be collected tomorrow, and that is opium." Occasionally, the woman with the knife would carefully remove the rather sticky opium from the knife blade and place it in a plastic container she had tied to her waist.

Clifford marveled at the hand labor required to grow the poppies and harvest the opium. "How much are they being paid for the opium?" Clifford asked. Lee Mui spoke to the men, and told Clifford, "This year they are getting 5,000 Baht a *joi.*" Clifford knew that 5,000 Baht was $250, but was not acquainted with the word *joi* as a weight measurement. Later, he was to ask Mr. Lee in Chiang Mai and discover one *joi* is the equivelant of 1.6 kilograms, about 3.5 pounds.

"How many *joi* can they harvest from this field?" Clifford asked. After another conversation with the Lahu men, Lee Mui replied, "They think they will get about one *joi.*" "They also asked about you and why you were asking so many questions."

"What'd you tell them?"

Lee Mui looked Clifford in the eye and said, "I told them you were alright and would not report anything to the authorities. That is true isn't it?"

"Yes, of course that's true. I appreciate your hospitality and will not report this to anyone."

Clifford did wonder what the Board of Directors of the Asian Inland Mission would think if they knew he was standing in an opium field and promising not to say anything about it. Clifford felt somewhat conflicted; he was certainly opposed to the use of opium as a recreational drug. Although he had no personal experiences of knowing people addicted to it, he had heard plenty of stories. He was also aware that much of this opium was refined to heroin and adversely impacted his own country. At the same time he could see the poverty of these people who needed a source of income. It was a dilemma he had not resolved when they left the field and continued on the trail.

It was a long walk, and Clifford remembered the words of the *Jin Haw* man at the house where he and the Akhas had stayed that first night of this trip, "I hope you like to walk." Clifford really did like to walk, especially to new places. They were going through an area of steep hillsides, with slash-burn fields cut out of the remaining forest. Most of the fields had been for hill rice, now harvested, but a few were for corn, which was also harvested, leaving the dry stalks standing. Opium fields were few and far between, but they did pass near two fields tended by Akha women. Clifford noticed that the Akha women wore their heavy headdresses, adorned with silver, even when working in their fields.

It was late afternoon when Clifford spotted a village of about 20 houses squatting on a ridge directly in front of them.. "Is that your village?" he asked Lee Mui.

"Yes it is; we are nearly home."

That was good news for Clifford, whose legs were tired and beginning to feel weak. Even the pack horses raised their heads, held their ears alert and picked up their pace. Clifford knew not to expect too much of a hill village, but this one struck him as being a rather depressing place. The houses were the usual bamboo structures elevated off the ground with roofs of grass thatch, however the bamboo on most of the houses needed replacing, and so did the roof thatch, which was old and dark. If not for the bare ground around the village it would have blended almost totally into the surrounding scrub brush. A few scrawny sway-backed pigs were wandering around, and a flock of small black goats could be seen grazing in an old hill field. They were welcomed into the village by several small children with grubby hands and faces wearing an assortment of shirt tops, but no bottoms. A girl of about 12 years of age seemed to be in charge of the children, and she was carrying one on her back. Two children ran up to the two Akha women, who picked them up, hugged them, and wiped their runny noses. The packs were removed from the horses and placed on the porch of one of the houses.

"This is my house. You can stay here," said Lee Mui. Clifford felt like he needed a bath after the long walk and asked where to go. "Just follow that path," instructed Lee Mui, "it will take you to a *hui*" (a gulley or small stream). Lee Mui spoke to one of his wives, who went in the house and came out with a plastic dipper, which she gave to Clifford. Clifford took a *pakama* (loin cloth) from his backpack, and found the *hui* about a half mile downhill. He took a dip bath while standing in the middle of the stream, where the water was about 10 inches deep. While he was there some of the village women came to get water, upstream from him. They filled several bamboo sections, which they carried on their backs back to the village. Clifford followed them and worked up a sweat before reaching Lee Mui's house.

That evening Clifford and Lee Mui sat down and ate rice together. It was not yet dark outside, but the Akha houses had no windows and the grass thatch roofs come down very low on both sides of the houses making the interior rather dark. An old man, who Clifford had not seen before, came out of an inner room and joined them. Lee Mui introduced him, "This is my father, his name is Jah Leh." Clifford acknowledged his presence with a nod of his head, but the old man did not speak. He did not appear to be in good health. The three of them sat in silence eating rice out of bowls with chopsticks. There wasn't much to go with the rice; just some chili pepper paste. Lee Mui apologized for the meal. "We have rice now, but not much else." "Never mind," replied Clifford, trying to be a good guest, "this is very good rice."

After the men had eaten, the women and children sat down to eat their meal. The men retired to one end of the room to drink their tea, which one of the women had poured into rather grubby rice bowls. Clifford was full of questions, and this seemed like a good time to ask them. "How long has your village been in this location?" he asked.

Lee Mui thought a minute and replied, "Five years."

"Where were you before that?"

"Further north, up near the border with Burma."

"Why did you move?"

"We had made our fields there several years and the soil was used up. We needed to move to a new place where the soil was good."

"So, is it better here?"

"It's better, we get more rice, and also good for other crops."

"What other crops?"

"*Fin*."

Clifford was a bit surprised. He hadn't thought of Lee Mui as an opium grower. "Do other people in this village plant opium?" he wanted to know.

"Most of them do."

"Aren't you afraid of the police?"

"The police don't bother us; the Chinese Army in Maesalong see to that."

"Do you sell to them?"

"Yes, we have to."

"What do you mean you have to? Aren't there other buyers?"

"Not around here. We wouldn't dare sell to anyone else. The Chinese know how much we plant and they come here to buy it. I keep some for my father, but the rest all goes to the Chinese. They can be...." he hesitated, "very rough. It is dangerous to cross them."

"What about that *Jin Haw* man? I thought you sold some to him."

"He works with the Chinese."

"Does your father use opium?"

"Yes, he has bad pains in his stomach. He smoked opium to relieve the pain, but now he is addicted. He can't live without it."

As if on cue, the old man got up and went into the inner room. He came back with an opium pipe, a lamp and a small lacquered box. Clifford watched as he lit the lamp, which was just an old tin can with a hole in the cover in which a small wick had been placed. Next, Jah Leh opened the box and took out a very small piece of the brown colored opium and rolled it between his fingers into a small ball, about the size of a BB. Clifford had observed that the pipe was simply a bamboo tube stuck into a hollow ceramic ball about 1 ½ inches in diameter. A very small hole was on one side of the the ball, and Jah Leh placed the opium over that hole. Next, he laid down on his side close to the lamp and put the opium to the flame. When it started to smoke he inhaled deeply from the bamboo pipe stem. He did that two or three times, and when the opium was all gone he took out another bit of opium from the box and repeated the process. He had to light the opium with each puff. When finished, he put the pipe down, but continued laying on the floor, with a peaceful expression on his face.

"My father usually smokes two pipes at this time of day," explained Lee Mui. "He will have two more tonight before going to sleep."

Clifford asked about the women, "Are both of them your wives?"

"Yes," replied Lee Mui, "the older one is my first wife, but her younger cousin became an orphan when her mother and father died, so I married her too."

"Do they get along alright?"

"Certainly, my younger wife defers to her older cousin. You can hear them talking together now in the women's side of the house."

Clifford had been hearing their voices, but was not aware of Akha house plans. "What do you mean by 'the women's side of the house'?"

"Our houses all have this divide across them," explained Lee Mui, pointing to a shoulder high partition. We are in the men's side and they are in the women's side."

"Must they always stay there?"

"No, no, we all go where we want, but we have our space. The men's side is also where guests would stay. If you had brought your wife she would also sleep on this side."

"I have no wife."

"Well, if you did."

Clifford wanted to ask how they had babies if they slept in different locations, but was too shy to ask. Anyway, it was getting late and he was cold. He stood up to retrieve his sleeping bag from his back pack and Lee Mui spoke over the room divide to one of the women who came in and spread a mat on the floor for Clifford. He unrolled his sleeping bag, crawled in, and removed his trousures while he was in the bag. He rolled up his trousures and used them for a pillow. They were a bit aromatic, but he was soon asleep.

Clifford awoke in the morning to shouts and excited voices at one end of the village. He hurriedly pulled on his pants and went out to stand on the porch. He could see four or five men, with muzzle loaders strapped on their backs, carrying something into the village. One of the men began to beat a tattoo on a section of bamboo, using it like a drum. There were more shouts as people came out of their houses and joined the celebrants. Lee Mui was already up and Clifford saw him pick up a knife and head toward the group. Clifford slipped on his shoes and joined him. "What's going on?" asked Clifford.

"Hunters were out last night and have returned with a wild pig they shot."

"Is that good news?"

"That's very good news. We'll all have meat to eat."

"Will the hunters share?"

'Yes, that is our custom."

The pig had been placed on a bamboo platform about three feet high. Other men were arriving with their knives. Before cutting into it, however, a fire was built and the pig, held by four men, was passed over the fire to singe off the bristles. When well singed it was placed on the platform again and some of the men started scraping it to remove the remaining bristles and soot. When it was well scraped, it was opened up and the entrails, liver, heart and other organs were removed and placed in buckets. While the body of the pig was being cut into pieces some of the men were washing the entrails in buckets of water. Both the inside and outside of the intestines were washed. In a few minutes the pig was all cut up and some given to all households. The hunters got an extra share, as did two other men. "They," explained Lee Mui, "are our village headman and our *dzoe ma.*" (village priest). Clifford noticed that Lee Mui also received an extra portion. "The hunter who shot the pig," Lee Mui explained, "was using my gun, so I get and extra share also."

Lee Mui carried his share of the meat back to his house wrapped in a banana leaf. Clifford noticed it also contained some pieces of fat and intestines. The two women immediately started heating the fat in a pan to extract the lard. Some of the lard was saved in a crockery container, but the remainder was left in the pan and pieces of the intestines, cut in one inch lengths, was added and fried until crispy. Rice had been cooking at another fireplace, so bowls of rice and the fried intestines was the breakfast menue. Clifford, who had just seen the dripping entrails from the pig, was a bit hesitant to try them, but he did and found them delicious. It was a great meal.

Nothing had been said about how long Clifford would stay in this village, so he brought up the subject. "I should be getting back to Chiang Mai soon, would it be safe for me to walk back alone to where my Land Rover is parked?"

"You'd better not go alone," replied Lee Mui. "A man from this village wants to go to Chiang Mai, so he could go with you."

"Sounds good; can we leave tomorrow morning?"

"I'm sure that will be a good time, I'll ask him to be ready."

Clifford was curious about something Lee Mui had told him when the pig meat was being divided and asked about it. "Lee Mui, you told me an extra portion of the meat of the wild pig was to be given to the *dzoe ma*. Who is he?"

"He is a very special man in our village," replied Lee Mui. "He leads in all our ancestral offerings, and any village ceremonies that relate to the ancestors."

"Is he the one who makes offerings to the spirits when they are offended?" asked Clifford.

"Oh no," Lee Mui quickly replied, "That is another person; the *dzoe ma* is the ceremonial village leader, like when we repair our village gate each year, or like where to make our hill fields, when to plant, what to do when someone is sick, what kind of sacrifices to make. Many things like that, so the spirits will help us and not be angry with us. He is very important for us Akha. Soon it will be time to clean and repair our village gate. He will set the date for that."

"Village gate," exclaimed Clifford in surprise, "I have seen no gate. There is not even a fence or wall around your village."

"There is a gate. I'll show it to you."

Lee Mui got up and Clifford followed. They went to the upper part of the village, beyond where the pig had been butchered, and there it was -- a ceremonial wooden structure. Not really a gate like Clifford was expecting to see. There was no door to open or shut, but just a row of posts planted on either side of the path, with cross bars on top, like a series of upside down U's. Since the village had been there five years, there were five sets of these posts. The whole structure was adorned with carved wooden objects, and strings of decorative pieces of bamboo. It was what was alongside the gate, however, that immediately caught Clifford's attention. He was a bit shocked. In fact, he was really shocked. There were two life sized wooden figures carved from the trunk of trees; one obviously male and one female. They were anatomically correct, and in a position of sexual intercourse. Clifford didn't ask, but Lee Mui explained. This is our spirit gate. They can come

THE SECRET RETIREE: DRUGS AND DEATH

and go here. The male and female figures will remind them that we need to be productive; better crops, more animals, and more children, so our Akha way of life can continue. Clifford realized what the figures represented; they were fertility symbols. He had heard of such things, but had never seen any.

On the way back to Lee Mui's house Clifford noticed a house that was down slope and some distance from the other houses. "Why is that one house separated from the other houses?" he asked.

Lee Mui hesitated before replying, "That family used to live up here close to the other houses but they had a great misfortune."

"What happened?"

"Twins were born to them."

"What's so bad about that?"

"For us Akha people that is a great catastrophy. Such a birth is not normal. It means the spirits are angry with that family because of something bad they did, or for not following the Akha way."

"So, what about the twins?"

"Such abnormal births are killed immediately and they are buried in a hidden place in the forest."

"Why is the house separated from the other village houses?"

"First of all, it must be torn down and then rebuilt at some distance from the other houses. It must also be downhill, so it cannot contaminate other households."

"In my country we do not do that. Twins are even admired."

"That is not the Akha way." Lee Mui appeared uncomfortable with the subject and said no more.

That evening they ate rice and a soup with wild pork in it. Lee Mui's father smoked his two pipes of opium and went to sleep. Lee Mui brought up a subject that had been bothering him. A man and wife in the village wanted to ask a favor of Clifford, but Lee Mui didn't know how Clifford would react. Finally, he went out and brought the couple to his house. The man did not speak Thai, so he spoke to Clifford in Akha, with Lee Mui translating. This couple were very concerned for their daughter, who they said was 14 years old and named Mi Ja. A Thai couple had visited the village two or three months ago and this man and his wife had given permission for their daughter to go with them to Chiang Mai. The couple said they owned a restaurant and needed a girl to work in it.. She would earn a salary to send home to her parents, and could live with them in a safe place. The Akha couple knew nothing of city life, and were wondering if they had done the right thing. Clifford thought they had likely not done the right thing, but did not want to alarm them. "I will try to find her," he replied.. "Where is this restaurant?" All they knew was that it was near the *Pratu Chiang Mai* (Chiang Mai gate) in the old city wall.

Early the next morning, Clifford heard the women stirring around and smelled wood smoke coming from the fireplace. He got up and dressed, packed up his back pack and was ready to go. Clifford wanted to leave something for the family, but didn't know what. Reluctantly, he withdrew his flashlight from his pack and gave it to Lee Mui. It was a good flashlight that contained three batteries and projected a light like a spotlight. He knew he could buy another one in the Chiang Mai market and was happy to see how pleased Lee Mui seemed to be with it. They ate rice and pork again, and Clifford received a bundle of rice in a banana leaf to eat on his return trip. It was just getting light when the villager Clifford was supposed to walk with came by. This time there was no horse. Clifford shouldered his pack, lightend by the absence of a flashlight, and followed his new companion.

It was a silent trip, as the Akha who accompanied Clifford did not speak Thai. They retraced their steps on the same trail to Mae Salong and stayed in the same house. Not wanting to be a burden, Clifford went to the market and came back with some raw pork and vegetables, which the woman in the house cooked for their evening meal The next day they walked out to the house where Clifford had left his Land Rover.

The only person home was Mee Bu, who seemed a bit startled to see Clifford. She conversed in Akha with Clifford's companion for a while and then turned to Clifford, "I would like to invite you to stay here tonight, but I think it best you find accommodations elsewhere. *Khun Nai* (boss) is not here." She lowered her voice and continued, "Someone else stayed here one night. He is a Hmong, and he and *Khun Nai* do some business together. He saw your Land Rover and demanded to know who owned it and where had the driver gone."

"What did *Khun Nai* say?" Asked Clifford.

"He said he didn't know; just some foreigner who wanted to visit an Akha village."

"What is the Hmong's name?"

"I think it is Sae Yang."

Clifford could hardly believe it. Could it really be the same unfriendly man he had met in the Hmong village? The same man the Thai headman had warned him about? It could be. Clifford had no desire to meet him again, so hastily declared he had to get back to Chiang Mai immediately.

Clifford threw his backpack in his Land Rover, and motioned to his companion to come. The man did not get in, so Clifford asked Mee Bu to tell him he was leaving for Chiang Mai right now. The man replied, through Mee Bu, that he did not want to travel any more today and would take a bus tomorrow. Clifford nodded, waved to Mee Bu and took off. That night Clifford holed up at an inexpensive guest house, mostly occupied by young European travelers, located on the south bank of the Mae Kok River in Chiang Rai. He was tired, but sleep eluded him. He had heard bad things about Sae Yang, and had been advised to stay away from him. Had he been followed? No, must have been a coincidence. Sae Yang and the *Jin Haw* man just had some business to discuss. Clifford decided it was likely not good business, but he would keep his nose out of it. He heard a night guard strike a gong three times. That meant it was 3:00 A.M. He drifted off to sleep and woke with a start with sunlight flooding his room. It was 8:00 A.M., well past his usual rising time. He dressed hurriedly and ate breakfast at the restaurant attached to the guest house. He ordered American Fried Rice, which turned out to be fried rice topped with a fried egg and accompanied by a small, pink sausage, masquerading as an American weiner.

Driving back to Chiang Mai Clifford realized he might have made a promise to the parents of the 14 year old girl that he couldn't keep. He was aware that young Tribal girls were sometimes tricked into the sex trade. They were easy to control, because they were naïve and often did not speak Thai. Clifford was sure this girl did not speak the Thai language, and, anyway, he didn't even know what she looked like. How would he find her? Besides that, Clifford couldn't imagine walking into a brothel. He needed some local person with street smarts. He didn't want to involve the bank manager or his Karen language teacher, or heaven forbid, his landlady. She was a good woman, but how would he broach the subject? "Would you please go with me to a brothel?" No, no, that would never do.

He was approaching Chiang Mai when he thought of Ai Tia, the man who had a pickup truck and delivered things around town. He had delivered the prison made furniture Clifford had purchased to his house. Whenever he saw Clifford around town, he waved and greeted him. Ai Tia certainly knew his way around. Resolving to speak to him, Clifford drove straight to the main fresh market, near the Ping River, where he knew Ai Tia would likely be hanging out waiting for customers who had completed their evening shopping. Ai Tia was just leaving the market with a load of produce to be delivered to a restaurant, but Clifford flagged him down. "Ai Tia, please come to my house tomorrow morning; I have something to ask you."

"I can come about 9:00," replied Ai Tia, "Will that be alright?"

"Good, I'll see you then."

When Ai Tia arrived at Clifford's house he expected to be asked to haul something. He was surprised when he was invited up into the Foreigner's home, and was served one of the worst cups of coffee he had ever drank. "What do you want me to do?" he asked. Clifford was almost tongue tied. He was embarrassed by the subject, and asking for help from a man he did not know well.

"Ai Tia," Clifford began, "You know your way around this city, so I would like you to help me find a young girl. I would pay you for your time."

"Oh," replied Ai Tia, "so you like young girls."

Clifford blushed. This was not going well. "No, no, that's not what I mean. I met the parents of this girl in an Akha village and they asked me to find their daughter who went off to work in a restaurant in Chiang Mai."

Clifford explained what he knew, and Ai Tia began to understand. There were still a lot of gaps, but Ai Tia was getting the picture.

"How old is this girl?"

"She's only 14."

"Did she, or her parents, know what she was getting into?"

"They thought she was getting a job in a restaurant, Don't you think that's possible?"

Ai Tia thought this foreigner was just as gullible as the parents of the girl, so he spoke plainly. "Mr. Clifford, when someone from the city goes up to a Hill Tribe village and recruits a girl who can't even speak Thai to work in a restaurant you should know its not true. She's going to be placed in a *sawng*" (brothel).

Clifford could speak the Thai language well, but that word was new to him. Ai Tia had to explain what a *sawng* was, and Clifford blushed again. He knew there were such places, of course, and feared that may have been the real destination for the girl. "Can't she just leave?" he asked. "No way," replied Ai Tia. "The people who recruited her will keep her locked up so she can't run away."

"Isn't there a law against that?"

"Maybe for someone that young, but the police won't do anything; they're paid off. I've seen girls younger than that in those places."

"You've been to a *sawng?*"

"Why not, I'm not married."

Clifford was disappointed. He didn't think Ai Tia would help, and was sorry he had asked him. Ai Tia, however, had more to say. "I really hate those people that trick girls that young. If a woman wants to *khai tua* (sell her body), that's her business, but deceiving *dek* (children) is evil. Sure I'll help. What's the girl's name?"

"Her name is Mi Ja, and the restaurant where she is supposed to be working is near *Pratu Chiang Mai.*"

"No surprise; lots of those kind of places over there."

"How can we find her?"

"I'll ask around in that area and try to find out if there is a *Sawng* owned by a man and wife who recruit young Hill Tribe girls."

"What if you find such a place?"

"If I find such a place, you and I are going *Thio Sawng*" (visiting a brothel).

"What?"

"You heard me. I'm going now, but I'll get back to you."

CHAPTER TEN

MI JA

Mi Ja had lived 14 hard years in her home village. Her mother and father scratched out a living on rather unproductive hill fields. From the time she was five or six years old, she had cared for her two younger siblings, carrying the youngest on her back. Later, she worked with her parents in their fields, clearing land, weeding, harvesting, threshing the rice by beating the sheaves over a mat to collect the grain, and carrying the rice back to their home. It was backbreaking work, and her hands were course and calloused. She knew there was a wider world outside her village; it was called Doi Maesalong. Once she accompanied her father there, and she was amazed at all the shops selling beautiful things, and people who dressed differently and spoke languages she could not understand.. She wished she could live there and be a part of that wider world. Back in her home village she listened when men spoke of an even larger world. There were big cities, like Chiang Rai and Chiang Mai, where thousands of people lived. "How can they all find land to farm?" she asked. The men all laughed at her, except her father's friend, Lee Mui, who explained that people could live by making money selling things, and buying their food. Mi Ja was determined to go to one of those cities some day, and see such things with her own eyes.

She was there when the Thai couple came looking for a girl to work in their food selling place. She could not understand their language, but they looked like her people, the Akha. Lee Mui translated what they said into Akha, and Mi Ja immediately ran to find her mother. "Let me go to the city," she begged. "I will earn money and bring it home when I come to visit." Mi Ja's mother spoke to her husband, and they agreed to let her go. It had been a bad year; rain didn't come at the right time, so the rice did not grow well. There was some to harvest, but after the rice had been cut, and the bundles still laying on the stubble to dry, there came a three day period of rain. They managed to save some, but much of it was moldy, and tasted bad. Mi Ja's father and mother didn't know how they were going to live, and feed their three children, for another year. Maybe Mi Ja could help, so they let her go.

That very day, Mi Ja, barefooted, and wearing her homespun Akha clothes, set out on what she believed would be a great adventure. She followed the Thai couple on the trail back to Doi Maesalong, where they stayed one night in a cheap guesthouse. The couple slept on a bed; Mi Ja slept on the floor. The following day, they walked on a well traveled trail to the highway, where they boarded a bus. When they came to a town, Mi Ja thought it must be Chiang Mai, but it was only the small district town of Mae Chan. It looked big to her. The next town was huge; she didn't know so many people could live in one place, but that was only the provincial capitol of Chiang Rai. It was dark when they finally arrived in Chiang Mai; a very confusing place for Mi Ja. They were at a bus station; hundreds of people were milling around, and buses were constantly coming and going. In a few minutes, Mi Ja saw more people than she had ever seen in her whole life.

The couple, dragging Mi Ja with them, walked a short distance and boarded a mini-bus holding about 12 people. No one wanted to sit next to Mi Ja. Neither her, or her clothes, had been very clean when she left home. After two days of walking in the hot sun and sleeping in her clothes at night, she was beginning to smell. Being car sick on the bus that day had not helped. That night she couldn't understand what people in the bus said when they looked at her, "*Chow Khao sokaprok,*" but she remembered those words. Later, when she understood Thai, she felt ashamed that people had looked at her and said, "dirty Hill Tribes."

The mini-bus drove through street after street, letting people off as new ones boarded. Shops, bright with electric lights, lined the streets, buildings, some four stories high, amazed her, and everywhere were people, masses of people walking the streets and entering the shops. It was all too much. Mi Ja could not comprehend her new situation.

Finally, the bus stopped in front of a two story building, and the Thai couple stepped out, dragging Mi Ja with them. They took her in through the open door and walked through a large room filled with tables where people sat eating. At the rear of the restaurant they entered a small room where a middle aged Thai woman sat behind a desk. A conversation between the three adults ensued, that got a bit heated at times. The lady behind the desk got up and walked over to Mi Ja to look her over. She felt Mi Ja's arms and legs and her small breasts, wrinkling her nose in disgust as she returned to her desk, where she opened a drawer, took out some paper money, and gave it to the couple. Mi Ja didn't know it, but she was now the property of the woman behind the desk.

That woman called one of the waitresses in the restaurant, who took Mi Ja upstairs to a bathroom, undressed her and proceeded to give her a bath, dipping water out of a large crock and scrubbing her with a bar of soap. She even washed Mi Ja's hair, and dried her with a towel. The waitress had done this before; she knew just what to do. She opened a cupboard on one side of the room and took out clean clothes, consisting of underpants, a long Thai skirt and a tee shirt top. Mi Ja dressed herself, even stepping into the underpants, something she had never worn before. The waitress led her to another room, where there was a mat and blanket on the floor. Mi Ja understood she was to sleep there. The waitress left, but soon came back with a plate of rice and curry and a bottle of water. She set those on the floor and left. When Mi Ja finished eating, she thought she should return the dirty dish, but found the door locked. She spent the night in that room, alternately sleeping, and alternately being homesick.

The lady at the desk was called *Khun Pa* (Aunty). She came up to check on Mi Ja once a day. When she was satisfied that Mi Ja was keeping herself clean she made a telephone call to a favored client. She knew what he wanted. "*Ai*" (elder brother), I have one here; just the kind you like".

"What've you got?"

"I have a *sao borisut* (virgin). I guarantee, she's never been touched."

"How much?"

"800 Baht."

"You're never cheap are you?"

"I carry good merchandise."

"I might be by tonight."

Ai came in about 9:00 that night. He ordered food, and washed it down with imported whiskey he brought with him. He was just a little tipsy when he went looking for Khun Pa in the back room. "Ready?" she asked. "Yeah," he replied, "Let me see what you've got." Khun Pa held out her hand, and *Ai* gave her eight red 100 Baht bills. She led the customer upstairs, unlocked the door to Mi Ja's room, let *Ai* in, closed the door, and returned downstairs.

Mi Ja fought. She was tough and wirery, but *Ai* was big and strong. He got what he came for. He left, locked the door behind him, as he had done several times before, and left the restaurant. Mi Ja hurt. She spent the night curled up in a fetal position. Her blood stained her sleeping mat. She wept, but no one came to help. That month, she was sold as a guaranteed virgin to three other men.

It was during that time, when Ai Tia returned to Clifford's house. "Tonight we *tio sawng*" (visit a brothel), he announced.

"What have you found out?" Clifford asked.

"I think I know where that girl is."

"How'd you do that?"

"Well, I know a waitress at a restaurant. She told me a few things."

"So, what are we going to do?"

"Tonight we go to that restaurant, and you, my friend, will be a Foreigner looking for a young girl. I will introduce you. You are not to speak Thai. Understood?"

Clifford understood, but he was very apprehensive. "What if someone I know sees me there?"

"No one you know goes to those kind of places."

"If she's there, how do we get her out?"

"That might be tricky, but I have a plan. Bring a lot of money with you, and, you know, it will be up to you to find a place for her. She can't stay with you; what would people think!"

"Maybe I'll ask my landlady."

That night Clifford had his first visit to a whorehouse. It looked just like an ordinary restaurant, except the customers were all men. Ai Tia ordered food and drink; beer for himself and Coca Cola for Clifford. Before the food arrived, Ai Tia took Clifford through a door into another large room. Clifford was amazed. That room was divided by clear glass, like a show window in a department store. Clifford, Ai Tia, and some other men were in the smaller part of that room. From that vantage point they could look through the glass into a larger room, where there were about 15 young women, dressed in colorful, but skimpy outfits. The women looked rather bored; some were talking to one another, some were knitting, some just sitting alone. An older attendant was with them. The men were in a viewing room, and made their choice of which girl they wanted. When they made their choice, they pointed to the girl and the attendant took her out. The man left, and met his choice for the night in a small room with a bed. Clifford was appalled; "Like a meat shop," he thought.

Ai Tia took Clifford back to his table and went on to the back room, where he spoke to Khun Pa. "I have a Foreigner with me. He likes young girls from the mountains. Do you have someone for him?"

"I might. It would cost him 800 Baht."

"Make it 1,000 Baht, and return 200 to me."

"You know how to do business don't you?"

"Maybe I do, and I can bring more Foreigners in here too."

"You do that and I'll make it worth your while. Bring your friend in here; I want to see him."

"Just as soon as we finish eating."

Ai Tia returned to their table, and told Clifford what he had learned. Clifford had not finished eating, but now he was too nervous to eat. Ai Tia had to eat most of the food they had ordered. A waitress came to replenish Ai Tia's beer glass, and Ai Tia spoke to her in a low voice. "Have the back door unlocked," he told her. "I'll give you 200 Baht." She nodded her head. Ai Tia finished his beer, and led Clifford to the back room. Khun Pa looked at Clifford and spoke to him in Thai, asking where he came from. Clifford pretended not to understand, and shrugged his shoulders. Khun Pa turned to Ai Tia, "Are you both going to use this girl? That'll cost you more than 1,000 Baht."

"No, no," replied Ai Tia, "Just the Foreigner. I'll wait outside the door in case this Foreigner needs help."

Khun Pa laughed. "He does look kind of *dip*(green)." She held out her hand, and Ai Tia told Clifford to give her 1,000 Baht. Clifford did so. She led them upstairs, and let Clifford into Mi Ja's room, making sure Ai Tia stayed outside. "When he's done come back to my room. I'll have 200 Baht for you." She left.

Clifford entered the room, and saw a girl huddled in one corner. He came close, knelt down, and softly spoke her name, "Mi Ja." Mi Ja looked up, startled to see a Foreigner. Clifford again said, "Mi Ja," and held his finger to his lips, warning her to be silent. He took Mi Ja by her hand and helped her up. Slowly he led her to the door, opened it and looked out. Only Ai Tia was there. Mi Ja was fearful, but the Foreigner knew her name; that gave her hope. The three of them, Ai Tia in the lead, went down a hallway to a fire exit door. That door was always kept locked, but that night it was open. They stepped outside onto the stairs, but Ai Tia turned to Clifford and said, "Take the girl to your truck, get in and start the motor, but don't turn on your headlights. I have one more thing to do."

Ai Tia went back inside, and Clifford led Mi Ja to his Land Rover, parked near the restaurant. He had just got Mi Ja inside and started the car, when Ai Tia came alongside and jumped in the front seat with them. "Go," he said, and Clifford turned on his lights and took off. There was little traffic, so Clifford drove down the streets at a rate of speed unusual for him. *"Cha, cha,*(slow) cautioned Ai Tia, "We don't want the police to stop us." When Clifford had slowed down a bit, Ai Tia handed Clifford 200 Baht. "What's that?" Clifford wanted to know.

"I got a special discount because I'm so clever!"

Clifford had no idea what he meant, but kept his attention on the road. Ai Tia did have a good heart; he had used his own money to pay the waitress.

"Where are we going?" asked Ai Tia.

"I guess we had better go to my landlady's house."

"Didn't you ask her?"

"No, things have been happening kind of fast."

"Oh my, I thought you Foreigners alwas planned ahead."

It was really late when they got back to Pa Chintana's house. Not a light was on; obviously she was sleeping. Clifford took Mi Ja with him to the house, and knocked on the door. It took a while, but eventually a light came on and Clifford's landlady came to the door. She was not happy. "What do you want?" she demanded.

"Would it be possible for you to let this girl stay with you for a few days?" Clifford pushed Mi Ja into the light comeing through the doorway.

"Who is she?"

Clifford explained about Mi Ja. At first, Pa Chintana shook her head and was about to refuse when she took another look at the girl standing in front of her door. "She's only a child," she said, "and how did you say you met her?" She looked at Clifford suspiciously. Clifford had to explain again about meeting the girl's parents, and how they thought their daughter was to get a good job in Chiang Mai. Ai Tia had come up to the house, so Clifford explained how the two of them had spirited the girl out of her locked room at the brothel.

"Men," complained Pa Jintana, "They cause most of the trouble in this world." Clifford could tell that his landlady was beginning to soften. "Well, c'mon in," she fumed, "Why are we standing out here in the middle of the night." They stepped in, and Pa Chintana continued to examine Mi Ja, who had still not looked up.

"You say she can't speak Thai?"

"Not a word." replied Clifford, "but her name is Mi Ja."

"Might as well leave her here tonight; wouldn't do to have her sleep in your house."

"That's what I told him," chimed in Ai Tia with a smile.

Pa Chintana glared at the two men, "Now get out of here, and let's all try to get a little sleep tonight."

Mi Ja was bewildered. She didn't know what was going on. The two men seemed nice; one of them even knew her name. He must have talked to her mother and father. The woman, whom the others called Pa Chintana, talked to her, but Mi Ja did not understand. She was taken to the kitchen, where Pa Chintana took some leftover food out of the *tukopkhow* (food cupboard), started a charcoal fire in her stove, and heated the food in a frying pan. She placed the food in a plate and gave it to Mi Ja, who started to eat with her fingers. "*Dio, dio* (just a minute)," said Pa Chintana, in a not unfriendly voice. She took out a fork and spoon from a drawer and gave them to Mi Ja. Mi Ja had always eaten with her fingers, and handled the utensils rather clumsily. Pa Chintana showed her how to hold the spoon in her right hand and use the fork to push the food onto the spoon. She learned quickly, and Pa Chintana smiled at her.

After eating, she had a bath, by herself, and put on a long sarong that Pa Chinta had laid out for her. She tied the sarong up high, above her breasts, just like the sarong Pa Chintana was wearing. When Mi Ja came out of the bathroom, Pa Chintana was tying up a mosquito net over a mattress on the floor. Mi Ja slept well that night. She sensed the people she had met tonight would help her. She had had a terrible experience, but, unknown to her, she was also fortunate. The woman at the restaurant had already sold her to a brothel in Bangkok. Someone was to take her there the following day.

The next morning, Clifford came over to see how things were going, and discovered all was well. Mi Ja's hair was neatly combed and tied in a ribbon. Pa Chintana was teaching Mi Ja the names of objects around the house, and had already taught her how to *wai* (curtsy), according to Thai custom. When Clifford came in the house, Mi Ja curtsied to him, with her hands together and raised to her face. Pa Chintana beamed and clapped her hands.

"If she's a bother to you, I might be able to find another place for her," ventured Clifford.

"What other place?" retorted Pa Chintana. "We're getting along just fine. She's a very clever girl. You just leave us alone."

That's just what Clifford wanted to hear. "However," he told Pa Chintana, "I need to get word to her parents that their daughter has been found, and is in good hands."

"I suppose you must, but tell them she is a comfort to an old woman who never married. She can stay with me for as long as she wants. I need some help around here anyway, what with my tenant pounding on my door at all hours of the night."

Clifford was able to get word to Mi Bu, the Akha woman who lived near the beginning of the trail to Doi Maesalong, and she forwarded a message to Mi Ja's parents. Mi Ja continued to live with Pa Chintana, learned the Thai language, and, at Clifford's suggestion, started attending a government adult night school. He paid her school fees.

CHAPTER ELEVEN

CLIFFORD BUILDS A STUDENT HOSTEL

Clifford resumed his life; studying Karen with Po Swe, attending the Sunday service at the bank manager's house, and making occasional trips to Karen villages, especially to the home of Saw Pa Heh and his family. As Clifford's Karen language ability improved he was sometimes asked to preach at the Sunday service at the bank manager's house, which made him feel like a real missionary. It also gave him something to report back to the Asian Inland Mission.   Clifford had noticed that some Karen children from distant villages were living with the bank manager so they could attend school. "I see there are some students living with you," observed Clifford one Sunday.

"Yes," replied the bank manager, "there are no schools in their villages."

"It is very kind of you to do that."

"Someone gave me a chance when I was young, and God has been good to me. Now it is my duty to do the same. Even my Thai Buddhist friends know to do good; they have a saying, *tham di, dai di; tham chua, dai chua.*" (do good, receive good; do evil, receive evil)

Clifford recognized in that statement the Buddhist doctrine of Kharma, not the Christian doctrine of Grace, but had not Jesus taught to "do unto others as you would have them do unto you?" The bank manager was reflecting the love of Christ that he had experienced. Clifford thought this was a good time to ask a favor. "You know the Karen family I visit in Huey Fawn Village?" he asked. "They have a daughter named Naw Wa Paw who is of school age, but there is no school in that village. Would you have room to take her in?"

"Well," considered the bank manager, "one of the girl students is leaving, so I could probably take in one more. Her parents would have to agree of course."

The next time Clifford traveled to Huey Fawn Village, on the trail now familiar to him, he asked the girl's parents if they would like to send Naw Wa Paw to school in Chiang Mai. He told them about the Karen man who was manager of a bank and took in a few children to live with him and his wife so they could receive an education. Saw Pa Heh was favorable, but his wife, Naw Baw, had reservations. No one from their village had ever gone to school, and certainly no child had ever left home until they were grown. "We'll think about it," replied Saw Pa Heh, "and let you know tomorrow."

In the morning it was still evident that Naw Baw had not agreed. "We have no relatives in Chiang Mai," she argued, "How can we send our young daughter there?" Clifford had an idea. "I'll take you in my Land Rover, and bring you home again. You can see the place where she can live and meet the Karen man and his Thai wife who own the place."

Naw Baw had never been to Chiang Mai before, but she had heard it was a big city. "I suppose we could go for a look," she allowed.

That was how Naw Baw, Saw Pa Heh and their three children got to Chiang Mai. The following morning, after arranging for someone to look after Grandfather, they all marched down the mountain to the Thai village.

The Headman was surprised to see them. "Where are you all going?" he wanted to know.

Clifford explained the situation, and the Headman thought that was a great idea. "I've been urging those people to accept a school in their village, but they won't hear of it. If one of their children goes to school they may change their minds."

Clifford helped Naw Baw and her youngest child into the front seat of the Land Rover. Saw Pa Heh and the other two children sat in the back. The Headman's wife came out and picked some limes from a tree. She showed them how to hold them to their noses to help prevent car sickness. It seemed to help; only the two children in the back threw up while they were on the winding road going down the mountain. On the main highway going to Chiang Mai they were fine.

They arrived in Chiang Mai on a Saturday evening and Clifford took them directly to his house. He put mats down on the floor for them, and while they were washing off the dust of the trip in his bathroom Clifford made a hasty trip to a nearby evening market, where he purchased cooked rice, a vegetable curry, and some grilled chicken. He had stayed in the house of this Karen couple several times and was glad for a chance to repay their hospitality.

Pa Chintana, his landlady, was waiting for him when he returned. "Who are those people in your house," she wanted to know, "They look like *Chow Khao* (mountain people).

"They are," replied Clifford. "They're a Karen family from that village I sometimes visit."

"What are they doing here?"

"Maybe their daughter will enroll in a school. I know a place where she can live."

"Oh, well, I guess that will be o.k. Education will be good for those people. Mi Ja, the Akha girl you left with me is doing fine."

Clifford knew his landlady was a bit condescending, but she had a good heart. "They won't be staying long, will they?" she wanted to know.

"No, I'll take them back to their village Monday."

Clifford's guests had recovered from their trip in a motor vehicle, and enjoyed their food. Clifford was now able to converse with them in Karen, so he told them of his plan to take them to the Christian service at the Bank Manager's house the following evening.

On Sunday Clifford took them on a tour of Chiang Mai. Saw Pa Heh had been to Chiang Mai before, but Naw Baw had never been to a city before. They even stopped at Nai Lee's shop. Nai Lee's wife served them tea and gave candy to the children. It was a kind gesture, not lost on Clifford. He knew most lowland people would not be so nice to the mountain people. The small zoo on the north side of the city, however, was the big hit of the day. Most of the birds and animals were native to Thailand, but over-hunting had driven some to near extinction. The children had never seen some of them, and they all laughed at the antics of the gibbons and monkeys.

In the evening they went to the Bank Manager's house and attended the worship service. Po Swe, Clifford's Karen language teacher, was the speaker. He read the creation story from the Book of Genesis. Whether that was by accident, or design, Clifford didn't know, but it certainly caught the interest of Saw Pa Heh and Naw Baw. Pwo Swe went on to speak about the kindness of God in creating such a wonderful world, and how people everywhere could respond to God's love by showing love to one another.

It was mid-March, the end of the Thai school year, so the Bank Manager and his wife provided a meal after the service to celebrate the occasion. The students who lived there helped serve the food. Some of their parents had arrived to take their children home for the two month school break. Clifford introduced his guests, who felt at home among this group who spoke their own language. It's always important for Karens, when meeting other Karens, to try to find some relationship. Saw Pa Heh was pleased to discover that one of the parents of the students was his relative. He tried to explain the relationship to Clifford, but Clifford was soon lost in a tangle of distant cousins related by marriage. He didn't think it would count as a relation in America, but was glad for Saw Pa Heh, who seemed pleased to find this distant cousin. The Bank Manager showed Saw Pa Heh and Naw Baw the rooms where the students slept; one room for boys and one room for girls. "How old is your daughter," he asked Naw Baw.

"She's eight years old. I think that's too young to leave home." she replied.

"No, not at all. Really she should be seven to enter the first grade, but eight is alright."

"She can't even speak Thai. How can she go to school?"

"That is usually the situation for our Karen children. She may have to repeat the first grade, but after that, no problem."

Naw Baw looked to her husband for support, but he was no help. "I have a dream," he replied. "I have a dream that one day our village will have a school, and our daughter will be the first teacher."

"I'll think about it," she murmered.

Naw Baw did think about it, even though it was painful to contemplate her daughter leaving home at such a young age. The next day, Clifford took the family back to their home. Actually, just to the end of the road at the Thai Headman's house. They would walk alone from there. "I'll come to your village in two months just before the school year starts," he told them. "The decision is yours, but I can take Naw Wa Paw back to Chiang Mai if you agree."

Clifford had a lot to think about as he drove back to Chiang Mai. He appreciated what the Bank Manager was doing, but those few children staying at his house were only a drop in the bucket. Clifford thought about all the children he had seen at Huey Fawn Karen Village, at the Akha village, and the other mountain villages he had visited. No schools in any of them. Clifford knew the traditional way of life of the Mountain Tribes was changing. Their preferred life of separation from the dominant Thai culture and economy was under assault. Already, the Royal Thai Forestry Department was forbidding the cutting of trees in many mountain areas. Preserving national resources was good for the Nation, but how could the Uplanders continue to make their fields by cutting and burning trees as they always did?

Clifford had often witnessed merchants taking advantage of the Mountain People. Uneducated people were always taken advantage of; the products they sold did not receive full value, and they were over-charged for what they bought from the merchants, because they could not speak Thai or add up the value of their own products. Clifford began to develop a plan. He was thinking of building a student hostel in Chiang Mai where children of all the Tribes could live in a safe environment while attending schools. Maybe it was just a dream, like Saw Pa Heh's dream for his daughter to become a teacher.

It may have been a dream, but Clifford had a stubborn streak. He wrote to the Asian Inland Mission informing them of what he wanted to do. They had no objection, but said he would have to raise the money himself. They did send a few more names of potential doners, and Clifford wrote more letters. He had been neglecting to keep in touch with his financial supporters, but now, reinvigorated by his dream, he wrote to everyone he could think of. He described the villages he had visited, he wrote about the children , he wrote about the injustices faced by the Mountain Tribal people, and slowly money began to come in; mostly from widows and working class people who had known hardship themselves. Their gifts were small, but they came from their hearts. Students in a small Midwestern high school started an "Education For The Hill Tribes" project and raised funds from their community, as well as within the school. The Bank Manager was helpful, and advised Clifford to purchase certificates of deposit at his bank which gave 7% interest, so the accumulating funds continued to grow.

It was fortunate that Clifford had a lot of patience. He hoped for a big doner that would send $10,000, but that never happened. One day, the Bank Manager alerted Clifford to a plot of land that was for sale adjoining the Manager's house. "I advise you to buy it," urged the Manager, "It is not expensive, and since it is close to my house I can keep an eye on it."

"What can happen to a piece of land?" Clifford wanted to know.

"Lot's of things; it might become a dumping ground, or squatters may move on to it and be difficult to move off. Property in Thailand needs to be watched."

"Can I buy the land in my name?"

"No, foreigners cannot own land in Thailand, but it can be in my name and a lawyer can draw up a legal document stating that you, as a representative of Asian Inland Mission, can use the land for a non-profit student hostel."

Clifford knew the Bank Manager was trustworthy and agreed. It required all his accumulated funds to purchase the land and fence it. Now, he had to start raising money all over again for the building itself.

It took ten years for Clifford to finally raise the necessary funds to begin construction. Several times he almost lost heart, but another village trip would reveal more children in need of an education, and he would redouble his efforts. By that time Naw Wa Paw, who had received permission from her mother to go away to school, was a senior in high school and an honers student. She still wanted to return to her home village as a teacher, so Clifford arranged for her to attend the Chiang Mai Teacher's Training College. He paid for her school expenses, which was a further drain on his slowly accumulating funds.

However, the day finally came when enough funds had been collected, and the building was built. The Bank Manager arranged for a dedication service on a Sunday afternoon. The group of Karens who worshipped at his house sang some hymns, prayers were said, and Clifford was given the honor of cutting the ribbon at the doorway, and being the first to enter. The empty two story building smelled of new wood, and Clifford inhaled deeply, savoring the odor of success. It was the happiest day of his life.

Reality was soon to come. Clifford had been so intent on raising money for the building that he failed to think about ongoing expenses. The Bank Manager, ever practical, reminded Clifford that house parents to supervise the students and a cook to prepare food were needed. He did have a suggestion, "Ask Pwo Swe," he whispered into Clifford's ear after the dedication service. By that time Pwo Swe had married a young lady from his village and brought her to live in Chiang Mai. They already had two children and were struggling financially. Pwo Swe still had his job at the abattoir, but no longer taught Clifford the Karen language. Clifford did ask them, and they readily agreed.

"I will make an apartment for you and your family at one end of the hostel," promised Clifford, "You can supervise the students and also cook for them. Of course, board and room will be free."

Pwo Swe and his wife, Naw Ewa, had good suggestions. "The boarding students who will live here should bring rice as their boarding fee, and they should help prepare their food too." Clifford also agreed to provide a salary for Pwo Swe and Naw Ewa, but knew that would put a major strain on his own finances.

The students came; all of them children he had met in his visits to the Tribal villages. There were Karen, Akha and Lahu. The Akha children from the Doi Maesalong area, were the most needy. Teacher Chen brought them to the hostel in his pickup truck, and even provided some money for their expenses. He had changed his mind about returning to Taiwan when a woman teacher, also from Taiwan, came to teach at the school in Doi Maesalong. They had fallen in love, first with each other, but also with their students, and decided to stay. Teacher Chen had forgotten about the nightclubs of Taipei! Clifford found that Pwo Swe and Naw Ewa could efficiently run the hostel, so he left it to them and he returned to his life in the hills, living as frugally as was possible.

Clifford was certainly not a big spender. The rent for his Thai style house was very little. He lived off the local fresh markets, and maintained his ancient Land Rover, which he used to transport himself to the foot trails that wound up into the mountains. He would park his vehicle at a low-land farmer's house, shoulder his back pack and ascend into the rugged hills, staying for days among the Hill People. Those hospitable people fed him and gave him a place to sleep when he arrived on foot in their villages. He, in turn, earned his keep by providing simple medicines, news from the outside world and entertaining Bible stories. His intention was not to entertain. He strived to turn those villagers away from their animistic spirits and toward his concept of God. Mostly, however, his stories did no more than entertain. Living with the mountain people as he did, he learned to speak three of their tribal languages to perfection. No other foreigner had ever done so. He spoke as one of them, and was accepted almost as one of them. He was so at home with the Hill People he neglected his contacts with his supporting churches.

CHAPTER TWELVE

A VISITOR FROM THE AMERICAN EMBASSY

Monthly stipends for Clifford's living expenses, forwarded to him by the bookkeeping department of AIM, slowly diminished. Contributions needed for the student hostel continued to arrive in small amounts, but he kept those in a separate account at the bank. He did not touch those funds for his own expenses. It was true he did not need a lot of money, but he certainly needed more than he was receiving. His landlady assumed all Foreigners had a lot of money and nagged him when he was late with the rent. His battered Land Rover was using a lot of engine oil and needed a ring job, but he couldn't afford to have it done. Clifford had a hard life, but he loved it. He couldn't imagine returning to his home country. What would he do there? Here he was free to roam the forested mountains and live with the independent minded people he found there. He didn't want to leave his work. However, he knew he was not a fund raiser, and funds were what he needed. That's why he listened carefully when he received a visit from a tall American dressed in a safari suit who came from the American Embassy in Bangkok.

The American had appeared without notice one rainy day when Clifford was home recuperating from a bout of dengue fever. Dengue fever is not a pleasant ailment. Sometimes it's called " break bone fever", because it causes intense bodily aches and a high fever. It is mosquito borne, and Clifford's unscreened house provided easy access for those pests. Clifford was painfully aware of the condition of his house when he invited his guest inside. Never a meticulous housekeeper, his illness had prevented any effort to wash dishes or pick up the house. He apologized profusely, while wiping off two mismatched chairs and setting them around the small kitchen table on which he ate his meals. He filled two glasses with water from his filtered water crock and placing them in front of the chairs invited his guest to sit.

"I don't receive many guests," Clifford explained, "and I have been ill for about a week. Is there anything I can do for you?"

"Perhaps there is," replied the guest, "but first I should introduce myself. My name is Alex Scott and I work out of the American Embassy in Bangkok. We like to keep in touch with American residents in this country, just in case there should be a political crisis, you know. You never did sign in at the Embassy did you?"

"No, I never got around to that. Is it required?"

"Not required, but it could be useful to you sometime. Do you have a family Mr. Johnson?"

"No, I live here alone, and as you can see, I am not a good housekeeper. My missionary work among the Hill People requires me to spend much time with them."

"I understand that. Are you able to support yourself adequately?" questioned Mr. Scott, with a glance around the sparsely furnished room.

Clifford was getting a little irritated. His guest had arrived without notice. He had not removed his shoes when entering the house, an Asian custom Clifford followed, and if he had a reason for coming he was slow to get to the point of his visit. Clifford, well attuned to local sensitivities, also noticed that Mr. Scott had left his driver outside in the large American station wagon.

"Excuse me," murmured Clifford, "I'll take a glass of cool water to your driver."

"Oh never mind, he's o.k."

"No trouble. I'll be right back."

The driver appreciated the water, and Clifford chatted briefly with him. When he returned to the house he noticed Mr. Scott glancing at his watch. "Did you know your driver was from Isan, Mr. Scott?"

"Please call me Alex, and no, I was sure my driver was from Thailand."

"Isan refers to a region of Thailand, Alex, the Northeast Region. They speak a different dialect there which I find interesting. More like Laotian. Perhaps I will be able to talk to Montri some other day and learn more about his home dialect."

"Montri?"

"Yes, that's your driver's name."

"Really," exclaimed Alex with feigned interest. "Well, I have heard about your ability with languages."

Clifford had had no contact with the Embassy, and couldn't imagine how anyone there could know anything about him. "Can I help you with anything Alex."

"Perhaps you can. I would like to talk to you about an opportunity that may be of interest to you. I may be in a position to help you financially, Clifford, and you can be of service to your country as well. I work for the DEA."

"I'm sorry, I live a rather isolated life here. What is the DEA?"

"My God," thought Alex, "this weirdo really is out of it."

"The DEA," annunciated Scott, "is the acronym for the Drug Enforcement Administration of the United States Government. Perhaps you are not aware that harmful addictive drugs originating in Thailand, or neighboring countries, find their way to our own country and constitute a growing problem."

"Yes, I know there are some drugs here, but what does that have to do with me?"

"You spend a lot of time with the Mountain Tribes, and even speak their languages. Is that not true?"

"Yes, I do mission work among those people, but how do you know these things about me?"

"The Embassy is interested in your welfare you know. That's one reason why we're here, and perhaps you could use some supplemental income."

Clifford felt a dengue fever headache coming on. "Please get to the point, Alex. Just what is the purpose of your visit today?"

"The point is, Clifford, that you are a unique person. You know the Tribal people. You know their languages. You must know that drugs pass through those mountains and people involved in their transport hide in those remote places. You are in a position to help your home country, as well as keep drugs away from your parishioners, or whatever you call them. We just need some information on drug movements and who is involved. Of course, we would be prepared to reimburse you for your trouble. It would not be a small amount. What do you think?"

Perhaps it was his nagging headache, or the fact that he was again late in paying his rent, which made Clifford respond with some interest. "What kind of information are you looking for?"

"We would like to know who is involved in the purchasing and sale of drugs, specifically opium and heroin."

"What about those who plant opium?"

"That's the responsibility of the Thai police. We are especially concerned about the kingpins, the big guys, who are making fortunes while poisoning our country."

"I don't think I'm likely to meet people like that."

"Perhaps not, but you may hear of people who can point us to the big traffickers."

"Yes, I understand."

"We know that Burma and Laos produce even more opium than Thailand, but much of that is channeled through Thailand because of marketing arrangements worked out by international criminals. We want to know when large shipments are on the move, and we want to know where bush factories are located that convert opium to heroin."

Clifford was getting increasingly concerned. Yes, he needed money, but this was beginning to sound serious. "Could this be dangerous?" he asked.

"It should not be dangerous for you. Don't go around asking questions. Just keep your eyes and ears open."

"If I hear of something how do I contact you?"

"Do not contact me; we have an office right here in Chiang Mai located on the grounds of the American Consulate."

"So, I should go there?"

"No, no, I will give you a telephone number. Just call that number and someone will tell you what to do. What do you think, Clifford, can you help us?"

Clifford was not totally convinced that he should get involved in this matter, but replied that he would think about it.

"Good," replied Alex, "Think about it carefully, and I will arrange for a stipend to be sent to you each month. Do you have a Post Office box number?"

Clifford gave Alex his mailing address, and Alex gave Clifford a plain card with a phone number on it. "Call this number when you have something to report. If the information you provide is useful you will receive a bonus."

Alex stood up to leave and Clifford saw him to the door. When Alex Scott and his driver drove off Clifford swallowed two aspirins and went to bed. His head ached, his body ached, and he was not sure he had responded wisely to his visitor's request.

Alex was pleased. Obviously, the man he had just visited needed money. Clifford had not refused the monthly stipend, and from past experience, Alex was confident Clifford would keep the money and provide information.

After a few days Clifford was up and about and traveling to hill villages where he discretely enquired about drug movements. Most village people knew where opium was planted in their local areas, but Clifford knew that was not what the DEA wanted. They had in mind bigger fish they hoped to fry.

Clifford hated to recruit informers. He knew it could be dangerous for the informer; and Clifford had too much respect for the villagers. However, sometimes people came to him with information when they saw he was interested in drug movements. Also, the villagers knew that drug money was not good; it brought in outsiders who did not respect local traditions. On a trip to Clifford's favorite village, the Karen village he had first visited when he was newly arrived in Chiangmai, his old friend, Saw Pa Heh, confided to Clifford that he thought he knew where the heroin factory was located. This was the factory the Thai Headman had warned Clifford about many years ago. The Headman did not know its location, but knew there was one, and that the Hmong man, Sae Yang, was involved.

"You mean that factory is still in operation?" Clifford was amazed.

"Yes, I'm sure it is." replied Saw Pa Heh. "I was hunting in a wild area where no one lives and came across a trail that had been heavily traveled by horses or mules. I carefully followed the trail until I could see a horse corral and some buildings. I didn't go any closer, but there could only be one purpose for such a place."

"What is that?"

"It has to be one of those places where they make heroin. They would need the horses to bring in chemicals needed to convert opium to heroin, and to transport the heroin out."

"Could well be," admitted Clifford.

Saw Pa Heh drew a rough map of the area, showing the trail and location of the buildings and gave it to Clifford. Clifford was conflicted. This was the kind of information the DEA wanted, but he knew it was also dangerous to even know such things, not to mention passing on the information. "Saw Pa Heh," entreated Clifford, "Do not go to that place anymore."

"I'll be careful." Saw Pa Heh thought he had not been seen, but he didn't know how careful the drug people were. They had posted guards near the trail..

For the first time, Clifford made use of the telephone number given to him by Alex Scott. Clifford had no phone at his home. He had no use for one, so he called from a pay phone next to a large store near the Chiang Mai fresh market. His call was picked up at the first ring. "Yes," a woman's voice answered. Clifford was surprised. He was not expecting a woman to answer.

"My name is Clifford Johnson. I have some information."

"Ah yes, Mr. Johnson. Just a moment please while I arrange a meeting place."

After a short pause, the woman was back on the line. "Mr. Johnson, this evening at 9:00 P.M. go to the Kai Yang Restaurant on River Road. Sit at an outside table behind the restaurant under a big tree located there. An American man will meet you there. Do you know the place?"

"Yes."

"Good, arrive exactly at 9:00."

Clifford did know the restaurant. He had eaten there before, and as it's name indicated, the specialty of the house was *kai yang* (barbequed chicken). Clifford loved to eat the chicken with sticky rice and *som tam,* a spicy Thai salad. He was surprised, however, to have the meeting arranged at such a public place. He thought he would be going to a DEA office.

Clifford walked into the restaurant at exactly 9:00 P.M., and found the table with a Westerner seated there. "Hello," Clifford introduced himself, "I believe I am to meet you here."

"Yes, I believe so. My name is Steve. Please have a seat."

Clifford sat down, and Steve continued, "I have already ordered a roast chicken and a bottle of Singha. (Thai beer). What will you have?"

"*Nong,*" (younger sister) Clifford called to a waitress, and ordered a roast chicken, sticky rice, a Coke and *som tam,* the spicy Thai salad he liked. Steve complimented Clifford on his ability to speak Thai. Clifford didn't know what to say in this situation, so decided to leave the first move up to Steve. Their orders came, and there was silence as they both hungrily attacked their food. Clifford used his fingers to eat the sticky rice, which is really the only way to do it, but Steve thought that was rather strange. He had been briefed about Clifford, but only knew that he was a missionary, had lived in Thailand many years, and had a gift for acquiring languages.

Finally, Steve pushed aside his plate. "I hear you have some information for us?" he enquired.

"Yes, I have been told the location of a heroin factory."

"That's interesting, but we usually refer the them as labs. What is the source of your information?"

Clifford was reluctant to provide Saw Pa Heh's name and village, but just said his source was from a Hill Tribesman whom he had known for many years.

"Can you provide me with the location of the lab?" asked Steve.

"Yes, its in Chomtong District of Chiang Mai Province. I have a map that provides some details."

"That's strange," observed Steve as he studied the map, "Most of these labs are near the border with Burma. This one is not. Can you give me some major landmarks, so we can make some aerial observations."

Clifford described how he got to the hill village, and how the crude map was oriented to that village. "O.K , we should be able to locate the place. Thank you for your assistance Mr. Johnson."

A month passed. At first, after his conversation with Steve, Clifford was worried that something bad would happen, but as time went on, he was lulled into complacency. That was before Naw Wa Paw came to visit him at his home. She was now teaching in the new school in her village. She had some terribly bad news. She described how at dawn one morning about two weeks ago two men they had never seen before arrived at her parent's house. They did not speak Karen, but when Saw Pa Heh came out to see what they wanted, they pulled out revolvers and shot him several times. He died instantly. Naw Wa Paw sobbed as she told Clifford of this tragedy. "My father was such a good man. He allowed me to go to school, the first in our village. Why would anyone hurt him? Can you tell me?"

Clifford was also grief stricken; Saw Pa Heh was his first real friend in Thailand. "No, Naw Wa Paw, I can't imagine anyone wanting to kill him. Did they rob you?"

"No, they ran away. Later some of our men took their hunting guns and went looking for them, but found nothing."

Naw Wa Paw also told Clifford of another happening on a nearby mountain that she thought would be of interest to him. "One day, about three weeks ago, we saw three helicopters flying over our village. That was the first time we had seen them so close to us. Later, we heard from some visiting kinsmen that helicopters had landed in a clearing in a forested area on that same day. There were Thai police in them who raided something they found in that forest. We don't know what, but there was gunfire, and whatever they raided was burned up. Could that be connected to my father's death?"

Clifford was stunned. He felt sick with remorse. Had he indirectly caused his friend's death? Tears ran down his face and he could not speak. Naw Wa Paw tried to comfort him. "Please don't cry, because of you and my father, attitudes have changed in my village. Now they welcome the school, and send their children to learn. I have a good salary, so I can support my mother and younger brothers. As you know, they are already attending high school here in Chiang Mai and staying in the student hostel you started."

Clifford said nothing about his suspicions concerning the raid, which he guessed was on the heroin lab. Saw Pa Heh must have been seen in the area. Retribution came quickly. Clifford did not sleep well that night, nor for many nights thereafter. A few days after his meeting with Naw Wa Paw there was an envelope addressed to him in his Post Office box with no return address. In it was 5,000 Baht in cash, and a note, "WELL DONE."

Clifford was not so sure it really was "Well Done." There was no one he could confide in, so he thought about it constantly. He reasoned that the illicit narcotic drugs were bad; bad for the people of Thailand, and bad for his own country. It was good to reduce the amount of such drugs in the world. It was necessary to put evil people in jail who profited from those drugs. But the cost; that was the problem that nagged at Clifford. The cost was high. Saw Pa Heh was a good man. Were the results of Clifford's actions worth the cost of a good man's life? There was no clear cut answer, but Clifford knew he wanted to hurt the people who had killed his friend. He wanted to put them out of business. That was the one thing he could do for his friend, so he decided not to sever his relationship with the DEA.

CHAPTER THIRTEEN

CLIFFORD RETURNS TO DOI MAESALONG

Clifford felt like he needed a change of scenery, so when he received a letter from Teacher Chen at Doi Maesalong inviting him to come for a visit, he responded affirmatively. The last sentence in the letter puzzled Clifford; it stated, "There is something I want to talk about with you. You can stay with my wife, Quon Hing, and me in our new house."

Clifford decided to take a bus, rather than driving. He had heard from his Akha friends that the Jin Haw man, whose house yard he had used to park his Landrover, still lived with Mee Bu in the same house. Clifford did not like that man, and did not want to meet him. That's why he took the bus north of Mae Chan to the intersection where the trail to Doi Maesalong begins. This time he had to walk alone with no horse to help carry his pack. At the Akha village, half way to Doi Maesalong, he stopped to rest and eat the lunch he had brought with him. Some village children sat near him, watching the foreigner eat, when suddenly, in response to their mother's calls, they all got up and ran to their own houses. Clifford wondered if he had been considered a threat to the children, but that's when he noticed a caravan of horses and mules coming over a distant hill from the north. The trail they were on joined the Doi Masalong trail about where he was sitting.

Clifford thought he had a ringside seat to watch the parade go by, but a woman in a nearby house, where some of the children had disappeared, opened her door a crack and motioned for Clifford to come. Clifford thought she might know something he didn't, so quickly went into her house. Without saying a word she closed the door behind him and peered outside through a crack in the bamboo wall.

Clifford did likewise, just in time to see the first horses of the caravan pass by the house. What he saw next froze his heart and made the hair on the back of his neck stand up. Two mounted men with rifles slung over their backs were near the head of the caravan. Clifford had seen both of them before. One was Sae Yang, the Hmong man Clifford had met when he got on the wrong trail many years before and reached that man's village by mistake. Several people, including the Thai headman, had warned him about that man. The other mounted horseman was the Yunnanese man. The one Mee Bu lived with.

Clifford immediately realized what he was seeing; it was a large amount of drugs being moved out of the mountains. Besides the two riding horses, Clifford counted 22 pack horses and mules, each one heavily loaded with bulging back packs. In addition, there were guards on foot who were armed with automatic rifles. The two mounted men were in charge of the caravan, and where the two trails met, directed the caravan to turn eastward, toward the highway where Clifford had started his trek that day. "How bold," murmured Clifford to himself, "Here they are in broad daylight." Still, with 10 armed men they weren't taking any chances.

As the caravan passed by, not a sound was heard in the village. No one was to be seen; they were all hiding in houses. The caravan rounded the corner and were soon out of sight, but still no one opened their door. Clifford started to thank the Akha woman for likely saving his life, but she put her finger to her mouth, and continued to look out the crack. Soon, one more armed man on a horse came by and followed the caravan. He was the rear guard. After he had passed by, doors opened and children ventured out to play. Clifford wanted to express his appreciation to the Akha woman, but she motioned for him to leave. Clifford realized his presence put her in danger. He left, and continued westward on the trail to Doi Maesalong, away from the route taken by the caravan.

It was evening when Clifford arrived at the Chinese settlement of Doi Maesalong. He found Teacher Chen's house and the teacher came out to greet him. "Welcome friend! Please come in and rest. You must be tired." Clifford took off his shoes and stepped into the house just as Teacher Chen's wife, Quon Hing, came to the door. Teacher Chen proudly introduced her to Clifford. "Welcome to our house in the mountains," she said graciously. "I know you must be tired. That long walk to the highway is very difficult for me."

"I've offered to get you a horse," ventured Teacher Chen.

"I'm afraid of falling off the horse, anyway I'm quite content to live here in these mountains."

Clifford noticed that Quon Hing's English ability was better than her husband's. She was also a beautiful woman, and Clifford understood why Teacher Chen was no longer homesick for Taiwan.

"You're probably ready for a bath," added Quon Hing, "I'll show you to your room."

She led Clifford to an enclosed porch at the rear of the house where a bed had been prepared for him, and showed him the bathroom, complete with a shower.

"Wow," exclaimed Clifford, "I have never stayed in such a luxurious place in all of my trips to the mountains."

"No, its just a simple house," laughed Quon Hing, "Make yourself at home."

Clifford enjoyed a refreshing bath and changed into clean, though wrinkled, clothe that had been packed in his backpack. He followed the aroma of cooking food back into the main room of the house. The table was set, Chinese style, with bowls and chopsticks. "We're having Yunnanese food tonight," announced Quon Hing, "Most of the people who live here at Doi Maesalong came from Yunnan Province, in southwest China, so it is the easiest type of food to obtain. I hope you will like it."

"I'm sure I will," replied Clifford, "It smells delicious."

Clifford was famished after his long walk. Although he was curious to find out why Teacher Chen had invited him here to talk about something, that could wait. Clifford dug into the pork stew and steamed buns that Quon Hing served him. He recognized the meat cuts that were used in the stew. In Thai they are called *mu sam chan,* which means three layered pork. Those cuts come from pork bellies, and can also be used to make bacon. They are the cheapest part of the pig, but Quon Hing had stewed the meat with Chinese herbs, resulting in the most delicious pork dish that Clifford had ever eaten. The hot steamed buns were eaten with the stewed pork, and there were two vegetable side dishes.

After the meal, they sat around the table eating watermelon seeds and drinking a strong aromatic tea, that Teacher Chen said had been produced locally. Clifford told of his experience that day with the drug caravan. Quon Hing inhaled sharply and held her hand over her mouth, while glancing at her husband. "I'm sorry you had such a frightening experience today," Teacher Chen said, "But it relates to what I have to tell you."

Teacher Chen explained that General Tao, commander of the 93rd KMT army located at Doi Maesalong, had spoken to him about something very secret. "Actually, the General had hardly spoken to me before I married Quon Hing," explained Teacher Chen, with a fond look at his wife, "But it seems that Quon Hing's father is a rather important man in the Taiwanese government and now that government is pressing General Tao to make some policy changes here at Doi Maesalong. The General is willing, but must be very careful. Such changes could be dangerous."

Clifford was feeling a bit uncomfortable, "I don't think this involves me," he asserted.

"If you are willing, you may be able to help us in this matter," interjected Quon Hing, "And the danger would be to General Tao, not to you."

"I'm confused," said Clifford, "I think you had better explain just what you have in mind."

"I'm sorry," apologized Teacher Chen, "My wife can explain things better."

With her better command of the English language, Quon Hing explained that General Tao, and the entire 93rd Army that he commanded, supported themselves by engaging in the production and marketing of illicit drugs. They purchased the opium from local Tribal people, converted the opium into heroin, and sold it to international drug traffickers. Quon Hing explained that the United States and

European governments were aware of these arrangements, and also that Taiwan sponsored the Chinese outpost in Doi Maesalong. All of this was causing some embarrassment to Taiwan, so they wanted Doi Maesalong to cease involvement in the drug trade. Quon Hing further explained that her father was using her and Teacher Chen to secretly communicate this sensitive matter to the General.

"Why doesn't the Taiwanese Government just order General Tao to quit his dependence on the drug trade?" Clifford asked.

"Its more complicated than that", responded Quon Hing, "Those involved in the drug trade have become very powerful. They have a worldwide network and can inflict tremendous pressure on countries like Thailand and Taiwan. My father believes the only way to proceed is for a powerful country, like the United States, to catch the drug lords, indict them of serious crimes and put them in prison for long terms; or even better, execute them."

"So, why doesn't Taiwan deal directly with the United States?"

"That's where we come in, and you, if you are willing. My father has informed me that there are U.S. Government people in Thailand attached to an agency that aids the Thai Government in drug suppression; I believe it is called the Drug Enforcement Administration."

Those words really shook up Clifford, but Quon Hing's next words relieved him somewhat. "General Tao believes we need an ordinary American citizen who is fluent in local languages and is well acquainted with the Tribal People. The General is in a position to provide real damning information to this American Agency, but he cannot be seen talking to them. He can't even trust his own staff. He knows that Americans are sometimes seen together at social occasions, so perhaps if one of those Americans had such information he could pass it on to the right people. He asked us if we knew of such an American. We thought of you. You don't have to do this if you don't want to, but we invited you here to ask you. What do you think?"

Apparently, Teacher Chen and his wife did not know that Clifford already knew about the DEA. Clifford was certainly not going to tell them. It did not take Clifford long to make a decision. Yes, he would help. It was not the money. It was a personal thing. He would help because of what those drug people had done to Saw Pa Heh.

"I am willing to be of assistance in this matter," answered Clifford, "Just tell me how."

"Oh, that would be great," exclaimed Quon Hing, "Your experience on the trail today is an example of how brazen these people have become. They're not afraid of anyone, but everyone is afraid of them."

"I really don't want to get deeply involved in this matter," explained Clifford, "But I could pass some information on to the right people."

"We understand," Teacher Chen replied, "We do not want you to be in any danger. It will, however, be dangerous for General Tao. It will soon be noticed that he will not be providing protection to the heroin labs and drug movements."

Quon Hing continued, "General Tao has had a real change of heart. We think his daughter has been a good influence on him."

"He has a daughter?"

"Yes, and she has become a Christian, like you. We know she has been trying to convince her father that the time has come to leave his old ways and find other sources of income to support his army."

"Does she live here?"

"No, her father has a house in Chiang Mai and she lives there most of the time."

"I didn't know that."

"Not many do. She prefers not to be recognized. She just wants to live a normal life."

Clifford had never met General Tao, and never would. "Better if you're not seen together," explained Teacher Chen.

Clifford did, however, have two enjoyable days in the cool weather of Doi Maesalong. Teacher Chen took Clifford to see extensive tea farms on the hillsides around the town, and also visited families who were growing the large brown shitake mushrooms. Both enterprises had received help from experts sent from Taiwan. "Already tea and mushrooms bring in a lot of money," asserted Teacher Chen. "Doi Maesalong does not need to be dependent on drug money."

"You don't sound like the same Teacher Chen I met here several years ago," teased Clifford, "At that time you couldn't wait to get back to Taipei."

"Yes, I have changed, and you have been a good example."

"What do you mean?"

"Your life has meaning. Getting that student hostel built in Chiang Mai and helping Tribal children live there to get an education is great."

"Well, I've noticed you have stayed here to teach in the Doi Maesalong School for many years now."

"Yeah, well, these kids need me. No one ever needed me before."

"I'm sure Quon Hing has had some influence on you too!"

Teacher Chen chuckled, "Yes, she's a determined woman. She wants to clean this place up and prove to her father that she can do something."

"Doesn't he think so?"

"Don't get me wrong, he's a good man, and noted for being one of the 'clean ministers' in the Taiwan Government, but Quon Hing is his only child. He and his wife would probably have preferred a son. We Chinese are like that you know."

"So I've heard. But her parents must have helped her receive a good education."

"Yes, that's true. She graduated from our best university with honors." Her parents thought she was throwing her life away to come to this remote place to teach school. Also, she was disappointed when she discovered that the Chinese Army here supports itself with the drug trade. I lived here for many years, but did nothing about it."

"What is she doing?"

"She contacted her father, and he, in turn, has convinced the highest levels in our government that Taiwan should not be involved in this trade. That is why General Tao is now under pressure to change his ways."

"Is he willing?"

"Yes, he is willing, but also cautious. I have already told you it could be dangerous for him. Some high ranking people are making a lot of money on the drugs from here."

Clifford was glad for this conversation with Teacher Chen. He knew he had made the right decision to help this young couple in their fight against the Drug Lords. The following morning he was fed a big breakfast, and provided with food to sustain him on his trek out of Doi Maesalong. Just before leaving, Quon Hing warned him to say nothing about their conversations concerning the drug business. "In a few days," she confided, "Someone will give you a letter containing very confidential information. Make sure it gets into the right hands."

CHAPTER FOURTEEN

A SECRET LETTER

Clifford walked back to his car, and drove all the way to Chiang Mai in one day. During the next week he checked his post office box daily, but nothing appeared, not even a small check from a supporter of his mission work. One day, when Clifford was parking his car near the downtown market, a motorcycle came by. The driver, a man unknown to Clifford, handed him an envelope through the car window, and drove off. Clifford's name was on the envelope, so obviously, he had been followed by someone who knew what he looked like. He carefully opened the letter with his pocket knife and studied what was written on two pages of typewriter paper. "Holy Moses," he muttered, and instantly gave up on food shopping that day. He carefully folded the letter, put it in his pocket, and walked to the nearest public phone booth. He couldn't help looking behind him, but no one seemed to be following.

Clifford had memorized the phone number he had been given, and, as before, a woman answered after the first ring. "This is Clifford Johnson," he announced, "I need to see someone immediately."

"It may be a few days," a sweet voice replied, "Our agents are quite busy these days."

Clifford was a very polite person. He had never raised his voice to anyone, especially a woman, but that day he lost his cool. "Listen," he demanded, "I need to see someone today. I have some information that can't wait, and if I can't talk to anyone here I'll call your office in Washington, D.C." Clifford had no idea who to call in Washington, but he did get results. "Just a minute Mr. Johnson." The sweet voice was no longer so sweet. A man's voice came on the line. "Mr. Johnson, just what do you have that can't wait?"

"Can I talk on the phone?"

"No, don't do that," the voice replied with a disgusted tone. DEA agents often had to deal with over excited informants who thought they had the most important information ever in the history of the world. The man Clifford was talking to was Agent Denning, the Chiang Mai Station Chief. He was writing reports that were due at the head office in Washington that night. He hated writing those detailed reports, and doing so always put him in a foul mood. "O.K. Mr. Johnson, I will see you in 30 minutes at the coffee shop located inside the Chiang Mai Bowling Alley. Don't be late, and this had damn well better be worth my time." Click, the line went dead.

Clifford had never bowled, but he knew where the bowling alley was located. He parked about a block from it and waited in his car. At 25 minutes after the call he left his car and walked to the bowling alley. He and a heavy set man entered at the same time. The man asked, "Are you Mr. Johnson?" Clifford said he was, and they sat at a table in the nearly empty coffee shop. "I can't stay long," the man said with obvious irritation, "What do you have?"

Clifford took out his letter and handed the contents to the agent; who first glanced at it hurriedly, but than went over it again, and again. Finally, the agent looked at Clifford, "Who gave you this information?"

"I would rather not say."

"You have to tell me where and how you acquired this letter or I cannot accept it."

"I am concerned about the safety of some people."

"Listen, the DEA is no Mickey Mouse outfit; all sources of information are strictly confidential. No exceptions. Maybe you wrote this yourself; how do I know."

There seemed to be no choice, so Clifford told the whole story of his visits to Doi Maesalong, and of the two teachers he had met there. He told about Quon Hing's family connection with the Taiwan government. He also told of General Tao's rather reluctant decision to quit the drug business, and how the letter had been passed to him in the market area. "I'm sure the information in this letter is trustworthy," asserted Clifford.

The agent studied the two pages again. "Have you read this?" he demanded.

"Yes, I have."

"Can you wait here a bit more? I need to go back to my office and check out something."

"Sure." replied Clifford.

The agent almost ran to his car and drove back to his office so fast he left pedestrians and pedicab drivers shaking their fists at his ordinary looking Toyota sedan. At his office building, on the grounds of the American Consulate, he first went to an adjoining office where the CIA Station Chief was located. "I have a fast moving situation here," he explained. "I think you'd better drop everything and work with me on this one." He handed the letter to the CIA Station Chief.

"Wow!" the chief exclaimed. "You want me to check out something?"

"Yes, my informant mentioned two Taiwanese who teach at that Chinese school in Doi Maesalong. Their names are Teacher Chen and Quon Hing.

The CIA chief turned to his computer muttering, "We have a lot on that place, and old General Tao, but you can't touch them you know. The Thai government has some deal with the General, and even Taiwan is involved." Soon the screen lit up with loads of information about Doi Maesalong. "Ah yes, here we are. There is a Lee Chen, who has been there for many years, and Wang Quon Hing who arrived just last year. Those two are now married. Whoa! This is interesting, Wang Quon Hing's father is a minister in the Taiwan Government. Is that important?"

"Very important. It corroborates what my informant told me."

"Need anything else?"

"Not now, but maybe later. Why don't you photo copy this letter and send it on to your people. That's your business of course; I don't mean to intrude."

"We'll encrypt it and send it on. I'm sure it will raise a few eyebrows at Langley."

The DEA agent drove back to the bowling alley at a slower pace, reviewing in his mind what the letter had said. It gave detailed information on the shipment of 950 kilograms of pure refined heroin from Doi Maesalong to the fishing town of Mahachai on the Gulf of Siam. It gave names and aliases of all involved in the shipment and who would be protecting it along the way. There were some high ranking police officers on that list. The fishing vessel, that would receive the drugs, was named and even the point of rendezvous on the high seas where the shipment would be transferred to a tramp steamer, also named. Map coordinates were even provided for the labs that had converted the raw opium to heroin. The letter had not been signed, but it had to be either a complete hoax, or written by someone within the drug ring that knew everything. The DEA already knew about General Tao, but could not touch him. It would make sense if he was the author of the letter. The CIA file had confirmed that Mr. Johnson was in touch with people who had important contacts. It might all be true, and it might be more than the Thai Police Department wanted to know. This could be a headache. A much bigger headache than the unfinished reports still waiting for his attention.

Clifford had waited at the Bowling Alley, so the Agent questioned him some more. His story held up, so he was told to go home, but not leave town in case he was needed again. "Whatever you do, don't go near Maesalong until this matter is cleared up," warned the Agent.

DEA Agent Denning had decided he could not ignore the contents of the letter, and he could not wait for permission to proceed from his superiors. According to the letter, the shipment was already assembled at a house owned by a Yunnanese man who lived near Maechan just off the trail head that led to Doi Maesalong. The DEA knew about that man. They knew he lived with an Akha woman, named Mee Bu, and had unsavory friends, but had no hard evidence against him. "Hang the reports," thought Agent Denning, "I'm going to Bangkok."

In two hours he was on a flight to Bangkok. His destination was the office of Police General Manoon Sripanluang, commander of the Narcotics Control Division. All the DEA could do was pass incriminating information on to the Thai police. They would make the arrests, if they wanted to. To the frustration of agents like Denning, they often didn't want to. Agent Denning usually dealt with General Manoon's deputies, but in this case he knew he would only talk to the top man. He had already phoned the General's office and made an appointment.

Upon his arrival at Police Headquarters, Agent Denning was ushered directly into General Manoon's air conditioned office, which, Denning noted, could have been the office of the CEO of a large corporation. No metal file cabinets, no police radio, but a spacious room with carpets on the floor and matching drapes for the windows. Intricately carved wooden cabinets, in the old Thai style, were placed against two of the walls. On a highly polished table, made from a single slab of teak wood, were two very large elephant tusks, arranged to form an arch. Elegant celadon bowls were placed on the table under the tusks. Photographs, diplomas and awards of various kinds were mounted on one wall. Above them were large framed photographs of Their Majesties, The King and Queen. A Buddha image on an elevated carved table was against another wall. Three burning incense sticks were placed in a black lacquered bowl in front of the image. The aromatic smoke from the incense wafted up around the image and throughout the room. The General sat behind a large teak desk that matched the table on which the ivory tusks were placed. The desk was bare, except for some papers in a folder and a photograph of a young lady.

General Manoon stood behind his desk and greeted Agent Denning in impeccable English, with more than a trace of an English accent, betraying the fact that he was a graduate of Sandhurst, the English military academy. "Did you have a good flight?" he enquired. Denning assured him that he, indeed, did have a good flight. He also apologized for this hurried meeting, and for keeping the General in his office.

"No problem at all," stated the General, "My staff have left, but it seems my work is never done. However, I believe I could arrange for some coffee; or would you prefer tea?"

"Coffee would be fine, thanks"

The General pressed a button on his desk and a police woman entered. *Kafae sawng ti,*" (two coffees) He ordered. The police woman was soon back with two cups of coffee on a silver tray. Denning took a cup, but refused cream or sugar. The woman placed the other cup on the General's desk, and added two lumps of sugar and a generous amount of cream. When she left, the General continued with small talk. "Do you have a family Mr. Denning?"

"I have a daughter, but she is living with her mother in America."

"Do they visit you from time to time?"

"My wife and I divorced five years ago."

"Ah, that is too bad. You must miss your daughter. How old is she?"

"She is 14. I will see her next year when I return to America."

"I too miss my daughter," sighed the General, glancing at the framed photograph on his desk. "Her mother is dead, so she is all I have. She has been studying at a university in England, but will soon return for a term break."

Agent Denning was not accustomed to such formalities. He wanted to present the information he carried in his suit pocket and urge the General to move on it. Finally, the General drained the last of his coffee and opened the folder on his desk. "Mr. Denning," he began, "I see you have been working in Thailand for nearly two years now; have you had good cooperation from my police officers?" Denning was not expecting such a question, but diplomatically replied that he usually did. "You can be frank with me," urged the General, "I suspect that some of the police in my Division would like to get rich quickly, and, unfortunately, drug money may have tainted some."

"Well," Denning replied cautiously, "There have been some occasions when information my office has provided was not followed up. Perhaps there were reasons I was not aware of."

"Perhaps," replied the General, "But what do you have now.?"

Agent Denning took the two-page letter from his pocket and handed it to the General, who perused it quietly. He looked up at Denning with raised eyebrows, and read the letter again. The General was first, and foremost, a police officer, who had risen through the ranks to his present position. He knew how to interrogate. He questioned Agent Denning in great detail. Denning, in turn, had become a station chief because he knew how to gather information, and present it in a concise manner.

"Strange," mused the General, "How you Foreigners can find such information. What have my police been doing?" Denning did not reply. "We know, of course," the General continued, "about what is going on at Doi Maesalong." He did not tell Denning what he really thought. He thought the previous Prime Minister and his military advisors had made a deal with the Devil when they allowed the Republic of China's 93rd Army to settle at that remote outpost, known as Doi Maesalong, and freely engage in drug dealing to support themselves. That Prime Minister was known to have said, "Drugs are not a Thai problem; they're the Foreigner's problem." General Manoon knew better. He knew that drugs were rapidly becoming a serious problem in Thai society, and he believed the information brought by this American agent was true. He would move on it, but carefully.

He thanked Agent Denning for bringing this information directly to him, and not through the usual channels. He stood, shook Denning's hand and assured him, "We must move fast on this, and we will. Keep in touch."

General Manoon was a good man, and a loyal subject of His Majesty, The King of Thailand. Just a few months back, senior police officers, including himself, had been called to the palace for an audience with His Majesty. The officers stood at attention while His Majesty addressed them. The King's message was a lecture on two evils infecting Thai society; corruption and drug addiction. "As police officers you are responsible for maintaining order in our society," warned the King, "You cannot do that if your own hands are dirty." The police officers were not accustomed to be so directly told of their own shortcomings. His Majesty continued, "I am very concerned about the damage drug addiction is doing to Thai society, especially our young people. This problem is related to the first. Drugs and corruption always go together. Cleanse your own hearts, so you can serve our nation."

Thailand had not had a ruling monarch since 1932, but Thai people retained their sense of awe and loyalty to their kings. Police General Manoon was touched by the earnestness of His Majesty, and vowed to do his part to root out corruption and police involvement in the drug trade. He secretly investigated the personal wealth of the officers in his division. Those found to have accumulated wealth far in excess of their salaries or family status were quietly transferred to positions where they had no influence. At the same time, he developed a ring of young officers who wanted nothing to do with corruption, or involvement in matters detrimental to Thailand. The General was convinced he knew who he could trust, and who he could not. After the American agent had left, he wrote down a list of names to give to his secretary, who was still waiting in the outer office. She was the police officer who had served coffee. She was also the General's niece. He trusted her, and all those named on his list. As he was leaving his office, he spoke kindly, but correctly, to his niece. "Lieutenant, please contact all the people on this list tonight asking them to meet with me at the Conference Room at the Erawan Hotel tomorrow morning at 0900 hours. There will be no excuses."

Everyone invited was at the meeting. General Manoon skipped formalities and got right to business. "You are a select group whom I have called together. I know that everyone of you is a loyal citizen of our Nation, and a loyal subject of His Majesty. Now is the time to demonstrate your loyalty." General Manoon proceeded to describe in detail what he knew about the big drug shipment; not only what he had learned from Agent Denning, but from his own sources as well. "We have a great opportunity, not only to seize the largest shipment of heroin I have ever heard of, but, more importantly, to catch those involved and put them away in prison for a very long time."

He revealed that the drugs were assembled under one roof near Mae Chan, in Chiang Rai Province. "I have it under surveillance. If we just want the drugs, now is the time to take them, but we also want those who are involved in this transaction, and those protecting it. Therefore, we will watch the shipment closely all the way to the port city of Mahachai and nab all involved when it leaves our shore." What the General did not reveal, was that he had a close friend who was an admiral in the Thai Navy. They had been students together. The Admiral himself had promised to be on the Navy patrol boat that would interdict the drugs.

The officers sitting around the conference table that day were given their instructions. They were to dress in civilian clothe and follow the progress of the shipment without being detected. Not all of them at once, but in a relay system, so suspicion would not be drawn to them. Secrecy was of utmost importance. They had one big concern, and Police General Manoon knew what it was: fear of retribution. Some of the people protecting the shipment were big names. Some were police, some were military, some were politicians and some were well known business tycoons, often in the news seen donating to charities. "We must, and we will, be successful in this operation," said the General. "We'll put them away and they will not be able to harm you. Now, go in the name of Country, Monarchy, and Religion. Do your duty."

CHAPTER 15

HEROIN ON THE MOVE

The shipment of pure heroin was always under observation as it moved from Maechan, to Lampang, to Nakornsawan and, finally, the fishing town of Mahachai on the Gulf of Siam. It was always in some kind of truck, covered up with local agricultural produce. The trucks had to go through a number of police checkpoints, but were always waved through without being stopped. Sometimes the drugs were even in Thai Army trucks, which would not have allowed a police inspection anyway.

The DEA Office in Chiang Mai was mostly left out of the loop, much to the frustration of Agent Denning, who was greatly relieved when he finally received a hand delivered note from Police General Manoon "THE FISH YOU ENQUIRED ABOUT WILL SOON BE ON A FISHING BOAT. YOUR HELP IN TRACKING IT WOULD BE APPRECIATED." Agent Denning knew what the "fish" was, but what, when and how he was to track it remained a mystery. He alerted someone at the American Embassy in Bangkok that he would need help soon in tracking a large shipment of drugs on a fishing boat. After that, he could only wait.

General Manoon was also waiting. From the information on the letter Agent Denning had shown him, he knew the drugs were to be delivered to a sea going fishing trawler named HOI TALAE (sea shell), but the time was not mentioned. Some of his undercover police were working as stevedores, unloading fish from incoming vessels, and loading ice on outgoing vessels. One of them had discovered a ruse. There had been a trawler named HOI TALAE, but that name had been painted over, and replaced with MALAENG KAPUN (jelly fish). The police officer who discovered that ruse was well trained. He was curious as to why fish were being loaded onto that boat, rather than unloaded. "Being shipped to Singapore," someone said, but that did not make sense. Why not ship freshly caught fish to Singapore? That night he hid in a very smelly place under some old discarded fish nets at the waters edge near the trawler. At 0100 hours a truck without lights backed up near the dock where the MALAENG KAPUN was located. Six men exited from the truck and carried many packages onto the boat The police officer knew that had to be the heroin shipment. To the officer, the packages appeared to be the usual 10 kilograms each, and were sealed in waterproof plastic. In the hold of the boat the fish were shoveled to one side, and the packages placed underneath. Afterwards, the fish were shoveled back on top of the packages. It was a stinky, messy job, and when the men had completed their task, they sat on the dock drinking Maekong whisky until they were ordered back on the truck, which drove off into the darkness.

The police officer had noted that six men came out of the truck, but only four got back in. Obviously, two were left on board to guard the shipment. The officer knew he had to get word to General Manoon, but the moon was too bright to sneak away from the beach. He was relieved when clouds began to form, and covered the moon. When it was very dark, he quietly crawled out from under the nets and returned to his group command station, located in a rented room above a coffee shop. The officers working as stevedores slept there at night. The officer who had been on duty watching the trawler dug out a small radio, provided by the DEA, that had been hidden in their old smelly work clothes, and radioed to one of their men in Bangkok on a band not normally used by the Police. All he said was, "Produce loaded on the Malaeng Kapun."

As ordered, the police woman, who had received the message,

immediately called General Manoon and gave him the message. General Manoon, in turn, called Agent Denning, who had been sleeping on a cot in his office waiting for such a call. After Agent Denning received the message he radioed to his contact at the American Embassy in Bangkok. That person notified someone at CIA Headquarters at Langley Field, Virginia, and that person notified the technicians operating the spy satellite hovering over Southeast Asia. A lot of people were awake that night.

The camera in the sky could zoom in on the fishing trawlers anchored at Mahachai, Thailand, but the operators had to wait until they were told which boat to track. Another officer, from the plain clothes police in Mahachai, was sent out to observe the MALAENG KAPUN. A crew soon boarded, and it put out to sea. Several trawlers left at that same time. Police General Manoon, however, had taken no chances. Unknown to his own police, the General had placed someone else on the Mahachai docks who was indebted to the General. That person was a low level civil servant who worked for the Fisheries Department recording approximate weights of fish brought to shore. He had been caught selling drugs to the workers, and the General had made him an offer he couldn't refuse. "Do one job for me," the General had told him, "or I'll put you away for life." The man had no choice but to cooperate. He had been able to slip one fish into all the fish that had been loaded into the MALAENG KAPUN. In that fish was a tiny radio beeper. The General had received some of those gadgets from the DEA, but had never used them. This seemed like a good time. Once again, the phone calls and radio messages flashed around the world. Agent Denning was ecstatic. "That old fox," he exclaimed. "The General never said a word about that until now."

The technician controlling the spy satellite got the message, and picked up the signals coming from one of the trawlers. He tracked that boat out into the Gulf of Siam. The General had notified one other person; the Admiral waiting on a Thai Navy patrol boat, whose puzzled crew had no idea what an admiral was doing on their ship. His radioman also got the signal emitted from the fish deep in the hold of the MALAENG KAPUN, and the Admiral, standing on the bridge, ordered the ship's captain to follow that signal at full speed.

The trawler was also built for speed, so it took three hours for the patrol boat to overtake it. By that time they were far from shore. Using a bullhorn, the patrol boat's captain ordered the trawler to shut down its engine. It did not do so immediately, so the Admiral ordered a gun crew to fire warning shots from quad .50 caliber machine guns mounted on the bow of the patrol boat. That did it; the trawler stopped dead in the water. The Navy ship pulled alongside and attached lines to the MALAENG KAPUN. A contingent of armed sailors, including the Admiral, to the astonishment of the sailors, boarded the fishing trawler.

The fish in the hold were just a cover and had been inadequately iced. They stunk! Under the guns of the sailors, the entire crew of the fishing boat, including their captain, were ordered to carry the fish up to the deck in baskets and throw them overboard. Eventually, the packages wrapped in plastic, were found and transferred to the patrol boat. Not until then, did the Admiral send a brief radio message to his old friend and classmate, Police General Manoon: "950 KG of fish are on my ship. Where do you want them delivered?" General Manoon replied, "Take them to Klong Toey and let me know when you are nearly there." He also sent a message to Agent Denning, "In about four hours fish will be delivered to Customs House at Klong Toey. You may inspect for quality." Agent Denning prepared for rush trip to Klong Toey, the seaport for Bangkok.

Police General Manoon had been busy all day. Shortly after the fishing trawler, Malaeng Kapun, had left the port of Mahachai, he issued orders to his subordinates to bring in a long list of suspects and hold them for questioning. Some of those people, complete with evidence against them, had been prepared by the DEA. Some were on a list kept by the General. He gave orders that none were to be allowed bail, nor were they allowed to communicate with anyone. Many on those lists were not accustomed to be handled in such a manner.

No one had notified General Tao in Doi Maesalong about the events in the Gulf of Siam. Ever since his decision to send the damning letter to an American, who he did not know, he had not slept well, even after doubling the guard around his house. With pressure applied from Taiwan, he really had no choice. Even his daughter, living in Chiang Mai, knew of his involvement with the drug trade and wanted him to quit. He was very fond of his daughter. She reminded him of his wife, who had died of Cholera in Chungking before the Communists took over. It had not been an easy trip overland from China to Burma, and on to Doi Maesalong. "Mao Tse'tung may have had his Long March," he liked to say, "but so did my daughter and I."

When they first arrived in Doi Maesalong the General's daughter stayed with her father, but eventually tired of the isolation. She wanted to live in Chiang Mai. General Tao thought he ought to have a house in Chiang Mai anyway, so had one built in a quiet part of the city. It was built to his specifications, with two walls around the compound and a strongly reinforced house. Some of his soldiers were sent there on a rotating basis to guard the house, and some of the General's female relatives also lived in the house with his daughter The General often visited.

If General Tao had known what was going on, he would have had reason to be uneasy. Those who made money off the drug trade would not easily accept the loss of 950 kilograms of pure heroin. That represented a huge investment, and a staggering loss when it was seized by the special police and Navy force. Most of those involved, of course, had been rounded up and were unhappily sitting in isolated cells in Klong Prem prison. Police interrogaters were promising them extended stays, up to 30 years, unless they cooperated and named others. Most would not do so. Thailand did not have a witness protection program, and they feared retribution. Anyway, the big shots among them were confident they would soon be released. It might be costly, but a lot of money could buy a lot of influence among high ranking politicians in the government. They all knew their loss was the result of an inside job. Someone who knew all about that big drug shipment had betrayed them. Who was it? They had time to think. That damn *Jek* (pejorative for a Chinese) was on the minds of several of the imprisoned.

The drug bust was big news. Police General Manoon had invited members of the press, both Thai and Foreign, to view the drug haul, and inform them that a Thai Navy ship had interdicted the shipment somewhere in the Gulf of Siam. It was front page news, complete with pictures in all the Thai newspapers. Most major papers in Europe and the United States also carried the news. General Manoon had a reason for releasing the information. He knew some of the imprisoned had powerful friends who would exert pressure to have them released.

With the drug bust as world wide news, that would be more difficult. General Manoon received the most satisfaction from a news release from Chitlada Palace, in which His Majesty the King praised all those involved in seizing the huge drug shipment. "True citizens, of whom we can all be proud." he wrote.

Teacher Chen and Quon Hing read the news in a Chinese language newspaper. They were quietly exultant. Quon Hing's eyes filled with tears a few days later when she received a letter from her father: "My dear daughter, I am very proud of you. You are a credit to our surname, Wang." Teacher Chen bought a guard dog, which they left in their house at night.

Agent Denning was stunned by his good fortune. Delaying his monthly report to meet the missionary in the Bowling Alley was the best career move he had ever made. He received a letter of commendation from the Director of the Drug Enforcement Agency in Washington, DC. He also requested a large bonus for his informant, Clifford Johnson.

Clifford did not know if the letter he had passed on to Agent Denning had done any good, until he read the newspapers. "Wow! 950 kilograms just like it said in the letter," he murmered to himself. He postponed a trip to Doi Maesalong, but took no further precautions. He was very sure no one, but the DEA, knew of his role in this matter.

A few weeks later a nondescript van was driven into an empty lot close to the wall around General Tao's Chiang Mai house. Some people saw the van parked there, but thought nothing of it. About 9:00 P.M. on a Sunday evening a huge explosion rocked the city of Chiang Mai. Nothing but a hole in the ground remained where the van had been parked. A mentally handicapped man lived nearby. Nothing was left of him or his house. Two substantial two story houses, rented to missionary families, were not far away. One was completely destroyed, the other was left standing with the walls blown off. No one was home at either house. Other houses in a two block radius from the explosion suffered considerable structural damage. Houses and businesses several blocks away had broken windows and roof damage. An elementary school for the children of expatriates was near the General's house. It suffered considerable damage, and one wing needed to be rebuilt. It was fortunate the explosion did not occur during school hours. Everyone in the city heard, and felt, the explosion.

It was obvious the bomb had been intended for General Tao's house. The van had been parked up against the outside of the wall, as close as possible to the General's house, and that portion of the wall was blown to smithereens. The house had been strongly constructed and was still standing, although the windows and doors had all been blown off and the house contents mostly blown out the gaping windows. The general and his daughter were not home. That evening they had decided to eat at a restaurant. After the explosion, they drove by their house, saw the damage, and disappeared for a few days. The police reported one fatality; the mentally handicapped man. There were rumours of fatalities among the guards at the compound, but no mention was ever made of them.

Tourism was a major source of income for the Thai economy, so when foreign tour companies starting canceling tours to Chiang Mai it was a serious matter. The Prime Minister met with his top police generals. "What's going on up there in Chiang Mai?" he demanded. "Put a lid on it; this is bad public relations for our country." The big police generals, in turn, met with General Manoon, who was only a little general. "Clear up this problem with the drug trade," they told him. "No more bombs."

General Manoon decided to get tough. "Keep those drug prisoners on rice gruel and water," he ordered his subordinates, "until they give us names." He sought out General Tao and had a secret meeting with him. He told the Chinese general that he was sure the information that led to the big drug seizure had come from him. "That was a good first step, but now you must cooperate fully with me. I need the names of all the people used by the KMT at Doi Maesalong to market drugs."

It was General Tao's nature to keep such things to himself, but he had indeed been the one who released the information about the drug shipment, after pressure from Taiwan and his own daughter, so there seemed to be no need to stop now. Also, he was furious about the attempt on his, and his daughter's, life, so he wanted revenge against those who had tried to kill them. General Tao was an astute man; he could see times were changing. He knew he and his daughter could never return to Mainland China, and he preferred to live in Thailand, rather than Taiwan. To do so, he had to adjust to Thai law. "I'll give you all the information I have," he told the Police General, "if you can guarantee the people I tell you about will be put in prison for a long time." General Manoon was honest and spoke frankly, "I will put them in prison and keep them there as long as possible, but eventually there will be trials. I cannot guanrantee the results of those trials, but if any are released they will be kept under close observation."

General Tao knew that was the best deal he was going to get, so he agreed. He spent the next few days preparing a list of names, aliases, and where to find those people. He used a trusted relative as a courier to deliver the list to the Police General in Bangkok. He also sent his daughter to Taiwan. She was reluctant to go, but he insisted. "Just stay there a while until things cool down." he told her. General Tao returned to his home at Doi Maesalong and changed his bodyguards. He may have bowed to pressure in regard to the drug trade, but a tiger does not really change his stripes. He only hired guards who had wives and children. The new guards stood at attention before the General while he gave them instructions. He asked each one if they would be totally loyal to him, and looked each one in the eye as he waited for a positive response. "I will now make you a promise," he vowed to the men before him. "If anyone betrays me, that person, together with his wife and children, will be killed. Your parents and grandparents will be killed. If they are already dead and buried their tombs will be dug up and their bones scattered. If I am killed by betrayal I have instructed those loyal to me to carry out this sentence of death." When the guards were dismissed they silently returned to their duties, with the General's chilling words reverberating in their minds. They had no doubt the General's orders would be carried out.

Police General Manoon was getting a lot of information, both from those already imprisoned, and from Doi Maesalong. He ordered a round up of all who were implicated in major drug dealings. According to Thai law, suspects could be held for several months before appearing in court. Eventually, however, they had their day in court, and Clifford was asked to testify.

CHAPTER SIXTEEN

A THAI COURTROOM

Clifford was surprised to be asked to testify.. He really didn't want to be a witness. He hadn't bargained for such a public involvement in drug cases when he agreed to provide the DEA with information. He had assumed his connection to the DEA would remain a secret. Indeed, the names of informers were usually not given to anyone, but because this case was so big, General Manoon had insisted that Agent Denning provide him with the names of all involved. Agent Denning had done so, but neglected to inform Clifford, who had never even heard of the General, and was surprised, and very concerned, when a police officer came to visit him one evening at his house. The officer came in a police car with a driver, introduced himself as an aid to Police General Manoon, and delivered a letter from the General asking Clifford to cooperate with the Police Department by testifying against the accused. Clifford decided he really had no choice. As soon as the police car left, Clifford's landlady, Pa Chintana, came over to see Clifford. "Why did the police come to see you," she demanded, "are you in trouble?" Clifford assured her he was not in trouble, but simply had to appear in court as a witness. "What did you witness?" she wanted to know. Have you been hanging around with bad people?" "I really can't say,"

Clifford told her. "The police told me to keep quiet about it." That was really not true, but Clifford did not want his involvement with drug dealers to be gossiped about.

Clifford had never been in a courtroom before, and certainly not as a witness to a crime. He had seen movies of American courtroom scenes, but the Thai situation was quite different. When he was asked to testify he stood at a small podium directly in front of the judge, who was sitting behind an elevated desk. On the podium was a sheet of paper with three oaths printed on it. One was for Buddhists, one for Muslims, and one for Christians. Clifford was asked to select one and read it aloud. The oaths were all written in the Thai language, which Clifford could read with no problem. He selected the oath to be used by Christians, and read it with a slightly trembling voice. It was an unnerving experience for Clifford. High ranking police officers and government officials filled the courtroom. The judge, behind his desk, looked down upon Clifford as he read the oath; promising to tell the truth, only the complete truth, and if he didn't, he would be cursed by God and all kinds of evil things would happen to him.

The judge had already been provided with the details of the case against the drug dealers, so he was the one who questioned Clifford. "Do you desire a translator?" he asked. Clifford replied that he did not, and the judge congratulated him on his ability to understand and speak Thai. The judge proceeded to question Clifford about those details of the case that involved Clifford: The letter, that had been presented as evidence, was shown to Clifford, and he was asked how he had received the letter, and if this actually was the one he had received. Clifford had to relate that he had passed it on to the American DEA Agent. After about 30 minutes of such questioning, Clifford was thanked and informed that his presence would not be needed in the court anymore that day, but to remain available in case he was needed any other time during the course of the case.

Most of the defendants had hired capable lawyers, so their cases moved slowly through the court system. After five or six months, the delays ended. The judge pronounced guilty verdicts on all the defendants, and they received prison terms ranging from 10 to 30 years.

There was a collective sigh of relief from many people. Police

General Manoon was satisfied. In his view, justice had been done. Chinese General Tao was relieved, and hopeful that he might yet live a long life. Teacher Chen and Quon Hing knew they had done the right thing, and were confident that none of the bad people knew of their involvement. The conviction was a rare success for the DEA. Agent Denning basked in the glory of a successful operation.

The whole experience had been an education for Clifford. He had learned there is evil in the world, and goodness does not always overcome it. He was heartened by the long prison terms given to the drug people, but he was wise enough now to know it might not be all over yet. He returned to Huey Fawn Karen village to tell Saw Ba Heh's family the news. "The killers of your husband and father are likely among those who were sent to prison." he told them. He wanted them to know that. Clifford missed his old friend, and, if the truth were to be told, he was still bothered by a feeling of guilt. Saw Pa Heh had died because he was looking for drug information to pass on to Clifford.

CHAPTER SEVENTEEN

A KAREN WEDDING

However, the trip to the Karen village also brought joy and satisfaction to Clifford. The village school had added another classroom, and another teacher had been hired; a male teacher, who had also been recruited by Clifford to attend school in Chiang Mai and live in the student hostel. With a demure smile, Naw Wa Paw asked Clifford to return the following month at the time of the full moon to "*aw taw nya*" {eat pork). Clifford had seen the big fat pig that Naw Wa Paw was raising in a pen next to her mother's house. He also knew that the bride's family must provide the pork for a wedding feast, so to "eat pork" was a euphemism for a wedding "Will your man be the other teacher?" Clifford asked. Naw Wa Paw nodded her head, blushed, and covered her face with her hands. "I will certainly be here to *aw taw nya*", replied Clifford. Naw Wa Paw had one more request. "*Thra* (teacher), will you perform a marriage service for us like the Jesus People do?" While living in Chiang Mai, both Naw Wa Paw and her husband to be had attended Christian weddings. They had been impressed by the vows made between husband and wife, and by the invoking of the name of God to bless the marriage. Clifford replied, "I would be honored."

When Clifford returned to Chiang Mai there was another envelope in his post office box with no return address. Inside was a check for a very large amount. So large it made Clifford gasp. He went directly to the Siam Commercial Bank and bought a certificate of deposit that gave 7% interest. Clifford had began to think of his possible retirement in a few more years. This would help.

Clifford returned to Huey Fawn Village the day before the full moon. He drove his new car, a Toyota pickup, to the Thai Headman's house over a new road. As always, he asked permission to park besides the house, and commented on the new road. "The new road is great; very easy to drive here now."

"Yes," the headman replied with a laugh, "it helps that my oldest daughter is married to the *Nai Amphur* (district officer). She thinks we should move to town, but we won't. This has been our home for many years. We'll stay here." Clifford mentioned he was going to a wedding at the Karen village. "Yes, I know," replied the Headman. "I'll be there too. That village is part of my jurisdiction, so when the two teachers get married I should be there."

There may have been a new road to the Thai village, but it was the same old foot trail up the mountain to the Karen village. He remembered his first trip up this mountain, following Saw Pa Heh and his father in law. This time he went slower; pausing often to rest. Clifford could tell he was getting older. Besides, he carried a bulky package tied to the top of his backpack. It was a modern padded quilt; a gift to the bridal couple.

Clifford stayed in Naw Wa Paw's house, together with her mother, Naw Baw. The grandparents had died, and the two boys had already married and were living with their wives in another village, where they were school teachers. Following Karen custom, Naw Wa Paw and her husband would live in this house.

Very early in the morning, before light, Clifford heard the squeals of the fat pig being sacrificed for the wedding feast. Naw Wa Paw's two brothers, and other male relatives, had volunteered to take care of the main course. After slaughtering the pig, the carcass was placed on a bed of banana leaves and cut into pieces. Cubes of fat were thrown into a huge wok placed on a tripod over a fire. When the lard had melted, the rest of the meat and fat were also put in the wok. The men stood by for several hours stirring the meat with a wooden paddle, adding dried herbs for flavor, and an occasional pail of water to prevent the meat from drying up. The cleaned intestines had been chopped up and, together with the eye balls, thrown into the wok. The liver was cut into thin strips, skewered on slivers of bamboo and barbequed, by placing them around the edges of the fire. Nothing was wasted.

Meanwhile, Naw Wa Paw, assisted by her mother and numerous friends, was getting dressed in the inner room of the house. Her face was powdered and lipstick applied generously. She wore, for the first time, the garb of a married woman, consisting of a newly woven skirt and blouse; mostly in red, but with designs of yellow and blue. Her attendant was still single, so wore the white shift of an unmarried woman. Both were adorned with many strings of seed bead necklaces.

The marriage service was conducted in front of the school building at mid-day. All the villagers, and a few of the groom's relatives, gathered in a semi-circle around a desk that had been borrowed from the school. A chair had been placed behind it for Clifford. The groom and his best man stood nearby, dressed in black pants, white shirt and tie and wearing a traditional Karen pull-over shirt. The bride, and her retinue, had already moved from the house into one of the class rooms. Clifford had to send someone back to the classroom two times to inform the bride that it was time for her to appear. Finally, Naw Wa Paw and her attendant appeared and walked over to stand in front of the desk. The modest bride appeared to be studying her new shoes; she never looked up. She kept her eyes averted when Clifford motioned for the groom and his friend to join them in front of the desk.

This was the first Christian service that any of the villagers had ever seen. They were curious. There had been no indication of any interest in becoming Christians, but it had been under discussion for many months around the kitchen fire in most of the homes. Clifford had provided Bibles in the Karen language and taught some of the people to read Karen. Other than that, he kept his distance and waited for the villagers to come to their own conclusion. He knew such a decision would take time until they eventually arrived at a consensus. At that time either everybody, or no one, would accept Christianity.

Clifford made the most of his opportunity. He preached a sermon that started with Creation and ended with the Apostle Paul's admonition for married couples to love one another. All the Karens were acquainted with the concept of a Creator God, and Clifford entreated God to bless this union. Stepping from behind the desk, he asked the bridal couple to hold hands. The groom was willing, but it took a while for the bride's hand to appear and clasp the hand of her husband to be. They were standing about three feet apart, and Clifford knew he was not going to get them any closer, so he concluded the ceremony with a prayer and declared them to be man and wife.

After the ceremony, mats were placed on the ground, and bundles of cooked rice wrapped in squares of banana leaves were placed on the mats. Enameled wash basins, heaped with pork, were placed in amongst the rice. Naw Wa Paw's brothers urged everyone to sit and partake of the feast. Each person sat down in front of a bundle of rice, opened it, and using the banana leaf like a plate, scooped out pork from the basins with spoons and mixed it with their rice. The brothers kept urging people to eat their full, and replenished the rice and pork as it disappeared. One of the bride's uncles had brewed up a batch of rice whiskey in a homemade still. He made it available to those who wanted a drink, and the drinkers, both men and women, congregated on one side of the meeting place. They soon became red faced from the effect of the alcohol, and erupted in loud laughter when bawdy stories were told.

That evening, Clifford returned to Chiang Mai, and resumed his usual life. He was studying Akha with one of the boarding students at the Student Hostel, preparing sermons in Karen for the Sunday service at the Bank Manager's house, and making occasional village trips. More years passed. He was content with his life.

He knew time had been passing when he received a letter from Teacher Chen and Quon Hing inviting him to a celebration of their son reaching the age of one month. Clifford didn't even know they were expecting a child, even though they had been married for a few years. He replied immediately: "Congratulations; I'll be there."

CHAPTER EIGHTEEN

ALL PATHS CONVERGE AT MAESALONG

Clifford was not only pleased to visit his friends, but was glad for an excuse to leave Chiang Mai and head for the uplands of Doi Maesalong, where it would be about 10 degrees cooler. It was the first week in April, and April is the hottest month of the year. It is hot and dry, but the soon to come monsoon season raises the humidity to uncomfortable levels. April does have its compensations, however. Mangos of a variety, known as *Ok Rong*, were ripening, and Clifford dearly loved the Thai dessert made from sticky rice cooked with sweetened coconut cream and served with those sweet and aromatic mangos. He knew that dish might not be available in Doi Maesalong, so he treated himself to this special dessert daily before leaving town.

There was also another good reason for leaving town. The first week in April is when the traditional Thai New Year, known as *Songkran*, is celebrated. In former times it was a rather sedate festival, during which people returned to their original homes and villages to visit relatives. Young people would pour water on the shoulders and hands of their elders. The water was a blessing, and a sign of respect and honor. In later years, the celebration had morphed into a riotous one week frenzy of throwing water on everyone. Chiang Mai, the Rose of the North, had become a favorite destination. Since the weather was hot and dry, no one objected too much, even traffic police got drenched, but the crowded streets were a bit much for Clifford, especially since Foreigners were a favorite target of the water throwers. Every time he ventured out he was doused with water, ranging from small dippers of colored water thrown by pretty girls to huge buckets of not so clean water poured over his head by grown men. The whole affair had become a bit tedious to Clifford, so he looked forward to a trip to the uplands, and to a different culture, where *Songkran* was not celebrated..

Unknown to Clifford, two young ladies from Bangkok had also flown into Chiang Mai to participate in the festival. Kultida, the daughter of Police General Manoon, and her good friend, Wipha, had received permission from their parents to travel together to Chiang Mai. General Manoon, ever vigilant of his daughter's safety, had made hotel reservations for the two friends at a first class hotel, and, unknown to the young ladies, had requested the manager of the hotel to check on them from time to time. Both of the young women were in their mid-twenties, and had studied abroad, so they were confident of being able to take care of themselves in their own country. They did not tell their parents of more exciting plans they had in mind. While living in England, Kultida had read an article in a newspaper about a place in northern Thailand known as Doi Maesalong. She had never heard of the place, and was intrigued by the article, which gave a more detailed description of the remnants of the Chinese Nationalist Forces located there than Thai newspapers were allowed to print. The English reporter, who had visited Doi Masalong, described in glowing detail the beauty of that upland area, and the comfort of the more temperate weather. The two friends decided to visit that remote place, and tell their parents about it when they returned home.

It had been five years since the big round up of drug kings, and those people were still in prison, but Police General Manoon was not naïve enough to believe that he had caught them all. Even the imprisoned could command some of their henchmen on the outside to exact revenge against those who had betrayed them. Prison officials had intercepted some messages that indicated General Manoon was a target.

He had been targeted before, and knew the risk went with the job. His house was guarded, he had personal bodyguards with him when he appeared at public events, and he always carried his police issue 9 mm. revolver. The General wanted his daughter to have a normal life, and not be fearful of events beyond her control. The trip to Chiang Mai to celebrate *Songkran* seemed harmless enough. If he had known the full extent of his daughter's plans he would have been horrified and nixed the whole adventure.

Kultida and Wipha did check into their hotel in Chiang Mai, and had two *sanuk* (fun) days throwing water, getting soaked in return and eating food from street vendors; some of the things they had missed while living abroad. They visited two of the ancient temples and worshipped in front of the Buddha images, presenting flower garlands and lighting incense sticks, so their presence would by noted by the spiritual forces in this northern city.

On the third day, they checked out early in the morning and took a bus to Chiang Rai, which was a full day's trip. They could have taken the 30 minute Thai Airways flight, but wanted to see more of their country. The *Songkran* festivities were diminishing in the city, but still going strong in the countryside. Upon arriving in Chiang Rai, they checked into a tourist guest house and set out to explore the city. They noted that the main part of Chiang Rai was laid out nicely in straight streets. They were unaware that the city planning had been done by an early Presbyterian medical missionary, who had also supervised the building of the provincial government building and a prison, using bricks from the old city wall, that had fallen into disrepair. They ate Chinese food at the Clock Tower Restaurant, and discovered that most of the shops closed by 9:00 P.M.

Back at the Guest House, they met the young Chiang Rai couple that owned the place and enquired about traveling on to Doi Maesalong. The owners asked if they had ever been to Doi Maesalong before.

"No," they replied, "but we hear it is an interesting place and the weather is cooler."

"That is true, but it is a rather difficult trip," stated the wife, with a dubious look at these two young Bangkok ladies. "There is no road, so you must either walk or ride horseback. Are you prepared for that?"

"Oh yes," replied Kultida, "I learned to ride horses when I lived in England."

"Well, this will be quite different I'm sure. There are no rest stops along the way; no food or water, and overnight lodging in Doi Maesalong is rather primitive.

"No problem," piped up Wipha, "We have lived in primitive conditions before." What she had in mind was a Girl Guides outing to the ocean beach at Hua Hin, south of Bangkok. The middle school girls had been provided with tents, food, restrooms and adult supervision.

"Well, if you really want to go, I can arrange for Ai Seng, a Lahu man, to be your guide. He often guides groups of Foreigners to Hill Tribe villages."

"Sounds good; we'll go," eagerly replied Wipha.

Kultida, just slightly more cautious, asked, "What is a Lahu?"

"The Lahu are one of the Tribal groups; we Thai often call them Mussers." She continued, "It's best to travel light, be here in the morning at 7:00 O'clock ready to go. You can leave excess baggage in our office. I will arrange for Ai Seng to meet you here at that time."

At seven O'clock Ai Seng had already eaten his breakfast and was sipping his second cup of tea. He expected the Bangkok women to be both late and inappropriately dressed, but he approved of what he saw when they came out of their room. First, he noted they were good looking, and, secondly, only about 10 minutes late. They were also dressed in slacks, long sleeve blouses, floppy cloth caps, and wore no makeup. Ai Seng thought they might even make it to Maesalong.

Ai Seng was a man of some experience. He had been born in a Lahu village in the Shan States of Burma, and, together with most of his extended family, had slipped across the border into Thailand when he was a teenager. He had started school in Burma, and studied a few more years at an elementary school in Thailand before dropping out. He was intelligent and picked up languages easily. In addition to his native Lahu, he could speak Shan, Northern Thai and Central Thai, all of which are related, but also spoke Burmese, Akha, English, and a bit of Chinese. He had roamed all over northern Thailand and knew where the Tribal villages were located. When he felt like it, he made a good living as a guide. When he didn't feel like it, he went hunting with some of his friends. Most of the time, he guided groups of Foreigners and had formed opinions about the various nationalities he encountered. In his opinion, Israelis were the most difficult, Japanese wanted to do everything together and took endless photos, Americans were o.k., but European young people were more adventurous. They did, however, embarrass him sometimes, by skinny dipping in streams or rivers. Ai Seng knew such behavior offended villagers, so he advised against it; not always successfully. He had experienced a few encounters with robbers while trekking with groups in remote areas. He always carried a .32 revolver in his pocket, but never showed it to his customers.

He seldom guided Thai people; they seemed to have their own contacts, and were not much interested in visiting Tribal villages anyway. Most of the people who went to Doi Maesalong were Chinese and did not require guides. On this day, he was burdened with two young Thai women from the big city. Well, not much of a burden. He had immediately noticed their beauty, and that they were dressed appropriately for such a trip. It was unusual, however, for Thai women to travel to such a remote place without male companionship. He introduced himself, led the way to his pickup truck and placed their travel bags in the bed of the pickup. "Better if you sit in front," he told them. "Too much dust in the back." Anyway, with three in the front seat they had to sit snugly together. Ai Seng liked that arrangement.

They drove north out of Chiang Rai on the road to Mae Chan, and Ai Seng enquired about their interest in Maesalong. He was surprised that one of them had learned about the place from a newspaper in England. "I've taken some of those reporters around," he remarked. "Might even have been the one who wrote that article." The young women asked about Maesalong, so Ai Seng told what he knew about that upland area, and the Chinese army that had located there. He even mentioned that it had been infamous for drug running, but was much better now.

At Mae Chan he turned west and drove a few kilometers over a dirt road. "The road ends soon," he informed his customers. "We will have to either walk or find some horses."

"Oh, we would really like to ride," implored Kultida.

"I'll see what I can do," replied Ai Seng, although he was sure he could easily rent some horses near where the trail began.

He stopped at a rather nice two-story house, got out of his car and called "Mee Bu." He hoped Mee Bu was home. He knew her man, a Yunnanese he had never liked, would not be home. He was in prison on drug charges. Mee Bu came to the door and they spoke in Akha. She knew Ai Seng well, and teased him about the good looking cargo he had in the front seat of his pickup. "Well, you know how it is," replied Ai Seng with a grin, "I just can't keep these women away."

"Looks like you're well supplied; what else do you need?"

"I need three riding horses. I'm afraid these city girls would never make it to Maesalong on foot and I would have to carry them; one on each shoulder."

Mee Bu laughed out loud. "Pick out three horses out of the corral behind the house. They'll cost you 20 Baht a day. You can pay when you return."

Ai Seng noted that Mee Bu was happier these days, now that her "husband" was in prison. He was aware of the situation, and that the Yunnanese man was not really her husband, but had taken advantage of her poverty. He parked his vehicle behind the house and selected three horses from the corral. Kultida was not pleased with their rented mounts. "They're so small," she complained, "Not like English horses."

"Yes, they're small, but also tough," replied Ai Seng. "Anyway, better than walking."

Mee Bu came out with two saddles. "Your two friends can use these. They're all I have." Ai Seng pretended to be disappointed, but he really didn't mind riding bareback. "I think you ought to reduce the rent 10% for my horse." he kidded. "Maybe I'll add 15% for the two saddles," she added.

Their conversation had all been in Akha, but now Ai Seng spoke to his two customers in Thai. "These mountain women drive some hard bargains. We'd better get going before this woman adds on some more charges." With a smile at the two Thai women to show she understood, she helped them tie on their bags behind their saddles and waved goodbye as they headed toward the uplands of Maesalong. The ladies thought Ai Seng was very clever when he was able to find horses so easily.

As Ai Seng and other travelers often did, they made a rest stop at the Akha village, which was about half way to Doi Maesalong. Gultida and Wipha were glad to stretch their stiff legs, and unobtrusively, massage their rear ends while walking around the village. Ai Seng climbed up on the porch of one house to talk to the occupants. He also borrowed a mat to cover the floor. He called for his two customers to come *kin khaow* (eat rice), which they did rather reluctantly, thinking they were to eat village food. In their eyes, the village was poverty stricken, dirty, and very strange. They were relieved, however, when Ai Seng began to pull bundles of food out of his large shoulder bag. "I went to the Chiang Rai market this morning," he explained, "and bought some *khao mun kai* (chicken with rice cooked with chicken fat). All Thai people know that dish, and the women hungrily devoured it.

Ai Seng had requested the Akha woman of the house to boil water for tea. She did so, and came out of the house with a soot blackened teapot and three Chinese style tea cups. She gave her guests a big smile, exposing her teeth stained red from chewing betal nut. Ai Seng poured some tea in each cup and cleaned them out by using his thumb. Next, he poured some tea in the cups and rinsed them again. Finally, he poured tea in each cup and offered them to the Bangkok women, who were fascinated, and a bit dubious, of the whole procedure. They did drink it, however, and found it strong and smoky, but not unpleasant.

They were soon on the trail again, but Ai Seng was deep in thought. He had heard some disquieting news back in the Akha village. One of the village men had told him of seeing Sae Yang, the Hmong man, pass through the village the day before headed for Doi Maesalong. Ai Seng knew about Sae Yang. He was involved with drugs and had a vicious reputation. People who crossed him often ended up dead. Ai Seng thought the man was in prison. "Didn't he go to jail with the rest of those drug dealers a few years ago?" he had asked.

"He should have, but the police missed him."

"Didn't he hang out with that Yunnanese man? You know, the one Mee Bu lived with."

"That's the one. He was caught and put in prison, but Sae Yang hid out in Burma across the border. Now he's back."

Ai Seng was a little worried to know that character was likely in Doi Maesalong, but he put it out of his mind. He had no quarrel with Sae Yang. Anyway, he had drunk too much tea in the Akha village and needed to relieve himself. That problem occupied his mind. Unfortunately, at that point on the trail there were no trees; just grass. Ai Seng gritted his teeth and managed to make it to a place where the trail crossed a small stream. There was a dense growth of trees and brush on both sides of the trail, so he dismounted and was about to dash into the shelter of the trees, when he noticed the two young women watching him with questioning eyes. He hastened to explain, using an expression he had learned from Karens. "I have to catch a rabbit," he said, and headed for the trees. Ai Seng should have known there is no such expression in the Thai language. He was dismayed to see that Wipha had hurriedly dismounted and followed him into the trees. "I want to see how you catch a rabbit," she exclaimed. Ai Seng was quite embarrassed, but managed to explain what his true errand was. In turn, Wipha blushed crimson red when she understood what those words meant, and hurried back to her horse. Kultida was laughing so hard she had to dismount to keep from falling off her horse. "Let's you and I catch a rabbit on this side of the trail," she suggested to Wipha, choking with laughter. They tied their horses to a tree and disappeared into the underbrush. After all the rabbits were caught, they proceeded to follow the trail. Not a word was said. Ai Seng was riding ahead, but close enough to hear bursts of giggles from the young ladies. They were amused by Ai Seng's ears, which were a glowing pink. Ai Seng felt he had lost face. If he had only known: the girls thought he was cute.

Kultida and Wipha were a bit saddle sore when they arrived at the Chinese settlement of Doi Maesalong, but they were also amazed. "It's like being in China," Wipha exclaimed. "We seem to have ridden our horses up the mountain to a different land. All the signs are in Chinese, and look, there is a school, but the flag over it is the Chinese flag."

"The old flag," corrected Kultida. "Now its only the flag of Taiwan."

Ai Seng had been to Doi Maesalong many times and knew his way around. He took them to the best hotel in town, which, he knew, also had a good restaurant. "Imagine;" sighed Wipha, "We're actually arriving at a hotel on horseback. How exotic! None of our friends have ever done that."

"None of our friends have ever caught a rabbit on the trail either!" commented Kultida. "They've all led such protected lives, just like us."

Ai Seng went in to arrange for a room, and discovered the hotel also owned some guest houses adjoining the hotel. He explained that possibility to Wipha and Kultida, and they inspected one of the houses. "This will be wonderful," exclaimed both the young ladies, "Our own place in Shangrila." Ai Seng, with a very limited education, had no idea what they meant, but they were obviously happy. He had carried out his responsibility as a guide.

"I'll take care of the horses," Ai Seng said, "and stay with some friends of mine."

"Oh, do come back and eat dinner with us in about two hours. You seem to be well acquainted around here."

Ai Seng had recovered from his perceived loss of face, and agreed to meet them later. He had been pleasantly surprised by these two young ladies from Bangkok, who obviously were from wealthy families, able to send their children to foreign universities. They had made the long, and somewhat tiring, trip to Doi Masalong with no complaints. Now they had invited him to eat with them; something many others of their social class would not have done.

Ai Seng took the horses to some Akha friends of his who lived on the outskirts of the town. No one was home, but they had a corral behind their house where he released the three horses. Back in the house he removed his clothes and tied a *pakama* around his waist. A *pakama* is just a piece of cloth, but with a multitude of uses. He used it as a loin cloth, so he could take a bath from an outside water faucet next to the corral. It can also be used as a belt, head covering, swim suit, back pack, hammock for a baby, used to carry a baby on one's back, and many other uses. After his bath Ai Seng tried to take a nap, but worried about the presence of Sae Yang in Doi Maesalong. The Akha family who owned the house came back and invited Ai Seng to eat with them, but he declined. "I have a date with two beautiful Thai women from Bangkok," he replied, with a sly smile. "I've been with them all day and now they want me to eat with them in the hotel restaurant." "Can't be your looks," replied the Akha woman, "Must be your money." They all laughed at that comment. They knew Ai Seng well, and knew he did not accumulate either money or property.

Later in the evening, Ai Seng appeared at the ladies' guest house dressed in Black Lahu clothing, of black trousers, an embroidered tunic, and with a new *pakama* of red and white checks folded to about four inches wide and tied around his waist. At the restaurant the ladies asked him to order the food. His Chinese language ability was limited, but he managed to order a number of dishes. First, he ordered a clear soup with bits of chicken and water cress leaves in it. He knew the large mushrooms, known as shitake in Japanese, were grown in Doi Maesalong, so ordered a plate of them sautéed with black bone chicken. That breed of chicken has black feathers and actually does have black bones. It is delicious, but the Chinese also consider it to be medicinal. "This will restore our bodies after a hard day," he told the young women. He also ordered *pla chon* (snakehead fish) steamed with a plum sauce, bak choy cabbage with pork, and, of course, rice. They all ate with a good appetite, while Ai Seng regaled them with stories of his life experiences.

It had been a long day for Kultida and Wipha, so when their eyes began to droop Ai Seng escorted them to their guest house. "There are bad people to be found everywhere," he warned them, "so keep your door well locked." He assured them he would come by in the morning and make more touring plans. "Don't come early," they chorused in unison. They were tired, and slept well. Neither they, or Ai Seng, would have slept well if they had known about some very bad characters who had been following Kultida, and knew exactly where she was. Their plans for retribution were really aimed at Police General Manoon. However, he was too clean to blackmail, and too closely guarded to assassinate, so they turned their attention to the one most dearest to him; his daughter.

Clifford was already in Doi Maesalong. He had walked in the day before and was staying with Teacher Chen and Quong Hing. He had no idea that Chinese people considered a one month of age celebration to be an important milestone in a child's life. Perhaps it had started in ancient times when there was high infant mortality. If a new baby lived for one month, it would likely survive to adulthood. Clifford had brought some baby clothes, purchased in the Chiang Mai market, with him as a gift. Clifford knew nothing about purchasing gifts for a baby, so had wandered around the area in the market that sold children's clothing, asking the women shop owners what he should buy. "Is it a Foreign baby?" they wanted to know. "No, its for a Chinese baby up at Doi Maesalong," he had replied. As soon as Clifford made his purchase and left the market, one of those ladies went to a phone and reported what she had heard. Clifford should have been more circumspect. The big drug bust was over, and many people, including Clifford, had nearly forgotten about it, but not all had forgotten, including former "big men", who wanted revenge.

Quong Hing had hoped her mother and father could come, but there was a crisis in the Taiwan Government at that time, and her father was involved in solving the problem. Her mother would not come alone, but she had sent the red eggs and ginger that were traditional for a one month of age celebration. The eggs were dyed red, and the sliced ginger had been boiled in sugar water. Quon Hing and Teacher Chen had prepared a feast, to which they had invited their friends. There were many dishes, but the red eggs and ginger reminded everyone of the purpose of the gathering. The center of attention, of course, was the new baby. He had been sleeping before the guests arrived, but made his presence known when the party got noisy. General Tao arrived late, and did not stay long, but felt he had to at least make a presence. He knew Quon Hing's father was a government minister in Taiwan, so the minister's new grandson could not be ignored. He brought a gift of red eggs and ginger in an elegant container, made a brief speech to all assembled, and left with his bodyguards. He was a very careful man.

Sae Yang, the Hmong drug dealer, had arrived in Doi Maesalong the same day as Clifford, but well after dark. It was not a coincidence. He had been hiding out with a very big drug trafficker, called Khun Sa, across the border in Burma, who maintained his own private army. Sae Yang was safe from the Thai Police there, and was in no rush to leave. Khun Sa, however, was in radio contact with some of his men stationed in Chiang Mai, and he also received some messages for Sae Yang. The ones who sent the message were exultant. They couldn't believe their good fortune. They had good intelligence, and knew all their targets were in one place. The message was in the Hmong language and brief, There were no Thai police who understood Hmong, so that language served as a code. Sae Yang knew he had no choice but to obey. "GO TO DOI MAESALONG AND ELIMINATE GENERAL TAO, THE FOREIGNER KNOWN AS CLIFFORD, AND THE THE POLICE GENERAL'S DAUGHTER." There were some more details about who to contact in Doi Maesalong and where to get assistance for carrying out the assassinations. Those were orders he could not refuse. He left immediately.

Sae Yang rode his horse to Doi Maesalong, arriving at the house of one of his contacts in the middle of the night. His contacts knew the General was at his house, well guarded, and they knew Kultida and her friend were staying at one of the Hotel guesthouses. They also knew a Foreigner was staying with a couple of school teachers, and might be their target. "We'll help you with the Police General's daughter, and maybe the Foreigner," they told Sae Yang, "That should be easy, but getting the Chinese general will be tough. We won't do it for less than 100,000 Baht, payable in advance." Sae Yang argued with them. Now was the time to get all three. "I'll get the money for you after we've done the job." he assured them, but they wouldn't budge. Sae Yang knew he would have to either eliminate the General alone, or just go after the other two. He decided to go for the woman and the Foreigner first, but keep the Chinese General as an option if an opportunity arose. That was before he discovered that his contacts were not amateurs. They revealed to Sae Yang that hidden in their house was a 30/06 rifle with a scope sight, and some plastic explosives. They also knew how to set up a timer fuse, using a clock. That was useful information, but Sae Yang needed more.

He slipped out of his safe house and went to a tea house in the market area, next to the Chinese temple. He knew old men were always there gossiping and playing checkers. Sae Yang spoke the Yunnanese dialect and engaged the elderly men in conversation. "Anything going on around here these days?" he asked.

"Not much," was the reply, "just a military parade tomorrow morning."

"What's the occasion?"

"Just one of those Kuomingtang political affairs. After the parade General Tao will review the troops."

That caught Sae Yang's attention. "Where will that be?"

"Where they always have such things; on the ball field in front of the school."

"What time of day?"

"After the parade; should be about 11:00 O'clock. They put on quite a show. Everybody will be there."

Sae Yang paid for his tea, and left to inspect the parade ground. Some men, using powdered white lime, were marking lines on the ground where the soldiers would stand in ranks the following morning. Another group were putting up a review stand. Obviously, that was where General Tao would sit to review his troops. "Perfect," murmered Sae Yang.

Sae Yang returned to his house and told his contacts what he had discovered. "This is a perfect set up," he argued. "All you guys have to do is make a bomb, set it to go off at, let's say, 11:15, and bury it under the review stand. Our other targets will likely be there watching, and in the confusion after the blast I'll take care of them."

The contacts were a bit reluctant, so Sae Yang hit them with a clincher. "If you refuse to do this, I will inform Kun Sa, and he will let some of his contacts on this side of the border know of your unwillingness to act at this opportune time."

That did it. Those were hard men, but they knew enough to fear those who were more powerful. They agreed, and immediately set about to make a bomb. They used more than ample explosives, shaped it to explode upward, and laced it with ball bearings and nails. "Chinese fireworks," they joked, and set it aside to be buried under the review stand late that night. Sae Yang carried an 11mm. Revolver, but decided to add a knife with a foldout 6 inch blade to his armament. In his hands, the knife would be just as lethal, but much quieter. He intended to escape on his horse, and would need the revolver if pursued. He didn't care what his contacts did. They would have to fend for themselves.

Late that night, those men carried their bomb to the parade

ground. They stood in the shadow of a tree for some time. No guards appeared, so they proceeded to the reviewing stand, crawled under it and dug a hole, into which the placed the bomb. They had already inserted a detonator into the plastic explosive wired to an alarm clock set for 11:15. They covered the hole, put the excess soil in a bag to be taken away, and sprinkled dried grass over the spot where they had disturbed the soil. They thought their job was done, so that very night they walked back to the highway and took an early morning bus to Chiang Rai, where they holed up at a brothel on Old Airport Road.

CHAPTER NINETEEN

TERROR

At about 8:00 A.M. the following morning, Ai Seng knocked on the door of the Guest house, where the two women were staying.

"Who is it?" Kultida sleepily replied to his knock on their door.

"Your favorite guide. Are you ready to see the wonders of Doi Maesalong?"

"Just a minute, we'll be right there."

Actually, they were still in bed, but hurriedly dressed, and appeared to be ready for the day. "Please, no horseback riding today," begged Wipha. "My legs still ache."

"How about some breakfast?"

"Sounds good."

Ai Seng took them to an open-fronted restaurant in the market area and ordered *khaow tom* (watery boiled rice) with pickled cabbage in it He also ordered sticks of fried bread and hot soybean milk. A good Chinese breakfast. They were still eating, when a Foreigner entered the shop and tried to order food in Thai. No one understood him, so he pointed to Ai Seng and the young ladies' table, and indicated he wanted the same.

Clifford had awakened early that day and took a walk around town in the early morning coolness. He noticed several people entering a building that was obviously a church. The building was constructed of cement blocks white washed a gleaming white, with a cross on top painted red. He entered and sat on a pew in the rear of the church. People looked at him curiously, but no one spoke. One woman handed him a book that appeared to be a hymnal. Clifford leafed through it, and saw it was all written in Chinese, except for a flyleaf inside the front cover on which were the English words, "PRINTED IN HONG KONG." The hymns had numbers instead of notes, which Clifford had never seen before. Someone stood up and said a prayer, someone else suggested a hymn from the hymnal, and all stood up to sing the hymn with wavering voices. A man holding what appeared to be a Bible read some verses and spoke for about five minutes, another hymn was sung, and finally, a closing prayer. The service appeared to be morning devotions. Clifford was well acquainted with the structure of morning devotions, such as this service, but did not understand one word. He sat in his pew and prayed for this congregation, and for his friends, Teacher Chen and Quon Hing, including their one month old son. When Clifford exited the church an old man, with most of his teeth missing, was waiting for him. "Did you come to see the parade?" He asked in broken English. "What parade?" Clifford asked. In his limited English, the old man explained that this was a special day, and there would be a parade ending at the field near the school. "Even General Tao will be there." exclaimed the old man, as he walked away.

After morning devotions, and not wanting to bother Teacher Chen and Quon Hing, he wandered over to a restaurant in the market to order breakfast. That's where he met two women and one man who were speaking Thai. Ai Seng, always looking for business, introduced himself to this Foreigner and enquired if he had any need for a guide. "No," replied Clifford, "I have friends here, and come to visit from time to time."

"We noticed you speak Thai," spoke up one of the women. "We're from Bangkok, but that language doesn't do us much good here."

"No," agreed Clifford, "Not much good at all."

Ai Seng was curious about this Foreigner showing up in a remote area without a guide. "How did you get here?" he wanted to know.

"I walked in."

"By yourself?"

"Yes, I've done that before, but the first time I came with some Akha people."

Now Ai Seng was really intrigued. "How did you meet Akhas?"

Clifford told of meeting some Akha people in Chiang Mai and returned with them to Doi Maesalong, and on to their village.

"What was the name of their village?" asked Ai Seng.

"I never learned that, but I traveled with a man named Lee Mui."

"Lee Mui! I know him well. In fact, I used some of his horses for this trip, and left them with his relatives here. I'm also staying there."

"Must be the same place I stayed when I came here with Lee Mui," replied Clifford.

Clifford and Ai Seng continued to carry on an animated conversatiion, and learned more about each other, until Clifford noticed the two women were being left out of the conversation. Always polite, he attempted to include them, and asked their names. Wipha gave her first name only, which is the usual custom. Kultida, however, was a bit irritated about being left out of the conversation for so long, and with some sharpness in her voice replied, "My name is Kultida Sripanluang." Both men were surprised to hear her surname. Ai Seng knew there was a Police General with that same last name, who had been in the papers a few years back because he was instrumental in rounding up some big drug traffickers. Clifford was the first to speak. "I don't suppose you're related to Police General Manoon Sripanluang," he asked. "He's my father," was the quick response. "Do you know him?"

"Yes, I did meet him once," replied Clifford hesitatingly. He really didn't want to talk about his role in those drug cases, but Kultida was curious.

"Did you meet him socially?"

"No, I had some police business with him."

"And what would that be?"

"It had something to do with drug trafficking, and your father told me not to talk about it."

Ai Seng did not interrupt this conversation, but he sure was listening. The more he heard, the more worried he became. He never dreamed that one of these young women from Bangkok was a police general's daughter. If anything happened to her, he would be in deep deep trouble. What about the other one? Was her father the Prime Minister! Ai Seng was also concerned about this Foreigner, called Clifford, who had just told him he was a missionary. How could he have drug trafficking business with a police general? He must really be one of those secret agents from America that snoop into drug business. Ai Seng had been around. He knew what villages were planting opium, but he kept that information to himself. He had even smoked a little opium when staying overnight in those villages. He had no intention of talking about that to anyone. His real interest had suddenly become getting his two clients back to Chiang Rai safe and sound.

"Does your father know where you are?" he asked Kultida.

"He knows I'm with my friend somewhere in the North."

"We came to celebrate *Songkran*," interjected Wipha.

"There is no *Songkran* celebration here in Doi Mae Salong."

"Well, we did celebrate *Songkran* in Chiang Mai," Kultida defended herself, "Everybody goes *tio* (travel for fun) during *Songkran.*"

Ai Seng wanted a definitive answer. "But does your father know that you and your friend are here in Doi Maesalong at this very time?"

"I don't suppose he does. Is that any of your business? We can take care of ourselves."

Clifford decided to speak up, "Perhaps you are not aware that a lot of opium is grown in this area, and even converted to heroin. Doi Maesalong does have its charms, but it does have a history of drug trafficking and some violence."

"I can't believe that," retorted Kultida. "My father would not allow it."

Both Kultida and Wipha had been living abroad for some time. They were also rather naïve about some of the dark secrets of their own country. Obviously, Kultida's father did not tell his daughter about some of those secrets. The two men knew they would not be able to convince these two Bangkok women otherwise, so when Ai Seng suggested they reclaim their horses and start back down the trail, Clifford assented. "Yes, why don't we all go. If I can get a horse, I'll go with you."

"No way," the two women wailed, "we haven't seen enough of

Maeslong yet. You promised us some more touring today," they asserted, while glaring at Ai Seng.

Clifford had an idea. "I heard there is going to be a parade today sometime before noon. Why don't we all stay to watch it, eat dinner, and leave."

"Great idea," Ai Seng chimed in. "What kind of a parade?"

"Some Chinese occasion," was all Clifford knew.

Ai Seng went to the restaurant owner to pay for their breakfasts, and asked him about the parade. He returned to report that it was some kind of Kuomintang Military affair, and there would be an impressive parade, complete with a band, and General Tao would review his troops. "The parade starts about 10:00, and the review about an hour later," reported Ai Seng. "Let's go. You can tell your parents you saw a Chinese Military event right here in Thailand."

Ai Seng suggested he would take the young women on a brief tour of Mae Salong before the parade started. "We'll see how they grow the Shitake mushrooms and where they process the tea that is grown around her." Clifford said he would return to where he was staying and pack his bags. They agreed to meet under the large rain tree that grew next to the school.

Teacher Chen and Quon Hing urged Clifford to stay a few more days. "What's your rush?" they asked. "Enjoy the cooler weather up here." Clifford explained that he had met two young Thai women and their guide in the market that morning. "They didn't tell their parents where they were going, so their guide thinks they should start back. I will accompany them."

"Oh, they must be beautiful," Quon Hing chimed in.

"Sounds like romance to me," added Teacher Chen.

Clifford blushed. "No, no, nothing like that," he insisted. "Remember when you helped convince General Tao to provide inside information on drug trafficking?"

"Yes, that was a few years ago."

"One of these women is the daughter of the Thai Police General I met at that time.

"Oh well, take good care of her then." The two teachers thought it was funny.

"Maybe I am foolish," thought Clifford, "but the Police General's daughter seems to have no idea of the vicious enemies her father makes just doing his job."

He left his packed bag at the teachers' house and went back to the restaurant, just as Ai Seng and the two women arrived. Already, they could hear a marching band and the tramp of the soldiers feet as they marched down the street, passing by the restaurant. In front, mounted on horses, were officers, their highly polished cavalry boots shining in the sun. The men were rather indifferent marchers, and Clifford noted quite a disparity in their ages. There were older men, and young men, boys really. Nothing in between. He mentioned that fact to Ai Seng. "Yes," Ai Seng replied, "that's the way it is. The older men are what's left of the original soldiers who fought the Communists in China. The boys are recruits from Tribal villages around here."

The soldiers marched on down the road past the market and returned on a parallel street. The school, and its sports field, was located in between those two streets. The column turned off the street, and flowed onto the parade ground. General Tao, and his entourage of high ranking officers, were already seated in the reviewing stand. The band assembled on one side of the field, and continued playing while the soldiers were ordered into ranks facing the review stand. Hoping for a better view, Ai Seng, the ladies, and Clifford walked over to the edge of the field, as several other people were doing. They were quite close to the stand and Clifford noticed a young woman seated next to the General. "Who is that woman?" he asked Ai Seng. "The General's daughter," Ai Seng replied.

It had been a gorgeous morning; bright sun shining on marching and mounted troops, flags unfurled in a slight breeze, with a background of martial music. A scene right out of 1930's or '40's China. The last hurrah of the remnants of the Army of Nationalist China. You would think the weather might have continued to cooperate, but it didn't. April can be a time of rapidly changing weather. The forward elements of the coming monsoons may result in short, but violent, changes in weather. That's what happened at Doi Maesalong that day. The sky suddenly clouded, there was thunder and lightning, mixed rain and hail descended, blown almost sideways by gusts of wind reaching 80 miles per hour.

The roof blew off the reviewing stand, the ranks of soldiers wavered, and finally broke, as each person fled for shelter. General Tao, and the others on the stand, were escorted back to the nearest army billets by the General's personal guard. They had just left the field when there was an enormous explosion. First, a flash of light, immediately followed by a shock wave of sound that knocked everyone within 100 yards to the ground. The remains of the reviewing stand, reduced to small smoking pieces of wood and bamboo, were scattered over the field. Horses panicked, throwing their riders, and galloped wildly through the debris.

"What happened," screamed Wipha, as she and the others were still on the ground in shock.

"We've been struck by lightening," cried Clifford.

Ai Seng was the first to realize what had really happened. "It was a bomb," he contradicted. "Let's get out of here, now."

Sae Yang had recognized his targets, and was standing nearby, ready to knife them when the opportunity arose. "Might as well take out all four of them," he thought to himself, "and get the men first, so they can't protect the women." He was expecting an explosion, but the force of it surprised him. He too was knocked to the ground by the concussion, and only stood up when he heard Ai Seng say, "Let's get out of here." Sae Yang pulled out his knife, unfolded it, and lunged at Ai Seng, driving the blade into his chest. Clifford reacted rapidly; putting himself in front of the terrified women. "I know you," grunted Sae Yang, and turned his attention to Clifford. Sae Yang held his knife high, ready to plunge it into Clifford's throat, when a shot rang out. Sae Yang stopped his forward motion, his legs collapsed, and he fell at Clifford's feet. Clifford, and the women who were too terrified to even scream, turned in horror to see Ai Seng, revolver in hand, collapse on the ground.

Clifford now understood it was an assasination attempt, and further attempts would likely be made on their lives. He went to help Ai Seng, and discovered he was not dead, but gravely wounded. Blood was soaking his shirt. He took the revolver from Ai Sengs's hand and put it in his own pocket. He motioned for Kultida and Wipha to help, and they managed to get Ai Seng to his feet. "We'll take him to a house nearby," ordered Clifford. Ai Seng was in great pain, but managed, with the help of the three, to stumble to the house Clifford had in mind; the house of Teacher Chen and Quon Hing.

The two teachers, frightened by the explosion, were standing on their porch trying to see what had happened. From their house they could not see the school or the playing field, but did see their friend, Clifford, and two young women, helping a wounded man toward their house. They came down to help and eased Ai Seng onto a mat in the open area under their porch. "What happened?" they wanted to know.

"We don't know," answered Clifford, "but there was a terrible explosion. I think it was near the reviewing stand."

"What about the General and his daughter?"

"They had already left because of the storm, so they must be alright, but this man needs help," urged Clifford, looking at Ai Seng.

"Who is he?"

"He's the guide that brought these two women here."

Quon Hing ran to get her sewing scissors and cut off Ai Seng's shirt. A bleeding wound was revealed on the upper left side of his torso. Teacher Chen brought a bottle of iodine and one of his clean undershirts. He poured iodine on the wound, which continued to bleed. He spoke to his wife in Chinese, and she ran to their bedroom and came back with two sanitary napkins, which Teacher Chen placed over the wound. Using the scissors, he cut his undershirt open and tied it tightly around Ai Seng's chest, holding the sanitary napkins tightly in place. His first aid attempt helped some, but blood was still oozing out from under the makeshift bandage.

"Is there a hospital here?" enquired Clifford.

"There is a clinic," replied Quon Hing, "and there is a doctor there. I suppose this man was injured in the explosion."

"No, he was knifed. I think the man who did it wanted to kill all four of us."

Teacher Chen did not know Ai Seng, but couldn't believe what he had just heard. "Who are these women? Why would anyone want to kill them?"

Clifford pointed to Kultida, "This one is the daughter of the Thai Police General in charge of narcotic suppression. He's the one who caught those big dealers a few years ago."

Teacher Chen was beginning to understand, and connect the dots. General Tao, Clifford, and the daughter of the police general were all here at Doi Maesalong at the same time. Surely, it was an assassination attempt. He exchanged glances with Clifford. The two of them understood the danger they were in.

"Did you see the man with the knife?" Teacher Chen asked Clifford.

"Yes, and I have seen him before. He's a known drug dealer named Sae Yang"

"What happened to him?"

"This man," Clifford pointed to Ai Seng, "shot him after he had been knifed. I didn't even know he had a gun."

Teacher Chen was thinking clearly, "We're going to have to get this guide to the clinic, and you and the women will have to hide."

Quon Hing had gone upstairs to check on her baby, who, awakened by the blast, was crying. She rejoined the others, still holding her child, just in time to hear her husband say that Clifford and the women would have to hide. She looked at her husband. "No time to explain now," he told her, but Clifford and the women are in danger. Most likely from the drug dealers. Not all were caught."

The two women were trying to make sense of this conversation, but could not comprehend what was going on. "What do you mean hide," demanded Kultida. I think we had better go to the police station and report what happened."

Clifford knew they needed a full explanation, but there was not time. "Kultida and Wipha it seems there are some really bad people here. Some years back, when you were living abroad, your father apprehended some very big time drug traffickers and put them in jail. General Tao provided the information, and I passed it on to authorities. There has already been one attempt on General Tao's life when his house in Chiang Mai was blown up. He escaped that time, and today, it seems, he escaped again. The man who attacked us today is known by me. He is a drug dealer, and has a vicious reputation. I am convinced he knew of my presence here, and also of you, Kultida. I think they want to kill me because I passed on information and gave testimony in court. I think they want to kill you as revenge against your father. Most likely this man is not the only one. We must first hide, and then make our way to Chiang Mai."

Kultida had recovered from her panic, and asked some further questions. "What about our guide? Why was he attacked?"

"I suppose the attacker knew he had to get him before attacking you."

"Ai Seng is a brave man. He saved your life too."

"Yes he did.

"Whose house are we in?"

This couple are from Taiwan. They are teachers at the school here, and my friends. I came to visit them and see their new baby.

Kultida shuddered. Her father was a policeman, but she knew she had led a sheltered life. She knew nothing of what he did. She repeated, "Why don't we go to the police station?"

"Kultida," explained Clifford, "Doi Maesalong has been temporarily turned over to the former Chinese Nationalist Government. There is no Thai government presence here."

Teacher Chen wanted to help Clifford and the two women but he would not leave his wife and son at this time, so he went outside and called to a neighbor, who was also a teacher at the school. "I have a wounded man here. Can you go to the clinic and get someone to come with a stretcher. He needs to see a doctor, but I have to stay with my friends here. I'll explain later." The neighbor thought it must be someone injured in the explosion, and ran off to the clinic.

"We can't stay here," Clifford informed Teacher Chen, "Our presence would be dangerous for you."

"Where can you go?"

Clifford thought about the church he had visited that very morning. "I think we will go to the church; you know, that white building with the red cross on top." Neither Teacher Chen or Quon Hing had been in that building, but they knew of its existence. While Teacher Chen was mulling that idea over in his mind, Quon Hing took Kultida and Wipha with her to the kitchen. "Wherever you go, you'll need some food and water." She hurriedly filled two plastic containers with water, put some of the previous day's left-over food in another container, added three pairs of chopsticks, and put it all in a bag.

"This will be enough for today," she said kindly, and gave them both a hug. "Keep in touch. We'll help where we can."

Clifford had made his decision. They would go to the church. Churches have traditionally been places of sanctuary, not that he thought that would do much good here, but it was a place to go immediately. They could make further plans there. Before venturing out, Quon Hing handed the the bag of food and water to Wipha, and wrapped a cloth around each of their faces. Both Thai and Chinese women often did that when working outside to prevent the sun from darkening their faces. Teacher Chen gave Clifford a floppy straw hat with a wide brim that covered his face quite well. He also found a hoe in his workroom, and told Clifford to carry it. "Two women and a man going to their field to work," he smiled. That was before he noticed the clean, manicured fingers of the women decorated with red nail polish. "Keep those hands covered up," he admonished.

Clifford led the way as they straggled out of the house, heads downcast, and Clifford with his free hand on the revolver in his pocket. By that time the rain and wind was over and crowds of people had returned to the playing field to gaze in amazement at the hole in the ground where the reviewing stand had been located. Clifford went around the edge of the field, and up a side street where the church was located. After a furtive look around, he led the two women into the church. The church was deserted, so they hesitantly sat on a bench. No one spoke, until Wipha suddenly dissolved into weeping, which was starting to become hysterical. "I want to go home," she wailed. Kultida was proving to be the stronger of the two. She grabbed her friend by the shoulders and shook her. "Wipha, stop this! We'll be alright; this American will stay with us, and get us home again," she firmly stated, with a long questioning look at Clifford. "That's right," affirmed Clifford. "I will not leave, and I will get you home." Kultida knew nothing about this man, except that he had met her father. Mostly, she was trying to calm Wipha.

Now that Clifford was alone with the women, his old shyness came back and he did not know what else to say, but he knew he would not leave them. He would protect them and get them safely back to Bangkok. How would he do that? He started to think.

He knew the church was not a good place to hide. It was too public. If church members saw them they would certainly talk about it. Not good. It would do as a temporary place, but they would have to find a more secure location. Besides his friends, Teacher Chen and Quon Hing, the only other people he knew in Doi Maesalong were the Akha couple where he had stayed when he went with Lee Mui to the Akha village. He remembered that Ai Seng also knew Lee Mui and that couple. The more he thought about it, the more it seemed like a good place to go. Who would think of looking for two Bangkok women and a Foreigner in the simple house of a poor Akha family? That idea was even better than Clifford knew, as it was also the place where Ai Seng had left the three horses he had used when he guided the women to Doi Maesalong. Wipha was still trembling from their experience, and Kultida was not in much better shape. In a low, but reassuring, voice Clifford told the two young ladies what he planned to do.

"Kultida and Wipha, I am sorry we're in this situation, but we will have to use our heads to get us all home again. When it gets dark, we'll move to a house I know here in this town. It is an Akha house, one of the Hill Tribe groups. I have met the family in that house before, and Ai Seng also knows them."

"How do you know that?" asked Kultida

"I found that out in the restaurant this morning when Ai Seng and I were talking."

"That seems so long ago."

"Yes it does. A lot has happened since than."

Having a definite plan, no matter how limited, was reassuring to Wipha, who spoke up for the first time. "What about Ai Seng? I want to know how he is."

"At the Akha house," replied Clifford, "someone can go to the clinic and enquire about him."

They sat in silence for some time, until Kultida, looking around the interior of the church, asked Clifford, "Is this really a Christian church; it looks more like an ordinary meeting room?"

"Have you ever been in a church before?" asked Clifford.

"Yes, when I was in London I went to Westminster Cathedral. I thought it was quite grand."

"I have never been to London," replied Clifford, "but I'm sure Doi Maesalong is nothing like that city."

"But even Buddhist temples in small villages in Thailand are ornate and places of beauty," persisted Kultida, "and there is always an image of Lord Buddha. Why is there no image of Jesus here?"

"Some churches do have images," replied Clifford, "but they are not necessary. Christians believe God is a Spirit."

The rest of the afternoon was spent discussing theology. Kultida still thought a place of worship should be a place of architectural and artistic beauty. Clifford had to admit this Protestant Christian church building was very plain, but he explained that artistic beauty can also be a distraction, leading a worshipper away from true worship of a Living God. Neither convinced the other, but it did pass the time.

When evening was approaching, Clifford suggested eating the food Quon Hing had packed. "We had better eat before it gets dark, so we will be ready to move." Kultida and Quon Hing wanted to go back to their guest house and collect some items from their bags, but Clifford was adamant that they must not go there. He feared that place would be under observation. He unpacked the food containers and placed them on a pew between them. There were no plates, so they ate directly from the containers using the chopsticks. It had been a long time since breakfast, and the food was good. They consumed it all, and ended with water, drank directly from the bottles. Clifford saved the water bottles, but picked up everything else, stuffing it into a plastic bag. He did not want to leave any evidence of their presence. The food had a calming effect. With the cessation of fear and tension, they became drowsy and nodded off while sitting on the backless benches with their backs agains the wall.

Clifford awoke in the darkness with a start. He could not see to read his watch, but it seemed to him that some time had passed. He gently woke the others. "Time to go," he whispered. Clifford put the water bottles in his shoulder bag and collected the garbage, which he intended to dispose of when they were outside. It was pitch dark in the church, so holding hands, and with Clifford leading, they ventured outside. There was no moon, so it was not much brighter outside. There were a few streetlights, so Clifford was able to pick his way toward the Akha house. He threw the garbage bag under some bushes, which immediately caused a dogfight as several dogs contested for the bare remains of their food. No one challenged them, and they made it to their destination safely.

Clifford had been learning some Akha from one of the students at the student hostel. He was not proficient in the language, but what he did know came in handy. He led Kultida and Wipha up onto the porch of the house, and called softly to the occupants. Clifford remembered a couple with a baby lived in this house. It took three calls before there was a response. Clifford spoke a word or two in Akha, and the husband came out of one of the two rooms off the porch.

"What do you want?" the man asked in a surly voice. In the darkness he could not see who was there, and was surprised when Clifford replied that he was the Foreigner who had stayed in this house once before when he came with Lee Mui. Upon hearing that, the man called into the other room and another man came out. He spoke to Clifford, and immediately Clifford recognized his voice. It was Lee Mui. Clifford switched to Northern Thai, in which he was more proficient. "We need to talk. Let's go into your room. My friends and I believe we are in great danger." "I'll get a light," said the man of the house, but Clifford quickly stopped him. "No, no light. We must talk inside."

Lee Mui, the house owner, Clifford, and the two women, all filed into the unlit room and squatted on the floor. After the door was closed, Clifford allowed a lamp to be lit. The two Akha men were surprised to see the two young Thai women, but waited for Clifford to explain. Clifford felt he could trust Lee Mui, and, hopefully, the other man who was Lee Mui's relative. Clifford told the whole story, starting with the drug traffickers, his testimony in court, and that one of these women was the daughter of the Police General who had put the drug lords in prison. He told about the earlier attempt to assassinate General Tao, and they, of course, knew about today's attempt. When he told about Sae Yang's attack on them with a knife immediately after the explosion, they murmured in understanding. "We know about Sae Yang. He is a Hmong from Chom Tong District, and is known to be a very bad person. Where is he now?"

"Do you know a tourist guide named Ai Seng? asked Clifford. He is a Lahu."

"Yes, I know him well," replied Lee Mui.

"Ai Seng guided these two women here. They knew nothing about the drug situation in this area, and simply wanted to see Doi Maesalong. When we were attacked by Sae Yang, Ai Seng was stabbed, but he managed to shoot and kill Sae Yang before he killed the rest of us."

"Good, but what about Ai Seng?"

"He was badly wounded, but is now in the clinic. We don't know how he is."

"How did he get to the clinic?"

Clifford did not want Teacher Chen and Quon Hing to be involved in this at all, so he just replied that some helpful person took him to the clinic.

When Clifford had finished relating what had happened, Lee Mui and his relative spoke to one another for some time. They had already had one visit that day. Early in the evening KMT solders made house to house searches, looking for the ones who had tried to assassinate their general. They warned the occupants of every house to report any stranger they saw. Clifford could understand part of what was said. He gathered that because of their fear of both the drug people and the KMT, they were not anxious to get involved. However, Clifford had been Lee Mui's guest at one time, and, also, Lee Mui considered Ai Seng to be a good friend, and he remembered that Clifford had helped free the girl, Mi Ja, from a brothel in Chiang Mai. Lee Mui convinced his relative to help, and he spoke to Clifford. "We will try to help. It is not safe for you here, so you must leave. Going to my village is not good. If you are followed there, we would not be able to protect you. Best you return the way you came. From there you can take a bus to Chiang Mai."

"Sounds good," replied Clifford, "but how can we safely return on that trail, which will surely be watched?"

"We will turn you into Akhas."

"What!" Exclaimed Gultida. The Northern Thai being spoken was close enough to Central Thai so she could understand most of the conversation. "What do you mean, "turn us into Akhas?"

"All three of you would be easily spotted," explained Lee Mui. "You must dress in Akha clothes. I, and some others, will go with you."

It was not a perfect plan, but Clifford believed it was the best they could do. He spoke to Kultida and Wipha, "I think we had better do as they suggest."

"When do we leave?" both women asked. They were eager to leave this frightful place.

"Early in the morning," replied Lee Mui. "We leave before light, best you rest now."

In the other room Clifford could hear the woman of the house arguing with her husband. She was afraid of what might happen, and did not want to help the strangers. Her husband told her to shut up and give some blankets to their overnight guests. Sullenly, she gathered up three blankets and threw them in the guest room, narrowly missing the lamp.

If Kultida and Wipha were looking for new experiences, they were finding them. They were supposed to sleep in a small room in a Hill Tribe hut with two men; one Akha and one Foreigner. Wipha whispered to Kultida, "I have to go to the toilet, and I need a bath."

Kultida whispered back, "So do I."

Thai people bathe often; even two or three times a day in hot weather. Body odor is considered very objectional. Wipha and Kultida had not bathed all day, their clothe were dirty, and they could smell themselves, not to mention the two men in the same room. All of this made them very uncomfortable. Finding a toilet was even more urgent than bathing.

"Mr. Clifford," Kultida spoke in a low voice.

"Yes."

"Are you sleeping?"

"Not now."

"Sorry, but Whipa and I need to find a toilet. Can you help us?"

Clifford knew there was a toilet behind the house somewhere, but did not want to take a light outside. "Yes," he replied, "there is one outside behind the house. Come with me." They held on to Clifford's hand while he led them out onto the porch, down the stairs, and behind the house. It was so dark they could not see anything.

"I can't find it," said Clifford. "I think you had better do what you're going to do right here on the ground."

There was no response. With the exception of the day on the trail with Ai Seng, Kultida and Wipha could not remember ever going to the toilet on the ground. But, what had to be done, had to be done.

"Mr. Clifford."

"Yes."

"Please leave us. We'll call you when we're ready."

Clifford was terribly embarrassed. He was trying to help, but realized his direct and practical language was not appropiate. He could have used a more indirect wording. He went back to the front of the house and relieved himself standing next to the porch. Soon, he heard a call and went back to where he had left the women. He could only find them because he heard them whispering to one another. "Mr. Clifford," Kultida had one more request. "Is there anyplace we can wash our hands and face?" They had given up on the bath idea.

Clifford remembered the water tank for the horses. He felt around for the corral fence and the tank, which was on the other side of the fence. There was a hole in the fence above the tank, so it was possible to reach the water. He showed the women where it was, and they washed their hands and faces.

"Is this where these people bathe?" Wipha asked.

"No, this is a water tank for the horses." Clifford just couldn't help speaking the bare truth.

"Ai yaa," groaned Kultida, "horse water!"

Back to the house they went, and felt their way into their room. They wrapped themselves in their blankets, which were dusty, as well as musty. "Mr. Clifford?"

"Yes."

"Can we get our bags from the guest house in the morning? We need clean clothes."

"I think you had better forget about those bags. Goodnight."

Morning came very early; well before daylight, but rice was already steaming in the kitchen. Everybody had slept in their clothes. Kultida and Wipha had never done that before either! They felt sticky and stinky. Moreover, they had no comb, so could not even comb their hair. Rice was served, with vegetables and a bit of meat. They ate with chopsticks, sitting around a low table. After eating, the woman of the house took the two Thai women into the room where they had slept, and helped them dress in Akha clothes. That was a bit traumatic also. They had to strip to their underwear, which they didn't want to do in front of a strange woman, and put on Akha clothes, which had been borrowed from the Akha woman's friends. Kultida and Wipha had the common prejudices of Thai people toward the Hill Tribes, so assumed the clothes were not clean and probably full of lice. Besides, Akha women's skirts are short, only reaching to just above the knees. The two Thai women were taller than most Akha women, so that left a lot of leg exposed. More than they were willing to expose in public places, even after putting on Akha leggings from knee to ankle.

They were ready to mutiny, march over to their guest house, take a shower, shampoo their hair, and dress in their own clothes. Clifford wouldn't let them. They hated him, but he wouldn't budge. "Too dangerous," he declared. Clifford had also been provided with Akha clothes, and he still had the floppy straw hat and hoe that Teacher Chen had given him.

There was one more disappointment. There were only four horses in the corral, but seven people were going. The group included the two Thai women, Clifford, Lee Mui, the man of the house where they had slept, and two other Akha men. All four Akha men carried their muzzle loading hunting guns. Lee Mui had recruited the extra guards from among his relatives, who lived in Doi Maesalong. "It'll be safer to walk anyway," he told Clifford. "You and your two women friends can walk in between us men." Clifford didn't like the implications of those words, "your two women friends," but decided to let it pass.

Clifford explained the walking plan to his "women friends", which they readily accepted. They had not been looking forward to straddling horses while wearing miniskirts. Finally, Akha head gear, minus the usual silver coins, were put on the women's heads, and they were also handed hoes. If no one looked at them too closely, they might be able to pass as a group of Akha going to work in their fields.

CHAPTER TWENTY

FLIGHT

They were taking the proper precautions, but Kultida and Wipha really could have gone back to their guest house, taken showers and reclaimed their belongings. On the morning they left, no one in Doi Maesalong was seeking to kill them. Only three had been sent for that job; of those, one was dead, and the other two were losing their money and receiving a dose of gonorrhea in the Chiang Rai brothel located on Old Airport Road. There were, however, informers, who had seen Clifford and the two women in Doi Maesalong on the day of the explosion. Those informers also reported the death of Sae Yang, and the destination of the other two assassins About the time the group of seven were starting their trek, two rough looking men broke into the brothel in Chiang Rai and went searching room by room for the two explosive experts. They were soon found, and taken, half dressed, to a room over a car repair shop, where they were threatened by a man with a mask over his face; one of the king pins in the drug trafficking trade who had not been caught and imprisoned. There they were told how stupid they were, what their mother's occupations had been, and that they would soon be dead by unpleasant means if they did not get back to Doi Maesalong and finish their job.

"Sae Yang is dead," they were told, "and forget the old General, he'll be well guarded now, but get that Foreigner and the daughter of Police General Manoon."

"Yes sir, yes sir." The two men were on their knees.

"There is another woman with General Manoon's daughter. If she gets in the way kill her too, and don't try to run away. You will be watched."

"Yes sir, yes sir."

"Two men are waiting downstairs in a pickup truck. They will take you back to where the trail begins to Doi Maesalong. You will each be given a revolver and a knife. No bomb this time. I don't care how you kill them. I don't care what you do with the women, but if they're not dead within two days you will wish you were. Do you understand?"

"Yes sir, yes sir."

"Get out of here."

Within two minutes, the men were in the back of a pickup heading north. Two strange men sat in front, and one more in the back with them. "What happened? I thought we had that Chinese General nailed." they asked the man sitting with them.

"The only thing you guys did was blow the hell out of a flimsy reviewing stand with no one it. I'd hate to be in your shoes!"

One hour later the two badly frightened men were dumped off where the trail began. They were each handed a gun and a knife. Nothing more was said. The pickup, with the three men in it, turned around and started back to Chiang Rai.

The two disgraced men, Ai Mek and Ai Jek, were brothers, and had been *pern chow* (hired guns) before. They prided themselves on always getting their man, or woman, and vanishing without a trace. Their expertise with any number of weapons was well known in the criminal underground, so they commanded a high fee. They now knew they had really messed up doing the job at Doi Maesalong. Sae Yang must have messed up too. "We all got too careless," commented Ai Mek.

"Yeah, well, what do we do now?" asked Ai Jek, who always deferred to his elder brother.

"We'll start at a house I know."

"You know someone here?"

"Yes I do, and so do you, dummy."

"Look who's calling who dummy." They started to argue.

"Quit it!" shouted Ai Mek. "We're going to the house of that Jin Haw man who used to deliver the goods for the big shots."

"Oh Yeah, I remember him. Is that cute Hill Tribe woman still living with him?"

"I don't think so. He's in jail."

"You mean she's living there all alone?"

"I think so, but don't get any ideas; we need to pay attention to our job."

It was a short walk to Mee Bu's house, and they found her outside feeding her chickens. She knew who the two brothers were, and was not happy to see them.

"Mee Bu, how are you these days," asked Ai Mek.

"I get along alright."

"Mee Bu, I have a message for a young Thai woman who may be accompanied by a Foreigner. The parents of the woman are concerned about her and want her to return home. Have you seen them?"

Mee Bu remembered the two young Thai women that Ai Seng was guiding to Doi Maesalong . No Foreigner was with them that day, but they might be the ones Ai Mek was asking about. Anyway, she certainly was not going to tell Ai Mek about them.

"No, I have not seen anyone like that," she replied.

"Well, keep it in mind. Her parents are even giving a reward for finding her. We'll be looking for them, and will come back here again." Ai Mek was a very accomplished liar.

The two brothers were getting a little desperate. They stopped at a few other houses and asked the same question. Getting no results, they decided their targets must still be in Doi Maesalong, and started walking on the trail to that place. When they came to the Akha village they stopped to rest, and were sitting on the porch of a house when another group of Akha came walking through. There were seven of them, five men and two women. "Nice legs," remarked Ai Jek, gazing at the two women. "Come on, let's go," demanded Ai Mek, who was thinking about what would happen to them if they did not find their quarry.

Lee Mui, and the other Akha men, were concerned that the disguised Thai women and Foreigner would be spotted, and commented on, by the Akha people in the village along the trail. They hurried on through without stopping, even though they knew the people in that village. They noticed the two strangers resting on the porch of one of the houses.

Kultida and Wipha had time to think during the long trek, and they spoke to one another along the way. They knew they had been in danger, and were still in danger, but they had met people who had been very helpful. Ai Seng had been a good guide, and perhaps he had even given his life to save them. The Foreigner, Mr. Clifford, had, at first, seemed like a shy man, but he had taken care of them too; not allowing them to do foolish things, like returning to their guest house. They were also changing their attitudes toward the Akha. The society in which they had lived did not appreciate the customs and cultures of the Hill Tribe people. Indeed, those people were considered stupid, dirty, and even as illegal aliens who were detrimental to Thailand. Some of them had entered Thailand by simply crossing the border with Burma. Some negative things about them were often reported in Thai newspapers, such as the cutting and burning of forests to make their hill fields, and the fact that some were known to plant the opium poppy. However, an Akha family had given them shelter in their house, which city people would have called a hut Those people had fed them, and now were guarding them at great risk to themselves. The woman in the house where they had spent the night had never spoken to them, but had obviously gotten up very early to cook rice and *kop khaow* (food eaten with rice) for them. They had enjoyed eating the *khaow daeng* (red rice) and vegetables a ways back on the trail. The rice was red because the villagers removed the rice hulls in their own rice pounder, which removed the inedible hull, but left the red colored bran layer on the rice grains. In their own homes they were only served milled rice. Red rice was considered inferior, even though it was more nutritious. The two Bangkok women had learned that red rice tasted very good, and that the people who had prepared it and were now guarding them were good people.

It was late in the afternoon when they had descended from the hills and were approaching the main highway. Lee Mui led them off the trail and told them to conceal themselves in a clump of bamboo. He went on alone to Mee Bu's house. "Mee Bu," he called and Mee Bu opened the door. He quickly entered, and told Mee Bu all he knew about the events in Doi Maesalong. She gasped when she heard that Ai Seng had been knifed.

"I think I have met the two Thai women," she told Lee Mui. They came here with Ai Seng to rent three horses."

"What about the Foreigner? You know, the same one I took to my home."

"Yes, I know who you mean, but he was not with the women and Ai Seng."

"Have you seen any strangers around here?"

"Yes, about two or three hours ago two men came here asking about a Thai woman and a Foreigner. They said the parents of the woman wanted to know where she was, and was offering a reward if she was found."

"Did you tell them anything?"

"No."

"Good. Can you describe them?"

Mee Bu described them, and Lee Mui realized they were the same two men he had seen in the Akha village sitting on the porch of a house.

"I saw them in the Akha village as we were on our way here. We have the two Thai women and the Foreigner with us dressed in Akha clothes. They are hiding near your house, and three of my relatives are with them."

"Those men said they would be back." Mee Bu told Lee Mui, in a voice edged with fear.

"Then we must hurry and get those three out of here and on the road to Chiang Mai."

"How can we do that?"

"What about the Landrover parked by your house?"

"You know that belongs to the man who took me here. He's in jail, but he told me not to let anyone else drive it."

"Can you drive?"

"No."

"Is there anyone around here who can?"

"Well, there is a man in a house nearby who drives a pickup taxi."

"Quick, go and ask him if he will take three people to Chiang Mai. Tell him he will be well paid."

"Why not just go to Chiang Rai, much closer."

"Too close. They'll be safer in Chiang Mai."

Mee Bu ran to ask the neighbor, and Lee Mui stepped out of the house to hide in the bushes where he could watch the house. Soon a pickup taxi drove up and Mee Bu hopped out. Lee Mui stepped out from behind the bushes. "This is Nai Tong," she said with a glance at the driver, "He will take the three passengers to Chiang Mai."

"Maybe I will, and maybe I won't," replied Nai Tong. "How much are they paying me?"

"You can ask them," replied Lee Mui, "but they are two wealthy Thai women and one Foreigner. I know they will pay you well."

"Where are they?"

"I'll get them."

Lee Mui hurried back to the bamboo and brought back the rest of the group. Nai Tong eyed the armed Akha with some suspicion. "These all look like Akha to me," Nai Tong muttered. Mee Bu had immediately spotted the fake Akha, and thought Nai Tong would come to that same conclusion, so she told a small lie. "These are tourists," she pointed to the three, "and have been on a trek to an Akha village. They wanted to dress like the villagers."

Nai Tong accepted that explanation. He knew tourists often did crazy things. "Do you want to go to Chiang Mai?" he asked Kultida and Wipha, who were standing together.

"Yes we do, and we want to leave now," replied Wipha.

"That will cost you 1,000 Baht."

"*Toklong.*" (agreed)

Nai Tong cursed himself. He should have asked for more. "Also, you must pay for the gasoline," he added.

"*Toklong.*" Wipha wanted out of there.

"I will also need a 500 Baht down payment."

Clifford reached for his wallet, and gave the driver 500 Baht. "Can we go now?" asked Wipha.

"Yes, we can go," replied Nai Tong, turning toward his vehicle.

"Just a minute," Mee Bu spoke up, and had a brief discussion with

Lee Mui in Akha. She was afraid that Clifford and the women could be easily noticed in the pickup. Lee Mui seemed to agree, so Mee Bu pulled some bundles of rice straw from a stack not far from the house, opened them, and threw the straw on the floor of the minibus. She brought more bundles of rice straw, which she did not untie, and fastened them to the sides of the bus with bits of string and wire. For the first time, she spoke to Kultida and Wipha, "This will be more comfortable, you can lie on the floor if you wish, and no one will be able to see inside." Actually, the rear of the minibus was open, but having the sides covered did provide some privacy. It was a thoughtful gesture; something no one else had thought of. "Who are you?" asked Gultida.

"Just an Akha. Have a safe trip." Gultida and Wipha both raised their hands, with palms pressed together, and gave Mee Bu a *wai (curtsy)*. Up until this day, they would not have been the ones to initiate a curtsy to a Hill Tribe person. They were in need, and people were helping them. They never expected to receive such an education on this trip.

Ai Mek and Ai Jek were almost to Doi Maesalong, when Ai Mek suddenly stopped. He stopped so fast that his brother, walking behind him, bumped into him. "They tricked us," he shouted.

"Who tricked us?" asked Ai Jek.

"Ai ya, we were really stupid."

"Who's stupid?"

"You are, and so am I." Ai Mek was raging mad.

"What are you talking about?"

"Remember when we were resting in the Akha village, and a group of Akha came walking through?"

"Yeah, what about it?"

"Have you ever seen an Akha almost two meters tall?"

"No, I guess not."

"Have you ever seen Akha women with nice white hands?"

"What are you getting at?"

"In that group of Akha, one man and two women were not Akha. I knew there was something different about them, but it didn't hit me until right now."

"You mean the two women with the nice long legs?"

.   "Yes, and if you had noticed more than their legs you might have seen who they really were."

"So, who are they?" Ai Jek was a little slow.

"You are really *ngo kwai* (dumb like a buffalo). Those are the two women and the Foreigner we have been hired to eliminate. We have to go back."

Ai Jek protested. He was tired and hungry. He only wanted to eat a good meal and rest his tired legs. Ai Mek, however, understood the danger they were in. They had to finish their job, or face the wrath of shadowy people, like the one they had met that morning in the room above the car repair shop. He turned around and headed back down the trail, knowing that his brother would follow. When they got to the Akha village they tried to ask about the group of seven that had walked through earlier in the day, but no one would talk to them. The villagers knew Lee Mui and some of the other men, so were not about to answer any questions about them, even if they were curious. It was strange that Lee Mui had walked right through the village without stopping, and, although it was normal for men to carry their hunting guns, why were the women carrying hoes; they had no fields around here. There was something strange about those women, and one of the men, too. They were not Akha, even if they were wearing Akha clothes. They would ask Lee Mui when he came through again, but for now, they were not talking to nosy outsiders.

Ai Mek and Ai Jek learned nothing in the Akha village, so hurried on down the trail, arriving at Mee Bu's house just at dark, exhausted and hungry. Ai Mek expected to bully some information out of Mee Bu, but was disappointed to find four Akha men eating in her house. Lee Mui and his group had decided to spend the night. When the two brothers showed up, the Akha men recognized them as the two men they had seen in the Akha village. Mee Bu did not want them around, but when Ai Jek, succumbing to the smell of newly cooked rice, asked if they could have some food, she followed the custom of Tribal hospitality, and gave them each a plate of rice and stir fried vegetables. They both wolfed down the food and held their plates up for a second helping.

After eating, and with everyone sipping on cups of tea, Ai Mek began to ask questions. He would have asked sooner, but the men did not seem very communicative, and interrupting their meal would not have helped. " I am looking for two Thai women and a Foreigner," he began. "The parents of the women are concerned about them, and asked my brother and me to find them. If found, there will be a reward, which can be divided among all who provide information resulting in their being found. Have you seen them?"

Lee Mui and Mee Bu were the only two Akha in this group that could speak Thai. Mee Bu spoke first. "You were here this morning asking about them. At that time I had not seen anyone like them, and have still not seen them." Lee Mui added, "I have not seen them either."

"They may be wearing Akha clothes," added Ai Mek.

"Lee Mui laughed, "I have never seen either a Thai or a Foreigner that wanted to be an Akha."

"Maybe they're hiding."

"Why would they do that?"

"Maybe you would know."

"Maybe the Foreigner has abducted the two women and is running away with them," Lee Mui said with a grin. He translated that last remark to the other Akha men, who laughed behind their tea cups.

Ai Mek could see he was getting nowhere, and decided to bear down a little harder. "My brother and I were in that Akha village on the trail to Doi Maesalong when seven Akha people came walking through without even stopping. The four of you were in that group. Where are the other three?"

"Yes, there were seven," replied Lee Mui, "The other three just joined us along the trail somewhere. We don't know where they went."

Ai Mek didn't believe them, but there wasn't much he could do about it. "Where did you start from today," he asked.

"Doi Maesalong," replied Lee Mui, "That's where we live."

Now Ai Mek was positive the missing three had been with this group. "They must have paid you something for you to escort them here. I can pay you a lot more if you tell me where they are, and besides, you will share in the reward money."

Lee Mui just shrugged his shoulders, "I know nothing about them," he asserted. Ai Mek's temper flared. He wanted to pull out his revolver and threaten to shoot them all if they did not answer his questions, but there were four of them, plus Mee Bu. The odds were not good. "Maybe you can tell us where to get transportation to Mae Chan," asked Ai Mek with a scowl.

Mee Bu was eager to get them out of her house. "Some of the houses on the road to the main highway have some pickups," she told them.

The two men left without even a word of thanks for the food, and hurried on down the road. "They know," said Ai Mek to his brother through gritted teeth, "but they're not talking. We'll try to find out if anyone has hired a vehicle today. If not we'll hang out around here. I think those Akha men will leave tomorrow, and we can question the woman until she talks." Ai Jek liked that idea. "I'll make her talk," he grinned.

They asked about pickup taxis or minibuses at two houses along the road until they learned something of interest. One woman, home with her children, told them her husband had a pickup taxi, but he had left about two hours ago taking three passengers to Chiang Mai.

"Did he often take passengers to Chiang Mai?" asked Ai Mek.

"No, this was very unusual."

"Did they come here to your house? Did you see them?"

"No, that Akha woman who lives in that house up the road, with her man in jail, came and asked my husband to pick them up at her house. She was in a big hurry, and said the passengers would pay well. I think I heard her say there were two rich Thai women and one Foreigner."

Ai Mek was disappointed, but he knew he had to get word to Chiang Mai. "Do you have a phone?" he asked.

"No, no one around here has a phone. You'll have to go to the Post Office in Mae Chan."

Ai Mek had one more question, "What kind of pickup does your husband drive?"

"It's a red Toyota, and has his name printed above the cab; NAI TONG."

"Thank you."

The two brothers had no choice but to walk to the highway, which was not far, and wait for a bus to come by. Not many buses followed a route after dark, so they had to wait about 30 minutes. Finally, one stopped for them and took them on in to Mae Chan. They found the post office and Ai Mek pulled a Chiang Mai telephone number out of his pocket, which he gave to the man in charge of long distance calls. The man made the connection and motioned Ai Mek into one of two phone booths to take the call.

That number had been given to Ai Mek when he and his brother had first been given the assignment to kill Chinese General Tao. He had been warned not to use it, unless absolutely necessary. Ai Mek was reluctant to make this call, but thought he had no alternative. "Who are you?" a man's voice answered. No hello, no greeting, just "who are you?"

"My name is Ai Mek. My brother and I were hired to do a certain job in Doi Maesalong, but we have encountered some problems."

The man on the other end of the line lowered his phone and conferred with someone else. Ai Mek could hear a conversation, but it was not loud enough for him to understand. The man came back on, "What's your brother's name?" he demanded.

"Ai Jek."

"Yeah, alright, what are you calling about?"

"The people you are looking for got away from Doi Maesalong. They are presently on a minibus somewhere between Mae Chan and Chiang Mai. Their destination is Chiang Mai."

"Who are you talking about?"

"A certain police general's daughter and a Foreign man. Another woman, a friend of the General's daughter is also with them."

"You're really a big screwup; you know that don't you?"

"We've had some bad luck."

"You're bad luck!"

"I have a description of the vehicle they're in." Ai Mek wanted to change the subject. "That will give someone in Chiang Mai an opportunity to get them."

"That might save you're neck. What is it?"

"They are in a red Toyota minibus with a name above the cab, NAI TONG. Most likely it will have a Chiang Rai Province license plate. Their destination is Chiang Mai, but I don't know where."

"Big help," was the sarcastic reply. "There are probably a thousand red Toyota minibuses in Chiang Mai."

"Yes, but they will have to come into Chiang Mai from the Lampang Road." Ai Mek had been thinking about the route they would take, and that was the most likely way. A direct highway from Chiang Rai to Chiang Mai was under construction, but was not finished.

"That could be. Got anymore information?"

"No."

"Come on down to Chiang Mai. You might be of help."

Click. The line went dead.

Ai Mek and Ai Jek caught a late bus to Chiang Mai, even if they were apprehensive of their reception.

Clifford and the two women were making good time; they were approaching Lampang about the time Ai Mek and Ai Jek were leaving Mae Chan. That put them about five hours ahead of the brothers. They knew that at Lampang their driver, Nai Tong, would turn west toward Chiang Mai. Clifford was worried. He did not intend to underestimate the ability of the drug dealers to know where he and the women were. If they knew about the minibus, they would also know the route to Chiang Mai. Some very bad people might be watching for them where the highway enters Chiang Mai. Clifford knew of another way that would be no further, but would allow them to enter Chiang Mai by a different road. He allowed the driver to turn west at Lampang, but then yelled out the window for him to stop. Clifford hopped in front with the driver, so he could give directions. "When you get to the Lamphun turnoff, go on in to Lamphun and take the road from Lamphun to Chiang Mai." requested Clifford.

"Why do that?" argued Nai Tong, "The main highway is faster."

"Just do as I say. We want to enter Chiang Mai on that road."

Nai Tong shrugged his shoulders. These people were paying him well, and either way was the same distance. It was about an hour's drive to the Lamphun turnoff. The highway went over a mountain pass, where there were many Buddha images near the road. Nai Tong honked his car horn, took his hands off the steering wheel and raised his hands together in a worshipful curtsy to the images. All drivers did that; they thought the power of the Lord Buddha would provide them protection from accidents. Clifford always hoped it wouldn't cause an accident.

As directed, Nai Tong turned off at Lamphun, and took the road that went north into the southern part of Chiang Mai. Clifford always liked that road in the daytime. It had been the old ox cart road connecting Chiang Mai and Lamphun, but had been paved over in modern times. Huge trees, planted along both sides of the road, provided shade and added to the beauty of the road. At one time the Highway Department was considering cutting those trees down, so they could widen the road, but His Majesty the King said that was a bad idea, so it was never done.

Clifford knew the hotels might be watched, so he decided they would look up Po Swe, his former Karen language teacher at the Student Hostel. The Hostel would be a good place to stay, but Clifford did not want to endanger the lives of the students. He had already witnessed what a bomb could do and knew they could not stay there, but he wanted to seek the advice of Po Swe. Clifford directed Nai Tong to the Hostel, and paid him his fee, plus a little extra. He spoke briefly with Nai Tong and complemented him on his driving expertise. "Nai Tong," Clifford asked, "Do you know your neighbor, Mee Bu, very well?"

"Yes, my wife and I know her. We help her out from time to time."

"Do you think she's a good person?"

"She's a very good person, but we don't think much of that man she was living with. We were glad to see him go to jail."

"I agree with you. He is not a good man, but Mee Bu was a big help to me and the two women today. Some people might not like that, and harm her. Could you kind of keep an eye on her when you get back home?"

"Sure, I'm gone a lot, but I'll tell my wife. Who would harm Mee Bu? She's a kind lady."

Clifford had decided he could trust Nai Tong, but did not want to tell him too much. "Some powerful friends of the Yunnanese man Mee Bu lived with tried to kill me and the Thai ladies from Bangkok. Mee Bu may be in some danger because she helped us."

"I can't believe it!"

"Well, I'm sorry to say it is true. I don't think those people know about you, but anything is possible. Just in case somebody wants to talk to you about a trip you made to Chiang Mai, please don't mention the three of us, or where you took us. O.K.?"

"I won't tell anyone."

To make sure he wouldn't say anything, Clifford added that one of the women was the daughter of a police general, who would not appreciate anyone giving out information about his daughter.

"My lips are sealed." Nai Tong held his hand over his mouth.

Although it was in the early morning hours, Pwo Swe came out of the hostel building to see what was going on. He was very surprised to see Clifford, two young women, and a driver with his minibus. "What's going on?" he asked Clifford in Karen.

Clifford took Pwo Swe aside and briefly told him of events in Doi Maesalong, and of attempts to kill him, and at least one of the women, who was the daughter of a police general. "Seems to be an attempt at revenge from drug traffickers," Clifford added.

"Come into the Hostel," urged Pwo Swe, "You can all stay here tonight."

"Thank you Pwo Swe, but there are real dangerous people looking for us. They even use bombs. I don't want to endanger the students."

"Why not go to the Police Station?"

"We don't want to drive into the main part of the city. Maybe they have a description of this minibus," Clifford nodded his head at the red minibus. "We need to hide somewhere where no one would think of looking."

"What about the driver?" Pwo Swe asked, "Can you trust him?"

"Yes, I think so."

"So, I will take you to the abbortoir. I still work there part-time. No one would look for a Foreigner and two Bangkok women there."

"Good idea. Let's go."

Clifford returned to the minibus, where Kultida and Wipha were still waiting, and Nai Tong was sitting behind the steering wheel. Clifford told the women they were going to hide in a very good place, and that word would be sent to Kultida's father.

"Where are we going?" Wipha wanted to know.

"To the *rong kha sot* (abbortoir)" replied Clifford.

"Oh Lord Buddha save us all," wailed Wipha. Thai people,

especially of Wipha and Kultida's class, did not want to go to such a place of violence where animal's were killed in large numbers every day, and where their spirits may be waiting to be reborn in another life. The smell was not so great either!

"Yes, I know," Clifford was sympathetic, "but that will be a safe place. I'm sure we'll not be there long."

Pwo Swe got in the front seat with Nai Tong to direct him to the abbortoir, while Clifford sat in the back with Kultida and Wipha, who were both weeping. "I want my father," moaned Kultida.

"Yes, Kultida," sympathized Clifford, "I think he will find you today. Do you remember your home telephone number?" Kultida did remember, and, between sobs, told Clifford, who wrote it on a scrap of paper.

The abattoir appeared to be deserted, and only a few dim lights glowed ineffectively in the darkness. Pwo Swe knew there should be a watchman on the grounds, so instructed Nai Tong to turn off his lights and stop under a tree outside the building. Not wanting to alert the watchman, Pwo Swe whispered to Nai Tong to wait while he led the other three into the building. There was only a quarter moon, but Clifford could see it was a rather large structure with a sliding door on one side. Pwo Swe led them in that door, opening it just enough for them to squeeze through. Inside, it was quite clean, but there was a pervading odor of blood, manure, and of even fear, lingering from the panic stricken animals killed in that place.

Pwo Swe led them to a small closet where cleaning supplies were kept. After they were in, he turned on a light to reveal benches and cupboards. He removed containers of disinfectant from some of the benches so they could sit. "I will leave you here," he whispered. "Who should I tell where you are hiding?" Clifford handed Pwo Swe the scrap of paper with Police General Manoon's telephone number. "Go to the Bank Manager's house immediately, and use his phone to call this Bangkok number," whispered Clifford.

"Whose number is it?"

"It's the father of one of these women; he's a police general. Tell him, and only him, where we are hiding. He'll know what to do."

"I'm going, but there is one more thing. Today is *wan pra* (Buddhist Holy Day), so no animals will be killed. A few people may come to clean up, so if you hear anyone, just lay down on the floor behind those cupboards."

Clifford turned off the light in the closet, and Pwo Swe silently returned to where Nai Tong was waiting. They quickly drove back to the Student Hostel. Clifford thought Nai Tong could be trusted, but Pwo Swe did not want him to know about the Bank Manager. "Where are you going now?" Pwo Swe asked the driver.

"I'm going home."

"That's a long drive."

" I know, but its kind of scary around here. Do you know that Foreigner?"

"Yes, I have known him for many years."

"Is he a good man?"

"He's a very good man."

"I thought so. Good luck to you and those three we left at the abbortoir. I'm going home."

As soon as Nai Tong left, Po Swe immediately walked over to the Bank Manager's house, which was close by, and knocked on the door. A dog started to bark, which woke up other dogs in the neighborhood, who also started to bark. Soon, the four-legged sentinels were in full voice. They quieted down when Pwo Swe was admitted to the house by one of the Bank Manager's adult sons. "I have to make an important phone call," explained Pwo Swe.

"Can't it wait until morning.?"

"No, I have to call now."

"Who are you calling?"

"A police general in Bangkok."

"You can't call a police general at any time, especially at 3:00 A.M."

"Wake up your father; he'll know what to do."

The son went to wake up his father, but Pwo Swe did not wait. He knew where the telephone was, and went right to it. Pwo Swe had used a phone only a few times, but he was able to dial the number given to him by Clifford. Direct dialing from Chiang Mai to other provinces was something new, but it worked. Pwo Swe heard the sound of a phone ringing for a long time before a gruff voice answered. "This had better be good." the male voice growled.

"Is this Police General Manoon Sripanluang?" Pwo Swe asked in a trembling voice.

"Yes it is, what do you want?"

"I believe you have a daughter named Kultida, is that correct?"

General Manoon was instantly alert, and his mind was racing. Was this going to be bad news? Was it a request for ransome? Was it something unthinkable? He had difficulty catching his breath, but managed to reply, "Yes, I have a daughter by that name."

"I know where they are. You're daughter is asking for you."

"Who do you mean by 'they'?" The General was beginning to think clearly.

"She is with her friend, Wipha, and a Foreigner named Clifford."

Without saying it audibly, General Manoon was thinking that Foreigner was a dead man if he had hurt Kultida in any way. Not hearing a response, Pwo Swe continued, "The Foreigner is a good man. You may have met him when he testified in court several years ago against those drug dealers who were put in prison"

"Is he a Christian missionary?"

"Yes."

"I do remember him. Where are they."

"They are hiding in the Chiang Mai abbortoir. The Foreigner, whom I have known for many years, is trying to protect your daughter and her friend."

"Who are you?" the General asked.

"My name is Pwo Swe, which is a name of the Karen people. My wife and I are house parents at a student hostel for Hill Tribe children in Chiang Mai started by the Foreigner, Clifford."

The General started to ask more questions, but Pwo Swe urged him to order Police to raid the abbortoir. "Your daughter, her friend and the Foreigner are in great danger. This man, Clifford, told me some of the drug traffickers who escaped jail are after them."

"I will do that," agreed the General. Where can I contact you?"

"I have no phone; best if you contact the Manager of the Siam Commercial Bank in Thailand, he will know where to find me."

"Thanks for your information." The phone line went dead.

By that time, the Bank Manager had appeared and heard what Pwo Swe had said. He sharply questioned Pwo Swe about calling a police general at this time of the night, and even giving the police his name. However, when Pwo Swe explained what Clifford had told him, and about the trip to the abattoir, the Bank Manager agreed he had done the right thing.

General Manoon did not notify the Chiang Mai police about his daughter; he was uncertain who he could trust there. Instead, he called the dispatcher for the police aircraft located at Don Muang Airport, and ordered their fastest plane to take him to Chiang Mai immediately. He called his driver, who slept in the guard house by the front gate, and ordered him to pick him up in five minutes. The General did call the police station in Chiang Mai and ordered a squad of armed police to meet him at the Chiang Mai Airport in two hours. He did not tell them why. General Manoon hurriedly dressed, strapped on his police issue revolver, and left the house. His driver was at the front door. "To the police plane hanger at Don Muang Airport, fast," he ordered, "and turn on the emergency lights and siren." They made it to Don Muang in record time. A plane was waiting on the tarmac with the engine warming up. The airport guards opened the gates for the police car, and the driver parked next to the plane. General Manoon jumped out of his car and climbed into the plane.

Nai Tong thought he was going straight home, but he encountered a major delay. Instead of taking the less used road through Lamphun, he went out of Chiang Mai on one of the major roads that leads to the highway. Just before the highway, a black Mercedes Benz suddenly pulled up alongside him and forced him onto the road shoulder. Before he knew what was going on, a man jumped out of the Benz and put a revolver to Nai Tong's head through the open window. "Turn off your engine and get out," ordered the man. Nai Tong did so; he had been robbed before, but never with someone driving a Mercedes Benz. A well dressed man with a scarf around his face came out of the backseat of the Benz and confronted Nai Tong. "Where are the three people you just brought down from near Mae Chan?" the man asked.

"I didn't bring anyone. I came alone." Nai Tong tried to bluff.

"Listen, you piece of pig turd," hissed Nai Tong's questioner. "We already know about you, Nai Tong, and your red minibus. I'm going to ask you one more time. If I don't get a truthful answer this man here with the gun will start shooting you in the legs and work upwards. Where are those three?"

Nai Tong could see the man's eyes above the scarf. There was no pity there. He knew he had to tell. "I left them at the abortoir," he whispered, and dropped to his knees, hands raised in supplication. "That's the truth."

"Get in this car and lead us there. If you have misled us, you're dead."

Nai Tong was ordered to sit in the front seat with the driver. The two other men got in the back, one with his gun pressing against Nai Tong's neck.

"Which way?" asked the man with the scarf.

Nai Tong directed the driver back the way he had come. Sometimes he directed the driver on side roads that slowed them a little, but they soon arrived at the gate of the abortoir. Someone, perhaps a night watchman, had shut it. "Did they go inside?" the voice in the backseat asked.

"I parked under that tree there, and they got out and walked toward the abattoir . I did not wait, but left immediately. I am *glua pi* (afraid of ghosts).

"Was anyone else with them?"

"No, just those three," Nai Tong lied. He didn't tell about Pwo Swe. "Come with us."

They opened the gate and all walked toward the abattoir; one man kept his gun pointed at Nai Tong. They found an unlocked door and entered. Immediately, they were challenged by a night watchman. "You there, you cannot come in here." One of the other men reached in his pocket for a gun and shot the watchman twice, killing him instantly.

In the dark closet, Clifford and the two women heard the shots. Kultida and Wipha clutched each other and moaned with fear. "Quiet," whispered Clifford, and led them to the rear of the closet behind some cupboards. Unfortunately, Wipha brushed against a bottle, which fell to the floor and broke. The noise alerted the men with the guns, who moved toward the source of the noise. They found the door to the closet, opened it, and peered inside. It was too dark to see anything. The man with the scarf took a flashlight from his pocket..

CHAPTER TWENTY ONE

SAVED

During General Manoon's flight to Chiang Mai he had time to think. Initially, when his daughter and her friend left their hotel in Chiang Mai during the Songkran Festival and disappeared, he had been angry. He was sure they were just traveling around somewhere, but Kultida should have notified him. He had police searching for them. Train departures, and airline flights were checked. Inquiries were made at all hotels in Chiang Mai, and neighboring cities of Lampang and Chiang Rai, but they were not found. General Manoon knew he had enemies; after all he had put a lot of people in jail. He worried that some of those enemies might try to get at him by hurting his daughter. "She might be a big girl," he thought, "but when she shows up she'll get a spanking from me." Now, however, it was fear that gnawed at his heart. What could she be doing hiding at an abattoir? Was it just a trick? What would he find in Chiang Mai, the City of Roses, Kultida's favorite flower? His wife had been dead for several years; his daughter was his life. He couldn't bear the thought of losing her. He knew, if he saw her today, he would hold her close, and tell her how much he loved her.

It was still dark when they arrived at the Chiang Mai Airport, but a squad of armed police in two jeeps were waiting. General Manoon returned the salute of their captain. He was given the front seat in the first jeep, while the captain crawled in the rear seat. "Where do you want to go?" asked the puzzled captain. "To the Chiang Mai aborttoir," ordered the General, "as fast as you can."

Early morning traffic was just picking up. Trucks of produce heading for the markets to stock the stalls of the market vendors were coming into the city from outlying areas. Many of those trucks were overloaded and moved slowly. General Manoon cursed their slowness, and urged the jeep driver to ignore traffic rules and speed up. He did so, even forcing some oncoming vehicles to take the ditch to avoid a collision. Both jeeps sped throught the open abbortoir gates and pulled up alongside the building next to a Mercedes Benz automobile, now just visible in the early dawn.

"Captain," ordered General Manoon, "it is my understanding that three innocent people are hiding in this abbortoir from vicious criminals who mean them harm. I don't know if the criminals have found them yet, or not. Order your men into the building and search it thoroughly. Do all you can to protect the lives of the three who are in hiding."

"Yes sir," replied the captain, who immediately ordered three of his men to cover the outside of the abattoir, while he and the rest of his men entered the building. One of the policemen found a light switch near the door and switched it on. That illuminated the inside of the building, ennabling the police to find the dead body of the night watchman. General Manoon groaned inwardly when he saw the body. He knew dangerous people had either been here, or still were. He took charge of the search. "Search all the rooms, and everyplace where anyone could hide," he ordered.

The police diligently went through the building, finding nothing. "What about that room there?" the General pointed to the cleaning supplies closet. A policeman opened the door, and was immediately fired upon. Severely, wounded, he fell to the floor. General Manoon drew his own weapon and stood outside the door, but to one side, so whoever was inside could not see him. He spoke in a loud voice to whoever was inside, "We are the Police. We are here in a large force and have you surrounded. Drop your weapons and come out. You will be treated humanely."

After a pause, a voice from within answered. "Don't shoot. We are coming out with three hostages. One of them is the daughter of Police General Manoon." It was the man with the scarf who was speaking. He had no idea that General Manoon himself was present, and had just ordered he and his cohorts to surrender. If only he had had a little more time, he could have carried out his asignment to kill the three, and make his getaway. Now he was desperate; his only hope was to use the three as hostages, and maybe he could still escape. He only thought of himself; the other two men were lowlife hired killers. He cared nothing for them, but they still had one use. They would all come out of the closet with their guns jammed up against the backs of their hostages, and force the police to hold their fire while they made it to their car and escaped. It might just work.

They came out, moving slowly. "If you shoot, we'll shoot these hostages," the man with the scarf warned. "Lower your weapons," General Manoon ordered the police. When Kultida saw her father she involuntarily called to him, *Khun Paw, Khun Paw* (Father, Father), broke loose from her captor and ran to him. The man with the scarf swung his revolver toward them, intending to shoot both father and daughter, but a single shot rang out and he staggered and fell. The other two men were momentarily confused by the loss of their leader. Within that moment of opportunity, two more shots reverberated in the cavernous building, and those two also fell, mortally wounded.

Clifford stood there, in a state of shock, holding Ai Seng's revolver, which he had pocketed when Sae Yang was shot dead by Ai Seng back in Doi Maesalong. It had been in his pocket ever since. It was heavy, and he was always aware of its presence, but he never thought he would use it. In fact, he didn't know how to use it, but the safety was off. All he did was point and pull the trigger three times.

It was the police who had shot the other two, now they cautiously entered the closet, but found it empty. Others tended to their wounded companion, who was bleeding profusely, but would survive. Some also had to attend to the Foreigner, who had fainted dead away. When Clifford revived, he saw, kneeling on the concrete floor, father and daughter clasped in a loving embrace. "Its over, its all over," Police General Manoon whispered in his daughter's ear. Wipha was in the arms of the Police Captain, weeping and moaning. The Captain didn't seem to mind at all! Soon, however, a semblance of normality returned. Everyone started to talk at once. Kultida and Wipha found their voices, and praised Clifford for saving their lives. Only Clifford remained speechless. He had been under great pressure, not knowing if he was doing the right thing by hiding in the abbortoir. When the three killers opened the closet door and exposed them in the light of a flashlight, he thought he had failed. It never occurred to him to use his gun at that time. If he had tried it, they all would likely have been shot down. It was only possible when the three killer's attention was diverted.

"Father," General Manoon spoke to Clifford, "can you go with the Captain to the police station to make a statement? I must attend to my daughter and her friend." General Manoon had once attended a Catholic school in Bangkok and called all male Christian ministers and missionaries by the title, "Father." Clifford said he could do that, although his legs were still a bit shaky. "One more thing, Captain," ordered the General, "this Foreigner must be guarded at all times, there may still be people hunting for him."

"Mr. Clifford," the General spoke to Clifford, "I owe you a debt of gratitude. I would like to speak with you at some length concerning the events of the last few days. I'll be in touch." The Captain left some of his men at the abbortoir, radioed for an ambulance, and also for a forensic crew to come and investigate the site where four men were shot dead, and one policeman wounded. After making those arrangements, he took Clifford back to the police station. General Manoon appropriated the Mercedes Benz and, together with Kultida and Wipha, drove to the first class hotel where the women had stayed during the Songkran Festival. There, the two women had long, lingering hot baths, shampood their hair, put on the dressing gowns that were provided in their hotel room closet, and crawled into bed, and slept the deep sleep of young people in a safe environment. General Manoon would not leave the room. He sat by a window watching the city come to life in a new day.

A little later, he called his housekeeper back in Bangkok to tell her he would not be home for a few days, and to ask her what size clothes his daughter wore. "Oh, *Khun Nai,* (boss) is Kultida alright?" The General assured her she, and her friend Wipha, were fine, but that he wanted to surprise her with some new clothes. The housekeeper, a very efficient woman, also found the phone number for Wipha's parents, and gave that number to General Manoon, who called immediately. Her mother answered the phone after the first ring. General Manoon told her that her daughter was fine, but had a long explanation about her absence to tell her parents. "She's sleeping now, but I will have her call you when she wakes up." Wipha's mother wanted details, but the General replied, "It's a long story; best you hear it from her." He also obtained Wipha's clothes size, which brought on a torrent of questions, but the General, a stubborn man, kept to his story; "Best she tells you herself. Just be glad she is alright." Next, the General called the hotel manager and requested that a woman staff member be sent to buy some clothes for his daughter and her friend. He gave the manager the sizes. "Have them sent to our room before noon," he ordered, "and put the cost on my bill." The manager, eager to redeem himself to the high ranking police officer, replied, "I will send someone immediately, and there will be no charge to you, General Manoon."

Captain Manat, of the Chiang Mai Police Division, was a meticulous man. This day he was doubly so, since General Manoon's daughter was involved in this case. It took most of the day for Clifford to complete his statement. Another police officer, acting as a stenographer, filled ten typewritten pages of Clifford's connection with the American Drug Enforcement Administration, and especially, of the last few days beginning in Doi Maesalong and ending at the Chiang Mai Abattoir. Frequent glasses of iced coffee kept him going, but he was totally exhausted when the statement was completed. Clifford had one request, "Please check on the Lahu guide, named Ai Seng, who was left at the clinic in Doi Maesalong." The Captain had just heard Clifford's report of how Ai Seng had saved the General's daughter's life, so he promised to do so. In fact, he immediately ordered a police helicopter, with a doctor, to return to Doi Maesalong, and, if possible, take Ai Seng to Suan Dawk Hospital in Chiang Mai.

"Now, Mr. Clifford," the Captain had also taken to calling Clifford by his first name, "would you like to return to your home?"

"Oh Yes, that's where I want to go."

"Good, I will send you there in a jeep, together with three policemen who will stay with you."

"Do you have to do that?"

"Yes, the General's orders."

So, Clifford returned home in a police jeep with three armed policemen. His landlady, Chintana, was so curious she could hardly wait to find out what happened. The policemen were surprised by the Foreigner's modest home. They had expected a large, foreign type house. Clifford was numb with fatigue. After providing some floor mats for his guardians, he crawled into his own bed. The caffeine contained in many glasses of iced coffee did not keep him awake. He was already sleeping soundly, when Chintana came with a basket of fruit, which was really her excuse to find out what was going on. The policemen, sitting in the shade under the house, questioned her rather closely. "Who are you?" they wanted to know. Chintana was a bit offended. "I'm the house owner," she declared, "and the Foreigner rents it from me. May I ask what you are doing here?"

"We've been ordered to guard him."

"Guard him! What for? He never gets in trouble."

"All we know is some people tried to kill him."

"What people?"

"I think they were drug traffickers. The Foreigner testified against them."

"That was a long time ago."

"Those people have long memories."

That caused Chintana to remember something. "Two men did come here asking for the Foreigner. That was two days ago." The police were interested, so Chintana told all she knew. She related that the men spoke with Bangkok accents, and seemed to know about her Foreign tenant. She told them he was gone, and did not know when he was returning, so they left. The police thanked her for the information, and told her to let them know if those two, or anyone, came asking for her tenant.

"I came over to bring him some fruit." Chintana wanted to see Clifford.

"He's very tired, and is sleeping now. We'll see he gets it."

Reluctantly, Chintana returned to her own house. The policemen enjoyed the fruit.

General Manoon had asked that a copy of Clifford's statement to the police be sent to him as soon as it was completed. It had arrived, and the General read it while Kultida and Wipha were still sleeping. He was thankful that his daughter and friends had been spared, but also sorrowful that Kultida would not be able to travel freely wherever she wanted to go. "Maybe I chose the wrong occupation," he said to himself, "I don't think my friend, the Admiral, has these kind of problems." At the same time, the General thought of the drug traffickers he had put away for long sentences. "Maybe it's worth it," he murmered.

The sound of her father's voice awakened Kultida. "Oh, that was a lovely sleep," she exclaimed.

"You've slept the whole day away," teased her father. "I'm getting hungry."

"We don't have any clothes to wear," wailed Kultida, "We'll have to order room service."

"You're right about your old clothes; phew! I threw them away already. Look in that closet."

In the closet Kultida saw four complete outfits; two for her and two for Wipha. They weren't exactly what she would have bought, but her father was a dear to think about them.

"Wipha, get up. We've got new clothes," she called. "We're going out to eat, so let's take another bath. This time we'll use the bath salts we found in the bathroom."

"You just had a bath," complained the General.

"Popsie," Kultida had borrowed some English words while living abroad, "do you know how long we went without a bath, and the kind of places where we hid out?"

"Yes, I do. I read all about it. Go take your bath."

Wipha whispered something to Kultida, who giggled and said to her father, "Wipha would like that police captain to join us for dinner."

"If you don't take your bath, we'll never get out of this room."

General Manoon was thrilled to see how Kultida and her friend had rebounded. Early this morning they were two dirty, exhausted, bedraggled and fearful young ladies. "Wipha," the General remembered, "you must call your parents right now." She did so, sounding like her old self, much to the relief of her mother and father. When General Manoon was able to get the phone, he called the police captain to join them for dinner at the Empress Room in their hotel at 7:00 P.M. "Bring that Foreigner, Father Clifford, with you too." he ordered.

Clifford was still sound asleep when Captain Manat came to pick him up. The Captain greeted the three guards, and walked into Clifford's bedroom, "Father Clifford," he shouted. "Time to get up. We have been invited to eat with General Manoon at the most first class hotel in Chiang Mai."

"I'm tired," mumbled Clifford.

"You cannot be too tired to refuse the General's invitation. It's a great honor; all my friends at the Station are envious of me."

Clifford managed to swing his feet out of his bed. "How should I dress?"

"In your best suit of course, but may I suggest that you take a bath and shave first," the Captain wrinkled his nose.

Clifford looked at the Captain, who was wearing a new khaki police uniform with tailored shirt and crisply ironed trousers. His aftershave lotion almost overwhelmed Clifford's body oder. "Alright I'm coming; just give me 15 minutes."

While Clifford was showering, shaving and getting dressed in his only suit, Captain Manat talked with the three guards, who informed him of what they had learned from the Foreigner's landlady. In addition, one of the policemen had enquired in the neighborhood, and found that the compound where Clifford lived had recently been under observation by men who were not locals.

At the hotel, Clifford and Captain Manat were shown to a private dining room where the General, his daughter, and Wipha were already seated. The setting was elegant. There was a brightly lit chandelier over the round table, which illuminated the sparkling crystal, ornate dishes and shining silver. The polished teakwood table, large enough for ten, was set for five, which gave adequate room for the large plates, salad dishes, bread dishes, water goblets, wine glasses, and an array of silver utensils that confused Clifford, who had never dined in such an elegant place. The three who were seated rose, and there were greetings all around. The General proposed a toast to Clifford for his brave and astute behaviour in saving the lives of Kultida and Wipha. Clifford was embarrassed by the honor and blushed, as he usually did in such situations. Somehow, in the confusion of seating, Wipha ended up sitting next to Captain Manat. Kultida had been waiting to ask a question, "Captain, what about our guide, Ai Seng, who we left badly wounded at Doi Maesalong?"

"Oh yes, Captain, he saved our lives too," added Wipha.

"I have ordered a Police helicopter with a doctor to go to Doi Maesalong early tomorrow morning to check on him," replied the Captain in a reassuring voice, "If he can be moved, he will be returned to Suan Dawk Hospital here in Chiang Mai."

"Oh, thank you Captain," Wipha smiled, "You are so efficient."

The dinner was a great success. Clifford was going to order the cheapest item on the menu, but urged on by General Manoon, he ordered a rack of New Zealand lamb. He seldom ate Western food, because it was more expensive, so enjoyed the roast lamb immensely. Kultida and Wipha told, and retold, their experiences, beginning with the Songkran Festival in Chiang Mai, sneaking away to Chiang Rai, and going on the guided tour to Doi Maesalong. Kultida told her father about the Akha people, who fed and housed them, even at great danger to themselves. She told about being given Akha clothes to wear, and being escorted by an armed guard of Akha men back down from the highlands to the house of an Akha woman named Mee Bu who could speak Thai and obtained transportation for them to flee to Chiang Mai.

"Don't be angry with me, Father," she pleaded, "I know Wipha and I did some stupid things, but we also had a great experience. We were strangers, but Ai Seng, our Lahu Guide, and the Akha people all risked their lives to help us. I will always be grateful to them."

"And so will I," replied General Manoon. He was a tough, no-nonsense cop, but he had a catch in his voice that betrayed his feelings.

Captain Manat told the General about the strangers who had been asking about Clifford. That news concerned the General very much. As the party was breaking up, he took Clifford aside and spoke seriously to him. Clifford had explained to the General that he was not a Catholic priest, and should not be addressed as Father. "Mr. Clifford," began the General, "I am sorry that bad people are looking for you. We didn't get them all, so now we must take precautions. My daughter will not be able to travel around so freely, and you will not be able to live here in Chiang Mai as you have done."

Clifford was astounded, "What can I do; Chiang Mai is now my home."

"Yes, I know, but if you stay here those people will kill you. You are a marked man because you testified against those drug traffickers years ago. The police guard at your house cannot stay long."

Clifford looked so crestfallen that General Manoon felt sorry for him. He was also grateful to him for looking after his daughter. "Never mind," the General said, "You can stay with me. I have a guest cottage in the rear of my compound; its yours for as long as you want it. My place is heavily guarded; you will be safe there."

"I'll think about it," replied Clifford. He was grateful for the magnanimous gesture, but did not think he would accept the General's offer. He was accustomed to roaming freely in the hills, and coming and going freely from his little house.

"Don't wait too long," urged the General. "I would like your answer by tomorrow."

The following day was Sunday, and Clifford spent most of the day at the Bank Manager's house. In spite of his protests, two of his police guards went with him. One stayed at his house. After the house church service, Clifford talked with the Manager and Pwo Swe at length. He told them of his involvement with the United States Drug Enforcemernt Administration, and of the events of the last few days. He left out nothing, including Gerneral Manoon's conviction that it would not be safe for Clifford to live in Chiang Mai, and continue his present way of life. He told them of the General's kind offer. "Now," Clifford looked at the two men, "You have been my mentor and my teacher. At this time I want your honest opinion. What should I do?"

The faces of both men reflected the pain within them. They had come to love Clifford and did not want him to leave, but they were also realists who knew the General spoke the truth. The Bank Manager spoke first, "For your own sake, it would be best if you accepted General Manoon's hospitality. Perhaps some day it would be possible for you to return to Chiang Mai." Pwo Swe nodded his head in agreement.

Clifford sadly returned to his Toyota pickup, and with his two escorts, returned home.

On the way home, however, he took a detour, and went to Nai Lee's shop in the market area. Sunday was no holiday for Nai Lee and his wife. Their little shop was open 12 hours a day, seven days a week. The only time it closed was for three days during Chinese New Year. They had aged since Clifford had first met them, and helped Clifford meet the Tribal people, who came to sell their forest products and chili peppers. Nai Lee was in front of the shop packing dried chilis in baskets when Clifford arrived. He greeted Clifford, but noticed the two policemen. "So, the police finally caught you," remarked Nai Lee.

"What do you mean?"

"I mean all those illegal things you have been doing in Thailand."

"I never do anything bad," replied Clifford, who knew his old friend was teasing him.

"That's it! I'm glad you have confessed."

"Confessed to what?"

"For living in Thailand and managing to stay away from both women and whisky."

"Is that illegal?"

"Some think so. Now, come into my old shop and my old woman will give you a cup of tea." Nai Lee's wife was wearing wide trousers made from shiny black material and a sleeveless white blouse. Her gray hair was tied in a knot and fastened to the back of her head with a comb. She greeted Clifford, and spoke Chinese to her husband in a disapproving tone of voice. "You see," exclaimed Nai Lee; "You have just arrived but she is aready taking your part and scolding me. That must be illegal."

"I can see your wife if very intelligent," Clifford said with a grin, "but there is one think I don't understand."

"What's that?"

"How come she married you?"

Nai Lee roared with laughter. "Is that why you came here, to insult me?"

"No, I have come to say goodby. I am moving to Bangkok."

Nai Lee's wife almost dropped the cup of tea she was serving, and they both looked at Clifford in surprise. Clifford did not want to explain everything, so he just said he had testified against some drug dealers years ago. Retribution had been slow in coming, but now there had been attempts on his life and he could not live here anymore.

"Ah, there are evil people in the world," murmered Nai Lee. "My woman and I have spent our life in this shop. We have raised seven children and sent them all to universities. Now we have grandchildren who will not have to labor as we have. We are satisfied with our lives, but some people are not satisfied with what they have. They want to get rich quick, and are willing to do evil things."

"Well, that's the way it is. Maybe I'll be able to return some day."

"Don't wait too long. We are getting old."

The two policemen had remained in the Toyota, curious about a Foreigner who stopped to talk to two old Chinese people in a run-down storefront shop. Clifford joined them and drove on home.

The guard who had remained in Clifford's house had a message for Clifford. General Manoon wanted to see him at his hotel room. That news really impressed the policemen, who looked at Clifford with new respect.

Clifford, with his two guards, immediately returned to the General's hotel. Police Captain Manat was there, and he had good news. "The Lahu man, Ai Seng, had received good care at the Doi Maesalong Clinic, and has been brought to Chiang Mai where he is now at Suan Dawk Hospital. He is weak, but will recover."

General Manoon added, "I have given orders that he be given the best of care, and the Police Department will pay for his medical expenses."

"Captain Manat arranged for him to be brought back to Chiang Mai," said Wipha, with an adoring glance at the Captain.

"That is very good news," replied Clifford, with a sense of relief. "I have been praying for him."

"Mr. Clifford," asked the General, "Have you considered my offer?"

"Yes, General Manoon, I have," replied Clifford. "I appreciate your offer very much, and I will try to live in Bangkok. Perhaps I can find something to do."

"Good, and I know of things you can do for the Police Department, but we'll talk about that later."

"When should I move?"

"The sooner the better. My guest house is ready for you. How about three days?"

"So soon?"

"Yes, your three police guards can deliver you to the airport and you can take a Thai Airways Flight to Bangkok. You will be met and transported to my house."

CHAPTER TWENTY TWO

LIFE IN A GILDED CAGE

And so it was. Clifford had three days to sell his Toyota pickup and a few other items. Some furniture and pots and pans he gave to the Student Hostel. He said goodby to some old friends, including Nai Prasong at the Prison Shop, and Ai Tia, the pickup driver, who made deliveries around town and had helped him rescue Mi Ja. That young lady was now the proud owner of a noodle shop, and was sending her two younger siblings to the Teacher's Training College. He stopped by her shop to tell her the news. She cried, and begged him to return some day.

Clifford had received his Alien Registration from the Immigration Department, so before moving he had to sign out at the Municipality Building and at the Police Station. Two guards were always with him, which made Clifford rather self-conscious. All of this took five days, but eventually he had to leave.

He didn't know how the word got around, but many people were at the Chiang Mai Airport to see him off. It was a Saturday afternoon, so the children from the Student Hostel were all there in their school uniforms. They formed a choir and sang several songs. An English rendition of "God Be With You 'Till We Meet Again," brought tears to Clifford's eyes. Naw Wa Paw and her husband from the Karen Village were there, and gave him a Karen woven shoulder bag. Even Pa Chintana, usually suspicious of her tenants, was weeping as she pressed a bag of mangos into Clifford's arms, as if such fruit was not available in Bangkok. The Bank Manager placed a *dawk pumalai* (flower garland) around Clifford's neck, and assured Clifford that he would help look after the Student Hostel. A Thai Airways flight attendant, in her blue and purple outfit, had to call Clifford twice, before he left his friends, and, with a heavy heart, boarded the plane.

Clifford had a window seat, and after takeoff looked down on the mountains he had so recently been traversing by foot. He spotted several Hill Tribe villages, located on ridge top clearings. He prayed that he would be able to return, but if not, gave thanks to God for the opportunity that had been his to meet so many wonderful people.

At Dawn Muang Airport in Bangkok he was met by more police, who escorted him to a Mercedes Benze with tinted windows. Still clutching his mangos in an old paper bag, he was taken to the compound of Police General Manoon on a *soi* (side street) off of Sukumvit Road. The General was at work, but Kultida, together with a housekeeper, showed him to his new quarters, a guest house behind the General's house. Kultida spoke of it as "only a little guest house," but never had Clifford lived in such a luxurious place. It was built of teakwood, oiled with a wood preservative on the outside. Antique furnishings and cupboards of polished teak enhanced the parquet floor and silk drapes of the interior. The living room, dining room and bedroom all had ceiling fans. "If you prefer," said Kultida, "the bedroom has an air conditioner, but most Thai people prefer not to use it. Suit yourself."

"I am not accustomed to air conditioning either," replied Clifford.

"My father would like you to join us for dinner tonight at about 7:00, but come over anytime you want. Perhaps you would like to rest now."

The housekeeper had opened Clifford's two battered suitcases and hung his meager collection of clothes in the closet, which could have contained 10 times as much clothes. She showed him a hamper, and speaking in fractured English, told Clifford he could leave his dirty laundry there and it would be washed each day by the cleaning lady. She was surprised when Clifford spoke to her in fluent Thai. Clifford noticed something about her accent, and asked about her regional origin. "Are you from Isan District?" He ventured.

Surprised, she replied, "Yes I am; have you lived there?"

"No, but I'm interested in languages, so I picked up a bit of Isan. Also, I once met an Isan man who was a driver for an American government official."

"Where did you meet him?"

"In Chiang Mai."

"Do you remember his name?"

"Yes, it was Montri."

"That's amazing! I know a Montri from my village who had been a driver for Americans for many years. Must be the same one."

"Could be. I know the Isan District is in northeast Thailand, but I have met Isan people all over Thailand."

"Yes, that's true. Our land is not very good, and the rains often fail, so we must look for work elsewhere. There are many villages in Isan where only old people and children live. Many of our people are wage earners all over Thailand, so the old people stay home and care for their grandchildren."

Without even trying, Clifford made a conquest. From then on, Wattana, the house maid, took special care of Clifford. Even bringing him occasional snacks of *som tam* made by an Isan woman who had a little food stall on the street near the General's house. *Som Tam* is a Thai salad made from slivered green papaya, shallots, tiny dried shrimp, crushed peanuts, lime juice, and the fiery little chilies, known as *prik khi nu* (mouse droppings peppers.

That first evening, however, he ate with the General and Kultida in their large, two-story house. It also was filled with teak furniture. The General preferred rather austere surroundings, but his deceased wife and Kultida had added silk drapes and fired pottery from kilns in northern Thailand. The dining room floor of smooth marble blocks felt cool to Clifford's feet. His threadbare socks provided little protection. He learned to wear heavy socks when dining with the General. The dining room table was amazing; made from one slab of teak wood. Clifford knew that had to be an old table, as there were no more teak trees that large.

A maid served rice and chicken curry, with side dishes of raw vegetables. The General assured Clifford that the curry was made from native Thai chickens, not those broilers, with their soft meat, imported from the United States. The base for the curry was coconut cream and the cook's secret curry sauce. It was spicey hot, but Clifford could manage that with no problem. For dessert a large bowl of Thai fruit was placed on the table, containing mangos, bananas, mangosteen, rambutan, putsa and langsaat. The General told Clifford an old Thai fairy tale about rambutan, called *ngaw* in Thai. It is of red color, hairy on the outside, and not very attractive, but the fruit inside is delicious. The story was about a king who announced that whoever won a contest of strength and skill could marry his daughter, a beautiful princess. The contest was won by an ugly, hairy man. When he came to claim his bride, the princess did not refuse him, but declared her loyalty to him. At that moment, the ugly outer skin and hair of that man fell off, and a handsome prince was revealed, and, of course, they lived happily together ever after. "You see, Kultida," he addressed his daughter, "filial piety and obedience has its rewards." Kultida wrinkled her nose at her father.

As they ate the fruit, General Manoon talked to Clifford about what he might do to put his time to good advantage. "I realize time may go slowly for you confined to this compound, so I have a suggestion." The General went on to explain that his drug supression department often conducted wire taps on people they suspected of drug dealing. Some of the conversations they recorded were in English. "We have police translators," he explained, "but they only know proper English. They are confused by idioms and slang. Would you mind listening to those tapes and making translations for us?"

Clifford had no reason to refuse, so agreed to give it a try. Later that evening, back in his quarters, Clifford began to really confront the reality of his position. "I'm living in a gilded cage on someone's charity," he reasoned, "with nothing to do but help the Thai Police. That was not why I came to Thailand." Actually, he did have other things to do. He started writing a Thai-Karen dictionary. Kultida was of great assistance with the Thai words. He also continued to perfect his conversational ability in the Isan dialect by conversing with Wattana.

The translation of English language wire taps proved to be an interesting experience. He knew the meaning of most of the slang words, even if he never used them. Clifford was amazed by the number of English speaking people who were involved in drug trafficking. Most were for small amounts that an individual could carry back to their home country concealed on, or in, their bodies. Women had a convenient cavity. Both men and women often swallowed heroin packaged in condoms. Sometimes, the condoms broke open in the stomachs of the "mules", as the carriers were called, resulting in death. Many of those "mules" were Africans from English speaking countries, who came from impoverished families. What really caught Clifford's attention, however, was one conversation that apparently involved him. It was between a Thai man, speaking poor English, and an American, whose English consisted largely of swear words and crude expressions. The American owed a large drug debt to the Thai man, who was willing to forgive the debt if the American, named Tony, did a job for him. All the American had to do was kill an American missionary living in Chiang Mai who had become bothersome. "Sure, I'll do it," replied the American, "Just give me the details of where this guy lives." That's when Clifford finally realized he was not going back to Chiang Mai. Indeed, he could not live, unprotected, anywhere in Thailand.

General Manoon tried to make Clifford happy. He arranged for a generous salary to be paid to Clifford for his work with the wire taps. He allowed Clifford to use his telephone, and Clifford occasionally called the Bank Manager, now retired, in Chiang Mai, to check on the Student Hostel. There were never any problems at the Hostel, or, at least, none that the Bank Manager revealed. Clifford felt like he had nothing to do of any importance. He loved the freedom of trekking through the mountains of northern Thailand. He loved the people he met there, and missed them terribly. He rose early every day, and in the morning coolness walked around and around the compound trying to decide what to do. Clifford had not had a happy childhood. Only in his adopted country of Thailand had he felt a sense of self worth. Here he could do things; learn languages, relate to people, and enable Tribal children to attend school. In truth, he feared returning to his homeland.

Clifford devoted himself to completing the Thai-Karen dictionary. He had already obtained an English-Karen dictionary done by Baptist missionaries in Burma. Kultida possessed an excellent Thai-English dictionary, so they collaborated on this new project. General Manoon was glad to see his daughter absorbed in work that kept her safely at home. As the dictionary neared completion, the General, a man of some intellect, realized it was something that would be useful to his country. The Karen population was the largest of the Tribal groups in Thailand. Also, Karens in Burma were in insurrection against the Burmese government, and that conflict often spilled across the border. The General was among the few who realized that better communication was needed with this ethnic group, and that a Thai-Karen dictionary would be useful to military, local government officials, police, Health Department, and Education officials.

It took nearly a year, but when the dictionary was completed Clifford had come to a decision about his future. First, he saw to the printing and distribution of the Thai-Karen dictionary. Actually, General Manoon did most of that. One evening, after dinner with the General and his daughter, Clifford revealed his future plans. "I owe you a debt of gratitude," he explained, "but I cannot live here any longer. I am very comfortable living with you, but it is too confining for me. I have decided to return to my own country."

Both the General and Kultida urged him to stay, but Clifford was adamant. "I must go," he argued, "I hardly know my own country anymore." That was true; Clifford had lived in Thailand for 30 years without ever returning to his homeland. Stipends from the Asian Inland Mission had been reduced to a trickle. He was almost forgotten. A new generation of staff at the home office of the AIM had never seen Clifford. However, Clifford's economic situation had never been better. His regular stipends from the Drug Enforcement Administration, plus several large bonuses, had left him with adequate funds to retire. Since moving to Bangkok his Police Department salary had added to his retirement fund. The retired Bank Manager of the Chiang Mai Branch of the Siam Commercial Bank had been wisely investing Clifford's money in certificates of deposit, which yielded at least 9% interest. Money wise, Clifford was not hurting.

"But where will you go? Do you have any family?" Kultida asked. Thai people could hardly imagine anyone without family or relatives.

"No, there is no one," Clifford replied, "but I have read about a retirement community in Ashmore, California that sounds like a good place for me. I have been in correspondence with them, and they have a small house available for me."

Kultida was quite upset when she thought about Clifford leaving their home and going to a place where only elderly people lived, and none of them were relatives, or even friends. "That is a common American practice," Clifford assured her. "I can live there for the rest of my life, and if I become incapacitated they will care for me."

"Where is Ashmore?" she wanted to know.

"Its in Southern California, near the city of Los Angeles."

That information reassured Kultida somewhat. "Oh, I know about LA; many Thai people live there, and there is even a Thai Town. I will ask some of my old friends to visit you."

Clifford, with help from General Manoon, arranged for his departure. First, with help from the Assistant Chief Executive Officer at the Palm Gardens Retirement Community in Ashmore, Clifford located a bank and made a small deposit to establish an account. The retired Bank Manager in Chiang Mai, who had power of attorney for Clifford, forwarded all Clifford's funds to that account. Clifford booked a flight from Bangkok to Los Angeles over the phone, and General Manoon sent one of his men to pick up the tickets. Clifford tried to pay the General for the cost of the tickets, but the General would not accept his money. "You saved the life of my daughter; I am indebted to you.." Clifford's American passport had been renewed when he still lived in Chiang Mai, but he did need to sign out of Thailand at the Immigration Department and a nearby Police Station. The General provided a car with guards, and a letter to the officials at both places. The letter worked wonders; Clifford was treated like a VIP, and completed the formalities in record time.

Clifford departed Thailand on a night flight. Before leaving the house, Wattana, the maid, presented Clifford with a package containing *nua sawaan,* which are thin sheets of dried beef that has been marinated in soy sauce, sugar, chili peppers, and other spices, before drying over a fire; a typical Isan snack. General Manoon, Kultida and Wipha went to the airport to see him off. The General informed Clifford about some good news he had just heard from Chiang Mai, concerning the

Lahu guide, Ai Seng. Ai Seng had been out of the hospital for several months, but was not well enough to return to work. However, he had now returned to Chiang Rai and was busy guiding tourists once again. He had been warned about the possibility of danger to his life, but insisted he could take care of himself. He did, however, avoid Doi Maesalong.

Wipha, at Kultida's insistence, told of her own news. "Captain Manat came to my parent's home here in Bangkok, and we had a *mun wai* (engagement ceremony). We plan to marry in about six months."

CHAPTER TWENTY THREE

HOME TO DISASTER

During the long flight to his homeland, Clifford thought about the last 30 years of his life. They had been good years, but he also felt conflicted about what he had accomplished. "I came to Thailand to share my faith in God," thought Clifford, "but have I done that?" That question nagged him until he fell asleep. He slept through two movies, awakened briefly to eat two meals, and slept some more. He arrived at the Los Angeles Airport more refreshed than most of his fellow travelers.

Clifford may have lived abroad for 30 years, but he was not a seasoned traveler. By the time he located the correct luggage carousel, his two battered suitcases had been unloaded and placed on the floor next to the carousel. At an information booth he was advised to take a shuttle bus to the Palm Gardens Retirement Community in Ashmore. There were other passengers in the bus, who disembarked at various places along the way, so it took nearly two hours to reach Ashmore. By that time, he was the last person on the shuttle bus. Clifford was amazed by the traffic, which never ceased, and by how extensive the urban area was. He expected to reach the end of Los Angeles and see open country before reaching Ashmore. That never happened; there were houses all the way.

The bus entered Palm Gardens through a gate with bouganvillia vines growing alongside. That had been his favorite flower in Thailand, and their presence was reassuring. "You people living here sure travel a lot, which house is yours?" asked the driver.

"I'm just arriving for the first time," replied Clifford.

"In that case, I'll take you to the Administration Building. Good thing I know my way around this place."

At the Administration Building, a middle aged woman, named Miss Karinski, greeted Clifford and took him to his new home. "This is one of our smaller units," she explained. "I believe you did request such a place."

"Yes, I did. This is fine." Clifford noted the house had more floor space than the one he had rented in Chiang Mai. Not being elevated off the ground, of course, there was no shady area under the house to park a car, or sit and read. Clifford decided that was probably not done in California anyway. After signing a few papers, and being advised of the location of the dining hall, Clifford became an official resident of Palm Gardens.

The house was only partially furnished, but Miss Karinski informed Clifford that second-hand furniture and household items could be purchased very inexpensively at a storeroom filled with items donated by fellow residents who had downsized when they moved into smaller assisted living facilities. Clifford did not need much, and what he needed was found at the used furnishings place.

Clifford, shy by nature, was not accustomed to socializing with so many people of his own nationality and language. He was always polite with fellow residents when they spoke to him, but was quite content to live his own life without much interaction with others. He was accustomed to trekking in the hills of northern Thailand, so started taking long walks in the mountains near Ashmore. He made lists of the plants and birds he saw, most of which were new to him, and developed a nodding relationship with other solitary trekkers. He slept better after a late night walk, so got in the habit of regularly walking around the grounds of Palm Gardens between 9:00 and 10:00 at night. One night Clifford was walking through Pratt Garden when he heard a sound behind him. He turned to see the hooded figure of a man approaching him with a club in his hand. "Who is this?" thought Clifford. That was the last thought Clifford ever had.

Captain Gallager was stymied. The murder of this man, Mr. Johnson, just didn't make any sense. First, there had never been any violence reported from Palm Gardens. The residents, mostly retired ministers and missionaries, were not the type to go around bashing people over the head with blunt instruments. A blunt instrument, by the way, that had never been found. Anyway, the murder victim was a new resident who couldn't possibly have made such a violent enemy in the few weeks he had resided at the retirement community. Besides, the victim had not been robbed. His billfold, containing a few dollars, was still in the dead man's pocket when he was discovered. Marvin Schuster, the resident who had made the gruesome discovery, checked out. He was a retired minister who had pastored a few parishes in the Midwest. Captain Gallager contacted police departments in those towns, and discovered that the Reverend Marvin Schuster had never been in trouble with the law. In fact, he was a peace advocate, and had been well liked in every community he had served as a Methodist minister.

Records at the Palm Gardens administration office, concerning Mr. Johnson, were sparse. He had served as a missionary in Thailand under the auspices of the Asian Inland Mission. He had only contacted Palm Gardens two months before arrival. He had paid his entrance fee and first month's rent with a check from a local bank. Armed with a court order, Captain Gallager had obtained Clifford's bank records. There was nothing unusual. He had a checking account, and an interest bearing savings account, totaling $302,500. Those funds had been forwarded from a bank in Thailand. Palm Gardens reported that Mr. Johnson had no known heirs or relatives, but they did provide an address and telephone number for the Asian Inland Mission.

Captain Gallager contacted the Asian Inland Mission, and had a rather unsatisfactory telephone conversation with the Managing Director, who, at first, insisted they had no missionary named Clifford Johnson. However, when Gallager mentioned he had been murdered, leaving a bank balance of more than $300,000, the Director became much more interested. "Just a moment please, I'm asking my secretary to recheck our list of active missionaries."

"Yes, please do that."

After a pause, the Director again spoke, "I'm sorry to keep you waiting. Yes, we do have a missionary listed with that name, however we are mainly an agency to transfer funds to our missionaries. The missionary is responsible for finding his, or her, funding, and we have not forwarded any funds to Mr. Johnson for several months."

"I see; and where did Mr. Johnson perform his missionary service?"

"Thailand."

"Would you please send me whatever information you have about Mr. Johnson, such as when he arrived in Thailand, where he lived, and names of people who knew him there?"

"We will do that, but what about his money? That is a substantial amount, and must consist of funds we have sent to him over the years. It should be returned to us."

"You may submit a claim if you wish. Send it together with the information I have asked for."

That conversation left two people puzzled. Inspector Gallager was somewhat surprised that a missionary who had spent his career in Thailand would have that much in liquid assets. The Director of AIM was very surprised when, upon his request, his financial officer revealed the amount of money that had been sent to Mr. Johnson over the last 30 years. They didn't know how anyone could survive on such a paucity of funds, even a single person living in a developing country. "What did he do, live in a cave and eat grass?" remarked the Managing Director of AIM.

Inspector Gallager had been assigned the Johnson Case. He was known to be a thorough investigator, but soon became frustrated with a lack of progress. One night, after his regular hours, he shut himself up in his office and reviewed all he had learned about Mr. Johnson. The murder victim's brief stay in the United States at Palm Gardens revealed nothing. "Perhas the solution to this case is to be found in Thailand," he mused, "and nothing is known about his life there." If it was possible, Gallager would have pursued the case to Thailand, but Ashmore's Police Department did not have that kind of budget.

This case intrigued him, partly because he had a personal interest in Palm Gardens. His mother was a resident in the Palm Gardens Health Center, which did receive people from the community, even if they had not been ministers or missionares. Captain Gallager would have preferred to care for his aged mother in his own home, but he was a widower and had long working hours. That just wasn't possible. He was very pleased by the loving care his mother received at Palm Gardens, and was disturbed by the thought of a murderer at loose on the grounds of that institution.

Once more, Gallager looked through the contents of Mr. Johnson's desk that had been collected and placed in an evidence envelope. This time he noticed a name card that he had previously ignored. He had ignored it because the words on the side he had looked at were written in a foreign language that was unintelligible to him. This time, he noticed there were also words in English on the other side.

POLICE GENERAL MANOON SRIPANLUANG
ROYAL THAI POLICE DEPARTMENT
NARCOTICS SUPPRESSION DIVISION

An address and a telephone number were included. This information answered no questions; it only raised more questions, but it intrigued Captain Gallager very much. He felt some kinship with this man in a distant country who had the same profession. Why was his name card in the possession of an American missionary who had returned to his homeland with very few possessions?

Gallager had a hunch this high ranking police officer could provide some useful information that would help him solve this case. But how to contact this General? One doesn't just pick up the phone and call a Police General halfway around the world. The Thai Embassy; of course; that was the way to go. Captain Gallager was a small town cop, but he did not have a small time brain. Just because he had never had the occasion to interact with police in a foreign country, did not mean he would not do so. So, he sat down and called the Thai Embassy in Wahington, D.C.

A woman, who spoke excellent English with a slight accent, took Gallager's call, and listened, with some impatience, to Gallager's explanation about a murder in a small town near Los Angeles that might have a Thai connection, and perhaps a Thai Police General could provide some useful information. Finally, she interrupted, "Captain Gallager, may I suggest that you contact the Thai Consulate in Los Angeles. I believe they may be able to help you." She provided an address and telephone number. Gallager felt a bit foolish; he was not aware that there was a Thai Consulate in Los Angeles. He gave his thanks, and hung up.

"Well, at least I learned something," muttered Gallager as he dialed the Los Angeles number. Again, a woman's voice. Again, Gallager explained the reason for his call. This time the woman he was talking to forwarded his call to Vice Consul Pricha, and Gallager repeated why the Ashland, California Police Department would like to contact a Thai Police General, named Manoon Sripanluang. Vice Consul Pricha was not about to offer any information over the phone, but suggested they make an appointment. "Would it be possible for you to come to my office next week?" asked the Vice Consul, "and bring that name card you mentioned with you." Gallager agreed, and an appointment was made.

The Thai Consulate was located in a section of Los Angeles known as Thai Town. Gallager found the building and parked on the street nearby. There were many shops, and restaurants, all with names written in a language Gallager assumed was Thai. He looked at the Police General's name card, and yes, it was written with the same kind of letters. There were two signs over the door of the Consulate, one in English, and one using those same exotic letters. The inside lobby was decorated by color posters and photos of scenes from Thailand. Captain Gallager was escorted to the office of Vice Consul Pricha. Gallager introduced himself, and although he was dressed in his police uniform, he showed his official I.D. to the Consul, showing that he was, indeed, a legitimate police officer.

They talked briefly about the traffic situation in Los Angeles, and the Consul spoke into his intercom ordering two cups of coffee. The coffee was brought in by a young woman dressed in a long skirt and matching blouse with long sleeves. Gallager noticed the beauty of the young lady, but failed to appreciate the fact that her clothing was made from elegant Thai silk. He had never noticed what his wife had worn either, much to her irritation. The young lady departed, and the Consul brought up the business at hand.

"May I see the name card you mentioned over the phone?" Gallager fished in his pocket for the card, and handed it to the Conul, who studied both sides of the card.

"Where was this card found?" the Consul wanted to know.

Gallager explained it was found in a desk drawer in the residence of the man who was murdered. He went on to explain that the deceased, Clifford Johnson, had been a missionary in Thailand who had only recently returned from that country. Very little was known about him.

"Well," continued the Consul, "there is a Police General in Thailand named Manoon Sripanluang who is in charge of drug suppression. Do you know if this man who was killed had anything to do with Thai police?"

"Not that I know of," replied Gallager, "we know little about this man."

"I could go through Foreign Ministry channels and contact General Manoon. We can inform him of the death of this man and your investigation. Would you like me to do that?"

"I would like that very much," replied Gallager. "Please contact me immediately if you find out anything."

"I will certainly do that."

Captain Gallager returned to his office, and was pleased to see an envelope from the Asian Inland Mission had arrived with his mail. The contents of the envelope, however, were disappointing. It consisted mostly of stipends sent to Clifford Johnson over the last 30 years. There was a note stating that he had no living relatives, and that his primary place of residence in Thailand had been in the city of Chiang Mai. Gallager noted that the stipends, while never large, had decreased greatly during the last few years of Mr. Johnson's residence in Thailand. "Perhaps he had another source of income," thought Gallager, "he could not have survived on such small amounts." There was also a separate letter on AIM stationary requesting that any money owned by Mr. Johnson at the time of his death be returned to AIM.

That same day, Kenneth Faust, the Chief Executive Officer of Palm

Gardens, came to see Captain Gallager and brought a hand written will that Mr. Johnsons had left at the Administration Office. Mr. Faust was very apologetic. "I'm sorry this was not found sooner; a new employee had misfiled it." It was a simple will, written by someone, obviously Mr. Johnson, who did not know proper legal language. The will directed that any money owned by himself (Clifford Johnson) at the time of his death be sent to the Tribal Student Hostel in Chiang Mai, Thailand, in care of Khru Praphan, retired bank manager of the Siam Commercial Bank in that city. Three witnesses had signed the will; one was the new employee who had misfiled it. The other two were Palm Garden residents.

"Thank you for bringing this to me," said Captain Gallager, "it may be of help in my investigation"

"Do you have any leads?" asked Mr. Faust, "The residents of Palm Gardens are very concerned about this murder."

"Well, its still early in the investigation."

"Yes, of course, but please let me know if I can be of any help."

"You might check your files."

"We did. There is nothing more. I'm sorry this will was overlooked. Is it a legal document?"

"That will probably be for lawyers to decide. The Asian Inland Mission may contest it."

Captain Gallager was discouraged. Two weeks had passed since the murder, and he was getting nowhere. His chief would have already pulled him off the case, except for the fact that Palm Gardens was a well established and historical institution in the city of Ashmore. Some City Council members had family ties to Palm Gardens, and they really wanted this case to be solved. That's why Gallager was glad to receive a call from Vice Consul Pricha. The Vice Consul had been reluctant to even try to contact General Manoon. He had had his fingers burned before. Thai police generals did not like anyone delving into their private lives. The Vice Consul had been very diplomatic. His letter to the General, sent by diplomatic pouch, mentioned the American police investigation of a local murder of a man named Clifford Johnson that might have a Thai connection. He also included some newspaper clippings concerning the murder that he had received from Captain Gallager. If the General wanted to respond, he could, but, if not, the Thai Consulate in Los Angeles would inform the American police of their inability to find any connection between the deceased and the Thai Police Department.

Vice Consul Pricha had been surprised to receive a telephone call direct from General Manoon, and he immediately called Captain Gallager to share what he had learned. The Vice Consul related that General Manoon was very upset. He had explained how an American missionary named Clifford Johnson had saved his daughter's life, and that Mr. Clifford, as he called him, had lived with the General for several months. General Manoon wanted details. Was the murdered man really a missionary who had lived in Thailand for many years? How was he killed? Were there any leads? He had even hinted that he might have some information that could be useful to the American police in charge of the investigation. Finally, he had asked for Captain Gallagers telephone number, and if it would be acceptable to call him.

Captain Gallager assured the Vice Consul that he would be glad to receive a call from the Thai Police General. Sure enough, a few days after his talk with the Vice Consul, Gallager's phone rang again. General Manoon had not waited. "Hello, is this Captain Gallager of Ashmore, California?

"Yes it is."

"I am Police General Manoon from Thailand. I think you know about me."

"Yes sir, I do. The Thai Consulate in Los Angeles helped me contact you."

"Maybe I can be of some help, but my English is not good. I will let my daughter speak for me. She speak good English."

A woman's voice came on the line, "Hello, my name is Kultida; General Manoon is my father. Is it t rue that Clifford Johnson has been murdered?"

"Yes, unfortunately it is true."

"That's terrible; he was such a good man, and he saved my life." A man's voice could be heard in the background, and Kultida continued, "My father wants to know if the newspaper reports you sent are accurate."

"Yes, they are basically correct."

The General, with Kultida translating, had many questions. Gallager could tell he was dealing with a fellow police officer. Finally, Captain Gallager asked a question in return. "Do you know of anything that happened in Thailand that could have some bearing on this case?" There was a pause before Kultida began to speak again. "My father says Mr. Clifford testified in court against some drug traffickers, but it's a long story. He will prepare a report of what he knows and send it to you by a special courier. That courier is Captain Manat of the Thai Police, based in the city of Chiang Mai."

"That would be most helpful. Please thank your father."

"My father has a personal interest in this case, and so do I."

"When can I expect the courier to arrive?"

"He will probably be on a flight to Los Angeles tonight. We will call again with the flight information. Can you meet his plane and arrange for a few days lodging?"

"Yes, I can arrange that. Thank you very very much."

Actually, Captain Gallager was not sure how he was going to arrange that. He doubted his chief would approve of hotel and per diem for a foreign police officer. The phone soon rang again, and Kultida gave Gallager the flight details. Captain Manat would be arriving at LAX in the morning. Gallager wanted to ask if the Thai Police Department was providing travel funds for this courier, but thought it would sound ungrateful, so he did not.

Later that morning, Mr. Faust called from Palm Gardens. He wanted to know if there was any progress in the Mr. Johnson murder case. News of the murder had gotten around, and applications for residence at Palm Gardens had dropped significantly. "This will have an adverse affect on our budget," sighed Mr. Faust. That's when Gallager had an idea. "Mr. Faust, there may be a break in the case. Just between you and me; a Thai police officer is arriving in the morning with information I expect will be very helpful."

"Well, that's good news."

"It is, and maybe you can help. I know Palm Gardens has some guest rooms. Could you provide one of those rooms for this man? It may help the investigation if he is lodged where the murder occurred."

Mr. Faust demurred, "Our residents manage those guest rooms, and any guest must have a sponser who is a Palm Gardens resident."

"Fine, my mother will make such a request."

"Oh well, really, I'm not sure."

"The Police Department is counting on your cooperation, Mr. Faust."

"I'll see what I can do."

Captain Gallager's mother made the request to reserve a guest room for an "acquaintence", and it was approved. Gallager drove to LAX to meet Captain Manat He had no idea what the Thai policeman looked like, so carried a sign with CAPTAIN MANAT printed on it. Gallager was surprised when a young Asian man approached and identified himself as Captain Manat. He was expecting an older man. They shook hands, and the Thai policeman explained, "My English is not the best, so please be patient with me. I have never traveled outside of Thailand, but I studied English in school."

"Never mind, I'm sure we will get along just fine," replied Gallager.

"I knew Mr. Clifford in Thailand, and was present when he had problems with some very bad people. I think that's why General Manoon asked me to come on this trip. I hope I can be of assistance."

"I'm sure you will be," assured Gallager. "I understand Mr. Johnson saved the life of General Manoon's daughter, Kultida."

"That's true, and also the life of Kultida's friend, Wipha, who is now my-- how do you say-- someone I am promised to marry.."

"Fiance?"

"Yes, that's it, my fiance."

"That's amazing! I know nothing about Mr. Johnson's life in Thailand. I'm sure you can fill in some gaps."

"I hope so, but General Manoon said the first thing I must do is give you a written report of what the Thai Police know about Clifford Johnson and some of his enemies, so here it is." Captain Manat handed Gallager a large manila envelope sealed with tape.

On the drive back to Ashmore, Captain Gallager learned more about Mr. Johnson, including his stay with General Manoon for several months. Gallager came to understand why General Manoon had a personal interest in this case. Gallager explained that he had arranged for Captain Manat to stay at Palm Gardens, the retirement community where Mr. Johnson had stayed briefly, before he was murdered. "That's good," commented Captain Manat, "In Thailand after the culprit is caught we conduct a re-enactment of the crime. This criminal is still loose, but I can familiarize myself with the setting. Thank you for thinking of that."

Gallager did not mention that it was really an economy move that placed the Thai policeman at Palm Gardens. Gallager had also prevailed upon Mr. Faust to provide meals for Captain Manat, arguing that his presence would help in the murder investigation. After leaving Captain Manat's luggage in his guest room, they both went to Captain Gallager's office in the Ashmore Police Department building, where Gallager read through the report concerning Mr. Johnson's activities in Thailand. As a policeman, Captain Gallager could appreciate the value of the evidence Mr. Johnson had provided to the Thai police, and how it had placed him in danger. Gallager understood how vicious and unforgiving the big-time drug traffickers could be.

The contents of that report provided Gallager with a motive for the murder; revenge. Not only revenge, but a lesson to other informers to keep their mouth's shut. The report included some of the wire taps that Clifford had listened to and translated into Thai. It was the English language tapes that were of great interest to Gallager, especially concerning the American man named Tony, who had been sent to kill Mr. Johnson in Chiang Mai shortly after Johnson had left that city for the protection of General Manoon's compound. "Now all we have to do is find an American named Tony who has spent some time in Thailand and likely has a criminal record," Gallager told Captain Manat. "Can you do that? I've heard you American police use computerized search methods." "Well, that narrows our search down to perhaps only a thousand." replied Gallager sarcastically.

"I can contact General Manoon," volunteered Captain Manat, "and suggest that he request our Immigration Department to conduct a search of names of American men entering, or leaving, Thailand in the past several months."

"That's a great idea," declared Gallager appreciatively. "Can you do that?"

"Sure. If I can use your telephone tonight I'll call General Manoon directly. The Immigration Department will listen to him."

"Why not right now?"

"Right now its the middle of the night in Thailand. I wouldn't dare call the General at this time."

Captain Gallager was getting excited, and, for the first time, realized that the Thai police officer could be of real help. Previously, he had thought of him only as a courier who had brought the police records concerning Mr. Johnson, Now he understood this man could call a high police officer in his own country and get things moving. Gallager enjoyed the chase of hunting down criminals, even without much information. There were things he could do immediately. With a few calls, he commenced a search for men with a police record residing in California with a first name, or nickname, of Tony. If no information showed up in California, he would try other states.

Captain Manat had one other bit of information that surprised Captain Gallager. "There is something that was not included in this report," Captain Manat informed Gallager, "but General Manoon asked me to tell you something else, and to please be discrete with this information."

"Yes, what is that?" asked Gallager.

"General Manoon knows that Mr. Johnson was in contact with an American government agency, known as the Drug Enforcement Administration. It seems he provided information on drug movements to them. "Wow!", exclaimed Gallager. The possibilities of this case were getting explosive.

Captain Manat was in Gallager's office most days, but spent his nigts at Palm Gardens. No one knew who he was. When asked, he replied, "I'm just visiting from Thailand for a few days. Mr. Faust arranged for me to stay here." Captain Manat was a fitness buff. In the morning he jogged several laps around the track at a local college, and at night he took long walks before going to bed. He had been involved in the sport of Thai kick boxing before his duties as a police captain left him with little time for such activities, but he still worked out and was in good physical condition.

Captain Manat was intrigued by Palm Gardens. He had never seen a senior retirement community before. Such places were virtually unknown in Thailand, except for a few administered by the Social Welfare Department for indigent elderly who had no family to care for them. Like most young people, Captain Manat did not think much about his future, when he too, would be advanced in age. He just assumed he and Wipha would have children, and eventually they would live with one of those children, surrounded by grandchildren. That was the Thai way.

Captain Manat's night time walks often took him past the place where Mr. Johnson had been murdered. It was a dark, shaded place, where a killer could hide before attacking his victim. Captain Manat was absolutely convinced that Mr. Johnson's murder was a direct result of his courtroom testimony against the drug traffickers, and he so advised Captain Gallager.

Following up on what Captain Manat had revealed about Mr. Johnson's relationship with the Drug Enforcement Administration, Gallager had contacted the DEA Office in Washington, but they were tight lipped. First, they claimed ignorance of ever having an informer in Thailand named Clifford Johnson. When pressed, they would only allow that such information was classsified and could only be revealed if a federal judge presented a court order. Gallager knew that would be a time consuming endeavor, so put that line of investigation on the back burner to be pursued later, if necessary. He turned his efforts to finding Tony.

Captain Manat, in touch with General Manoon, had received information from the Thai Immigration Department about an American named Tony Hernandos who had arrived in Thailand on a tourist visa about a year ago. This man had renewed his tourist visa three times before departing Thailand two weeks before the murder of Mr. Johnson. He had boarded a flight bound for Los Angeles.

When Gallager contacted the United States Customs and Immigration Services, they confirmed that an American with that name had arrived at LAX on that flight, and they even provided Gallager with an address in the city of San Bernadino, not far from Ashmore.

Gallager thought he was making progress, but when he and other police officers went to that address, hoping to arrest Tony, they only found an old abandoned house. Neighbors told them that no one had lived in that house for years. Obviously, Tony had used a false address on his travel documents. This did place more suspicion on him, however, and now Gallager and Manat were both sure this was their man. All they had to do was locate him.

Gallager's earlier search for men named Tony with a police record had produced no results, but when he ran the full name, Tony Hernandos, he got a hit. A man with that name had been indicted in Los Angeles three years before for drug possession and for selling small amounts of heroin. It was small time stuff, but Gallager did receive a physical description, and even a photo. No current address was available, but Gallager was making enough progress for his chief to keep him on the case.

Gallager again interviewed Marvin, the man who had discovered the body at Palm Gardens. From Marvin he heard of other residents who walked their dogs at night, and Gallager interviewed them all, and showed them the picture of Tony Hernandos. An alert reporter at The Ashland Herald, however, ran a story that irritated Gallager. This reporter had been covering the story, it was, after all, big news in Ashland. The reporter had learned from Mr. Faust that a man staying in a guest room at Palm Gardens was really a policeman from Thailand, where the murder vistim had lived for many years. He had also learned that Captain Gallager had obtained a photo of the murderer. That reporter was hanging around the police station when Marvin was interviewed by Gallager, and, to Gallager's dismay, the next edition of the Ashland Herald ran a story implying that a resident of Palm Gardens, named Marvin, had actually witnessed the murder and could I.D. the murderer. That story was totally false, and Gallager was furious.

CHAPTER TWENTY FOUR

TONY HERNANDOS

Tony Hernandos' fortunes had changed. He had been born poor, and had grown up poor.

His heroin addiction did not help. Tony had once been told by a dealer that the best heroin came from Thailand, and was cheap if you lived in that country. Going to the source seemed like a good idea to Tony, so he intensified his regular occupation, which was home breakins, and scraped up enough money to buy a one way ticket to Thailand. Tony rented a room in a cheap hotel near the Hualampong Train Station. He was inconspicuous there, because many foreigners from a variety of countries lived in that district. Some were young people with backpacks traveling around the world on the cheap. Others were like Tony, who made a living outside the law. Those people seemed to recognize one another and traded useful information, like where to get the cheapest drugs, and where the brothels were located. Tony had never had it so good. He took the train to Chiang Mai a couple of times, but always returned to Bangkok, staying in different inexpensive guest houses and hotels. When he ran short of money, a man like Tony knew what to do. Those young backpackers were his cash cows. They may have been traveling on the cheap, but many of them came from well to do families in the United States or Europe. They had expensive cameras and body belts where they hid their money. Some had come to Thailand to try out the drug scene, but had been warned of long prison sentences if caught by the police.

Tony passed himself off as a long time expatriate who knew his way around, and offered to purchase the drugs for the backpack crowd. Even after Tony doubled the price, the young people thought they were getting a good deal. If they were careless with their cameras or money pouches, those items were soon in Tony's possession, and he commiserated with them over their loss. "You have to be careful in this country," he told them, "you can't trust anyone." Tony soon became known in the Thai underworld who hung out around the Hualampong Train Station, because he frequently had good cameras to fence, and was a steady customer for heroin and other drugs.

Tony had dreams of becoming a big operator. He wanted to make a lot of money before returning to the United States and live in luxury for the rest of his life. That's when he began to buy drugs on credit. He would buy a sizeable stash, sell it to international travelers, and repay the dealer. That was a good deal all around; both Tony and his suppliers sold more drugs that way. Tony had street smarts; he never left his supply of drugs in his room, but always stashed them on his body. He had a tailor make a sport coat for him that was about two sizes too big and had a number of inner pockets. Tony was a walking narcotics store. His attire was not very suitable for hot and humid Bangkok. He perspired a lot, but his stash was safe.

Safe, that is, until he stole a camera from one of his customers and got caught. If he had just stuck to drugs, he might have ran a successful street business, but Tony was at heart a thief. He could easily pick the locks of the hotel room doors, and did so regularly. One day he sold some heroin to two young Australian men who were going on a shopping expedition to one of the large outdoor markets in Bangkok. One of the men mentioned he did not want to carry his camera into the crowds of people at the market, so had hidden it in his room. They invited Tony to go with them, but he declined. As soon as they left, Tony went to their room, picked the lock and entered the room, closing the door behind him. It took him about 30 seconds to find the camera, wrapped in a dirty shirt and hidden under the bed. He took it, and immediately went to a pawn shop, where the owners never asked questions. It was a $200 camera, but Tony only received Thai money worth $50. He knew better than to argue; take it or leave it seemed to be the motto of pawn shops around the world.

Tony, however, had been observed breaking into the room occupied by the Australians. A housekeeper had been in the linen room at the end of the hall. When she heard a noise in the hallway, she opened the linen room door a crack and peered out. She saw Tony pick the lock, enter the room, and soon come out with something in his hand. She knew a theft had probably been committed, but did not tell her boss, whom she called a "stingy old *Jek* (Chinese)." She planned to inform the two foreigners when they returned, and perhaps earn a tip.

That's exactly what she did. The two Australians looked under their bed, and found the camera missing. They immediately went looking for Tony and found him at a coffee shop next to the hotel. They pretended to be interested in making another drug purchase. "Got any more of that good stuff?" they asked, "You know that Triple 0 Brand." Tony knew what they wanted. The Triple O Brand had a reputation of always being pure dope, not cut with chalk dust or powdered sugar. "I sure do," replied Tony. "Let's go outside." Tony led them to a nearby alley where he often made his sales. No one was in sight, so the Aussies pushed Tony up against the wall of a building and demanded the return of the camera. "We know you took it; someone saw you do it and told us."

If Tony had been smarter, he might have admitted the theft, took the two angry young men back to the pawn shop and redeemed it. Tony knew that would cost him about $200, the true value of the camera, so he denied everything. "I was never in your room, and I never stole anything," he asserted. The Aussies, however, were done talking. One held Tony's arms behind his back while the other one used him for a punching bag. Tony begged for mercy, but didn't get any. His knees buckled and he fell to the street, where the two furious Aussies continued to kick him into unconsciousness. When their fury abated, they searched Tony's pockets and were amazed to find a hoard of cash, and a large amount of drugs, neatly packed in small plastic bags. They took it all, but had second thoughts about the drugs. "What if we're caught with this stuff," the camera owner said, "We'll rot in a Thai jail for 30 years." They ended up dividing the money between them and throwing the drugs in a nearby *klong* (canal). They went back to their room to collect their luggage, tipped the cleaning lady 500 Baht, which was equal to a months pay, went to the nearby train station, and took the night train to Nong Khai on the Mekong River and crossed over to Laos on a taxi boat. With their infusion of new funds they could continue on their trip around the world.

Regaining consciousness was a painful experience for Tony. He hurt. He hurt from head to toe. Just sitting up, leaning against a wall, caused him to groan. When he discovered his hidden pockets were empty of all money and drugs, he moaned again. He had just restocked his drug supply from his usual suppliers, on credit of course. In two days, maybe three at the most, they would want their money. These were not kind people. When they came to collect their money they expected to receive it, or else. Clifford did not like to think about what those words meant. He was in big trouble, and he knew it. If he had been able, Tony would have moved across the city, or better yet, taken a train or bus to some place far away, but he could barely stand up; not to mention the fact that he was broke, completely broke.

With great difficulty, Tony made it back to his room and slowly reclined on his bed. Alerted to his condition, the hotel manager came to see him. The manager was appalled by Tony's condition. He didn't speak much English, but managed to say, "I call police, o.k.?" "No, no, don't do that," Tony groaned, "Just let me rest a few days. Maybe you can bring me some food." Many of this hotel's clients were rough characters, so the manager was not surprised when one got beat up. He did ask the cleaning lady to bring Tony a bowl of *khaow tom* (watery rice gruel) twice a day. She didn't mind doing so, and appeared quite cheerful, which was unusual for her.

On the third day after his beating, Tony managed to get out of bed, and was sitting on it when the cleaning lady came with his rice gruel. She made a point of covering her nose. That motivated Tony to shower and shave. He also had visitors that day. They were not unexpected; Tony was wondering when they would show up. Three men appeared at his bedside when Tony was napping. He recognized two of them as the ones he bought drugs from on credit. They were a shifty eyed pair with bad colored skin. Tony was sure they were addicts. The third one was a man Tony had never seen before. He let the others do the talking, but it was clear the two dealers deferred to him. Tony explained, as best he could, about being beat up and robbed. The beating part was obvious; Tony was still black and blue. When he asked for more drugs on credit so he could repay his debt, the two dealers looked at the third man, who spoke for the first time, "No more for you. We come back tomorrow. You must pay all you owe. If no pay, you dead man." There was no pity in his eyes, and Clifford knew he meant what he said. He was the enforcer in a business that did not give second chances.

Tony needed 10,000 Baht just to pay his debts. Besides that, Tony was addicted and needed drugs for his own use. The need was gnawing at his insides, especially when he considered his future, or really, no future. A snort of heroin would take his worries away, and make him feel good again. "What can I do?" he groaned. "Go rob some foreigners," the man with the hard eyes said. "We'll be back tomorrow. Don't try to run away. You will be watched."

Tony had no scruples, he would have robbed some foreigners, even fellow countrymen, but he was still weak and had no weapon. He knew he couldn't do it, so he just lay on his bed contemplating a bleak, and short, future. On the afternoon of the next day the three men returned. "Got the money?" asked the man with the hard eyes. Tony knew he couldn't stall any longer. "No, I don't," he murmured, "I'm in no condition to go looking for money."

Tony's eyes were downcast, but he could feel the hard eyes boring into his skull. "You one lucky bastard," hissed the man. Tony looked up, and "Hard Eyes" continued, "Someone I know needs a *Farang* (white foreigner) to do a special job. You do it, and you go free."

"I'll do it," gasped Tony. "What is it?"

"Hard Eyes" explained. "Some *Farang* in Chiang Mai is being a problem. All you have to do is go there and kill him. Can you do that?"

"Sure, I can do that."

"You ever use a gun?"

"Many times."

"O.K., police are guarding this guy, but they won't be suspicious of a *Farang*. This evening you take the night train to Chiang Mai."

"I have no money; no gun."

"Never mind, we supply you."

"Who do I kill, and how do I find him?"

"Here's a round trip train ticket to Chiang Mai," the man pulled a ticket from his pocket. "Train leaves at 6:00 P.M.. You stand on the platform next to your car at 5:30. Someone will come and give you money, gun, name and address of dumb ass *Farang* in Chiang Mai. You do job, and we all clear. Besides that, someone in Chiang Mai will give you money to return your country."

The men left, and Tony gave a great sigh of relief. He had been a bit glib about his use of a gun. Actually, he had never carried a gun before, but had done a little target shooting with a friend's revolver. He knew he could point and pull the trigger. That was enough.

Tony packed his few belongings, painfully descended the stairs to the lobby, and stopped in mid-stride. He had forgotten about his hotel bill. By that time, the hotel manager had seen Tony and barked at him, "You there, I don't like the friends you keep. Some hoodlum paid your bill. Now get out of here, and never come back."

Tony was glad to leave. He walked the short distance to the Hua Lampong Train Station, found his car, and waited outside on the platform. Just at 5:30, a man Tony had never seen before approached him and handed him a small drawstring bag. Tony took the bag with him into his car, and into the toilet cubicle. Inside was 500 Baht, a sheet of paper and a .32 revolver. Tony put the money in his shirt pocket, shoved the gun in his pants pocket, and took the paper with him to his seat. He studied the crudely printed message, which said his target was a foreigner named Clifford Johnson. An address, and a map, giving directions to his target's house, was included. At the bottom of the page was a telephone number in Chiang Mai he was to call when he had completed his assignment. Tony folded that paper and stuck it in his other shirt pocket. His hands shook. He needed a fix. A clock out on the station platform read 5:40. Tony was streetwise, and knew the area around the train station. In a flash, he was out of his car and in the men's toilet within the cavernous station. He stood against a wall flicking through his slim roll of bills until a man approached him. Tony nodded his head, and the other man nodded his. They went into a cubicle together and 30 seconds later Tony had a small packet of powdered heroin, for which he had paid 50 Baht. By 5:55 he was back in his train car's toilet, where he opened the packet and snorted the heroin. He was flooded with a sense of well being. He felt invincible, he could handle anything. He was Tony Hernandos, an American Superman.

The drug people who had provided Tony with the train ticket had not been over-generous. The evening express train to Chiang Mai has three classes. A first class compartment, second class with a sleeper, and third class sit up. Tony's car was third class with hard seats and no air conditioning. Clifford hardly noticed; he was full of nervous energy, getting up often and walking up and down the aisle. At the Ayutaya Station he purchased a bundle of sticky rice and barbequed chicken wrapped in a banana leaf for 10 Baht. He returned to his seat to eat, and, between bites, smiled at the woman sitting in the seat facing him. Finally, she pulled out a magazine and held it in front of her face as she read. Eventually, Tony fell asleep and slept most of the way. He didn't wake up until the train arrived in Chiang Mai, which was also the end of the line.

No one met Tony; it was understood he was on his own. He stopped at a restaurant across from the train station and had a breakfast of fried eggs and toast. He had been picking up a few words of Thai and loved to order two pieces of toast; *kanom pang ping sawng chin*. Not that he was so fond of toast, but because the words tripped off his tongue like a line of music. After eating, and savoring his second cup of bad coffee, he studied the map given to him by the drug dealers. He knew it would be safer to walk to the home of this *Farang*, who was named Clifford. If he took a minibus, or taxi, the driver might remember him, and tell the police. He was tempted to hop in a pedicab, which were plentiful around the station. Their drivers called to him as he walked, but he ignored them, and continued on foot.

Chiang Mai was larger than he thought, and after making a few wrong turns, it was nearly noon when he found the house. At first, he couldn't see the house, even though he knew he was close. He had to ask a passerby where the house was, showing him the address written on his map in both Thai and English. He knew that might call attention to himself, but felt he had no choice. The passerby looked at the address, and pointed with his chin toward a house across the street, while saying the word "*poon.*" Clifford, of course, did not know that Northern Thai word, which means "over there." The gesture with the chin was more meaningful, so Tony went in the direction so indicated, and found a small wooden house located behind a somewhat larger wooden house of the same style.

Tony was only reconnoitering; he intended to come back after dark to complete his assignment, but was startled to see a police pickup truck parked beside the house. As he watched from behind a corner of the larger house, two armed policemen came out of the smaller house, descended the stairs, and took a box from the pickup back up into the house. "Probably their lunch," thought Tony. He had been told about the police, but thought he could still do the job. Breaking into houses while the occupants were sleeping was Tony's specialty. The police had not noticed Tony, so he quickly turned away, and continued walking down the street. He would return after dark.

He had only walked about 10 minutes when he came to an old rambling wooden house with a sign in front that said MANOP'S GUEST HOUSE. Tony went in to check it out . The building was divided up into small rooms, most of which were rented to young foreigners, who were lounging in their rooms with the doors open. It was obviously an inexpensive place. Just what Tony needed. He rented a room for 50 Baht a day; payable in advance each day. The place also served food, so after an afternoon siesta Tony went to the restaurant area and ordered a plate of American Fried Rice, which consisted of a generous plateful of fried rice, a small wiener and topped by a fried egg; all for 12 Baht.

Tony was keeping close attention to his financial resources. He hoped to finish his job that night, call the number on his map, return to Bangkok, and leave the country. He had had enough of Thailand. He needed a fix, but kept his mind on his assignment. He could celebrate after he had knocked this guy, Clifford, off. He was not even curious who this foreigner was. Tony was in a jamb; all he wanted to do was do the job and get out.

Tony went back to his room. There was no air conditioning, but he kept his door shut, locking in the heat and humidity. He sat up on a chair, so he would not sleep, until nearly 1:00 A.M, when he got up, checked his revolver, and made sure the map, train ticket, and remaining money was in his pockets. Tony quietly left his room, and walked back down the street to his target's house. The cool night air was refreshing, but he hardly noticed. All Tony wanted to do was complete his assignment, and get out of town.

At the compound where the foreigner lived, Tony eased open a gate that had been open when he was there the day before, and walked carefully to the small house. No police vehicles were there. "This is going to be easy," thought Clifford. He drew his gun and crept up the outside stairs, carefully stepping on the outer edge of each step. He had learned from experience, that stairs creaked less if stepped on at that location. He was surprised to find the door unlocked, but carefully opened it and slipped inside. He searched the three rooms, and found them empty. There were no personal belongings; just some old furniture. The man he was ready to kill had left.

Tony returned to Manop's Guest House and into his own room, but he could not sleep. The passage of time, together with the tenseness of the last hour, made him crave another fix. He got up and returned to the restaurant, where a mixed group of Thai and Foreigners were still sitting around tables drinking Singha beer and Mae Khong whiskey. "Anybody got any medicine?" Tony asked. No one responded, so Tony ordered a bottle of beer and sat alone. Soon, a man with a French accent came over and joined Tony. "What do you need?" he asked. "Something good to calm me down," responded Tony. "I can't sleep."

"Will this do?" The Frenchman extracted a small packet from his pocket.

"Yeah, that might help."

"It'll cost you 100 Baht."

"C'mon man, I get it for half that."

"I see you've been around here a while. Alright, 50 Baht."

Tony paid the man, put the packet in his pocket and returned to his room, where he immediately snorted the powder.

Now Tony couldn't sleep because he was on a high, so he returned to the restaurant, where he had seen a pay phone, put a one Baht coin in the slot and called the number that was on his map. The fact that it was 4:00 A.M did not bother him. Once again he felt like he was king of the hill. After many rings, a sleepy voice answered. Tony explained who he was and why he was calling. "O.k., o.k., where are you?"

"Manop's Guest House."

"Stay there, I'll pick you up at 8:00."

Tony started to explain, but the man on the line, obviously irritated, cut him off. "You can tell me when I see you." Click; the connection went dead.

Tony, wide awake, sat up in his bed until 7:00, when he returned to the restaurant and ordered a mug of hot soy milk and two pieces of fried bread dough a Chinese lady was frying in a pot of hot oil. Tony was getting a little tired of rice. Also, the soy milk soothed his stomach. He was ready for whoever was going to meet him.

It was nearly 8:30 when a man appeared in the restaurant. He scanned all the people sitting there, but zeroed in on Tony. "Are you Tony?" he asked in fair English. Tony acknowledged he was indeed that person. "Come with me," he ordered. Tony followed him outside to an older model Mercedes Benz where he was told to sit in the front seat passenger's side. His escort got in the rear seat. Another man, wearing dark glasses, was sitting behind the steering wheel. The man who had brought Tony to the car was obviously the one giving orders. He spoke to the driver in rapid Thai, and they were driven to a place not far from the guest house. Tony recognized what kind of establishment it was; he had seen such places in Bangkok. It was a drop-curtain *sawng* (brothel), so named because there were parking stalls where a car could be parked and hidden by lowering a curtain. Thus sparing a car's owner possible embarrassment from having his car seen at such a place. They stayed in the car; the man in the back seat just wanted to talk to Tony in private.

Tony, thinking he might be blamed for not doing his job, started to speak first "Hey, I went to the guy's house yesterday. Police were all over the place. I went again last night and he was gone. House was empty."

"Yeah, I know," replied the man in the back seat. "I already checked this morning. You were one day too late."

"Not my fault."

"O.k., o.k., calm down. We already know the police put him on a plane for Bangkok. You can still be of use to us, so we want you to return to Bangkok. We'll be in touch."

"Where should I go? I can't go to my old hotel near the Hua Lampong train station."

"You sure can't," snorted the man in back, "You outlived your welcome there."

"So?"

"So, we got another place for you. This one is in *Klong Toey* (the Bangkok Seaport area). Try not to mess up. People around there will do more than beat you up."

Tony wanted to ask who the "we" were that the man was always referring to, but thought it best not to enquire. He knew he was still in a precarious position.

The man in the backseat continued, "You've still got your return train ticket, right?"

"Yes."

"Alright, return to Bangkok tonight. Someone will meet you and take you to your new place of residence."

"I could use some more money," ventured Tony. Actually, he had enough to make it back to Bangkok if he continued to live very frugally, he just didn't like to live that frugally.

The man refused, so Tony ate plain fried rice again on the train that night.

Tony was met at the Hua Lampong Station by the same man who had seen him off two days before. The man led him out to a nearby street where a Toyota Corolla with tinted windows was parked, and told him to get in. It was the same arrangement as in Chiang Mai. Tony was in the front seat and another man was in the rear seat. Tony recognized him as the man with the hard eyes who had provided him with train tickets, and told him to kill the man in Chiang Mai named Clifford. That man spoke first. "Give me the gun." Tony extracted it from his pocket and handed it to him.

"I tried," said Tony, "Not my fault that guy left Chiang Mai."

Hard Eyes only grunted. The driver started the car and headed down Rama IV Road

"So, you promised me return air fare to America. I'd like to leave in a day or two."

"You not do your job yet."

"That man gone. Police guard him anyway."

"We know where he is. You kill him; you get air ticket to your country."

"Hire someone from this country. I told you I tried."

"A Thai man cannot get close to him. Maybe a *Farang* like you can get him."

"What'd this guy, Clifford, do anyway? He must be one bad dude."

"What mean 'Dude'?"

"Oh, it means like a tough guy."

"He not tough; just a missionary," Hard Eyes laughed.

Tony was surprised. "What could he do that was so bad?"

"He told police, and testified against us in court. No one can do that and live. Bad example."

Hard eyes lapsed into silence, and Tony looked ahead. They were driving through what Tony would call a slum. Old wooden houses falling apart, with rusty sheets of metal roofing. Narrow wooden walkways built over stagnant water led deeper into the slum. The driver stopped at one of the houses along a dirt road.

"You stay here," grunted Hard Eyes. "These people know us; you try to leave you dead."

Again Tony was hearing the words "us" and "we". Again, he did not ask questions. The driver stayed in the car while Hard Eyes took Tony into the house. Only an elderly Thai woman was home. She wore a long *pasin* (sarong), and a bra with no blouse. She was fanning herself with a fan made from coconut palm leaves. Her gray hair was cut short, almost like a man's, and she was chewing betal nut, occasionally spitting red saliva into a can. Heat radiated downward from the metal roof, and Tony began to perspire profusely.

"You stay here," Hard Eyes repeated. "When we need you we'll come for you."

That was the beginning of the hardest year in Tony's life. He almost went crazy in that house. Most of the time, he only wore a pair of shorts, but still he perspired. In the rainy season it cooled a bit, but the humidity also went up. The driving rain on the metal roof rattled his brains. The old lady fed him rice and curry twice a day; morning and evening. At midday she gave him some crackers and a cold soft drink. That was the only liquid he ever got that was cool. A toilet room next to his contained a squat toilet at floor level. His knees hurt every time he squatted.

He went through heroin withdrawal cold turkey. He cried and begged for a fix. The woman, and the two men who also lived in that house, knew what he wanted, but ignored him. Those men were gone most of the time. They slept in one room, and Tony had another small room to himself, with only a thin reed mat to sleep on. Laying on his side made his hips ache. Laying on his back made his butt ache. Cracks between the wall boards nailed to the sides of the house allowed hordes of voracious mosquitoes to enter from the putrid smelling water beneath the house. He was provided with a filthy mosquito net, but sleeping under it was even hotter. Twice, he tried to leave; the first attempt was in the daytime when he thought the old woman was napping. She heard him leave, and called out to a neighboring house. A man wearing only a *pakama* (loin cloth) came out and stopped him. Late one night he tried again, but the floor boards always creaked when stepped on. The two men of the house were home. They caught him before he got to the bottom of the stairs, and drug him roughly back up inside the house.

The next day Hard Eyes paid Tony a visit. "What do you think you're doing? You can't run away from here. Try it again and you'll never see your home country again."

"Why do I have to stay here?" Tony complained, "Show me where that missionary lives and I'll shoot him, so I can go home."

"Not that easy. He stays with a police officer and never comes out."

"So what's the use; I might as well leave."

"No, you stay; sooner or later police get careless. When that happens we call you."

Tony could have done something useful to occupy his mind, like writing about his experience, or trying to learn Thai from the old woman he lived with, but neither of those possibilities even crossed his mind. He longed for freedom. He longed for a chair, so he wouldn't have to sit on the floor all the time. He longed for a cold beer. He longed for a woman; a young one. Most of all, he longed for the drugs that would give him relief from his sense of hopelessness. There were days he even longed for a gun, so he could shoot himself, but there was only one boring day after another.

Even a visit from Hard Eyes was preferable to sitting alone with his knees drawn up and his back against a wall. Through the long days he moved around, so the wall he leaned against was not the one the sun was shining on, radiating heat to his backside. Hard Eyes did arrive one day and he had big news. "You go home now," he announced.

Tony could hardly believe his ears. "Do you mean I can really leave this hell hole?"

"What you mean 'hell hole', I grew up in place just like this. Yes, you go home."

"What about the missionary?"

"He leave Thailand. He went home to place called California."

"California! That's where I'm from."

"We know that. Your job not done yet."

"In his home he feel safe. Your job now easy."

"My job is now all over."

"No, you still kill him. We have not forgotten him."

"No one knows where he lives."

"We know."

"How can you know?" Tony was dubious.

"We read his mail."

"How could you do that?"

"Mailman one of us."

Tony's heart sank. Would he ever be free of these people who never forgot, and always retaliated.

"What do you want me to do," Tony asked.

"Here's the deal," Hard Eyes began, as he pulled a piece of paper from his pocket and gave it to Tony. "That man live at this place. You kill him, we all square. We forget about you; you forget about us." Tony read what was on the paper:

CLIFFORD JOHNSON
PALM GARDENS RETIREMENT COMMUNITY
ASHMORE, CALIFORNIA

There was even a picture of a mild looking man with white hair. "That's him," continued Hard Eyes. "He the one you kill. We give you airplane ticket and one thousand dollars. After that, you on your own. Don't get bad ideas; you will be watched. We have people in your country too. You fail; you dead. Understand?" Clifford understood. These people were relentless. "O.k.," he replied, "we got a deal."

CHAPTER TWENTY FIVE

THE STALKER

Tony got his ticket back to California. Some years before, he had lived in San Bernadino, but he avoided that place now. Instead, he moved in with an old friend who lived in a shack in the town of Fontana. That house was in a gritty part of town, just south of Interstate 10 and near a recycling plant. Tony was free of drugs, after what he called his imprisonment, and should have stayed off, but when his friend offered him some heroin he succumbed. Tony was too disorganized, and lacked the necessary willpower, to straighten out his life.

Tony, however, was mindful of his task. He feared what might happen to him if he neglected to complete his assignment. After his experience with the drug people in Thailand, he did not doubt that he was being watched. He became a little paranoid. Every time he saw an Asian face he imagined it was someone watching him. He spent $500 for an old beat up Ford, and began to spend a lot of time in Ashmore. He soon located the Palm Gardens Retirement Community, and one day spotted the man, named Clifford, returning to his house after eating his noon meal in the dining hall. He matched the photo that Tony carried in his pocket. Tony followed Clifford to his house.

Tony now knew where Clifford lived; all he had to do was learn his habits. Palm Gardens was not a gated community, so people from nearby streets often entered; sometimes to walk their dogs, so Tony's presence was not noticed. He soon learned that Clifford took nightly walks through the grounds of Palm Gardens, starting out at about 9:00 P.M. Tony felt a slight tinge of conscious; Clifford seemed to be a good person, and looked so harmless, but Tony knew what he had to do to save his own skin. It was not a hard decision for Tony. He found a section of one inch steel pipe near the recycling plant, and using his friend's hack saw, cut it back to three feet in length. It made a formidable weapon.

One night, Tony parked his car a block away from Clifford's house, and watched from across the street. The pipe was wrapped in a towel. A few minutes after 9:00 Clifford emerged from his house and started walking. He was a fast walker, so Tony had to step quickly to keep up with him. Tony wore tennis shoes, so was able to walk quietly. Also, he knew the route that Clifford usually took on his walks, so could stay some distance behind and still keep his target in sight. Tony picked up his pace when Clifford neared the secluded area, known as Pratt Garden. The night insects were buzzing, so Clifford did not hear the approaching danger. It was too late when he did hear a sound, and turned to see a man behind him swinging a metal object. The sound of a crushing skull was not unlike smashing a pumpkin with a club. That sound was heard by no one, except Tony, who quickly drug Clifford's dead body into the underbrush, rewrapped his weapon in the towel, and nonchalantly walked back to his car. His assignment was completed. He hoped he would never hear from the shadowy drug traffickers again.

Tony had never told his friend what he did during his night excursions, and certainly did not mention ever going to the town of Ashmore. He didn't read newspapers either, but his friend did, and often read articles in the paper to Tony about a vicious murder at a retirement community in Ashmore. "What's this country coming to," exclaimed Tony's friend, a man with a criminal record himself, "You can't even go for a walk at night without getting your head smashed in."

"Terrible," agreed Tony.

"What was it like in Taiwan where you were?"

"You mean Thailand?"

"Yeah, Thailand, whatever."

"It's a peaceful place; nothing much ever happens there."

Several days later, however, Tony's friend read another article from the Ashland Herald concerning the murder of the retiree, which shocked Tony. The words jumped out at him, "Ashland police have photo of the murderer, and a resident of Palm Gardens, named Marvin Schuster, witnessed the murder and can identify the culprit." That was the article, mostly untrue, which had made Captain Gallager furious. Because of that article, he was expecting a call from Mr. Faust, which soon came. "What's this I read in the paper," he demanded. "I just spoke to Marvin and he most certainly did not witness the murder. This whole matter is causing considerable stress among our residents."

Captain Gallager assured the angry Mr. Faust that he knew the article was not true, and had not given that information to the Ashland Herald reporter. Captain Gallager also called the managing editor of the paper and complained about the erroneous article. The editor promised to talk to the reporter responsible. Gallager neglected, however, to call Marvin and warn him of possible consequences. Gallager was a careful man; he seldom made mistakes, but the police captain had given Gallager other cases to work on, in addition to the Clifford Johnson case, and he was a very busy man with too much on his mind. He simply forgot.

Tony sure didn't forget. He knew he would have to take care of this other resident at Palm Gardens, named Marvin Schuster. He had learned from his erstwhile friends in Thailand to never leave witnesses. He needed to know where Marvin lived, without asking anyone, so he visited the Ashmore Public Library and looked in a telephone book for that city. There was a listing for a Marvin and Emily Schuster, and, Tony noted, their address was within the Palm Gardens Retirement Community. He already knew a lot about that place. Tony drove by the house that same day, and actually saw a man leaving the house leading a dog. "There's my man," thought Tony. As he had done for his previous victim, he continued his surveillance for several nights, and discovered that Marvin Schuster always walked his dog at 10:00 P.M.

Soon after returning home the lights went out in the house. It was the final walk of the day.

Mr. Schuster avoided the Pratt Garden, and that was fine with Tony. He thought rubbing out two people in the same location might be a bit risky. Mr. Schuster mostly walked around the perimeter of Palm Gardens, including Avocado Street on the west side, that looked more like an alley. It was a rather dark street, little used, and the occupants who lived on that dead end street mostly turned off their lights and went to bed early. "A dead end street," chuckled Tony, "Sounds like the perfect place."

Tony reclaimed his steel pipe from its hiding place under his friend's house, and returned to Palm Gardens one night during the dark of the moon. He parked nearby, and didn't even bother to wrap his weapon in a towel. There was a hedge along that street, so Tony hid behind it, beginning at 9:45. About a half hour later he heard steps coming. In the dim light from a street light some distance away he could see a man and a dog. The man was talking to his dog. "Well, Caliban we'll be home in a few minutes. You can sleep on your rug, and I'll crawl in with Emily, as I have done now for 52 years. She's a good woman, Caliban, even if she aggravates me once in a while." Tony firmly gripped his pipe and stepped out just behind Marvin as he passed by. He raised his weapon and was about to bring it down with a crushing blow to Marvin's head

Before he could so, Caliban went berserk. He was not a large dog, but with a loud bark and a fierce growl, he threw himself at Tony, pulling his leash from Marvin's hand. Caliban sunk his teeth into Tony's thigh, producing a painful yell from Tony, who tried to back up so he could swing the pipe at Caliban, but the dog just clenched his teeth harder and swung his head from side to side. Caliban had rat terrier in his blood, and old instincts clicked in. He did not let go, even when Tony let loose with a gush of expletives that would have put a mule skinner to shame. Marvin stood, rooted to the ground, not knowing what to think, or what to do. Tony might still have gotten to him, even with a little devil hanging to his thigh, but out of the darkness came another figure, who gave Tony a wicked kick to the groin, and another to his head when Tony doubled over in pain. Tony collapsed, unconscious, to the street, but Caliban continued worrying him, like a dead rat.

The man picked up Caliban's leash and handed it to Marvin, who was still speechless. "Maybe you should pull your dog away," said the man, "and call the Ashmore Police Department; ask for Captain Gallager." Marvin finally found his senses, and hurried off to his home, pulling Caliban, who would have preferred to wreak more damage on the prostrate figure lying unconscious on the street. "Good dog, Caliban, good dog; I think you just saved my life."

Marvin burst into his house, and immediately called the Police Department. Captain Gallager was working late, as he often did, and took the call. Marvin was not very coherent, "Captain, come quick. Someone tried to kill me, but my dog saved me, and there was also some man who suddenly appeared, and he saved me too. Come quick." A thoroughly confused Captain Gallager finally got Marvin to slow down, identify himself, and give a location of the incident. When Gallager realized the call was from Marvin Schuster he knew it was serious. "Mr. Schuster," he ordered, "stay in your house. Do not go out. Lock all doors. I'm coming." Gallager did not know what to expect, so he ordered back-up assistance, and drove as fast as he could to the dead end street where Mr. Schuster had apparently had a frightening experience. When he turned in that street his car lights picked up two figures; one standing and one on the street, trying to stand up. Gallager drove closer, and recognized Captain Manat as the one standing. He jumped out of his car and approached the two men. "Captain Manat!" Gallager exclaimed, "What happened?"

"This man," Manat pointed to a still moaning Tony, "is likely the murderer of Mr. Johnson. I caught him in the act of trying to kill Mr. Schuster."

"Where is Mr. Schuster? Is he alright.?"

"He's fine; I sent him home to call you."

Captain Gallager felt a great sense of relief. When he had received the excited call from Marvin Schuster, he realized he had been negligent in not warning Marvin to take precautions.

"Thank God he's o.k., but how come you happened to be here?"

"I was concerned about Mr. Schuster when that article came out in the newspaper. I take a walk every night and soon found Mr. Schuster also walked his dog about the same time. I got in the habit of silently following him, in case the murderer came back for him. In my country witnesses are sometimes silenced."

"In my country too," murmured Gallager, "I erred in not warning Mr. Schuster to be careful."

They were joined by the occupants of two more police cars, and a night security guard employed by Palm Gardens who had noticed the arrival of the squad cars with flashing red lights. Even Marvin showed up, leading his dog. He had disobeyed Captain Gallager's order to stay in his house. Closer to home, he had even disobeyed his wife, who had overheard Marvin calling the police and was in a nervous state. When she saw her husband preparing to leave the house with Caliban she tried to prevent him. "Marvin, don't you leave this house." Marvin, however, had seen the approaching police cars and was curious to see what had happened on Avocado Street. "Never mind, Emily, I'm taking Caliban with me. He won't let anyone hurt me." With those words, he was out the door and down the street.

Gallager was not happy to see him. "Mr. Schuster, I told you not to leave your house."

"Yes, I know, but when I saw the police cars I figured it was safe. Anyway, I took my dog with me."

Gallager glanced at the dog, "That mutt; looks like he wouldn't even go after a rat."

Captain Manat entered the conversation, "That dog saved Mr. Schuster's life. I was too slow, but that dog jumped on the murderer and bit him. That gave me time to come up and take his club away."

"Looks like you did more than take his club away," commented Gallager, with a glance at the man, now sitting up on the road surface.

"Well, that club looked dangerous, so I may have kicked him a couple of times."

Gallager now spoke to the other policemen, "Take this guy in, book him for attempted murder and lock him up."

As the police were pulling Tony to an upright position, Caliban growled at him again. "Keep that monster away from me," cried Tony, "he's a vicious dog." One of the policemen shined a flashlight on Tony, and Gallager recognized that face. It was the man on the photo they had received from the Los Angeles Police Department. It was the man they were looking for; the man who had returned from Thailand not long ago. Captain Gallager didn't say anything, but he knew his search was over. "Mr. Schuster," he said to Marvin, "can we go to your house, so we can go over what happened tonight, and I will write my report?"

"You sure can." replied Marvin, and he led the way to his house. Captain Manat and the Palm Gardens night watchman were included. Gallager questioned each one in turn, until he had the complete story. The night watchman had seen nothing unusual, but Gallager thought it good for him to be included. It might motivate him to be a more observant watchman in the future. "Always check out the dark places," Gallager told him. Marvin was advised to walk his dog earlier, and avoid those dark places. Marvin's wife, Emily, made a pot of coffee and served it with some leftover cake. The cake was not very fresh, but no one complained. She agreed with Captain Gallager, "Yes indeed, Marvin, I have told you many times not to walk that dog of yours so late." Actually, she had suggested that late hour for Marvin to walk Caliban in hopes the dog would not require an early morning walk. Marvin took a sip of coffee, and did not refute her.

It was Captain Manat who had the most interesting report. He told again of following Mr. Schuster on his late night walks. "I was worried about him being out late at night, and I had lots of time on my hands, so it was something to do. It was just a small thing."

"No, it was not a small thing," replied Gallager. "Thank God you were there." When questioned about how he was able to disarm, and disable, the murderer, Captain Manat described Thai kick boxing, and how he formerly participated in that sport. He was modest; failing to mention that he was a champion in the Thai Police Division. Marvin and Emily had seen Captain Manat around Palm Gardens, but like all other residents, did not know he was a Thai police officer, who was acting as an unofficial advisor on the Clifford Johnson murder case. Marvin had nothing but praise for him. "What you did was wonderful, maybe you should teach all us residents of Palm Gardens how to do Thai kick boxing, so we can defend ourselves." Neither Captain Manat or Captain Gallager thought that was a good idea. Neither did Emily, "Marvin, you can't even step into your under shorts in the morning without nearly falling over, how in the world could you do kick boxing."

It was now Captain Manat's turn to give praise, where praise was due. "Mr. Shuster, it was that dog of yours who was the real hero. He sure tore into your assailant. You should always keep him with you when you are out for a walk at night." Emily had been listening to all the narratives, and now she surreptitiously reached under the table and gave Caliban a piece of cake and patted him on his head. Caliban was rather surprised, but wagged his tail anyway.

"Was that man the one who murdered Clifford Johnson?" asked Marvin. Gallager was not ready to reveal what he knew, so he just replied, "Maybe, but we will need to investigate further." Gallager and Captain Manat left the house together. Before getting in his car, Gallager told Captain Manat that he recognized the man they had apprehended from the picture provided by the Los Angeles Police Department. "That man, whose name is Tony Hernandos, recently returned from Thailand, and he is the man that we received Thai immigration records about sent by your police general. I'm sure he is the murderer, but I will question him myself tomorrow."

"Very interesting," replied Captain Manat, "May I be present?"

"Yes, you may; in an unofficial capacity, of course."

"Of course."

CHAPTER TWENTY SIX

TONY IS SENTENCED

The prisoner had demanded a doctor's examination, with a lawyer present, before agreeing to a police interview. He had hopes of suing the City of Ashmore for a large sum of money. Since the prisoner had no funds, a public defender had to be found to serve as his lawyer. A local physician was called to the jail cell to examine the prisoner, who had refused to give his name. "Nothing seriously wrong with him; just a little swelling. He'll be o.k.," reported the doctor. "Do you want that in writing?"

"Yes," replied Gallager, "an official medical evaluation."

"I can do that. The prisoner may even be able to father children after a few months." added the doctor with a grin.

"Don't put that in the report."

"Just kidding."

It was late afternoon before Gallager was able to start interrogating the prisoner. He thought it best that the Thai policeman not be in the interrogation room, but observe and listen through one-way glass. The prisoner denied everything. "I was just out for a walk," he declared. "What's this country coming to, anyway, if a man can't go for a walk without being attacked by a vicious dog and almost kicked to death by some foreigner."

"Where do you live?"

"I live with a friend in Fontana." He gave the address, and Gallager sent an officer to check that out.

"Why come all the way to a retirement community in Ashmore to walk?"

"Safer over here, or so I thought."

"So, why carry a club?"

"Well, you never know. See what I mean? Me, a peaceful man was assaulted. That dog should be put down and the foreigner, whoever he is, jailed for battery."

Gallager held off on disclosing all he knew. He wanted to gather all relevant facts first. Anyway, the County Attorney's Office would have to be advised. Gallager hated the red tape, but it had to be done. Photos and finger prints of the prisoner were taken, and sent to the Los Angeles Police Department, who confirmed they matched what they had about a man named Tony Hernandos, who had a drug selling record. Gallager also sent the pipe to a police lab in Los Angeles. The pipe had been washed, but not good enough. The lab was able to find traces of blood and human tissue. From that they were able to perform a DNA analysis. Fortunately, Mr. Johnson had had a physical examination shortly after arriving at Palm Gardens. The examination, which included lab work, was located. Bingo! They had a match. The blood and tissue found on the pipe belonged to the deceased, Clifford Johnson.

All of this took several weeks, but the evidence was compelling, so Tony was kept in prison, and a judge ruled that bail would not be allowed. Captain Manat also telephoned Police General Manoon and informed him of the evidence implicating Tony Hernandos. He said nothing about his own role in apprehending the suspect, and preventing another murder.

Mr. Faust, the Palm Gardens CEO, was informed that a suspect in the murder of Clifford Johnson had been apprehended, and was being held without bail. He called a general meeting of all Palm Garden residents and informed them that a suspect was in jail. He hoped that would alleviate the fears of some of the residents, but there were still questions. "What about the man staying in the guest room," several people wanted to know, "Is he really a Thai Policemen?"

When Captain Gallager had assembled all the evidence, he again interviewed Tony. The prisoner's lawyer was also present. The lawyer demanded that his client be released for lack of evidence. Gallager was prepared; he presented the criminal records from the Los Angeles Police Department, the Thai immigration records, U.S. immigration records showing when Tony had arrived from Thailand, the audio tapes from Thailand implicating Tony in a plot to kill a missionary in Chiang Mai. Captain Manat had already provided evidence that Clifford Johnson had been an informant for the Drug Enforcement Administration. That fact was known by the Thai Police. Finally, and most damning of all, the police lab report that found Mr. Johnson's DNA on the steel pipe that had been in Tony's possession. Gallager thought it ironic that Mr. Johnson had listened to those audio tapes while he was living with the Thai Police General.

Tony and his lawyer saw and heard the evidence. Tony was amazed at the extent of information the police knew. The lawyer knew he had no case, so he requested permission to speak to his client alone. Permission was granted. Later, the lawyer approached Captain Gallager. "We're ready to make a deal."

"What's the deal?"

"My client tells me he has a lot of information about drug traffickers in Thailand, including some big names. He's willing to tell all, if he will not be given a death sentence for the murder of Clifford Johnson."

"I'll think about," replied Gallager.

Gallager consulted with the Los Angeles County District Attorney's Office about the lawyer's proposition. He mentioned that Mr. Johnson had been an informer for the United States Drug Enforcement Administration in Thailand, and that the prisoner, Tony Hernandos, likely did have information about drug dealers in Thailand. Gallager suggested that the District Attorney might want to contact the DEA office in Washington and ask for their input.

People in the DEA office had not been willing to talk to Captain Gallager when he had called them early in the investigation, but when given the evidence against Tony, they were eager to speak to the District Attorney. "We want to interview this prisoner; so make the deal," they urged. The District Attorney agreed, and so did a judge. It was agreed that Tony would be exempt from the death penalty if the information he gave was helpful.

Tony was interviewed over a period of several weeks, and spilled all he knew. He was able to describe people he had dealt with in Thailand, pinpoint residences, and even vehicles. He even mentioned the postal worker who had intercepted Clifford's mail. Tony had a good memory, and that was coupled with a desire to bring down those people who had given him a bad time. The DEA cooperated with General Manoon, and sent him copies of the interviews. Suspects were picked up in Thailand, and their photographs sent back. Tony recognized several and gave evidence against them. He knew he faced life in prison, but it gave him considerable satisfaction to know that he was not the only one going to jail.

The court system moved slowly, but about a year after his capture, Tony Hernandos was given a life sentence, with the provision that he would not be eligible for parole. Judicial proceedings progressed faster in Thailand, especially with a police general involved. Several drug traffickers were given long prison terms. They, in turn, implicated others, who were also jailed. General Manoon was greatly pleased by the progress he had made, but he was not so naïve as to think he had rounded the traffickers all up; especially the big operators who maintained a good public face, but also had a dark side in their lives. The General knew he had won a battle, but the war continued.

Captain Manat had returned to Thailand as soon as possible. His fiancé, Wipha, had started to make wedding plans. He had stayed on for a while, transferring information obtained from Tony back to General Manoon. He also provided audio and visual testimony that was used at Tony's trial. His "non-official" assistance to the case had been of immeasurable value. Captain Gallager knew that the Thai police captain had saved him from great embarrassment by covering his mistake. Marvin knew Captain Manat had saved his life.

Before Captain Manat returned to Thailand, however, Gallager planned a send-off dinner for him. He was thinking of a quiet affair at a local restaurant, and wanted to include Marvin and Emily, as well as Mr. Faust from Palm Gardens. Emily had bigger plans. Not only was she grateful to Captain Manat for saving her husband's life, but Emily was, at heart, a romantic person. She had heard that the Thai police officer was returning to his sweetheart in his home country, and would soon be married. "Marvin, we need to have a real party for Captain Manat before he leaves," she announced to her husband one morning. Marvin was not one to plan parties, and Emily knew it, so she went right to Mr. Faust.

Mr. Faust had no intention of getting involved in planning a party, but after a 30 minute one sided conversation with Emily, he agreed that Palm Gardens would host the party in their dining hall, and all residents would be invited for a gala evening dinner party. Emily organized a fund raising effort among residents, and purchased two gifts; one for Captain Manat, and one for his bride to be.

Although Tony's trial had not yet been held, it had become general knowledge among the residents of Palm Gardens that the man who had lived in their guest room for some time was, in fact, a Thai police officer, and that he had been of assistance in capturing the murderer of Clifford Johnson. The residents of Palm Gardens were very relieved to know that the murderer was behind bars. They all pitched in to help decorate the dining hall, until it was nearly unrecognizable as the place where they normally gathered to eat. Emily even found some entwined hearts, left over from a Valentine's day party, to decorate the speakers podium. "What a shame," she said to Marvin, "that the lovely lady from Thailand will not be here too." She had never seen Wipha, but somehow imagined her wrapped in an off the shoulder silk gown, a silver tiara in her jet black hair, and wearing exquisite golden slippers. Actually, at that very moment, Wipha was working with her mother in their orchid house. She was wearing blue jeans, a T-shirt, and bathroom flip flops. Emily's dream was partly true; Wipha was lovely, no matter what she wore.

The party was a smashing success. The Palm Garden cooks, with some help from the staff of a Thai restaurant, had prepared a Thai meal. There was aromatic steamed rice served with chicken curry, a vegetable stir-fry and sweet and sour fish. Dessert was a white gelatin made with cocoanut cream in a bed of sliced mangos. The residents thought it was very exotic, and it really was delicious. Mr. Faust had told the head cook, "Hang the expense, lets have a party to remember." He was in a good mood because some potential residents, who had delayed signing up because of the possible presence of a murderer on the grounds, had reconsidered. With the killer apprehended and behind bars those people were signing up. All the news about Palm Gardens had actually been good public relations.

There were, of course, a number of speeches during the party. The Mayor of Ashmore said some good words about international cooperation. The Ashmore Chief of Police praised the two captains; one Thai and one American, for the work they had done. Mr. Faust stressed the safety aspect. "In addition to our lovely location," he mentioned, "we can rest assured that the Ashmore Police Department is always on the job, and even willing to tap into foreign expertise when the situation demands it."

Finally, came the time to present the gifts to Captain Manat, who was scheduled to fly to his homeland the following morning. Emily did the honors. She gave a speech of her own; thanking the brave police officer from Siam, the Land of Smiles. In preparation for the event, Emily had read the book, "Anna And The King Of Siam" written by an English governess, with a runaway imagination, who had been hired in the 19th century to teach the children of the Thai Court. Emily thought it was very romantic. She had also read some recent Thailand travel brochures, and mixed things up a bit, to the confusion of most of the residents.

At the end of her speech, Emily presented the gifts she had purchased to Captain Manat. The Captain graciously accepted the gifts, and gave a short speech of his own thanking Palm Gardens, Ashmore City, and the Police Department for the hospitality he had enjoyed. He even invited everyone to come to his wedding. He returned to his seat, holding the unopened gifts, which Emily thought he would open for all to see. She was unaware that Thai people do not open gifts in front of the giver. They wait until they return home. Emily, however, was not to be denied the opportunity for all to see what she had purchased. "Oh Captain Manat," she urged, "won't you please open your gifts so we can all see what it is you will be taking back to your country."

A hesitant Captain Manat, acquiescing to the expectations of a foreign culture, opened his gift for all to see. Emily's romantic nature had known no bounds. The Captain received a pair of embroidered silk pajamas. Emily, not knowing his initials, had instructed the seamstress to embroider the words, CAPTAIN MANAT, with a pair of hearts under the words. The package also contained a matching bath robe and leather slippers. Captain Manat hoped that would satisfy everyone present, but, no, he had to open the other gift as well. The one he was to take home to his fiancé. That one also contained pajamas and bath robe that matched his own, and also a pair of fluffy bedroom slippers. Emily did not know the recipient's name at all, so had the seamstress embroider the word, SWEETHEART. Captain Manat had been a champion kick boxer, he had faced down dangerous criminals with blazing guns, but this completely did him in. He retreated to his chair with a flaming red face. It did turn out well, however. A month later Wipha was very impressed. "Oh *ti rak* (my love), you do have a romantic soul don't you."

Before his death, Clifford was hardly known around Palm Gardens. After his death he was famous. His murder had been big news, and was covered, not only by the local paper, but also by the L.A. Times and Southern California television stations. Some portions of his life in Thailand had been revealed during the trial of Tony Hernandos, but not what Clifford would have considered important. There was no mention of his friendship with the Mountain Tribal people, and nothing about the student hostel in Chiang Mai. Only the dangers he encountered while helping the Thai Police Department apprehend drug traffickers had become known. Clifford would have been disappointed.

Fame, however, is fleeting. The small house where he had lived at Palm Gardens was cleaned out, and someone else moved in. His meager possessions were disposed of, and his name again slipped back into obscurity. Occasionally, someone sitting around a dinner table in the Palm Gardens dining room would bring up the subject of Clifford. "Remember that resident who lived here a while back; Clifford Johnson I believe his name was?" Other diners would join in, "Yes, I remember him. A bit strange he was. Never said much."

"Lived abroad somewhere in Asia. Supported by some Faith Mission I believe."

"Came to a horrible end right here at Palm Gardens."

"Gave our place a rather bad name for a while; safety issues you know."

"That all seems to have blown over now."

Marvin Schuster never forgot. He now walked Caliban a bit earlier, and they often stopped at Pratt Garden. Marvin would say a prayer for the former resident he had never really gotten to know. He would contemplate on the meaning of that man's life, on his own life, and on all lives. A verse from the Bible often came to him, "From dust we have come, and to dust we return." (Genesis 3:19 kjv) Caliban, not being the philosophical type, would sniff around on the ground. Perhaps he remembered the body of a human he had discovered there. Perhaps not.

CHAPTER TWENTY SEVEN

REMEMBERED

In Thailand, Clifford was certainly not forgotten. A new sign in front of the student hostel proclaimed it to be the CLIFFORD JOHNSON MEMORIAL STUDENT HOSTEL FOR TRIBAL CHILDREN. That was quite a mouthful for the residents, but the house parents, Pwo Swe and Naw Ewa, often reminded the students of their benefactor. It is a Thai custom to have a religious ceremony 100 days after a death to honor the memory of that person. Khru Praphan, the retired bank manager of the Siam Commercial Bank in Chiang Mai, organized such an event. He set the date and sent out invitations to some people known to have been friends of Clifford. A personal note in each invitation urged the recipient to tell others about the occasion, which would be held at the Student Hostel. It was open to anyone who wanted to honor Clifford by their presence.

Khru Praphan was amazed by the turnout. There was to be a dinner served by the students at the hostel after the service, and it soon became obvious that not enough food had been prepared. An emergency phone call was made to some of the food stall owners at the market on Cheroen Muang Road ordering more food to be delivered to the hostel. People came on foot, by bicycle, pedicab, mini bus, pickup trucks, and expensive automobiles. Naw Wa Paw and her husband came from their Karen village in the mountains, where they were both teachers in the government school there. They had hired a minibus and brought 20 students with them in that vehicle that had a normal capacity of 12. The Thai village headman and family, where Clifford had often parked his Land Rover, came in their own pickup. His daughter drove.

A minibus load of Akha came from the Maesalong area, led by Lee Mui, who had invited Clifford to his village so many years before. Mee Bu, the Akha woman, had arranged for the red Toyota bus, owned by Nai Tong, to take them all to the Student Hostel. Nai Tong knew the way well. He had never forgotten that scary night when to had taken Clifford and the two Thai ladies to the Hostel, and on to the abattoir. He did not charge anything for this trip.

The Chinese merchant, Nai Lee, and his wife came, driven by one of their sons in a modest sedan. Ai Tia, the pickup driver who delivered things around town, came with Prasong, who had worked in the Chiang Mai Provincial Prison Store. Prasong had completed his prison sentence, but still worked selling prisoner made furniture.. The Lahu tourist guide, Ai Seng, came with his new wife. He had recovered from his wounds suffered in the shoot out at Doi Maesalong. His wife was a nurse he had met at the Maesalong Clinic. Pa (Aunt) Chintana came in a hired pedicab. She was already in tears before the service had even begun.

The two Chinese teachers from Doi Maesalong, Teacher Chen and Wang Quon Hing, arrived in a taxi. They had actually arrived in Chiang Mai the day before so they could visit the Hostel. They were good people, but had never thought of educating the Hill Tribe children. They had loved Clifford, but thought he was wasting his time building a hostel for such children. Their visit to the Tribal Hostel was an eye-opening experience for them. They could hardly believe that the children, neatly dressed in school uniforms doing their homework, were really Tribal children. They now understood what Clifford had been all about. General Tao, head of the Chinese Army at Doi Maesalong, sent a scroll with verses written in elegant calligraphy on it authored by a Chinese poet from ancient times that described the attributes of a good man.

Police General Manoon came in a chauffeured Mercedes Benz.

With him was his daughter, Kultida, and the newly married couple, Captain Manat and Wipha. The General even brought his housemaid, Wattana, who had cried when she heard of Clifford's death.

The American Ambassador from Bankok sent his regrets, but the Consul General from the Chiang Mai Consulate was there with a letter from the Ambassador promising to provide musical instruments for the hostel students. That news pleased the students very much.

Many more people from the hill villages, and trades people from the Chiang Mai markets, also came streaming in. One hundred folding chairs had been set up on the east side of the hostel. In late afternoon, when Khru Praphan opened the outdoor service, the chairs were nicely shaded by the building. There were not enough chairs, however, so the students brought out their sleeping mats for people to sit on. Honored guests, such as General Manoon and his family, Captain Manat, Wipha, and the American Consul General were seated on upholstered chairs in the front row.

The hostel students had gathered in front of the assembled crowd, and with a gesture from Khru Praphan they sang the King's Song. Everyone quieted, and stood in honor of His Majesty the King. The retired bank manager was a respected figure in Chiang Mai. When he rose to speak the crowd remained silent. He said a few words of welcome, mentioning the honored guests, but also including all the people who had gathered to pay respects to the Foreigner they knew as Mr. Clifford. Khru Praphan said a prayer giving thanks to God for the life of Mr. Clifford. All the people, who were mostly Buddhists, raised their hands, pressed together, in a universal gesture of worship. Khru Praphan read a portion of one verse from the Book of Psalms, found in the 90th Psalm, verse 9, "We live our life as a tale that is told." (kjv) He went on to tell about what he knew of Mr. Clifford's life, beginning when Clifford came to his bank to open an account, and how he stayed in his adopted country for many years where he became a friend to many, especially the Mountain People. "From my conversations with Mr. Clifford," continued Khru Praphan, "I found out that he came from a poor family that were not prominent in their society. His parents died rather young, but the son, motivated by his faith in God, overcame hardships to leave his home and travel to a distant country, where he served his God by serving his fellow men."

Khru Praphan concluded his brief message by holding up Mr. Clifford as a person to be emulated. "We would have a better world, if, like Mr. Clifford, we had life goals, not of achieving wealth or power, but of being a servant." Khru Praphan then invited anyone who wished to speak up and tell what they knew about Mr. Clifford. "If we live our lives as a tale that is told, please share with us something you know about Mr. Clifford, so we will learn more about Mr. Clifford's story."

At first, there was no response; only silence, and Khru Praphan thought he had made a mistake in asking people to participate. However, many people were just waiting; no one wanted to be the first to speak. Finally, Naw Wa Paw stood. Although she had been a teacher in her village school for many years, this day she was dressed in the traditional tribal clothe of her people, the Karen. She told of the first time Mr. Clifford had come to her village. She was just a small child, and fearful of this strange man who had come from the outside. She explained how he became a welcome guest, and after her father was killed by bad men sent by drug traffickers, he had helped her receive an education, so she could become a teacher in the first school in her village.

It was like a dam had burst; many people wanted to share their stories about Clifford.. Kultida and Wipha stood together and took turns telling about Mr. Clifford, who had protected them at Doi Maesalong, helped them flee to Chiang Mai, and saved their lives at the abattoir. The whole experience had changed their lives. They knew they were children of privilege, who knew little about the lives of people outside of Bangkok. Because of Mr. Clifford they had met Tribal people in the mountains who were kind and good, and even risked their lives to help them. Kultida explained how working on the Thai-Karen dictionary with Mr. Clifford had given her new insights into a different culture, and helped her appreciate the mosaic of peoples who made up the Kingdom of Thailand.

Lee Mui, the Akha man who had led Clifford to his village, and Mee Bu, the Akha woman who had previously lived with the Yunnanese man, told of their first meeting with Clifford, and of their experience in helping Clifford, Kultida and Wipha escape from the assassins. When they had finished, another Akha man stood up and asked Mee Bu to translate for him. He apologized for not being able to speak good Thai, but he had something to say. He told of a Thai man and woman who came to their village one day. They spoke the Northern Thai dialect, and explained that they owned a restaurant in Chiang Mai and needed girls to help clean and learn how to be servers. The woman said there were sleeping places above the restaurant where they would be safe, and that they would receive a salary which could be sent back to their parents. "My wife and I allowed our 14 year old daughter, Mi Ja, to go with them," the man's voice faltered. "We are simple people, and do not know city ways. Those two did not speak the truth, and our daughter had a horrible experience. However, Mr. Clifford saved her. She is not here today because she owns a noodle shop here in Chiang Mai, and must serve her customers."

Khun Pa Chintana suddenly stood up, "Here comes Mi Ja," she exclaimed, and went to hug Mi Ja, who had suddenly appeared.

"I closed my shop today. I had to come to honor Mr. Clifford." That was all Mi Ja could say. She and Pa Chintana collapsed in tears.

General Manoon had waited until last. "I knew Mr. Clifford was a good man," he began, "but I did not know the extent of his activities." The General told of his own fears when his only child, and her friend had disappeared. "As a father, I was not their to help them, but, at great risk to himself, Clifford escorted them out of a dangerous situation and defended them at the Chiang Mai abattoir. I owe him a great debt of gratitude, which now I can never repay, but I would like to erect a memorial marker at some appropriate place." He looked at Khru Praphan, "Perhaps you can help in this matter."

The service was drawing to an end when Khru Praphan announced that the hostel students would sing a song. The students, dressed in their school uniforms, shyly gathered in front of the crowd. They were directed by the hostel father, Pwo Swe, who had taught the Karen language to Clifford. The students sang Amazing Grace, a hymn they had learned from Khru Praphan. They sang it twice, once in Thai, and once in English. Khru Praphan sang along with them, remembering the day, so long ago, when he had sang that very hymn to the Foreigner who had arrived at his bank to open an account.

Finally, Khru Praphan invited everyone to stay and eat. The students quickly set up tables and served rice, chicken curry, and string beans cooked with pork. General Manoon, Khru Praphan, and the

American Consul General had stayed in their chairs discussing the General's proposal concerning a memorial marker for Clifford. The students brought each of them a plate of food, so they could eat as they talked. Khru Praphan suggested that the Foreign Cemetery, located alongside the old road to Lamphoon, would be a suitable place. "Can you make the arrangements?" General Manoon asked the American Consul General.

"The American Consul has no jurisdiction over the Cemetery," replied the Consul General. "I believe there is a Cemetery Board. I would be willing to ask them."

And so it came to be, that a memorial for Clifford was erected at the Chiang Mai Foreign Cemetery. At first, the Cemetery Board, consisting of some long time expatriates, had demurred. After all, there was no body. However, an Englishman, a former soldier who had been in the Burma Campaign during World War II, reminded the Board that there was a precedent. "You know, there is a bust of Queen Victoria in the Cemetery, and her body is certainly not buried there." An agreement was reached, with the stipulation that any memorial marker not be more than two meters tall. The Consul General notified General Manoon.

A month later, General Manoon delivered a plain marble stone, exactly two meters tall, that was erected in one corner of the cemetery. On one side was inscribed the following words:

IN MEMORY OF CLIFFORD JOHNSON

APRIL 17, 1912 - NOVEMBER 2, 1972

THE FOREIGNER WHO LOVED US

On the other side was the same epitaph written in Thai.

For many years after, various groups and individuals came to stand before the monument to remember Clifford. Mr. Lee, the merchant, and his wife came on Clifford's death day each year and burned joss sticks at the base of the stone. They continued to do that until ill health, and eventual death, made it impossible. Wipha and her husband, now Colonel Manat, came occasionally for many years. They brought their children, and told them about this man who had saved their mother's life. When the school teacher, Naw Wa Paw, came to Chiang Mai, she usually stopped at the cemetery, before returning home, to say a prayer for Clifford. Khru Praphan sometimes brought hostel students there, who cleaned up around the monument while Kru Praphan told them about the man who was their benefactor. Before leaving, they always sang Amazing Grace.

General Manoon stopped by when he was in Chiang Mai on business, until his diligence in rounding up drug traffickers finally caught up with him. One day, a car bomb blew up, killing him and his driver. The ones who did it were never apprehended. His daughter, Kultida, took it badly. After months of deep sorrow, she became a Buddhist nun, and joined a meditation center in Northeast Thailand. After two years, she rejoined society, with a vow to use her influence to do something about the problem of Tribal girls from the North being tricked into prostitution. Clifford was her inspiration. She remembered what the Akha man had related at Clifford's memorial service in Chiang Mai. That family had lost a daughter, but Clifford got her back She opened a woman's shelter in Bangkok. With her police connections, and prominent name, she was very effective in gaining the release of underage prostitutes. She sought out, and became a friend, of Mi Ja, the Akha girl Clifford had rescued from the Chiang Mai brothel. Parents of missing girls knew where to find Mi Ja at her noodle shop. Mi Ja would relay the information about such girls to Khun Kultida, who had the contacts needed to free the girls.

Clifford's influence did not end with his death. He was remembered.

The events that take place in this book, THE SECRET RETIREE; DRUGS AND DEATH, occur in two locations; a retirement community in Southern California, and Thailand. The author lives in a retirement community in Southern California, and previously lived for 33 years in Thailand. He is well acquainted with both locations. His previous book, JAI YEN MEANS KEEP A COOL HEART, is a non-fiction account of those years in Thailand.

Fiction can often convey more truth than non-fictiion. In this book, the author draws upon his 33 year experience in Thailand to highlight the customs, languages, food, and geography of that country. His affection and respect for the ethnic minorities in Northern Thailand, known as the Mountain Tribes, is obvious, and he wants to share his insights with others. Current social problems in Thailand caused by drug use and the trafficking of young women are heart wrenching realities.

The author grew up on farms in South Dakota and Iowa. He is a graduate of South Dakota State University and the University of Wisconsin. He was employed by the Montana State Extension Service, working on the Fort Peck Indian Reservation. He was an Agricultural Missionary in Thailand for 33 years. Together with Dee, his Hawaiin born wife of Chinese ancestry, he lives at Pilgrim Place, a retirement community for retired church related workers, located in Claremont, California. He continues to be involved in peace building activities, gardening, reading and writing.